THUNDER ROAD

THUNDER ROAD

COLIN HOLMES

THE LONELIEST ROADS LEAD TO THE DARKEST SECRETS.

CamCat
Books

CamCat Publishing, LLC
Brentwood, Tennessee 37027
camcatpublishing.com

Hardcover ISBN 9780744304978
Paperback ISBN 9780744304961
Large-Print Paperback ISBN 9780744304862
eBook ISBN 9780744304947
Audiobook ISBN 9780744304855

Library of Congress Control Number: 2021947759

Cover and book design by Maryann Appel

5   3   1   2   4

For Elisa, who may not believe in aliens,
but she believes in me.

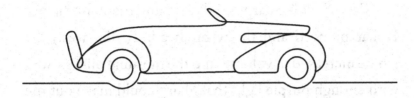

CHAPTER ONE

JUNE 1947

A thin flicker of flame licked the blue enamel coffeepot as Jefferson Sharp stirred life into the embers of last night's campfire. He broke his morning stare and cocked his head as a shiver brought him fully awake. The herd was moving, shuffling uneasily through the wooly ground fog. Somewhere off in the predawn darkness, a mechanical whine spooled up, echoing across the ranchlands of the Rafter B.

He shot a glance at the small oak where he'd tied Dollar the night before. The buckskin quarter horse flicked his ears and danced at the end of the lead rope, pulling the branch with him.

"Easy, fella." Sharp tried to calm them both, but Dollar pranced and threw his head. To the west, the whine increased in volume, and the morning mist glowed with enough purple light that Sharp could make out the terrain through the patchy fog. Whatever had the livestock spooked was just beyond a small rise.

Sharp buckled on his gun belt, and his hand found his Colt. Not the six-shooting cowboy revolver of Gentry Ferguson's King of the West movies, but a well-used Army issue .45 automatic that had followed him home from the European theater.

All through that war, Sharp had explained that, yes, he was from Texas, but that didn't make him a cowboy. He'd walked the beat as a cop before the war—didn't own a horse, have a ranch, or ever slept out under the stars or tended cattle. So naturally, here he was two years later, camped out on a ranch with a borrowed horse, guarding cows.

He patted Dollar's shoulder as if that would settle the horse, then hiked up the hill in the low crouch that had been driven into him on too many mornings in the infantry.

When he was two steps up the hill, the earth rumbled with the tremor of aggravated shorthorns thundering away from the noise and light. Sharp had been a special ranger for the Fort Worth and Western Stockmen's Association since the war, but he'd yet to be involved in a stampede.

Of course, it had to happen now, he thought. *Before sunup. In the fog.*

He had no place to hide as dozens of terrified red cattle came bellowing over the rise. He scrambled back to the campsite. He could see the white faces on the lead pair of Herefords when he yanked the Colt off his hip and fired twice into the air. The startled cattle reeled and parted right and left at the gunfire, the herd splitting to flow past the campsite like a stream around a rock. Luck and the good Lord favored the ignorant.

Sharp shooed the last of the stragglers past as the adrenaline drained away. "That," he said to the nickering quarter horse, "is enough excitement for today."

The mysterious whine disagreed. Pulsing lights strobing red, purple, and golden orange rose from beyond the hill. The apparition moved over the ridgeline, and the fog glowed. Behind Sharp, Dollar screamed a whinny and reared, trying for all his might to pull the scrubby tree out of the ground. The branch cracked. Sharp dove for the lead rope and dug his heels into the damp earth before Dollar could bolt. Something was out there with the man and horse, and the smarter one of the pair wasn't sticking around to find out what it was.

But the light show could move as well, and it did. The brilliant colors rotated in concert with the whine as it became a deafening howl. The hovering glow spun together into an intense white circle, levitated high over the hill, and disappeared into the morning fog. Instantly, the noise changed course and roared back over the camp. The lights flashed overhead, then vanished at incredible speed, leaving a dying echo and a breeze that moved the wisps of fog.

Sharp and Dollar stood frozen as whatever the hell it was blasted above them. They shared a look, and then the quarter horse went full rodeo, bucking, jumping, and twisting—anything to get out of this halter, off this rope, away from this tree, and back to the safety of the barn. Any barn. It took five minutes of profanity and cajoling, but Sharp finally calmed down the panicked gelding. He took a good hold on the halter and led them back to the campsite. "Look, I don't know what it is either, but I'm pretty damn sure it doesn't eat horses for breakfast."

Dollar's wild eyes and flicking ears suggested that he was not convinced.

Sharp remembered that something else was out there. Sixty-four head of cattle the Stockmen's Association was paying him to keep track of. Now, they were scattered from here to Mingus, and he and Dollar would be all morning rounding them up.

He gathered his blanket, saddle, and tack and put Dollar together. He'd just slid his lariat over the saddle horn when a second set of lights and mechanical noise came crashing from the direction the cattle had headed. A heartbeat later, a Studebaker stake-bed truck followed by a stock trailer busted through the mist.

The truck swerved to miss the tree and scattered Sharp's camp all over hell and back. The left front fender just missed Dollar, but the rusting hulk still managed to roll right over the campfire and crush the coffeepot.

Sharp caught the horse between crowhops and swung onto Dollar's bucking back cussing a blue streak. He found his stirrups and the quarter horse squatted, then took off like he was out to win the Kentucky Derby.

Halfway up the hill, Dollar found his stride and charged into a rising sun rapidly burning its way through the fog. Sharp ducked down behind the buckskin's bobbing head and spurred again. The rustlers tore across the prairie, the trailer bouncing left and right as the cattle trapped inside bawled in terror. Sharp slapped Dollar's rump, and the pair thundered across the ranchland, gaining on the rustlers.

Sharp unlimbered his Colt and shouted for all his worth, "Stockmen's special ranger. Pull over!"

The answer came from the passenger side. A great bearded ox of a man filled the window ledge. The ox bounced along with the truck as he produced a Winchester and leveled the rifle across the roof of the cab, aiming at Sharp. The rifle cracked, and Sharp yanked Dollar's reins, trying to put the trailer between them and the rifle. The truck swerved, exposing him again, and another round snapped off.

Sharp raised himself in the stirrups and unleashed his anger from the barrel of the Colt. He didn't care that at full gallop, firing between hoofbeats, he stood almost no chance of hitting the gunman, but his second round ricocheted off the cab and drove the ox back inside. The third shot tore the rearview mirror off the driver's side. So much for his expert pistol rating from Uncle Sam's army.

That was enough for the rustlers. The truck and trailer accelerated, the cloud of dust growing as it began to pull away. Sharp took aim at the front tire, and just as he squeezed off the shot, Dollar screamed and the world fell out from under him. The Ranger flew high over the horse's head for what seemed an eternity before slamming back down onto the hardpan prairie, sliding and rolling to a stop through yucca and scrub juniper, coming to rest in a stand of prickly pear.

Sharp lay there on his back, gasping to force air back into his lungs, slowly becoming aware of the pink morning clouds overhead.

It took him a long moment to get around to taking inventory. Both legs moved. He had a pretty good pain in his left shoulder. Might be a collarbone. He tasted blood but waved that off as a bit lip rather than anything internal. Slowly, he sat up. It was possible there was an entire cactus up his ass.

In the dusty distance, brake lights came on as the rustlers found the gap they'd cut in the barbed wire fence. Sharp groaned his way to his feet and shook his head, watching the truck and trailer turn onto the highway and head off toward town. He pulled a paddle of prickly pear from his backside and retrieved his crushed Resistol. As he slapped the battered hat against his leg, he turned, and a bad situation got worse.

Twenty feet behind him, Dollar was down, blowing air in great heaves. He thrashed, unable to get up. Sharp approached the broad buckskin. He and Dollar had their disagreements, but the big fellow didn't deserve this. His right foreleg had found a hole. Snake, armadillo, prairie dog. Didn't matter.

Sharp knelt. "Settle down, dammit. You're only making it worse." He put a hand to the horse's sweating neck and patted him. Dollar grunted through the pain.

The white cannon bone of the broken leg stabbed clear through the hide. He was a good horse, and he was in agony. Sharp checked his Colt then wrestled with his conscience. He walked a small circle, screwing up his courage and measuring his humanity, then put his last round into the suffering animal.

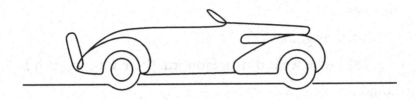

CHAPTER TWO

S harp limped the three miles back to the bunkhouse loaded down with a saddle, tack, bedroll, and busted-up camp gear. He had hiked farther, carrying more, and West Texas was significantly easier going than the Italian Alps had been, but his heaviest load was the guilt of putting down a good horse.

The situation hadn't improved two hours later as he explained events to Howard Estes, the foreman at the Rafter B. The headquarters building had indoor plumbing, so Estes stood on one side of a bathroom door while inside, Sharp twisted around with his pants around his knees, trying to remove the remaining prickly pear needles.

"So, they got away."

"My horse went down, Howard, there wasn't much I could do."

"And now I gotta shake loose a couple of hands to go mend the wire."

"I'd have one or two of 'em keep watch along that northeast stretch. These guys might be back." Sharp winced as he plucked a particularly deep set barb.

There was a harumph from the far side of the door. "Why exactly am I paying the Association if I've got to supply my own men to ride the fence?"

Sharp buckled his belt and opened the door. "The Association is law enforcement and investigation, not a security patrol. You know that, Howard."

"I know it's cost me most of a dozen yearlings on top of your too-damn-expensive dues. I aim to give Lavelle a piece of my mind about this."

He gave Sharp a nod and left him to find his own way out.

Relieved of his duty, Sharp loaded his gear into the trunk of his dusty blue LaSalle coupe. He'd collected enough poker winnings on the troop transport ship home to afford a good used car. Most of the men had gotten back pay before shipping out, and that made for plenty of easy marks if a guy understood the finer points of stud poker.

Sharp still had winnings from that trip stashed in a safe deposit box at the bank. He gingerly lowered himself onto the upholstery, thanking the interior designers at General Motors for the cushion on his abused backside. It was a long, slow drive back to town.

A couple of empty parking spaces waited in front of the brand-new building that housed the Fort Worth and Western Stockmen's Association. The jazzy architectural style was topped by a flat roof, supported by picture windows that angled down to a knee-high wainscot of stacked limestone. A pale green color someone told him was called "sage" framed the glass. The new headquarters building was just one more thing Sharp didn't particularly care for about the Association. In fact, about the only thing he did like was the paycheck.

A small cloud of range dust followed him through the front door and into the cavernous room packed with secretaries and stenographers hammering away at the cattle registrations and auction transactions that oiled the cash machine of the Association. Across the small sea of bobbing bouffants, E. G. Lavelle spotted him from behind the enormous window that overlooked his domain.

"Sharp! Get in here." Lavelle never left his throne. Sharp doubted the Executive Director of the Association could hoist his bulk out of the worn leather.

The bald, well-fed director stuffed papers into a manila folder and ignored Sharp as he entered. Finally, he dumped an inch of ash off his cigar and stabbed the foul-smelling stogie at the wooden chairs across from his massive desk.

"Sit down." He stuffed the stogie back under his famous walrus mustache and wallowed it around as he spoke. "I just got my ass chewed by Howard Estes at the Rafter B." He jerked a thumb at the telephone.

Sharp tried not to wince in front of his father-in-law as he eased his butt onto the hard Ranch Oak chair.

"They got away. There's two of 'em. They're using a truck and trailer and hitting before dawn. I think it's a Studebaker and—"

"You think? You're not getting paid to think. You're getting paid to stop cattle thieves." Lavelle's volume increased, and he punched the smoky air with his cigar.

"Why can't you do that? Stop them! Act, man! Don't just think."

"Well, there was something else, a light . . ."

"Did it steal any cattle? No? What the hell are you worried about it for?" The ladies in the typing pool tried hard to look like they weren't looking.

"This was unusual—"

Lavelle held up a chubby hand to stop him.

"Unusual. People have been stealing cattle for centuries, and you manage to find something unusual about it? You know, Sharp, I told Evelyn that I wasn't sure you were cut out for this. I told her you ought to go back to being a cop. That sitting around the Blackstone eating Spudnuts probably suited you more than the real, genuine work involved in being a livestock detective." Lavelle's words were even and slow now. Explaining the obvious to a child.

Sharp set his jaw. "E. G., I've had a reasonably shitty day. I've been in a stampede, hiked three miles, and had to put a horse down. I—"

"A horse? Dollar?"

"We were after the truck—"

"My Dollar?"

An unsettling silence followed.

Lavelle finally leaned back and took a long draw on his cheap Tampa cigar. He released a cloud of disappointment into the air and spit an offending particle of tobacco at the wall.

"I'm giving your cases to Smitty. He gets arrests."

"Of course he does!" Sharp threw up his hands. "But how many of those arrests end up in convictions? Arrests are easy. Getting them to stick and put people away is hard."

Lavelle studied his cigar. "That's what you don't understand about this business. An arrest takes these guys off the streets. Puts up good, visible numbers. That's what our membership wants. They don't care about convictions. They just don't want these sons of bitches stealing cattle. You don't get that."

"I want to put them away."

"That's not the game." Lavelle heaved his bulk to one side and dug out his wallet, then threw a ten-dollar bill on the desk. "Go home. Take Evelyn to a nice dinner. We'll talk about this tomorrow."

Sharp glared at the cash. "Let's talk about it today. What is it you aren't saying?"

Lavelle dumped another load of cigar ash and smoothed the enormous mustache. "Cattle get stolen right out from under your nose. I can't have that. The membership can't have that."

Sharp pulled a battered pack of Lucky Strikes from his shirt pocket and thumbed his Zippo, his hands trembling at the insult.

"Now, I have to figure out what to do with you. And I don't have time to do that right now." Lavelle reached for the next ever-present folder to dismiss his son-in-law.

Sharp took a drag of his Lucky and blew the smoke over his head to fight the cigar. He lost. He stood to walk out and stopped. Then turned with a glare and snatched the ten-spot off the desk.

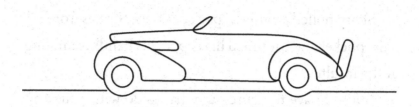

CHAPTER THREE

A Fort Worth Water Department crew jackhammered away at the curb next door to Sharp's modest West-side bungalow. One of them had parked a beige-and-cream Pontiac coupe in his driveway, so he parked on the street, in front of the yard he needed to mow.

He threw his gun belt over his shoulder and balanced his gear and bedroll on one hip as he opened the front door. He dropped the dusty saddle on the floor of the den, and was about to sit down when he heard Evelyn from the back of the house. She was working hard on an orgasm.

And it sounded like she had help.

Sharp paused at the bedroom door, watching as Smitty's narrow ass humped under the sheet. He pulled his Colt from the gun belt. Few sounds are as recognizable as a fresh magazine being snapped into an Army issue Colt .45 and its slide chambering a new round. Smitty froze in mid-stroke.

"Oh, God, don't stop!" Evelyn was nearing the finish line.

"Y'all let me know when you're done. I just need to get a few things out of the closet." Sharp slid the Colt back into its holster as much for his safety as theirs.

Smitty jumped backward like he'd peed on an electric fence. He grabbed for the sheet leaving Evelyn stark naked, squirming to hide under a pillow.

"Sharp?" He was bruised, battered, caked in horse's blood, dirt, and three days' worth of beard, but Smitty's eyes were locked on the gun belt and the semiautomatic pistol resting under his hand.

"Smitty. I believe her daddy wants to see you." Sharp's eyes moved deliberately to the pistol. "I think you'd rather be there right about now."

Evelyn found her voice. "What the hell are you doing home?"

Sharp answered with a narrow-eyed stare.

Smitty grabbed his pants from the bedpost and nearly busted his ass trying to hop into them. For an instant he looked like he wanted to say something but Sharp beat him to it.

"You better git. I've had a bellyful of you today."

Smitty grabbed his boots and ran. Outside, the jack-hammering stopped as the Pontiac's tires chirped and he sped to safety.

"You leave him alone!" Evelyn scrambled out of the bed, wrapping the sheet around her.

"Shut up, Evelyn."

He went to the dresser and stuffed underwear in the duffel. Then to the closet where he piled suits over one arm and topped the load with his city hat.

Evelyn stamped her foot like the spoiled little daddy's girl she was. "What are you even doing home?"

"It's where my mail comes. I thought I'd stop by and check it." Sharp was holding it together well, he thought. Nobody was dead yet. "Sorry if it cramped your social calendar."

She cocked her fist to her hip defiantly. "This isn't about me!"

"It sure as hell doesn't appear to be about me."

"You're never home." She followed him to the front door, tripping over the sheet.

Sharp grabbed his saddle and evened the load. "I doubt I ever will be again."

He slammed the door behind him.

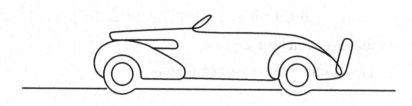

CHAPTER FOUR

S harp paused for a long time at the yield sign at the end of the block. He lit a Lucky, and the morning caught up with him. He exhaled into the windshield and slumped deep into the seat. *Now what?*

Angry, tired eyes stared back at him from the rearview mirror. He wasn't surprised. Not even disappointed. There hadn't been much of a marriage there for the better part of a year. But he hadn't really expected it to end quite this abruptly. Now it seemed his entire world had been reduced to the car and its meager contents.

He shifted into first with more determination than he really felt, promising himself that no matter how much he appreciated the LaSalle, it would not become his new residence.

The first stop was the Rexall drugstore. He picked up some basic toiletries and mercurochrome for his more delicate wounds. The elderly woman at the counter frowned at his appearance and the smell of three days on the range. He removed his battered hat and nodded an apology.

Ten minutes later, he pulled through the drive at the Skyline Motel on Highway 199. Not the swankiest place on Thunder Road, but reasonably clean. At this moment, cheap rent spoke volumes. It would do short term. He left Lavelle's ten-spot as a deposit and parked in front of the door. It took two entire trips to the car to dump all of his worldly belongings on the bed.

The bathtub had a showerhead above and a faucet below. He turned on both, settled gingerly back into the tub, and then woke with a snort five minutes later, almost underwater. It had been a short night and long morning; drowning in a motel bathtub would be the icing on the cake. The shave and shower helped. He spotted on the neon pink ointment and stuck a couple of Band-Aids on the places that still leaked blood. His shoulder was sore as hell. He fingered the cotton ball out of his new aspirin bottle and popped a couple of tablets.

His stomach growled as he strapped Lieutenant Jacob's Hamilton timepiece to his wrist, and he found that not only was it lunchtime, but the watch's crystal had developed a thin crack during the morning's festivities. That figured. The watch had made it all across Italy, keeping excellent time and surviving the rigors of combat, but it marked today by cracking. He reminded the Lieutenant to rest in peace and himself of his promise to take good care of it. He'd have to stop by Haltom's and get it fixed. Right after lunch.

He headed into town. Fort Worth was a growing community, and new money had been putting up skyscrapers downtown. At the corner of Fifth and Main stood the Blackstone Hotel, twenty stories of art deco cream limestone sitting on top of what Sharp thought was the best lunch counter around.

He'd just about finished his chicken-fried steak when Roni Arquette batted him with a rolled newspaper.

"You . . ." She placed her copy of the *Fort Worth Examiner* on the bar. ". . . look like crap." She nodded to Peggy, the waitress behind the counter, and indicated she'd have the same blue plate special. "I mean, more than usual."

Every male eye in the place had followed her to the seat next to him at the counter. Veronica was just this side of gorgeous, with a figure that did amazing things for her blue dress. But to Sharp, she was still the tomboy little sister of his childhood buddy Dave. He'd also patrolled the Hell's Half Acre beat with her husband, Frenchy. He knew that behind the big brown eyes was a widow's soul who had lost her husband in Normandy and her brother in the Pacific.

Sharp eyed this older version of the pesky kid sister.

"Yeah, today's one of those days that just gets better and better."

"I'm sure I'm not taking that the way you meant it."

Sharp dabbed the corner of his mouth. "Nah. You probably are."

She socked his bad shoulder, and he winced.

"You're hurt?" There was genuine concern in her voice.

"Like I said, rough day."

"Why don't you just go home?"

He shrugged his arm around the bruised shoulder, wondering about the uncomfortable grinding feeling in the joint. "Well, home is complicated right now."

"Evelyn and you . . ." She let the assumption hang in the air.

"Well, Evelyn and somebody."

"Oh."

Sharp's eyebrows went up. "Oh?"

"People talk." She pulled out a compact and lipstick and did a little unnecessary touch-up.

"Just not to me. You knew about this?"

Her lunch arrived, and she concentrated far too much on measuring a spoon and a half of sugar into her iced tea. "I don't get into other people's affairs."

"I see." He swallowed the last bite and dabbed his mouth. "So, you know anybody with a room to rent?"

"Can you pay rent?"

"I have a little squirreled away."

She chased gravy around her plate. "How's that going to affect your job?"

"Yeah. I'm probably looking for one of those too."

"Back to the PD?" She was inhaling her chicken fry like a hungry woman with only thirty minutes for lunch.

Sharp thought a bit.

His time with the Fort Worth Police Department had been tolerable. He liked being a cop, and that had allowed him to go into the service as a sergeant instead of a PFC, but those days were behind him. The FWPD's chief of detectives was one of E. G. Lavelle's running buddies, and he had about a snowball's chance in hell of getting back on as a detective once Evelyn started covering her ass.

"I don't think so."

That reality hung in the cigarette-stale air while Roni cleaned her plate.

"Can you get a private investigator's license? We have lawyers who hire their own detectives." Roni was a reporter in Judge Rowan's district court.

"I've still got my peace officer's commission. That's through the state, even mighty E. G. Lavelle can't take that away." Sharp nodded to Peggy, and the waitress reached across the counter and refilled his coffee. "Any of your lawyers trade out for divorce work?"

"Some might. We don't get divorce cases in our court. But I can get you some names, if you're interested."

"In work or the divorce?"

Roni gave him a wink. "Yes." With that, she was up and off, swatting him again with her copy of the *Examiner*. "Here, check the classifieds–they have rooms, jobs, furniture—everything a newly minted bachelor needs."

He took the paper and watched Roni head back to work without appreciating what every other male in the room enjoyed.

The lunch crowd thinned out, and it dawned on Sharp he had nowhere to go and an excess of nothing to do, so he unfolded the classified section and ordered a piece of coconut cream pie. He borrowed a stub of a pencil from Peggy, who was infinitely more interested in the two potentially big-tipping businessmen at the other end of the counter. Left alone to his task, he circled three possible rooms to let, two small houses for rent, and a job listing for a man who could keep confidential information.

The pie came and he folded the *Examiner* to the news section. The shock hit when the first column above the fold revealed that mobster Bugsy Siegel had been shot dead in Beverly Hills. He had played a little poker across the table from Siegel on one of the gangster's frequent trips to see Doyle Denniker. Rumor held that some of the nightclubs on the outskirts of Fort Worth along the Jacksboro Highway were Mob-owned joints. Sharp smiled at the memory. His favored poker table was at Denniker's 2222 Club. That table was a six-seat, green felt combat zone centered in a hidden room in a secret nightclub left over from Prohibition. He'd won a bundle from Bugsy that night. And again the next night when the gregarious mobster returned to try and win it back.

The wire report was filled more with juicy gossip and speculation than news beyond the fact that the mobster had been killed. But it made Sharp think. He hadn't been to the Four Deuces in a long while. Evelyn hated the place and he'd tried to be a good husband. He shrugged, took a sip of his coffee and knew exactly how he'd spend his first night of bachelorhood.

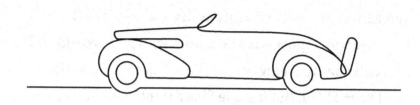

CHAPTER FIVE

S harp tossed his suitcoat onto the motel bed and eyed his handcrafted Italian leather shoulder holster next to it. His patrol had liberated a small town in the foothills of the Alps, and the local harness maker had shown his appreciation by cobbling together pieces for the five survivors in the platoon. Sharp hadn't really wanted the rig but found it to be a comfortable way to carry his .45, and the old man was purely thankful that his wife and two toddling grandchildren had been saved from the Nazis.

He slipped into the harness leather and slid his cut-down Colt home. In the mirror, the suit coat hardly even bulged. He gave a mental thank-you to Woo, the tailor who'd altered the suit to work around the holster. He knew most of the patrons at the club wouldn't be armed, but as a former cop, a former army officer, and now a former livestock detective, he felt naked without a sidearm. Came with the territory. He slid his hand into what Woo had called his detective's pocket, a hidden opening in the lining of the jacket that could hold an entire legal folder and leave the wearer's hands free. Sharp thought the main reason Woo had added it was because it tacked two dollars onto the price of the suit. Woo was a helluva salesman. But it did come in handy when he wanted to appear to be an empty-handed ordinary Joe, and then, from out of nowhere, serve an arrest warrant on a cattle thief.

He went to the closet, where he'd carefully placed his hats, his battered Resistol cowboy hat and his city hat, a two-and-a-half-inch brim gray felt with a wide silk band and a more stylish crease and crown. It looked better with the subtle gray suit and the paisley tie. And like he told folks, despite the boots he wore, he really wasn't a cowboy.

He locked the hotel room behind him and wheeled the LaSalle onto what the maps called Highway 199. Most people in Fort Worth called it the Jacksboro Highway as that was the next town of any consequence down the blacktop. But the old-timers who worked and lived along this stretch knew it as Thunder Road.

His grandfather, the original Jefferson Sharp, told him stories of bootleggers roaring away from the speakeasies during Prohibition and hauling beer and liquor north and west to thirsty cowboys and equally parched oilfield roughnecks. The old man had winked and talked about making hay while the sun shone on that ripe market. Sharp had heard the booming exhaust pipes on the flathead Ford his grandfather continually tinkered with and understood what put the thunder in Thunder Road. He also understood his grandfather was no angel.

These days, Thunder Road was a festival of neon. Nightclubs, restaurants, and motor court hotels. Bright signs split the night everywhere. Everywhere except the Four Deuces Club. The four twos of the address were neatly lettered on the intentionally ordinary mailbox beside a simple residential driveway that climbed a small, wooded hill to a white two-story house. It looked to all the world to be the handsome home of a well-to-do businessman.

Sharp drove past the mailbox and pulled in next door, where Rico's Mexican Dining Salon had its own neon circus blazing in pink, yellow, and blue glass tubes. Large painted windows fronted the roadway advertising Tex-Mex favorites and air-conditioning. Smaller signs near the road pointed to a rear parking lot filled with upscale autos.

He found an empty spot between a Mercury and a Packard. Rico had thirty cars in the lot, but just three patrons visible through the window paint. Sharp smiled at the maroon Cord 812 convertible parked at the base of the hill. Gentry Ferguson was here; it'd be an interesting night.

Like the rest of the parking lot patrons, Sharp didn't head to the Mexican joint. Instead, he walked to a stone path that wound behind the hill and continued past an ivy-covered wall and into the woods. Sharp paused at the ivy and knocked on the door hidden behind the foliage. A small window slid open.

"Hey, Dutch. Jeff Sharp. I'm alone."

The door opened in. The short, round attendant in the tuxedo gave him a once-over. "Mr. Sharp! Good to see you again. Anything to declare?"

"I declare it's good to be here."

"Come on in." Dutch stole a look around and ushered Sharp into a dark anteroom. Sharp paused as his eyes adjusted and waited for the diminutive gatekeeper to open the hidden interior doorway. A buzz came from behind, and one wall panel swung away.

"Push the door closed behind you, please," Dutch said for likely the hundredth time that evening.

Through the door, the cramped hallway angled up and bent twice to the left. Sharp came to the third door and tapped out Shave and a Haircut. A gorilla-sized bouncer in an expensive suit opened the door into one of the most impressive nightclubs this side of Havana.

Sharp smiled.

He'd made some decent money in this room once upon a time. The smell of gin and beer and cigarettes mingled with a whiff of fine perfume.

Home.

"Jefferson Sharp."

He looked to his left and found the proprietor, Doyle Denniker, with a broad smile and an extended hand.

"Hello, Doyle. Good to see you."

"You've been missed, my friend." The stout, fiftyish, balding owner of the Four Deuces was wearing his signature white dinner jacket and black bow tie.

"Been working. Out of town."

"Chasing cows for E. G. Lavelle, I hear." Doyle casually examined the burning end of his cigar.

"Well, a man's got to eat."

"Your talent isn't livestock. You belong at the table. Gentry's in town for a game, if you'd like to join us." He pointed his cigar to a door on the far wall with PRIVATE lettered in fine gold leaf.

Sharp considered it for less than a heartbeat. "I'll sit in a hand or two. If you've got an empty chair."

Denniker smiled. "For you? Always. My room opens at ten. I'll even stake your ante." Doyle was pushing a loophole in Texas gaming law that said he could host games of chance in his private home. Sharp admired Denniker's three-level, 6,500-square-foot "residential" game room, thinking this probably wasn't what the legislature had in mind when they envisioned little old ladies betting kitchen matches on a game of dominoes.

"I'll be there." Sharp put two fingers to his brow to say thanks.

He surveyed the room. Doyle had a crowd at the two roulette wheels and four craps tables, all of which could fold into panels in the walls. To his left, a separate area housed a pair of rows of one-armed bandits. In case local authorities got too nosy, Sharp had seen them disappear under tables to be covered with floor-length linens, ornate silverware, and tea sets.

He didn't figure those authorities were in a hurry to discover anything, because the county sheriff was throwing dice on one wall, while the wife of the district attorney was hypnotically feeding dimes into a slot machine near the main bar. The local law enforcement scene was covered. The real worry would be the Texas Rangers.

Sharp turned toward the bar and winked at Jimmy the bartender's wide grin.

"Mr. Sharp, good to have you back. Usual?"

Sharp nodded. "Good to be here." Jimmy slid a rocks glass across. Scotch, three ice cubes, and a splash of water. Sharp took a sip and smiled. Scotch just tasted better here.

He tipped Jimmy and shook a Lucky out of the pack. Money was in the room tonight. On the small corner bandstand, a tall man with ebony skin and a white handkerchief was mopping his brow and tucking his brass horn into a case. A doghouse bass lay on its side, and the tip jar on the piano overflowed with cash. He caught the trumpeter's gaze and raised his glass. Louis nodded and returned his famous grin.

Sharp shook his head. Figured he'd just missed their set, but it explained the crowd. Word got around in these circles when Doyle had a private show. People came from miles around.

"Well, look what the cat dragged in." Sharp turned to find Leo Fuller looking over his martini.

"Hello, Leo." He shook the newspaperman's hand. "You're looking dapper tonight."

Leo's ability to overdress was legendary and the occasional target of his rival newspaper's cartoonists across the Trinity River in Dallas. Tonight, the *Fort Worth Examiner*'s publisher was in a spotless tuxedo adorned with a perfect white carnation. Sharp hadn't seen spats in twenty years, but on Leo, they worked.

"What brings you out tonight? Celebrating or drinking away your troubles?"

Sharp cringed.

Very little happened in Fort Worth that publisher Fuller wasn't wired into. Especially when it concerned his friends and acquaintances.

Sharp qualified on both counts, having learned the ropes of dealing with the press from Leo, back when the publisher had been the *Examiner*'s star police beat reporter.

"Doyle asked me to join him at his table. I assume you'll be there?" He didn't really want to explain his situation to Leo.

"Of course. Gentry's here tonight as well. But that doesn't answer my question." The brains behind Leo's thick, round spectacles had moved him from the police beat to the city desk and then to editor in chief.

By the time the war ended, ambition and a partnership of other people's money had made Leo Fuller the publisher, majority owner, and a wealthy man. But Sharp knew he was first and foremost a curious reporter.

"Everyone comes when Louis is in town." Sharp tilted his head to the bandstand.

"Is that what brings you in? Or are you job hunting?"

Sharp spoke the truth. "As far as I know, I still work for the Association."

So did Leo. "Trust me, you don't."

"What's the word?" Sharp inquired as to his own condition.

"E. G. booted your ass out the door, and Evelyn gave you the heave-ho."

"Well, that's one way to tell it. But I haven't seen anything that says all that," Sharp said with more confidence than he felt.

"My bet is that'll happen within the next twenty-four hours. I don't think you have to worry about going back to the Association."

"I'm not. I'm done there." While Leo's star had risen during the war, Jeff Sharp had come home with a battle-field promotion, a handful of medals for making it through the war, and the scars to prove how difficult that had been. But he landed with little more than his poker winnings and no prospects for a civilian job when the boat docked.

Every former GI who'd ever wiped Cosmoline off a rifle snapped up the postwar jobs at the police depart-ment, and if not for Evelyn's old man at the Cattlemen's Association . . . well, he didn't want to think about that. Although the cactus in his backside was a healthy reminder.

Sharp checked his bare wrist, forgetting that he'd dropped Lieutenant Jacob's Hamilton at the repair shop. "What time is it?"

Leo pulled out a gold pocket watch. "Nine thirty-five. Pawn your watch?"

Sharp tapped out another cigarette and blew the smoke over Leo's head. "It's at Haltom's getting a new crystal, smart guy. Busted it chasing cattle rustlers."

"Oh, joy. So you and Gentry will be talking shop all through the game."

"Gentry deals with a better class of rustlers than I do. Mine aren't in the Screen Actors Guild, and they shoot real bullets."

"Why is it gunfire seems to follow you around?"

"It's a gift."

Leo's eyes moved past him and Sharp turned to follow his gaze.

"I figured you'd be here." Roni wagged an accusing finger as if demanding an explanation.

Sharp studied the end of his cigarette. "It's my first night out in a long time. But you? This is a little risqué for an upstanding member of the judicial branch."

"Pshaw. Judge Rowan is here all the time. Mr. Fuller, how are you?"

Leo toasted her. "Even better now that you've brightened the room, Mrs. Arquette."

She kissed the air next to his cheek. Sharp rolled his eyes. "Seriously, Roni, this isn't your kind of joint, what's up?"

"I have a date."

Sharp's eyebrows went up. "On a Tuesday?" He looked around and didn't see anyone unusual.

She pointed her clutch behind Sharp, and he turned to see a ghost. Walking toward him with a noticeable limp was an Army Air Force major in full uniform. His pencil-thin mustache gave him a hint of Clark Gable, and his dark eyes went from Roni to Sharp and back again with a flash of recognition.

"Son of a bitch." Sharp knew the flyer immediately. Roni punched him in the arm again. This time he didn't flinch.

The major stopped in front of Sharp, and they locked eyes. Finally, they said almost in unison. "I thought you were dead." Then each smiled, and they embraced like long lost brothers.

"I'll be damned." Sharp shook his head again.

Leo and Roni watched the entire scene play out. Finally, she said, "I take it you two know each other?"

"We damn sure do," said the major, busting into a wide grin. "But I can't tell you your name to save my life."

Sharp followed suit. "Well, we were never formally introduced. I'm Jeff Sharp."

"Jerry Cartwright. And I feel bad since you really did save my life."

"Right after you saved mine."

Roni looked from one to the other. "This is a story I need to hear."

Sharp doffed his hat and ran a hand through his hair. He heaved a great sigh and nodded. "I found the major hanging in a tree somewhere outside of San Marino. He'd just saved our butts by strafing a German artillery encampment. Those guys were good with their artillery—we were waiting for the last round to fall on us when the major here played the guardian angel in his P-38 and took them out."

The major chuckled. "They weren't just good with the arty, their ack-ack crews were damn good."

Roni looked at Leo. "Ack-ack?" The newspaperman fitted a cigarette to his holder to buy some time. He looked uncomfortable.

Sharp grinned. Leo had been 4-F and missed the fun and games that had been the Second World War. "Anti-aircraft. It's a big machine gun that makes that nasty sound. We heard them open up on you while we were running for the trees, I looked up in time to see the round take one of the tail booms right off your plane." He raised his glass to the major.

"Makes 'em damned hard to drive when they do that." The pilot nodded back.

Sharp's gaze focused on the memory. "Half an hour later, I'm wandering through the woods, cut off from what was left of my platoon, and I hear this voice up in the trees asking if I've got a knife. I look up, and there's the major, hanging twenty feet off the ground with his parachute tangled in the trees."

"As I recall, you tried to catch me when I cut myself loose." He shrugged at Roni's horrified expression.

"I was pretty sure you were going to break your neck."

"Nope. Just my leg. In training, they told us that the air pressure would just suck us straight out of the cockpit, that bailing out of a P-38 wouldn't be any problem." He tapped the cane against his stiff leg. "They lied."

Leo tapped his pocket watch. "Gentlemen, I would remind you that Doyle is big on punctuality."

"Some things never change." Sharp eyed the bar and considered another drink.

The major looked quizzical. "You're at Doyle's table?"

Sharp nodded. "Used to be a regular. Things . . . kind of got in the way."

Roni piped up. "His wife wouldn't let him come play."

Sharp shot her an irritated look. "When you're trying to make things work, you don't stay out playing cards every Tuesday."

"Apparently, that helped the situation a great deal," Leo said with a wink. "Good to see you, Mrs. Arquette.

Major. Sharp. I'll see you at the table, best of luck this evening." He turned and went to have his martini refreshed.

The major looked at his date. "You want something before we start?"

Roni smiled. "A gin fizz."

"Be right back."

Roni's smile melted as the major limped to the bar. "Now you've done it. Thanks a lot, Jeff-er-son." She drew out the pronunciation the way his mother had when they were kids, and he was in trouble.

"What'd I do?"

"He and I were going to have a long talk tonight. He thinks this is a great night out—takes me to a hideaway club on a Tuesday so he can play poker."

"Huh. So you're dating?"

She flushed and searched his face for a hint of disapproval. Then she looked at her shoes, and her voice became soft. "It's been three years, Jeff."

Her eyes were moist when she looked up.

He swallowed hard. "Hey, no. Roni. I think that's great. I'm happy for you. Really. You deserve a break. You're due some good times."

"You mean that?"

Sharp bobbed his head toward the major, at the bar. "Of course and hey—look, I don't know him well, but he saved my ass in Italy, so he's a good guy in my book."

"A good guy. Yeah, but he thinks I like sitting around yanking a slot machine while he plays poker. It's boring." She feigned a yawn.

"Maybe he's had enough excitement for one lifetime."

"Yeah, his idea of excitement is getting cherries in his Coke."

"So dump him." The idea seemed obvious to Sharp.

"Is that your advice as a recent dumpee?"

Sharp acknowledged the barb with a raised glass. "Touché."

"Besides, it looks like you two are pals."

"I wouldn't call us friends, but if he hadn't shown up when he did, I'd still be in a hole in Italy. I spent two days dragging him through a forest. He got beat up pretty bad when they shot him down. He was out of it most of the time. What's he doing here?" Sharp tinkled the ice in his glass. He was due for a refill as well.

"He's got some big-deal job over at the airbase. Runs off at the drop of a hat. Just leaves me hanging. Asks me out, then calls the day of to tell me he's got to go to Alaska or Nevada or Washington or somewhere. Although one time he did it, and two weeks later I saw him talking to Howard Hughes in the newsreels."

"That Howard Hughes? The multimillionaire?"

"Jerry says he's forgotten more about airplanes than most people ever know."

"Hmmm." Sharp pondered a moment. "Maybe he's working on the atomic plane."

"There's an atomic plane?"

"Must be, I saw it in *Popular Mechanics* at the barber-shop." Sharp moved, and this time she punched his good arm.

"She slug you all the time, Sharp?" The major had returned with their drinks. Sharp noticed the major's had two maraschino cherries.

"Ever since she was eight. Her brother hit her back, but my mom wouldn't let me hit girls."

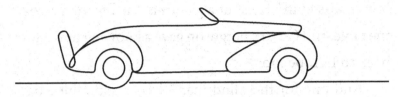

CHAPTER SIX

The hanging Tiffany lamp gave a glow to the cloud of cigarette smoke and the green felt poker table below, but the rest of the room, with its textured red velvet wallpaper and rich oak paneling, remained in the shadows.

". . . you went to find a medic, and not ten minutes later the German patrol showed up," the major explained to Sharp over his cards. "I saw the rest of the war through the barbed wire around different stalags and POW hospitals."

Sharp felt a pang of regret. "Yeah, I was a lot of help. Running around the forest yelling for medics like it was blindman's bluff." He shot a glance at the big man across the table, and Gentry Ferguson gave a knowing nod. He'd been to Europe too.

"And one for the blind man." Doyle slid a blue-patterned playing card facedown to Sharp, who slipped it off the felt with the practiced ease of a man who'd done it ten thousand times. The five of clubs nestled neatly between the five of hearts and the five of diamonds in his left hand. A pair of jacks looked on.

His eyes moved slowly to the stacks of chips in front of him. Then he casually selected a few and tossed them into the pile in the center of the table. "I'll see your ten and raise two."

Across the table, the famous blue eyes flicked between the center pile of chips, his own hand, and his old friend Jeff Sharp. Every person in the building knew Gentry Ferguson. The King of the West. He and Chief, the Wonder Horse, were big boffo box office in Hollywood, but at Doyle's table, he was just another hand of poker. He came to Fort Worth to get away from the flashbulbs and the fans and didn't have to hide the receding hairline under a ten-gallon hat.

"Damn shame about Bugsy." Sharp put a pack of Luckies to his mouth and pulled out a cigarette.

Gentry's eyes met his, looking for more meaning in the comment.

Leo chimed in, "Occupational hazard, I believe. If the cops have guns on you and the Mob has guns on you, crossfire is a genuine possibility."

Doyle leaned in, watching to see how the man who'd brought Bugsy to this very table would play it. Gentry rolled a ten-dollar chip across three fingers and looked from his cards to Leo, then Sharp. Gentry had a tell or two, and Sharp now knew the actor would be bluffing.

He had a habit of toying with the chip when he didn't have the cards.

"Mr. Publisher, Bugs and I go way back. If you're looking for a word against him for your editorial page, it's not coming from me." Gentry adopted a menacing look, which made Sharp think that while Gent was a good actor, he wasn't that good an actor.

"Not at all," Leo lied and adjusted the thick spectacles that had kept him home while men like Sharp and Gentry had gone off to Europe to fight the Huns. He pushed his chips onto the growing pile. "I'll raise five."

Gentry frowned and pushed in chips. "I'll stay in."

Between Gentry and Major Cartwright sat a drunk whom Sharp had never seen before. He'd been introduced to the table as Myron, a landman who enjoyed a good game. Usually, this was a friendly game, and strangers weren't invited, but when Sharp shot Doyle a questioning look, the table's owner rubbed fingers and thumb together to indicate the guy was loaded and could be an easy mark.

And he was.

Myron tossed down his drink, and angrily folded his hand. "I'm out. Again."

Sharp looked at his stack of chips and calculated that he'd taken almost twenty bucks off the drunk. The guy should stick to old maid. Sharp smiled and pocketed his smokes and Zippo. When he looked up, Myron, the drunken landman, had a surprise. A snub-nose .38, pointed right at Sharp's noggin.

"You palmed that card." The drunk's tongue was thick. He'd been guzzling gin and tonics for an hour and a half. The gun wavered over the pile of chips.

Sharp slowly moved his hands to the tabletop before answering. "Easy there, friend."

"Don't 'friend' me! You're pullin' a fast one here. I see what's goin' on."

Sharp paid him some attention now. Behind the gun was an expensive suit, tailored, so he hadn't noticed the bulge of the shoulder holster. And now this doughy drunk had the drop on him. His mind kicked into gear.

"If I was cheating, don't you think I'd be winning?" Sharp pointed two fingers and a cigarette at the pile in the middle of the table. Leo was winning the evening.

"Sharp doesn't cheat." Doyle coming to his defense helped, but the gun swung to him.

"You're in this too! You prob'ly get a cut."

Doyle's eyes widened and then immediately narrowed as his face reddened, and his angry jaw tightened.

The gun swung back to Sharp. "Let's see 'em."

Sharp put the Lucky in his mouth.

"Slowly," the drunk slurred.

Sharp almost bit off the end of the cigarette. He deliberately counted out his five cards, face down on the table. His eyes never left the drunk.

"And the sleeves." This drunk was really getting his goat. "Slowly. Smart guy."

Sharp's stare bored through the smoke. He shot his cuffs. "Nothing."

"I don't allow cheating in my place." The gun wavered back to Doyle. You had to have more stupid than moxie to put a gun on Doyle Denniker. Very few were still around to brag about that. "Or gunplay."

The drunk's voice rose. "I'm out almost fifty bucks!" He jumped to his feet, his chair crashing back into the wood-paneled wall. The noise took the drunk's attention, and Sharp came to his feet, jerking the Colt from his jacket. The drunk turned back to a face full of Sharp's .45. He blinked a bit to clear his eyes.

"I . . . uhh . . . I don't want no trouble."

"No, you really don't. Now, why don't you put that Smith on the table before I change the way you part your hair."

He'd been on the wrong end of a gun more than once, and the feeling always ticked him off.

The drunk wavered.

"Slowly," Sharp reminded him.

Just then, the door to Sharp's right opened, and one of the cigarette girls came in spilling out over the top of her red bustier.

"Do you gentlemen need any—oh, shit."

That was the opening Gentry Ferguson needed. The movie cowboy came out of the chair with a big right fist that caught the drunk on the chin and put his lights out. The studio PR machine made sure the world knew

Gentry had genuine guts and had parachuted into the French coast the night before D-Day.

And, as the drunk had just learned the hard way, Gentry did his own stunts.

Sharp holstered his Colt and gave an impressed nod to the actor. "Thanks."

Gentry flashed his celebrated grin. "Thanks, hell. The sonavabitch was going to cost me the pot." He flipped over his cards and proudly revealed two pair: threes and sevens.

Sharp smiled. He'd picked up the tell and Gentry hadn't disappointed. His full house would bring home this pot.

But Leo had other plans. "No, he wasn't." He grinned, and it made his tortoise-shell cigarette holder tilt up at a jaunty angle that Leo thought made him look like FDR.

It didn't.

He laid a pair of eights on the felt and then another pair of eights next to them with a king high.

"Shit, Leo." Doyle, Gentry, and Sharp all said it at once.

Leo gave a sly smile and pulled his golden pocket watch from his tuxedo. "Gentlemen, it has been a true pleasure this evening, but I really do need to go put the

Examiner to bed." He raked the pile across the table while Doyle stepped to the door and waved for a couple of bouncers.

Gentry frowned. "Now, I need a chance to win that back."

"How long are you here?" Leo calculated a chance at additional winnings.

Gentry thought a beat. "At least another week. We're shooting in Utah the end of the month."

Leo nodded. "Beautiful place."

Gentry grinned. "We're just there to fill in the gaps in the scenery for VistaScope. God knows there's no place hotter than Monument Valley in July. I think Ford's trying to kill us."

The major chimed in, "Are you chasing Indians or bank robbers this time?"

Gentry laughed. "I think it's a train heist. Just got the script. Chief has to outrun a locomotive."

"Quality cinema." Leo filled his handkerchief with chips and waddled out to the cashier across the main floor to collect his winnings.

Doyle's gorillas collected the snoozing drunk from the carpet and escorted him to a side door. Sharp knew from a past rapid evacuation of the premises that the door led to a long tunnel that opened through what appeared to be a walk-in freezer door in the kitchen of Rico's Mexican joint next door.

The drunk would wake up at a table with a cup of cold coffee and a hangover, and never know how he got there.

Doyle picked a business card from the carpet where the drunk had been sleeping. He frowned. Then gave Sharp a look. "Can we talk a moment before you leave? In my office?"

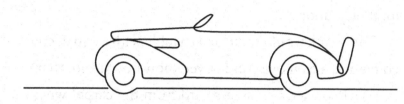

CHAPTER SEVEN

S harp worked his way across the crowded casino to a far door with the word OFFICE lettered neatly in black on the frosted glass. Another gorilla stood guard and raised a hand as Sharp approached. "Just a minute." He growled, and it came out as "Jessaminite."

Sharp figured that the bouncer went six-foot-three and 280, and that Doyle kept him around for his pleasant demeanor and elocution. From the far side of the door, he could hear Denniker tearing someone a new butthole. Doyle didn't really seem like the kind of gentleman who would raise his voice, much less to this level. But apparently, the fact that someone with a gun had gotten into his establishment, and brought said gun to his table, was not on his list of favorite things. He conveyed this with volume, clarity, and a promise that should there be a next time, this gorilla would need to have Doyle's expensive shoe surgically removed.

The door opened, and the gorilla stepped out, exchanging chagrined glances with the door guard on his way past. He, too, was a sizable character, but Doyle had clearly put some serious fear into him. Behind him, Doyle smoothed his hair and straightened his white suit coat. Sharp put a hand in his own coat, remembering his .45 waiting there and swallowed uncomfortably. The door gorilla gave him a wary eye. Doyle beckoned him in, and the door closed behind him.

On a clear night like this, the picture window of Doyle's office looked out over the modern art deco skyline of Fort Worth in the distance. Not much by New York or Chicago standards, but cattle and oil money did what they could, and the cityscape had become an impressive view.

Doyle had everything right here in his darkened office. One wall held a signed one-sheet movie poster featuring

Gentry astride a rearing palomino. Against another wall sat a mahogany humidor, a side table with an Atwater-Kent cathedral radio, and one of the largest freestanding safes Sharp had ever seen.

Doyle opened the humidor and produced a pair of cigars. They went about the ritual of clipping ends and lighting the Cubans. Sharp pulled his Zippo, and Doyle waved him off.

"Don't use that." He opened a small box on the desk, and out came two wooden matches. "Lighter fluid contaminates the tobacco. Changes the flavor."

Sharp nodded but thought that he'd never noticed it hurting his Luckies. But then a carton of his smokes was a fraction of the cost of this single Montecristo.

They puffed the cigars to life, and a small cloud of expensive smoke filled the room. Doyle gestured to a seat across the desk.

He turned and stepped to the big window and the distant skyline.

"So, what are you going to do now, Jeff?"

"Do?" Sharp questioned. "What do you mean?"

"Leo tells me your career as a livestock detective has come to an abrupt end."

"Leo talks too damn much."

"About some things, yes. He's a newspaperman. He can't help himself."

"Yeah, well..." Sharp took a deep drag to give himself a moment. "I haven't really had time to give it a lot of thought." Just that morning, he had been gainfully employed and not exactly happily married. It had been a busy day.

Doyle took his seat at the desk and handed a business card across. "The drunk dropped this when Gentry tagged him."

Sharp frowned when he read it. "Myron Williamson, Sales Agent, Robert Caples Real Estate and Investments." He knew the name. "Bobby Caples? Over here?"

Doyle studied his cigar. "Caples has been wanting a good reason to horn in on Fort Worth for a long time. We've had a gentleman's agreement. He stays in Dallas, I stay here."

Sharp thought for a heartbeat. "You figure he's rethinking being a gentleman?"

"As much as I am." Doyle looked out the window to the world beyond the Fort Worth skyline. "Are you open to a proposal, Jeff?"

Sharp thought hard. Doyle was a great guy. He was an excellent host, and the Four Deuces was the classiest joint between Hollywood and Havana. But he also cultivated a bit of mystery. He might, or might not, be tied to the Mob.

Rumors held that was why Bugsy had been a frequent visitor. And now Bugsy was an obituary.

"What are you thinking?" Sharp inhaled and appreciated the expensive cigar, wondering if it was just cheap bait.

"I need someone who can find out what's behind that card. Was this bum just here to play, or is Bobby fishing? There's too much about Caples I don't know. I need to fix that. I'd like you to do some looking. Find out about his associates, businesses, girlfriends, boyfriends, pets. Everything. I want to know what he had for Thanksgiving dinner last year and who sat next to him."

"Why me? Don't you have people?"

"I want someone I can be sure Bobby doesn't know. Someone who has investigative experience and can be cool if things go south."

"You expect things to go south?" Sharp's voice carried a note of cautious concern.

"I don't know. That's part of what I want you to find out."

"Doyle, I'm not really a private eye. I chase cattle rustlers. I don't have a license or any of that jazz."

"Think you need it? If it'll make you feel better, get one. I just want some information." Doyle unlocked the desk. He pulled out an envelope, then stepped to the enormous wall safe and filled it.

He slid it across the desk to Sharp. "Call this a retainer. Let me know if you need more."

Doyle wasn't taking no for an answer. Sharp looked at the envelope, knowing what it meant if he picked it up. He took another draw on the cigar to buy some time. This was a big step.

But then again, he'd called the number in the lone ad he'd found in the *Examiner* classifieds that afternoon. Leonard's department store needed a security man. Watching for shoplifters and pickpockets or doing some real detective work?

Wasn't really a hard decision on the one hand. On the other, Caples's people were dangerous. Probably not the major leagues of the Mob, but very likely triple A. Getting killed was a legitimate possibility. Or, he thought, he could die of boredom somewhere between Men's Accessories and Ladies' Undergarments.

Sharp picked up the envelope. "I'll start first thing."

Doyle smiled. "I appreciate it. I don't know the best way to do this. You do reports?"

"I can. Or I can just come and tell you. That way, there's no paper trail, no evidence."

"I like that." Doyle studied his cigar. "How do I get ahold of you?"

Sharp thought a second. It occurred to him that he didn't exactly have a home phone number anymore. "I have no idea, right now."

Doyle had an extensive Rolodex on his credenza; he flipped through it and handed Sharp a card. "I sometimes use this answering service. Give them a call. They'll set you up a phone number you can call and get messages from anywhere."

He stood and put out his hand. Sharp shook it. He waited for it to feel like he was selling his soul, but that feeling didn't come.

It should have.

He slipped the unopened envelope inside his jacket's detective pocket and hit the door, nodding to the gorilla on his way out. Dutch let him out into the night, and he felt, more than saw, the tall man's presence outside the ivy wall. A cigarette lighter flared, and Sharp recognized Gentry halfway hiding in the darkness.

"You know, if you're going to be sneaky, you should lose the big white hat."

"Sneaky?" The movie cowboy's cigarette glowed. "You know that's not my style. I want men to see me coming."

"What's up, Gent? You waiting on me?" He and Gentry had spent many an evening across the green felt of Doyle's table.

"I am. We should talk. I think we may have a common concern."

"What's that?" Sharp pulled his Luckies and shook one out.

"Doyle." Gentry took a drag on his smoke for dramatic pause. "And Bobby Caples."

"Isn't this a little local for you? Fort Worth and Dallas bumping into each other?"

"Caples is local, but he's working for Meyer Lansky."

"The Chicago mobster? You've got a running buddy in the Mob?" Sharp searched for Gentry's expression in the darkness.

"Not Lansky, but a guy who wanted to be in the movie business. We did a little business."

"Bugsy."

Sharp could see the big man's eyes in the glow of his Chesterfield.

They said yes.

"Lansky had Bugs killed."

"And now you're involved?" Sharp thumbed his Zippo. It sparked, but he needed to replace the flint.

"Bugs and I did some business together. He was heading up a nice investment property working in Las Vegas. I had a small piece."

"Las Vegas? In New Mexico?" The confusion showed on Sharp's face.

"No, Nevada. Five hours by car from LA. It's gonna be big."

"Never heard of it. So, what would he want with Dallas? Or for that matter Fort Worth?"

"Lansky wants it all. Dallas, Denver, Vegas, all the way to the West Coast. But it starts here. He can't leave gaps in his rear guard."

The movie cowboy took a long draw on his cigarette.

"Doyle know this? About Bugsy?"

"I told him. I also told him I thought Bobby Caples pulled the trigger."

Sharp found a matchbook in his jacket and relit his cigar. Doyle hadn't bothered to mention that there might be Mafia entanglements. He wondered just how thick that envelope in his pocket was.

Money was one thing, but it took a sizable stack to stop a bullet.

Gentry looked off into the darkness. "All I'm saying is keep your eyes open. If you see anything you think I'd be interested in, I'd appreciate a heads-up. I'll do the same."

Sharp nodded. "You're going to be in Monument Valley in a month. I think you'll be away from trouble."

Gentry flicked the glowing butt toward the parking lot and followed it. "If you think these guys can't get you anywhere, you aren't thinking hard enough."

Sharp watched the big movie cowboy fold himself into his Cord convertible and roar away.

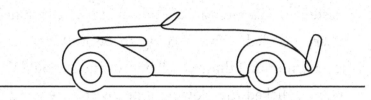

CHAPTER EIGHT

The morning light spotted the bed through the drapes of room 116 of the Skyline Motor Court. Sharp glanced at his naked wrist, then remembered that Lieutenant Jacobs's Hamilton was in the shop. The electric clock on the nightstand showed 6:45. The first day of a new life.

It began with a complete lack of hot water in the shower. Bracing, Sharp thought. Everything was just a matter of perspective. He'd bathed in a stream of melting snow coming down the Italian Alps. He scraped his face, applied a little Lucky Tiger hair tonic, and covered that with his Resistol. At the front desk, the clerk was on the phone to a plumber about the water heater. Sharp thought that was good service.

The Blackstone had a crowd for breakfast. He how-died to a couple of cops he recognized from his days on the force and found a seat at the counter. A charitable soul had left two-thirds of the morning edition of the *Examiner*.

Sharp hunted to see if the Cats, Fort Worth's local AA affiliate baseball club had done any good against Tulsa, but the charitable soul had kept the sports section.

Peggy appeared with a cup of black coffee, and he ordered the Number Two. The outlook in the classifieds hadn't changed in twenty-four hours. But that gig as a department-store dick did look a little more appealing in the morning light.

"You're here early. Hungover?" Roni took the seat next to him.

"You dogging me, Veronica? Every time I turn around, you're playing the bad penny."

"Me? I see you once every five years, and then here you are, all underfoot. And don't call me Veronica."

He grinned, knowing she'd hated the name since she was six. "I just came in for breakfast. You eat here every day?"

"No. But it's the judge's birthday, and Peggy has great cinnamon rolls." Roni nodded to the waitress.

Peggy heard her name and took the order for a half dozen to go. Then did a complete turn, and Sharp's breakfast magically appeared.

He pointed to the eggs with his fork. "You want something?" he said to Roni.

"I had grapefruit before I left the house."

"That's breakfast?" Sharp sprinkled Tabasco across his eggs.

"I'm watching my weight."

Sharp cocked an eye. "You've always been a skinny kid."

"Takes more work these days. Not so skinny anymore." She frowned at her image in the mirrored backsplash behind the counter.

Sharp paid more attention to his eggs. "So did you dump the major?"

She shook her head. "I did not. He's a good guy. He treats me nice."

Sharp looked to Dave's kid sister. "I'm happy for you."

"But he did say he was going to be working a lot and didn't know how steady things would be."

"So you've got an unsteady steady?" he backed the comment with an evil grin. It earned him the bop on the shoulder he fully expected.

"It's not that funny, mister."

"Would I laugh at your discomfort?" He tried to look innocent.

"Only all your life."

She noticed the newspaper on the counter and swiped it, looking at the front-page photo with a screaming headline: "Flying Saucer Crashes! Debris Brought to Fort Worth!" The picture was a staged shot in an office. In the foreground, an Army Air Force colonel was holding a sheet of shiny foil and some sticks. Behind him, trying to duck the camera, was an out of focus Air Force major that they both recognized as Jerry Cartwright.

Sharp mopped the last of his gravy. "Thrown over for a flying saucer and some little green men. You must be devastated."

She was deep into the article. "It says it crashed in Roswell. They brought the remains here."

A flag went up in Sharp's brain. "Remains? Like bodies?"

She read on. "Doesn't say. This is really a crummy article. Your buddy Leo needs better reporters."

"If I know the Army, that's all Leo's going to get out of any of them. And if I know Leo, he'll make up the rest of the story. No telling what the real skinny is." Sharp took the pages from her and analyzed the photo. "You know, I saw some weird lights out to the west the other morning. I bet the major is a guy who would know what's up with those."

Roni jotted a phone number on the edge of the classifieds and handed it over. "See if you have better luck with him than I do."

Peggy interrupted with a crisply folded white box and the glorious smell of fresh cinnamon rolls. Roni dug through her purse for four bits. "Gotta run, hon. Give me a shout sometime."

And with that, she was out the door and off to court.

Peggy and every guy in the Blackstone watched her walk out while Sharp finished his coffee. Peggy gave him the eye. "What she sees in you, I'll never know."

"Sees in me? Roni? Get out of here."

"Uh-huh." Peggy took his plate. "I have no idea what I'm talking about."

Sharp looked at the waitress, then to the door, but Roni was gone. He thought for a heartbeat. Roni? Nah. That wasn't happening. He shook his head at Peggy and went back to the newspaper story and Major Cartwright trying hard not to be front page news. Roni had mentioned a secret job at the base, and Sharp wondered if the atomic plane might be something that could be scaring cattle in the remote ranchlands west of Fort Worth. He and the major should chat.

A phone booth stood in the far corner of the diner. Sharp closed the door and dialed the number Roni had given him. A receptionist answered and asked if the major could call him back. He remembered that he didn't really have a phone number just yet and passed. He fished Doyle's answering service card from his pocket, and ten minutes later, he had a new phone number and someone to answer it. He scribbled his new number, BElmont-1225, on the back of the handy Bobby Caples Real Estate business card.

Caples wasn't famous, but he had a higher profile than Sharp was sure he wanted. He was known well enough for the nightclubs he owned in Dallas, notably the high-tone Bamboo Room and the more notorious Carousel burlesque club. Myron's business card claimed he was also a real estate investor. A trip to the Dallas County courthouse should help him uncover legitimate businesses Caples owned. He'd need to cultivate the rest of the inside information.

Sharp left a quarter under his plate for Peggy and paused just outside the door to look up to the cream limestone of the Examiner Building and the top corner office windows. Some days, one could see Leo Fuller, ten stories above, with his thumbs in his vest pockets, keeping watch over what he considered to be his empire to protect, the entire city of Fort Worth.

Before he got down to the business of Bobby Caples, Sharp would have to do a little erranding around Leo's fair city. In no time at all, he secured a new post office box, had his battered hat steamed and blocked, then dodged the trolley on his way to Haltom's Jewelers where he retrieved the Lieutenant's repaired and cleaned wristwatch. All before the bank opened so he could stash some of Doyle's cash in his safe deposit box.

That box was his little secret. He kept a few things in there that no one else needed to know about. It held a significant amount of poker cash he'd conveniently never mentioned to Evelyn, the title to the LaSalle, and a cut-down Colt semi-auto .45 that almost matched the one in his shoulder holster. There were also a few other trinkets and documents for an emergency such as the one he now faced—no home and no real job. He counted out seventy-five dollars of his stash and tucked the bills in his wallet.

He'd be okay. For a while. He paused for a moment at the open metal box and then unscrewed the gold wedding band from his left hand. It made a satisfying thump as it dropped into the box. He eyed it for a heartbeat and then locked that part of his life away in the bank's vault.

From the bank, he crossed two blocks back to the LaSalle and pulled out into the late-morning traffic. *First things first*, he thought, and steered toward the Stockmen's Association headquarters.

E. G. Lavelle watched him walk in, and Sharp saw the big man reposition his cigar and dig through his stack of manila folders. He rapped on his father-in-law's door frame.

Lavelle didn't say a word. He didn't even look up, just pointed to the farther of the two chairs across the desk, continued his paperwork archeology, and sucked on his cheap cigar. Sharp took the nearer seat and lit up a Lucky to combat the stench.

Lavelle thumbed through a final folder and exhaled a small fog bank. "Sign here." He placed the open folder on the desk and grubbed out a pen.

"What's this?" Sharp was genuinely curious as to how the fat man would handle this.

"Separation papers. You are no longer an employee of the Association."

"Do tell?" Sharp leaned back, an act that reminded him that cactus-perforated portions of his anatomy were still a little tender.

Lavelle smoothed the mustache and took a long draw on the cigar. "You sure you want to do this?"

"Are you? You're liable to hear some things about your precious little girl that a daddy might not want to discuss in front of the steno pool." Sharp gave a head tilt to the typists watching from the corners of two dozen eyes.

"She is not the reason for your termination. We discussed this."

"Oh, so she was the reason I got the job, but her screwing your top hand isn't why I'm getting the boot?" He swore he saw Lavelle wince.

"Affairs in your personal life have no bearing on the fact that you can't do the job."

"Affairs. Good choice of words, E. G."

Lavelle glared. His face was getting red, and it occurred to Sharp he'd never really seen the big man completely lose his temper. Lavelle leaned forward in the chair and placed his stogie in the ashtray. He put both hands on the desk and pushed his bulk to stand. His voice was even and quiet as he leaned forward, and it gave Sharp a cold chill. "Listen, you son of a bitch. You're going to sign these papers. You're going to give me your badge, resign your commission, and walk out that door. And I never want to see your sorry ass again."

Sharp nodded, reached across the desk and tapped his Lucky into the Executive Director's personal private ashtray.

"I'm good with part of that, E. G." He unpinned the steel star and tossed it to the desk.

"The badge is yours, but I'll keep the commission. Texas made me a peace officer, not you. And as for the papers, I'll have my attorney look them over and get back to you. Then we can talk severance pay."

"Oh?" Lavelle leaned back on his bootheels and crossed his arms over his gut. "I figured you'd be a smartass about this. I took the precaution of sending a severance check directly to your house yesterday afternoon. I talked to the bank this morning, and they said it had been deposited. That constitutes acceptance of terms."

"I never saw a check."

Lavelle retrieved his cigar and studied the ash end absently. "Your wife doesn't, by chance, have the authority to endorse a check for deposits at the bank, does she?" He rendered an evil smile, and Sharp stewed about it the entire drive over to Dallas.

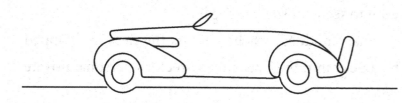

CHAPTER NINE

H ighway 80 wound across the river breaks to Dallas, and even though traffic was light, he found cause to cuss the few drivers in his way and rage to the windshield about the motorcycle cops hiding behind the "Welcome to Grand Prairie" sign as he rolled through. Once upon a time, they'd have been colleagues; now they were just two more members of a world that was pissing him off at every turn.

Sharp eased through Dealy Plaza, the WPA's monument to progress and the former Dallas mayor. The turrets of Dallas's "Big Red" courthouse looked like some out-of-place English castle, dropped onto the edge of downtown by Merlin playing a bad joke on the Round Table. A block away, the seven stories of the Sexton Grocery warehouse guarded the westbound side of the triple underpass. He parked on the street, fed the meter, and dodged traffic to get inside Big Red, where a placard implored visitors to please close the door to preserve the refrigerated air.

The hefty woman behind that counter ignored him for a solid two minutes of typing until, finally, her gaze left the file card she'd been tapping away at. "May I help you?"

Sharp looked at the clock on the far wall, then his boots. He flicked an imaginary bit of lint from his cuff. Today was not the day to play this game.

"Yes, I'm sure you can." He dug into his new notepad and retrieved a now-defunct business card.

"I'm Special Ranger Jefferson Sharp, Fort Worth and Western Stockmen's Association. I need to access your public records vault to verify some title information."

The woman looked over the card. Then back at Sharp. "Basement. Down those stairs." She waved a hand in the general direction of a hallway entrance and returned to pounding the keys of her Underwood.

"Thanks so much for your help." Sharp tried to sound extra sarcastic, but the woman immediately went back to ignoring the next person in line.

The public records vault was closer to a dungeon. Corridors of identical file cabinets stacked to the low basement ceiling were broken by reading tables in the middle of the room. It hadn't changed since he'd made detective in the fall of forty-one, just in time to have that promising career swallowed up by the Army.

He turned his thoughts to the Caples case and tried to push the mass that was E. G. Lavelle out of his mind. Gentry had given him a pretty good clue as to Caples's motive for bumping off Bugsy. Staying in good graces with Mob boss Meyer Lansky and his Chicago Outfit was a decent incentive. Now the trick was to see what Caples was doing about it next.

The files were indexed differently than he'd hoped. He grabbed a Criss-cross directory and found the few properties where he knew Caples was involved. Those addresses revealed a holding company name, which led to another few places. A couple of bars, a wholesale beer distributorship, a liquor distributor, and three residential addresses. One appeared to be Caples's own home at a relatively modest address off Greenville Avenue.

Not exactly Silk Stocking Row. Sharp made a note on two other places. Safe houses? Rental properties? Was Caples's real-estate business legit?

One cryptic entry stood out. Caples was in a partnership called Pegasus Petroleum. Everybody and their dog in Dallas was trying to get into the oil business, but the partners listing held two very interesting signatures. One scrawl was identified as Benjamin Siegel which Sharp knew was the given name of the late Bugsy.

The other was a familiar bold script that he recognized from the movie poster hanging in Doyle's office: his old buddy Gentry Ferguson.

A voice echoed through the dungeon announcing that the courthouse would be closing in fifteen minutes. Sharp double-checked it against the lieutenant's wristwatch: 4:15. Either the afternoon had gone quickly or he just worked slow. And missed lunch. His stomach growled.

He took the stairs two at a time, thinking he could beat the five-o'clock traffic if he hurried and pointed the LaSalle into the glare of the late-afternoon sun. An hour later, he pulled into the parking lot behind Massey's diner. Massey's was a Fort Worth staple with Formica tables and plenty of simple food. Sharp hung his hat on the rack between three other broad-brimmed cowboy hats. He noticed the hatter at Peters Brothers had placed a card in his hatband that read, "Like hell, it's yours, this hat belongs to Jefferson Sharp."

He ordered dinner, then opened his notes to mull while he ate. Caples, he thought, had a pretty good deal. He'd started with one small neighborhood bar. That had become a couple, which he'd sold and bought nicer or bigger joints. Then he'd added the beer and liquor distributorships that serviced his own bars. Assuming he had a place for illegal gambling, he'd taken Doyle's model to another level. The wholesale booze business could move a considerable amount of cash through transactions with the bars, and it could all come out looking perfectly legal. It would be a smooth way to launder a significant amount of money.

His steak arrived, and he chewed on both it and his theory. Caples might be a smart guy. And if he'd shown the ability to expand the business to this level, maybe Doyle had reason to be concerned.

His concentration was interrupted by the female half of an older couple at the table next to him, complaining loudly about their new neighbors. They played records too loud and had people over all the time, parking their jalopies in front of their house. It struck Sharp that she sounded far too much like Evelyn. Which reminded him of unfinished business. He paid his check, tipped his hat to the bitching woman, then steered the LaSalle right back toward his old address.

He steeled himself for a confrontation, but Evelyn wasn't home. His key didn't fit the lock. Apparently, someone had made a quick call to the locksmith. Then again, he'd said he wasn't coming back. Maybe she'd actually listened to him for the first time in her life. He walked around the house and hopped over the three-foot chain-link fence. He and Frenchy Arquette had built it to restrain Evelyn's obnoxious Pomeranian. Then the little devil dug under their hard work and gotten himself run over.

The back door was unlocked, and he let himself in.

Two apple boxes sat on the kitchen table, one with a piece of notepaper marked "Trash," attached to it with cellophane tape. Inside, Sharp found a pair of his boots, his military medals, a framed citation from the FWPD for having saved a citizen after a car wreck, and a bunch of other items he'd rather not lose forever.

The other contained his pride and joy Argus C3 camera, a secondhand photo enlarger he'd found at an estate sale, and some framed photos he'd shot and developed.

Photography had been a hobby most of his life, and the 35 mm camera was a quality setup. Plenty of great pictures in *LOOK* magazine had been taken with a C3, and he'd spent some serious cash on his darkroom. She was going to junk it. He bit his lip. This woman could really tick a man off. She hadn't removed his straw hat from the shelf in the closet, and he added it to the top of the stack. In just over fifteen minutes, he had packed up everything that had any meaning to him. Now, he didn't need to come back. He left the front door unlocked just to be ornery, and drove to the Skyline with the window down and the moon rising behind him.

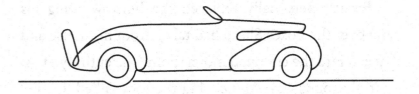

CHAPTER TEN

The bulb flashed and burned out in the bedside lamp when he pulled the chain, so he called the front desk, and the night manager promised to bring one down. His name was Barney, and it seemed to Sharp that Barney was a man bored out of his mind. As far as Sharp could see, he was one of only a couple of guests. The motel was typically used by visitors coming to town for business at the airbase or the big Fort Worth bomber factory. Early summer wasn't a big time for those travelers as folks got through first of the season vacations, weddings, school graduations, and things more important than working on warplanes during peacetime.

Barney personally replaced the bulb, winding his way over the boxes Sharp had taken from his house and packed into the cramped motel room. The entirety of his worldly goods wasn't much, but the boxes filled the tiny room and made finding a more permanent solution to his living space a priority. Sharp thanked Barney as he left and spread the afternoon edition of the *Examiner* on the side table.

The rooms-to-let section of the classifieds was slim pickings. He'd flagged a couple in the paper Roni had given him, but when he called, they'd already been spoken for. He tried two more from the afternoon edition of the *Examiner,* and the second one he called was still available. A two-bedroom, single bath for thirty bucks a month. The landlady was a talkative woman named Norma Hunnakee, and she'd be happy to show him the place right this instant.

The house was deep in the Fairmount neighborhood of bungalows and small family houses not far from the county hospital. Sharp pulled to the curb just past sundown. Still light enough to see that the small porch and gray asphalt shingle siding might need a little work.

In the drive, a compact pink-and-gray Nash Lafayette was parked in front of the sagging garage door. The front door and frame had been poorly repaired, and the paint was peeling. He was just reaching for the doorbell when an old woman's voice came through the darkness beyond the screen door.

"It's open."

Sharp stepped through, and the screen door creaked for want of any lubrication in the last ten years.

"Get the light, will you?" Sharp flipped the wall switch. It didn't help much. The walls were yellowed from tobacco smoke, and the simple schoolhouse fixture centered in the room made little light through the dust that covered it. The room smelled musty.

Ancient Mrs. Hunnakee teetered into the room. She was short and round with thin gray hair and arthritically knotted hands. She cocked her head like a bulldog and examined him through a pair of thick spectacles.

He stuck out his hand. "I'm Jeff Sharp."

"Norma Hunnakee. You want a drink?" Her free hand held a rocks glass of tinkling ice cubes.

"I don't recall ever saying no to that question, ma'am."

"Good answer. I need a refill. Follow me, and I'll show you the house."

She led him through an empty square dining room and into the small kitchen, flipping on lights as they went. The dining-room fixture was a fake chandelier, and Sharp noted it needed more bulbs than it didn't. The place was furnished in a plain and functional style, and that suited Sharp. The kitchen held a Kelvinator icebox and a sturdy O'Keefe and Merritt gas stove. One window looked out to a backyard of knee-high weeds and the other to a prewar Hudson filling the neighbor's driveway thirty feet away.

Mrs. Hunnakee eased herself into one of the three side chairs at an oval kitchen table that had seen better days. She pointed to the icebox. "Ice is up there."

A half-empty bottle of bourbon sat on the table by a wire napkin holder and the old woman's purse.

"First things first." She stated plainly, "You need to know that Mrs. Matthews died in this house about two months ago. You got a problem with that?"

Sharp cracked the lever on the ice tray. "I might, don't know enough yet to say."

She nodded. "She was ninety-seven years old. Her kids had rented this house from me when their dad died back before the war. She'd been here almost fifteen years. Died in her sleep." She pointed a bony finger toward the cabinet on the wall, and Sharp found a second rocks glass upside down on a folded towel. He dropped a few cubes in it and a couple more in Mrs. Hunnakee's glass as she extended it for the refill. He poured, and she let him go a bit more than three fingers full before she nodded "enough." He dumped the remaining ice in a bowl and refilled the ice tray at the sink.

"That doesn't sound so bad." Sharp filled his own glass and offered a silent toast.

"You have kids? Kinfolk?"

"No kids. One soon to be ex-wife. My folks have both passed."

"Kids don't always check up on their elderly parents like they should." Her statement felt like an accusation from personal experience. "Mrs. Matthews was gone a bit before the neighbors noticed."

"A bit?"

Mrs. Hunnakee took a sizable drink. "Three weeks. It wasn't pretty. Neighbors got worried. Called the cops." She took another belt and met Sharp's eyes. "Dumbass cops couldn't call the landlord to let them in. Oh no. That's too easy. They had to bust down the damn door. I would have let them in, but they couldn't be bothered. Cost me twenty-five bucks to have that fixed on top of everything else. And then the handyman did a shitty job on the repair."

Sharp spun the drink in his glass, "When was this?"

"Two months ago. I've had three different people in here cleaning and repainting and repairing. Don't get me started on contractors." She motioned for more bourbon, and Sharp obliged.

"Can I see the room?"

She left her drink on the table and ambled somewhat unsteadily toward the hallway. Sharp wasn't sure if that was a bad leg or the alcohol, but he followed.

The bedroom was surprisingly nice. New paint on the walls and the hardwood floor was freshly polished. The light fixture worked. The closet was newly painted, as well. Sharp was impressed.

"This is all new. I had the old stuff hauled off. Everything is fresh. Back room isn't this good." She snapped off the light, and she showed off the bathroom and the yet-to-be-refreshed back room before returning to the kitchen.

"So, what do you think, Mr. Sharp?"

"How much?"

"Thirty a month. I pay the utilities. Except the phone. You mow the yard."

"How about twenty-five a month, and I'll trade you out some work on the place? Repaint the rest of it. Fix that front door right. If you'll buy the materials."

She considered that and looked around. "Mrs. Matthews was a friend. Like I said, she was here fifteen years. I'd come over sometimes, and we'd play dominoes. Drink sangria wine." Sharp watched her get lost in the memories. Then she came back around to him.

"You handy?"

"As much as the next guy. I know which end of the paintbrush to use and the difference between a screwdriver and vodka and orange juice."

"Can you fix a swamp cooler? You'll need to, or it'll just be a fan."

"I think so—what's wrong with it?"

She looked at him over her bourbon. "If I knew that I'd have it working."

"Gotcha. I can give it a look. I bet I can get it fixed."

She smiled. "That's more than I can say for the last guy who tried. Tell you what, there's some tools in the garage. You can use those, and we do twenty-seven a month."

Sharp grinned to himself. She was a bargainer. He also figured this little rental might be one of her larger pieces of monthly income. He nodded. "I can do twenty-seven."

"I want a month's deposit and the first month in advance. Pay by the first of the month, late on the fifth. No pets, no loose women, no late-night parties."

"That sounds reasonable." Sharp peeled off five tens and a five from his Doyle Denniker stake. She took the money, tucked it into her purse, and came out with a key on string with a tag.

"Pleased to have you, Mr. Sharp." She raised her glass with one hand and handed him the key with the other, and kept the extra buck.

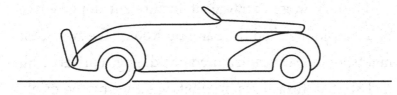

CHAPTER ELEVEN

B arney was excited to see Sharp step into the Skyline
Motel office. He was listening to the WBAP evening
news on the radio and swatting flies. Sharp figured
between that and washing towels, this was about as
thrilling as the clerk's life got. He was less thrilled to learn
that Sharp would be moving on.

Alone in the room, he spread out his courthouse
notes and information and began trying to connect dots.
The problem was that many of the dots were invisible,
waiting until the right time to reveal an answer. But right

now, Sharp didn't really know the questions, much less how he'd find the answer.

Caples's most extravagant investment appeared to be a ritzy joint called the Bamboo Room. The swankiest nightspot in Dallas, it featured fine dining, a private club that skirted Texas laws prohibiting liquor by the drink, and some of the best entertainment around. The house band was the twenty-one-piece Joe Reitman Orchestra, and they were as good as anyone west of Chicago. Sharp had never been in the place, but the word on the street was that an evening there could run as much as he'd just agreed to for a month's rent.

The cash cow of the Caples organization looked to be the infamous burlesque cabaret known as the Carousel Club. Sharp had walked a beat in Hell's Half Acre, Fort Worth's red-light district, so he was quite familiar with the ten-dollar words for strip club. The Carousel brought in almost double what the Bamboo Room did, according to the tax records.

The liquor and beer distributorships also paid serious franchise taxes, which impressed Sharp. It appeared Bobby Caples stayed between the lines when it came to paying his governmental obligations. That was a flag for Sharp.

A guy who was too good a citizen might be using that to keep people from looking too closely.

He lit a cigarette and flipped open his notebook. The lone entry on the page was circled. Pegasus Oil. He needed to have a longer conversation with his old pal Gentry. If he and Bugsy were partners with Caples drilling wells, yet Caples had bumped off Bugsy as Gentry said, this would lead to some very interesting board meetings. If Caples would put a hit on his own business partner, then a competitor like Doyle would have a real reason to be concerned.

This was going to require some investigating.

Sharp was staring out the window into the dark, waist-deep in thought when his head dropped to his chest, and he jerked back awake. He checked the lieutenant's Hamilton and decided he should get some shut-eye rather than try and think like a criminal.

The next morning he took a load of belongings by his new abode, then headed for breakfast, where he could build a list of things he'd need from the hardware store for repairs.

Peggy slid him a cup of coffee and asked if he wanted the usual. He nodded but wondered if he'd really been here enough to have a usual.

The eggs arrived a moment before the tap on his shoulder. The tall, slender stranger in the gray suit looked at him with a question. "You Jefferson Sharp?"

"Who wants to know?" he asked around a mouthful of biscuit.

The stranger stuck out his hand. "I'm Ben Wade, we've got a mutual acquaintance. Elmer Smithson." He wore a big grin.

"Actually, Smitty's kind of at the top of my shit list right now. What can I do for you, Mr. Wade?"

"So, you are Jeff Sharp?"

Somewhere way back in the back of Sharp's skull, an alarm bell rang, but as usual, his mouth was faster than his brain. "I am, why do you care?"

Wade nodded and stuck his hand into a hidden pocket in his jacket. Out came an oversized envelope which he presented formally. "You've been served, Mr. Sharp."

Sharp shook his head and gave a slight smile. Well played. Wade started to step away, his assignment complete. Sharp stopped him. "I have to ask . . ."

Wade turned warily.

He was a get-in-and-get-out kind of process server.

"Woo the tailor make that suit?"

Wade smiled. "Yeah, he did. How'd you know?"

Sharp nodded in professional agreement. "I've got that same pocket. Damn handy."

Wade put a couple of fingers to his hat brim, "Worth every bit of two extra bucks. Have a good day, Mr. Sharp."

Sharp opened the envelope to the handful of papers that informed the Great State of Texas and all of Tarrant County he was being sued for divorce. He tucked them back away and thought that was impressively quick, but then Evelyn had the full legal resources of the Association behind her. He was about to get steamrolled, but at least it would happen on a full stomach. He put a dab of Tabasco on his eggs and finished his breakfast.

Then he hit the Chickasaw lumber yard and left with boards hanging out of the window of the LaSalle, and the trunk loaded down with cans of paint.

Sharp spent the afternoon rolling paint on the walls and cleaning up his new house. The push mower needed the blades sharpened, and the broken handle on the edger had been put back together with black electrical tape, so the landscaping would wait for another day. But by six o'clock, he felt he'd earned the shower and dinner with a cold beer. He parked behind the stucco two-story building and ducked under the neon sign of the Mexican Inn. He'd just bitten into his taco when the proprietor walked through and gave a friendly nod. Tiffan Hall was a legendary gambler and restaurateur, though Sharp had never had much luck in the second-floor game room. Hall's tables might not be the straightest in the county. But he appreciated the fact that the dapper gentleman had kept the room going for more than two decades and had the best chips and salsa in town.

Sharp tipped the waiter and considered taking the stairs to the game room, but his more conservative nature kicked in. If he was going to wager his limited cash reserves, the Deuces offered a little better chance for a return on his investment.

He headed down Thunder Road to Doyle's establishment with the thought that not having a wife or a job to report to meant you didn't have much of a set schedule. He parked behind Rico's with a slight pang of guilt that he should have eaten there, but Hall's food was better, and Rico made a better living watching Doyle's back.

Dutch, the doorman, let him in, and he climbed the hallway to find a nearly empty room. Jimmy the bartender was polishing glasses. He nodded to Sharp and poured

Dewars over three ice cubes and hit it with a splash of soda. Perhaps, Sharp thought, he was a little predictable.

"So, what's up tonight?" Jimmy asked.

Sharp wasn't in the mood to celebrate, but it occurred to him that he should. Evelyn was on her way to history, he had a new place to live and an interesting case to investigate. Considering the week started with a cactus up his butt, people shooting at him, and his wife screwing one of his coworkers, it seemed a marked improvement.

"I think, Jimmy, it's going to be a fairly sedate evening." He toasted the bartender, who raised his own cup of coffee.

Sharp had barely tasted the whisky when he felt the presence next to him. A rail-thin spinster stared at him from three feet behind his left shoulder. He turned and slowly set his drink down.

"Can I help you, ma'am?" Sharp tried not to stare. The woman's floral print dress hung from bony shoulders, and she peered at him through wire-rimmed eyeglasses perched on a nose of impressive size for her small frame. The outfit was topped by a dowdy beige hat, and she stood in sensible shoes.

"Are you Mr. Sharp? Mr. Denniker said you were Mr. Sharp. I'm looking for Mr. Sharp." Her high-pitched screech grated. She eyeballed Sharp, and he noticed that one eye was lazy. Maybe glass. "Are you Mr. Sharp?" Everyone seemed to be asking that today.

"Yes, ma'am. I'm Jefferson Sharp. What can I do for you?" He puzzled over which eye he was supposed to be looking at.

She looked around, as though she were ashamed to be seen in the place and lowered her voice. "Is there somewhere we can talk? Somewhere private?"

Sharp showed her to a seat around the green felt of Doyle's personal card room and pulled the door mostly closed. His last experience in this room had been surprising, and he didn't really know what to expect this time.

The woman gave the room a disapproving once-over. "My husband comes here. He has a weekly card game on Thursdays."

Sharp shook a replacement Lucky Strike from his pack, offering one to her. She declined.

"Nothing wrong with that. I used to play here most Tuesday nights."

"Maybe you know him: George? George Griffin?"

Sharp thought a beat then shook his head. "Name doesn't ring a bell. But I've been out of pocket here for a bit."

"George has played here for quite a while. It started with some men from his work. But lately, he's taken to coming here more often." She met his eyes. "He says."

She removed a lace-edged cotton hanky from her needlepointed purse. Sharp noticed her eyes welling up. "I think there may be another woman."

Sharp prayed this wasn't a prelude to weeping. This skinny woman had a beak like a bird, and she tucked it into the hanky and blew a honk that Jimmy the bartender heard across the club.

"Mr. Denniker says you're a detective. I want you to follow George."

"Ma'am, I'm not really that kind of a detective. I'm mostly a—"

She sniffled. "Mr. Denniker said you could help me. He said you needed work and that you would be able to get me proof if George is . . . is . . ." Her lip quivered and the dam broke. The water works flowed like Niagara. Sharp mentally cussed Doyle Denniker. He hated to deal with a crying woman.

"What makes you think that . . .? Mrs. . . .?" Sharp had already forgotten her name. That wasn't a good sign. It occurred to him that this might be a good time to make use of his new detective's notepad.

He rolled out the lead in his new mechanical pencil.

"Griffin. Velma Griffin." She sniffed. "George has been working late. He's started traveling for work. He's home less and less."

"What does he do?"

The question seemed to perk her up. "He's at Consolidated. George is a lead engineer on the B-36 Peacemaker," she noted with pride.

Sharp nodded. "Nice job."

"At first, I thought it was just the job. The B-36 is a very large project."

"The Aluminum Cloud? Biggest plane I've ever seen. Loud too." Sharp drew a mental picture of the Army Air Force's new ten-engine strategic bomber. The behemoths were being built at the mile-long bomber plant on the west side of Fort Worth.

"George goes in early, stays late, travels to the West Coast, even Washington."

"And, you're suspicious." Sharp shook another Lucky from the pack, and mindlessly lit it. She took a pack of Old Golds from the needlepoint purse, and Sharp lit hers as well.

"There was lipstick on his collar." She stated the fact simply.

Sharp thought about an angle. How to approach an actual detective job. "Well, I can follow him. Get pictures. Write you a report on what I find out."

"That's what I want. I want to know what he's doing and if it's what I think."

"And then?" Sharp studied his cigarette, wondering if she'd thought this through.

"Then? Well, I . . ." She honked her nose again. "I don't know."

"Mrs. Griffin, I've been in your situation. There's a reason they say ignorance is bliss. Having to deal with the truth in cases like this can be difficult, and it will be life changing."

"If he's running around on me, I want life to change."

"And if he's not, you're wasting your time and money. And if he finds out you don't trust him, you could be the one in trouble. This cuts both ways." He met her eyes. Or eye. He still couldn't tell.

She considered that for a moment, but her mind was made up. "I'll pay you ten dollars a week, plus expenses. I want photos." She handed him a scalloped-edged snapshot of the two of them in a suburban backyard.

"He's a big guy." Sharp hoped that wasn't going to be an issue.

"He played defensive tackle at Rice."

Sharp had a couple of quick thoughts: a guy this size wouldn't be that hard to follow, but the consequences of not being discreet could be uncomfortable. However, ten bucks a week would just about cover his nut for rent, gas, and food. Greed won out over fear and good sense.

"I can start tomorrow."

"Very good. How do I get in touch with you, Mr. Sharp?" She tucked her cigarettes back into the needlepoint.

He thought for a second and remembered his new phone number, "I have an answering service—BElmont-1225. It's answered twenty-four hours a day."

She looked at him, waiting. Then dug through the purse for her own pencil and small notepad. "Mr. Sharp, as a detective, you should invest in some business cards."

Sharp nodded and passed on admitting he'd only been in the detective business for a couple of days. He turned over a page on his notepad and took down the particulars on George Griffin, then stood and shook Mrs. Griffin's hand.

She looked the place over one last time on her way out, making her disdain of Doyle's den of sin sufficiently obvious.

The next morning, the bell jingled as Sharp pushed through the door for what was becoming a routine breakfast stop at the Blackstone.

He scanned the room for an empty seat and started to head for the counter when a hand went up and caught his eye.

Roni gestured to the empty seat at her two-top table.

"You're early this morning." Sharp added his straw hat to the tree and took the offered seat.

"What? A girl can't go out for breakfast? I like this place." She'd finished her grapefruit.

"Yeah, but it's not right for a girl to just come eat by herself. Looks odd," he counseled his late buddy's kid sister.

Though now that he thought about it, the age difference didn't seem as vast as when he was ten and she was an obnoxious seven-year-old.

"Well, you're here."

"Sure now, but what if I hadn't shown up?"

"I figured you weren't getting a better offer." She smiled. She had a nice smile.

"Yeah. You've got me down pat."

Peggy arrived with an automatic cup of coffee, and Sharp took a hot sip.

They sat quietly for a moment and he watched Roni look distantly out the window.

"Hey. What are you doing Saturday night?" That question brought her back with a slight start.

"What?"

"Saturday night. I need to go over to Dallas and check out some establishments. You'd be good cover."

"Cover." The response had some frost on it.

"Well, it'd be the Bamboo Room, if that makes a difference."

Her eyes got even bigger than they usually were. They were a very deep brown.

"The Bamboo Room? I'd need a new dress and shoes."

Sharp thought a moment and covertly slid a ten across the table. Then added a five. "Get a nice hat too."

"Why, Jeff-er-son, is this a date?" A thought clouded her face, and she paused. "I don't really go out with married men."

"This is an investigation. I can go snooping around by myself, but if it's you and me looking like a couple out on the town, maybe I won't stick out like a retired ranch hand in the swankiest joint in town."

"You do know how to say just the right things to a girl, Mr. Married Man."

"Mr. No Longer Married Man." He waggled his ringless left hand at her. "Evelyn filed. I got the papers yesterday. You mentioned you might know a lawyer?"

She perked up, seemingly satisfied that if legal proprieties were being followed, she wouldn't be home-wrecking. "Tom Hall. Best around. Might not be cheap, but he's good."

The waitress refilled their coffees and took Sharp's order.

"So are you going to do the detective thing? Jefferson Sharp, Private Eye?" She held a cigarette to her lips.

He lit it and lowered his voice. "Nothing like that. Doyle wants me to get him some information on Bobby Caples. I'm doing a little digging. No big deal."

She blew her smoke sideways. "Silly, what do you think a private detective does? I mean that and following cheating husbands is pretty much the standard job description."

Sharp opted not to mention Velma Griffin and her cheating husband. Roni leaned in and whispered, "Jeff, Bobby Caples is a dangerous kind of guy. Are he and Doyle getting crossways? Do you need to be in the middle of that?"

"Well, the middle is where all the money seems to be, so that's where I am. How do you know Bobby Caples?" His Number Two arrived, and Peggy refilled their coffees again.

"He was in our court. Tax charges. And some of his associates got a little rough when the search warrants were served."

"I'm just doing research. Doyle assures me there's not any rough stuff involved."

"And Doyle, with his hidden gambling hall, who just might be tied in with the Mafia, has never misled anyone."

She had a point. He'd need to be doing better research. If his work had Caples squeaky clean, but he'd been in tax court, he could be missing something. Several patrons around them began to pay their tabs and depart. Sharp checked the lieutenant's watch; it was time to see what Mr. Griffin's day looked like.

Roni closed her paper and swatted his arm. "I have court this morning, so it's time for me to be off."

"So we're good for Saturday night? I'll get us reservations. Pick you up at seven?"

"It's a date." She pulled out a compact and rolled out her lipstick.

"It's not a date. When you're out with the major, that's a date. This is work."

She cocked her head behind the tiny mirror and shot him a dirty look. "Well then, I'll try and be good cover."

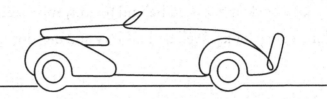

CHAPTER TWELVE

G eorge and Velma Griffin lived in a tidy white frame home between the huge Montgomery Ward store on Seventh Street and the Will Rogers Center, home of the annual Fat Stock Show. Sharp knew the neighborhood, but not well. Fortunately, George had a green Oldsmobile that wasn't too hard to follow. They wound through the streets, and Sharp stayed far enough behind to not be tagged as a tail.

It didn't hurt that he was confident he knew George was headed to the massive Consolidated Aircraft plant on the west side of town near Liberator Village. George waved to the guard at the gate of Army Air Force Bomber Plant No. 4 as he drove through, and Sharp took a left along the perimeter road, keeping the Olds in view. The bomber plant, as the locals called it, was one of the biggest buildings in the world when it had been constructed. Sharp worried that he'd lose Griffin in the vast parking lots, but George parked in a spot relatively close to the cyclone fence, and his giant size made him easy to spot as he was swallowed up by the huge engineering building.

Sharp parked across the road and made a few notes. He added a pair of war surplus binoculars to his list of things he hadn't known he needed to be a real private eye. He also needed to bring his camera. He promised to get pictures for Mrs. Griffin, and that was hard to do when the Argus was still in a box at the rent house. He considered if this private investigator bit was going to be a real, paying job, or if he might privately investigate a job at this enormous airplane factory. He'd seen a few security types riding along the fence in a jeep, and it looked more comfortable than chasing cattle rustlers.

Once upon a time, metal and glass and rubber had gone in one end of the enormous Consolidated Aircraft building in the morning, and a half dozen B-24 Liberator bombers had come out the other end by the afternoon. But now, with the war over and one plane and one bomb able to level an entire city, less demand for relatively cheap bombers had most folks thinking that men like George would be out of work.

Sharp lit a Lucky and watched the stragglers show up late to work, thinking how the Great State of Texas had politicians like Sam Rayburn and Cactus Jack Garner lobbying their days away in Washington, and Fort Worth had publisher Leo Fuller spilling barrels of ink to promote the region and occasionally wine and dine the president himself. When the time came to defend the peace, the plant magically transitioned from production of the slab-sided, twin-tailed B-24s to constructing the gargantuan ten-engine, atomic bomb-carrying B-36 Peacemakers that promised to keep George Griffin and fifteen thousand others busy for decades to come. Sharp considered that if he could get on at the plant as a security man, he could be set for a while.

He waited for most of an hour and figured that George was going to stay at work. Sharp got out of the car and stretched his legs with a stroll to the phone booth on the corner. He deposited a dime and called his new answering service. Both his clients now had the new number.

"Jefferson Sharp Investigations." A pleasant voice answered.

"Messages for BElmont twelve twenty-five."

"There are no new messages, sir."

"Okay, thanks." That was handy. The lieutenant's watch said 9:15, and that felt like a good time to get the detective business going. He could come back in a couple of hours and catch George if he snuck off for extracurricular activities at lunchtime.

The first stop was the post office, to see if mail had been forwarded to his PO box. Important things like severance checks, he thought, but the mailbox was empty along with all hope that Evelyn wasn't enjoying that check more than he ever would. He ran by Brumley's Printing and ordered business cards to make Mrs. Griffin happy and then, the Army-Navy surplus store.

The binoculars were brand new. Probably ordered when the Navy thought they were going to have to stage a full-on invasion of Japan. Sharp parked across the street from the lot where George's Oldsmobile sat right where he'd left it. He unwrapped the cellophane paper and tossed aside the official Navy technical booklet while wondering how dumb swabbies were if they needed operations manuals for binoculars.

In the distance, a steam whistle blew, and thirty seconds later, people began emerging from the various doors around the complex on their way to offsite lunches. Sharp sat, waiting for George and knowing the large commissary in the plant meant he could very well be wasting quality time during which he could have painted his rental. As if to read his mind, Griffin emerged from the building, laughing with three women.

"Jackpot." Sharp uncapped the binoculars and tried to find the quartet as he focused and unfocused the Bausch and Lombs. George appeared fleetingly in his blurry field of view. But he was alone. Sharp finally got the lenses focused, but by then, the women had vanished, and George had disappeared into the Olds. He set the binoculars next to the booklet that told how to focus the lenses.

Sharp followed discreetly as George drove down the street to the Bailey Bar-B-Q stand. He followed the big man inside and stood three people behind him. George had two chopped beef sandwiches with extra pickles and iced tea. Sharp opted for a smoked sausage sandwich, a Dr Pepper, and a seat in a repurposed grammar-school desk on the far side of the small dining room. George squeezed himself into his own too-small desk with a dexterity that told Sharp this wasn't his first visit to the joint. George ate his sandwiches, read the *Examiner*, and Sharp watched him do it. Then they both headed back to the plant. This was the exciting life of a private eye.

Sharp spent the afternoon working on the house, fixing the front door frame, rolling paint on the walls, and cleaning up the place. With a little work, he could turn the back bedroom into a darkroom for his photos.

He sharpened the mower blades and mended the broken handle on the edger, then put them to use so the place wouldn't look deserted, while the Bell telephone man installed a new Western Electric phone. Sharp used it to call Doyle and give his most prominent client his answering-service number. He had a few things to discuss with Doyle, but the man was headed out of town until Saturday night. They made an appointment to meet on Sunday morning.

At 4:45, he returned to Consolidated to discover the shift change had already happened. The lots were emptying, and George and his Oldsmobile were gone. He had a flash of panic but figured the best bet was to head straight to the Griffin residence and see if George was there. A block away from the house, he could see the Olds in the driveway and breathed a sigh of relief.

George was walking up the steps as he drove by and met Velma's eyes as he passed. He saluted, and she nodded in recognition. Yes, ma'am, no problem. Jefferson Sharp, on the job.

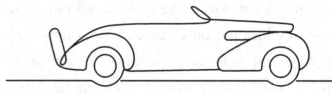

CHAPTER THIRTEEN

For the next few days, between trips to the courthouse records vault and the public libraries tracking down Bobby Caples's empire, he watched George Griffin get barbecue at lunch and drive straight home from work in the afternoon. He alternated between staking out the parking lot of the BBQ stand and casually entering like a regular patron. Sharp would take a seat with his back to big George and scarf down a barbecue sandwich. Occasionally, George joined some colleagues for lunch, but they were all male engineers, stamped out in the same white, short-sleeve shirts, dull ties, and scintillating conversation.

So far Sharp's eavesdropping had earned him little more than an education on carburetor icing issues on the B-36. Since the multiple prop-driven engines were mounted backward on the wing, the engine heat that usually prevented icing blew the wrong way. George's team was designing a bracket or a baffle or a baffling bracket to solve the issue. Sharp wondered if this type of fascinating aeronautical information would ever do him any good, or if he should just remember it for casual cocktail-party conversation.

He was sitting in the sweltering afternoon heat waiting for George to head home when he picked up a distant familiar whine that sounded very similar to the noise he'd heard on the Rafter B. The binoculars went into overdrive, scanning the far reaches of the base. Nothing. He dropped the LaSalle into gear and sped through neighborhoods. The tires squealed as he took Roberts Cut Off to Sansom Park and skidded to a stop on the high bluff that overlooked the bomber plant and the southern end of Lake Worth. He jumped out of the car and zoomed the Bausch and Lombs. He found the aircraft just outside a hangar near the end of the runway. It looked like some strange mechanical insect with a round glass bubble on one end and a ladder-like framework behind. A giant fan of four blades sat on top of the bubble.

The crew working on the craft swarmed over it, then one of them took a seat inside the bubble, and the others backed away as if the mechanical bug might come apart at any moment. The blades began to spin, slowly at first, then rapidly enough that Sharp couldn't even see them.

The familiar whine was still there, now accompanied by a weird rhythmic thumping.

The craft wobbled into the air, lifting straight up off the tarmac. It tilted slightly and moved down the runway, staying about a hundred feet in the air, then toured around but always remained within the perimeter of the base. Sharp's vantage point was a hundred feet higher than the runway, but the vehicle never went higher than he was.

After fifteen minutes and a series of maneuvers, the aircraft rattled through the air back to where it started. It stopped in mid-air, then slowly settled. The blades stopped spinning, and the crew came back out.

He lowered his binoculars as the flight line team attached wheels to the undercarriage and moved the flying bug back into the safety of the hangar.

Sharp gave a wry smile. He knew exactly what he was looking at. If this thing had lights on the ends of those blades, he could envision it as the mysterious monster that had scared the crap out of Dollar and the Rafter B cattle. Now he just needed to find out what the hell it was.

By the time Saturday night arrived, Sharp had mulled over the flying erector set from every angle. He'd also repaired the front door, painted the whole place, and replaced the screen in the back door. He had changed out the float switch and fixed the swamp cooler. The entire joint was clean from top to bottom, and he'd trimmed up the yard so it looked like a human being lived there.

His house was taking shape. So was the business. He was very close to finishing up his first case, having determined that either Velma was wasting her money or George and his secretary were getting hot and bothered in a supply closet at Consolidated. Sharp wasn't getting pictures of that. So far, he hadn't even taken his Argus out of the camera case.

He washed the LaSalle, and it sparkled in the late-afternoon sun as he locked the front door and waved to the neighbor kids playing tag.

Roni lived across Camp Bowie Boulevard in a nice house she and Frenchy had purchased before he had gone off to the war. The Sharps had dined a time or two with the Arquettes back in those simpler times. The men had a beer on the back porch and talked cop shop by the charcoal grill while the women chatted about marrying the entire police department in the den. It seemed like an awfully long time ago, Sharp thought as he pulled into the drive behind Roni's little yellow Pontiac coupe.

She answered the door in a robe. He instinctively tugged back the cuff of his gray pinstriped suit and looked to the lieutenant's wristwatch. He might've rolled his eyes.

She wagged a finger. "Don't start, mister. I'll be ready in a minute."

"I didn't say a word." He shrugged, thinking that there must be something with the female gender that made them unable to be on time for appointments.

Roni let him in and then padded back barefoot toward the bedroom. He could see the house was well kept, though he never really thought of Frenchy's widow as a homemaker. He set his hat on the coffee table and checked to see if she still hid the liquor where Frenchy had always stashed it.

"There's ice if you want to make a drink. I won't be a sec." She called from the back room. He took her up on it and found the Cats game on the radio. Fort Worth was down three runs in the bottom of the sixth.

"You want one?" he called.

"I'm good," came the muffled reply

A drink and an inning later, the Cats had two on and were mounting a comeback. Sharp was building another scotch when Roni stepped into the living room, pulling on long white gloves that accented the deep burgundy dress with a neckline cut down to Venezuela.

Sharp's eyes lingered a long moment, and he caught himself before he whistled. It was an impressive package.

"Jeff?" She looked at him strangely. "You okay? Something wrong?"

"Huh? Yeah. No. I mean, I'm good. Sorry."

"How much have you had to drink?"

"Drink? Um, this is number two. You, uh, want one?" He was off his game. This wasn't a Roni he was used to. "Um . . . you look great."

"Why, Jeff-er-son, thank you. I wondered if you ever noticed." She batted him with her clutch and walked into the den.

He even admired the walk.

"I thought we needed to get going?" She looked back at him over a bare shoulder.

"Um, yeah. We'll need to hurry if we're going to make our reservation." He gulped the scotch. When in the hell did Dave's pesky little sister turn into a bombshell?

The Bamboo Room was everything Sharp expected. A valet opened the door for Roni and whisked the LaSalle off to a remote parking area. The maître d' checked for the reservation and led them to a quiet table along the far wall.

Sharp didn't know if everyone noticed when Roni came down the steps, but they missed a good time if they didn't. Their table was draped in white linens, candlelight, and a centerpiece that looked vaguely nautical. The entire place had some sort of South Sea isles motif, but Sharp had played poker with a few marines who had hopped across South Sea islands, and their recollections painted a much different picture of the environment.

The waiter brought a round of cocktails, and Sharp ordered her the lobster and a steak for himself.

"You don't have to do that." She batted her eyes, but he was pulling out his Luckies and missed the flirt.

He reached across with the Zippo to offer her a light. "Hey, it's a business expense. It's on Doyle."

He wondered for a moment what he'd missed, as she rolled her eyes and said, "Tell Doyle thanks. I don't often get an evening like this."

"Me either. Or food like this." He chuckled as the waiter placed an appetizer of bacon-wrapped scallops between them. "I guess I'm going to need to learn how to cook."

She started to say something but caught herself. "You can't cook? Not even pork and beans?"

"I don't even own a pan. And if I ever did, I think most all of that is going away in the divorce."

"Peggy said you got served right in the middle of the Blackstone."

He grimaced and thought he should talk with the waitress about her mouth. "Yeah. I was officially cut loose by the Association too."

"Geez, so this really is your business now."

His hand went to his jacket pocket and retrieved his new business card case. "You get the very first one."

The crisp white business card proclaimed:

Jefferson Sharp, Confidential Investigations
PO Box 178
Fort Worth, Texas
BElmont-1225

"Impressive, very professional." She admired the card and tucked it in her clutch.

Their wine arrived, and Sharp uncomfortably went through the ritual of sniffing, sipping, and nodding. "This is a whole different world than it was two weeks ago."

Roni paused and looked around the room. "Is that so bad?"

Sharp raised his glass to her. "You know. It's really not."

She held his gaze a moment, and he swore she started to blush, but he wrote it off as the house lights dimming so the orchestra could assemble.

The conversation paused as they both searched for a direction to take things. They were saved by a pair of waiters arriving with a linen covered cart carrying a large silver dish. The lead waiter removed the lid with a flourish to reveal her lobster and his medium-rare ribeye. The sommelier presented, then opened and poured from another bottle of wine, and as quickly as they had arrived the tuxedoed waiters disappeared back into the atmosphere of the room.

The meal was perfect. He had to give the Mob credit—gangsters did know their food.

They ordered dessert, enjoyed a very nice bottle of wine, and Sharp lit his and hers after-dinner cigarettes.

She exhaled with a curious expression. "So, you met Jerry during the war?"

It took Sharp a beat.

"Jerry? Oh yeah, the major. Yeah. I drug him around a forest in Italy for a couple of days."

"Was it bad?"

"It wasn't a good time."

"Tell me about it."

He glanced around the elegant dining room. "I don't know if this is really the place for war stories."

"If you really don't want to, I think I understand . . ." She looked to the far wall then right into his eyes. "But my guys left home for that war and never came back. I'll never know what happened to them. How did you and Jerry make it back when Frenchy and Dave didn't? I want to know. I think I deserve to know."

Sharp thought back to Italy and looked back into her big brown eyes. He sighed. "You really want this? It's not exactly a fun tale."

She scooted her chair around and settled in, ready for story time. "The orchestra doesn't start for a bit."

"Okay." Sharp took a long drag on the Lucky and blew the smoke to the ceiling.

"We were getting shelled outside of San Marino, it was down to me and a corporal, two PFCs, and a radio messenger I'd never seen before."

He spun the drink in his glass as if to wind the clock back to that awful day.

"Radio and I are yelling, trying to get some cover while the German artillery is zeroing in on us. Boom. Boom. Boom. Walking these great geysers of dirt across the field towards us. There's not a damn thing you can do. About the time the last one is headed for us, Major Jerry Cartwright appears in his P-38, starts strafing the hell out of the German lines. The artillery stopped, but there's that one last round that's still in the air . . ."

Roni watched his mind go back there and wondered if this might not have been the best idea, but he didn't slow down.

"So, the round hit right next to our foxhole. Shrapnel got the corporal and hit me in the shoulder. This private and I go scrambling for the trees, but my rucksack strap is sliced through, and I'm tripping over the pack with it wrapping around my legs. I'm flat on my ass when I actually see the round that gets the major's plane. One of those deadeye German gunners took the tail boom right off his fighter. It just went to pieces, and this time, it's the better part of an airplane that's coming right at us. It was a big chunk of ragged aluminum spinning out of the sky like a giant saw blade."

Roni inhaled sharply, and it brought Sharp back to the moment. He looked around. The orchestra was tuning up. Other diners were enjoying an elegant evening, and the gorgeous, calm room was a complete contrast to the mayhem in his memory.

"What happened?" She leaned in.

He nodded and took another sip. "We died. The major crashed into the trees and exploded, and that big old chunk of aluminum cut me in half. Everybody died. Except the private. He runs a greeting-card company now."

She socked him in the arm.

"The plane came apart. It was dumb luck that it missed us. I never saw a chute, but I decided to get the hell out of there. The private vanished—I never saw him again. I knew the command lines were about a mile and a half to the south, so I started hiking. Half an hour later, I hear this voice above me. That's how I met your major. He was in a tree, hanging in his chute, asking if I had a knife. He cut himself loose, and I did a lousy job trying to catch him."

"That's why he limps," Roni observed.

"That, and I'm sure when the Germans found him, they didn't do him any favors. He really blasted them before they shot him down." He took another drink of scotch. "He passed out when he hit the ground. He'd lost a lot of blood, and I didn't have much of a first-aid kit left in my gear. I built a litter with my one good arm and then tried to drag him through the woods and back to our lines for two days. He was in and out of it." He was down to the ice in his glass.

"Finally, he woke up enough to tell me to leave him. It wasn't my favorite idea, but we both thought I could get him some help before the Germans got to him. I went for help, and half an hour later, they counterattacked again. He never had a chance."

"But you saved his life." There was sadness in her voice. "And you made it home." The war had taken the men she'd known more intimately than any others and here were two complete strangers giving each other a second chance.

Sharp saw the pained look in her eyes. "Everyone there was just trying to survive. When the counterattack caught up with me, I'd fallen in with a couple of other stragglers and we fought our way back to the Allied lines. Those guys were in bad shape too, but we got them back to the medics."

"What happened to you?"

"I was in the hospital for a month. The Army was all out of lieutenants, so they gave me that job and a platoon. We held our own across the Alps in spite of some idiotic command decisions, and when we got to Rome without getting everybody killed, they made me a captain."

He polished off his scotch-flavored ice and set the glass on the white linen with a degree of seriousness the moment needed. He found her eyes and took her hand.

"And that, is how I personally won the Second World War."

She laughed. She had a musical chuckle, and it made him smile.

"So what do you want to talk about now? Famine? Pestilence?"

She grinned. "How about the Cosa Nostra? It looks like Roberto Cappellini just came in."

Sharp followed her gaze. "Roberto Cappellini? You mean Bobby Caples?"

"I told you he was in Judge Rowan's court last month. On the docket, he's Roberto Cappellini."

He nodded and then noticed her hand was still in his. She noticed that he noticed and pulled it back.

"Sorry," he said.

She tilted her head toward the table they were watching.

"What is it?" He looked over as a few people began to loiter around Caples's orbit.

"That's the Dallas County DA," she whispered into the centerpiece.

"Which one?"

"In the tux. The older one is Augie Jenson, good lawyer. He's Caples's attorney." She knew all these players from court.

"So by good lawyer, you mean he's good at what he does, not that he's a good guy and a lawyer?"

"Doesn't being a mob lawyer automatically mean you're not one of the good guys?" She smiled at her own joke.

Sharp also noticed the oversized gentleman standing against the wall behind Caples's table. He appeared to be trying to hide a Sherman tank under his jacket. Sharp was reasonably sure the wall molding hid a door for quick escapes. An equally large fellow with a broken nose guarded the exit, and his awkward way of standing made Sharp bet a pistol was riding uncomfortably in the small of his back.

They finished the bottle of wine as a steady stream of glad-handers paused at Caples's table to give their regards to the mobster. Roni recognized more than a few: the

Dallas County sheriff, a couple of city commissioners, and the mayor pro tem.

The music began. The Joe Riechman Orchestra was as good as advertised. The tune was a mellow Glenn Miller number, and he met her eyes.

"You want to give the dance floor a go?"

"Jeff, I haven't danced in . . ." He watched as her widow's memory took her back to places both fantastic and horrible. He reached for her hand and gave a knowing, gentle smile.

"Yeah. Me neither. Let's give it a try."

They stepped hesitantly onto the rapidly crowding floor. It took a few steps, but they found their feet and fell into the natural rhythm of the melody.

"Hey, you're pretty good." Sharp wasn't as surprised as he sounded.

"While you and Dave were out playing baseball all summer, I was enduring four years of ballet. Mom was a stickler."

"It's done you more good than playing third base ever did me." The faint fragrance of her perfume blended with the music and the wine, and Sharp lost himself for a moment. It had been years since something had felt this nice. They stepped together and he glanced over her lovely shoulder as Bobby Caples stood to greet a group. It brought him back, remembering this was his late partner Frenchy's widow, Dave's kid sister, and the major's girl. He flashed anger at himself—he was supposed to be on a stakeout. He shook his brain loose and stole a look at Caples's table.

He began to make the mental notes an on-the-job, working detective should. Caples was drinking champagne—Moët. He was left-handed. Smoked Raleighs in a three-inch black onyx holder. A silver lighter. He carried the smokes in his right suit pocket. Judging from the way he held his head in conversation, he might be a touch deaf in his left ear.

"Any idea who that is with Caples? He looks familiar." He stepped a turn so she could see the table.

Three men stood over it, the one in the center was a tall guy with large ears.

"He's that congressman from Austin. He's running for the senate against Governor Stevenson. Landon Johnson? Landry?" They did a quick turn. "Lyndon. Lyndon Johnson." She all but snapped her fingers.

"Yeah, that's him."

"I wonder what he's talking to Caples about?" She peeked around his shoulder.

"A mobster, a lawyer, and a congressman walk into a bar . . ." Sharp never got to finish the joke. Johnson shook hands with Caples and turned away, and another large gentleman took his place. Gentry Ferguson. Sharp spun his back to the table.

"A little notice next time there, Mr. Astaire."

He maneuvered them to the opposite side of the floor as the number ended. Onstage, the bandleader went into his patter about the next tune, and Roni stiffened.

He saw her eyes widen and slid his hand from her back to her hip, where he could get to the Colt if he needed it. "Jeff, Gentry Ferguson just sat down at Caples's table."

"I saw that." They did a little box step so he could get a better look without being seen. The King of the West was parked there, signing an autograph as Caples's personal waiter was pouring champagne. Sharp thought they looked to be awfully buddy-buddy to be talking about Caples having shot Gentry's business partner Bugsy.

However that relationship worked, Doyle was not likely to be happy about this.

Almost on cue, Gentry stood in a huff and leaned his large frame over the table, jabbing an index finger at the host. Behind Caples, the two bodyguards exchanged concerned looks.

All the way across the room Sharp could see the goons were just waiting on their boss to give the nod. Sharp thought this might not end well for the big cowboy. Gentry spun on a bootheel and stomped from the room.

"Jeff..."

"Veronica?"

"Let's get out of here."

"What? Why?"

"I've got a funny feeling about this. I know Gentry's your poker buddy, but there's something fishy about this." She bopped his shoulder. "And don't call me Veronica. I hate that."

"Why do you think I do it?"

Her smirk was a good answer.

He steered her back to their table. "Let's give this a moment to cool down."

He motioned for a waiter. "Two coffees please. One with sugar."

"What was that?" Roni leaned in with a whisper and bobbed her head toward Caples's empty table.

"Could be a business disagreement."

"Your buddy, the movie star, is in business with the mob?"

"Gentry thinks he enjoys a little danger." Sharp lit each of them a smoke and watched Caples and his entourage toss napkins to the table and leave the room.

Roni watched with fascination.

"But I'm not sure he understands these guys don't just drop it when a director yells, "cut," to get him out of a tough spot."

Their coffee arrived as a clarinet player stepped to the front of the stage and the orchestra launched into "Begin the Beguine."

Roni watched the musician. "Did you know Jerry plays the clarinet?"

Sharp cocked his head. "The major? It wasn't really something we talked about what with the whole not-bleeding-to-death stuff to occupy the conversation." Sharp took a sip of seventy-five cent coffee.

"He's pretty good. Maybe not as good as this guy or Benny Goodman, but pretty good."

He watched her get lost in the music.

"You like him, huh?"

She blushed a touch.

"He's sweet. And smart. But I worry about some of the people he hangs around with." She blew smoke his way.

"Yeah, well, it's been a while since he and I wandered around the woods."

One of Caples's goons returned and took up his station against the wall. A new champagne bucket appeared and busboys reset Caples's table.

Sharp stubbed out his smoke. "You ready to get out of here?"

"Can we, please?"

He paid the impressive tab and she gathered her clutch.

Sharp gave his ticket to the hat-check girl and asked to have the LaSalle brought around.

Roni nodded toward a restroom sign. "I'm going to go powder my nose while you get the car."

She disappeared just as Caples and his second goon came around the corner from the restroom lobby and headed back to the main room. Sharp told the hatcheck girl he'd be right back and ducked down the hallway where three doors waited: GENTLEMEN, LADIES, and OFFICE. Sharp figured he knew what to expect in the gents and ladies, but the office was worth a look.

He tried the door, which was, predictably, locked, but with a cheap lockset. He pulled out his pocketknife and slid the blade between the door and the jamb. A push and a shake later, the strike slipped. He eased in quickly and closed the door behind him. The cheap lock didn't set. It was a reasonable bet that he'd broken it.

The room was dark, and there wasn't enough light from the transom to make out anything. He took a chance and turned on the desk lamp.

The desk was locked, and he might have broken that mechanism as well. He could be a bull in a china store when he was in a hurry. But the large drawer to the left held a rack of hanging files. Several were labeled with cryptic words like "Vegas" and "Flamingo," but he found one file halfway back marked "Panther City." Sharp smirked. His old Fort Worth patrolman's badge had featured the city's big cat mascot atop the shield.

The third page in the Panther City folder held a list of letters and numbers, and midway down was a slight surprise as he recognized the phone number of his old friend, publisher Leo Fuller. Behind that was a sheaf of papers that looked suspiciously like contracts for real-estate transactions with neighborhood names and lot numbers. It might as well have been in Greek. He pulled his notebook and started to copy down the information when footsteps paused at the door. He snapped off the desk lamp and dropped behind the desk just as the door opened. He stuffed the file folder into his jacket and quietly eased the drawer closed.

He couldn't see who stepped in, but the intruder closed the door quietly, and the broken lock rattled. Sharp imagined that things were going to get dicey when the guy came around that desk. He balled a fist and made ready to take him by surprise when a shapely ankle in silky nylons appeared.

"What the hell, Roni?"

She nearly jumped out of her skin.

"What are you doing here?" She whispered louder than if she'd simply spoken.

"Shhhh. What do you think I'm doing?" He moved her around the desk toward the door.

"Me too. I thought I'd help. I thought his office might hold . . ."

More footsteps at the door. And a knock. A man's voice.

"Mr. Caples?"

Sharp looked for a place to hide. The door opened, and he pulled Roni into his arms and kissed her as passionately as he could.

The awkward moment was exactly what he wanted.

"Uhhh, you folks can't be in here."

He released Roni, who blinked a couple of times and caught her breath, then Sharp got a good look at the surprised intruder. They had the same thought, but the other guy said it out loud. "Hey, I know you."

It was Myron Williamson, the drunk from the Four Deuces.

This time Sharp got his shot first and threw a right cross that tagged Myron's chin. He went down like he was getting good at it. Sharp grabbed Roni's hand, and they high-stepped over the stiff and out the door, turning down the hall where his hat was waiting with the check girl, and the LaSalle was idling at the curb.

The valet helped Roni in. Sharp tossed him a quarter as he jumped behind the wheel.

"That was close." He stated the obvious.

She straightened her hat and tried to calm down. "So, who are you going to kiss when I'm not around?"

"Probably a fist."

"That would serve you right."

They rounded the corner, and there at the Bamboo's private entrance, Gentry and a platinum blonde were getting into his burgundy Cord convertible.

"One thing for your buddy, he has a sweet car," Roni said.

"It's a one of a kind. Custom made. Supercharged. He let me drive it once, and it just roars." Sharp clutched the LaSalle and eased by quietly.

"What would have happened if he'd seen you back there?"

"Probably nothing, why?" Sharp asked.

"He scares me. I know he's a war hero and big movie star and all that, but something about him gives me the willies."

Sharp looked to the rearview mirror. Every now and then getting the willies was a good thing.

"So what happens next?" She cranked the window down a half inch and blew cigarette smoke to the night.

"Well, I have a tee time bright and early in the morning at Colonial. With Doyle." He steered the LaSalle onto the highway for Fort Worth.

"First the Bamboo Room and now Colonial Country Club? Living the high life, Mr. Sharp?"

"That's me: Mr. Big Spender."

"While I'm staying home doing laundry all day."

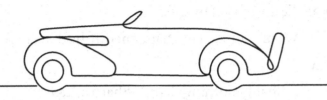

CHAPTER FOURTEEN

C olonial Country Club had gotten a lot of notoriety lately as Ben Hogan's home course. He was tearing up the pro tour and had won the Colonial tournament the last two years. Doyle had garnered a membership during the Depression by not mentioning the fact that he was a gangster and paying cash. Few places were more remote than the back nine, making it a grand place for a private discussion.

Sharp parked next to Doyle's Buick Roadmaster and gave Dutch a wave. The doorman also appeared to be

Doyle's chauffeur. Then he waltzed through the giant white columns of the plantation-style redbrick clubhouse like he owned the place. Sharp slipped the caddy master a couple of bucks so he and Doyle could carry their own clubs. He didn't see any need for additional ears around, no matter how young they were.

Doyle was, without a doubt, the worst golfer Sharp had ever seen. He took two cuts off the number one tee before he clipped a little dribbler that might have gone 40 yards. Sharp had only played a handful of times since the war, but watching Doyle, he didn't feel out of place at all.

He waggled for his tee shot and struck it straight and true, 175 yards down the fairway.

Doyle whistled, impressed. "Not bad, and with somebody else's clubs."

Sharp wondered where his own clubs were. He hadn't seen them since before the war and wondered if Evelyn had sold them or just thrown them away while he was across the pond.

They walked to Doyle's shot, and he picked up his ball. "Let's play from yours."

That was fine with Sharp, he wasn't a stickler for the propriety of golf etiquette and figured if the guy paying the bill wanted to play fast and loose with the rules, who was he to complain? Sharp took a par on the hole while Doyle added up his seven shots and three putts and had him mark a five on the scorecard.

Sharp waited until they were stepping to the second tee box to mention Gentry and Caples.

Doyle washed a new ball and explained, "Gentry has known Bobby for years. He told me after the drunk pulled a gun at our poker table."

"You're not concerned that Gent's in your place on Tuesday and having dinner with Caples on Saturday night?" Sharp asked.

Doyle took the honors on the second tee. "Not greatly. Gentry and I go back a long way. Longer than he and Caples."

He shanked the ball into the tree line on the right side of the fairway. "Let's make this more interesting—how about a two-dollar Nassau?"

"Sure," Sharp did some mental math and figured he could stand to make a few bucks. "But I'm keeping score."

Doyle agreed, and Sharp drove the ball a little left but about 180 yards down the par 4. Doyle took a Mulligan and snapped off a decent drive just about even with Sharp's shot at the edge of the trees. They walked down the fairway, and Doyle explained.

"Gentry is in a syndicate that's leasing properties for oil out towards Odessa. Caples is one of the members. That's how they met."

"Pegasus Oil." Sharp nodded. He'd seen that name in the Dallas county records. "Bugsy was in on that too."

Doyle was impressed. But Sharp was unsure. He'd wondered about Gentry's name showing up in connection with a known felon who had Mafia entanglements. The studio brass might frown on that. There was more to the King of the West than just a pretty face.

Doyle's second shot from out of the rough landed on the lip of the green. It was a helluva shot, and in the back of Sharp's mind, a little voice whispered, *Sandbagged.* He reminded himself that Doyle could be cold-blooded.

Sharp made the green in three and was fifteen feet from the pin; Doyle chipped from the fringe and landed inside his ball. Sharp two-putted, then Denniker lined up a five-footer.

"Know anything about Las Vegas, Doyle?" The mobster shanked the putt, and the ball skittered six feet beyond the cup. Denniker's poker face wasn't as good on the golf course.

"Nevada. Bugsy Siegel has—had—a place out there. The Flamingo Hotel and Casino—supposed to be a damned impressive joint." He gathered himself and drained the putt. They headed for the next tee box.

"Gentry seems to think things are happening out there." Sharp took the honors and teed up.

"Gentry? Well, I've never accused him of thinking too much, but Bugsy might have been right—the Army is reopening the air base there, and the Atomic Energy Commission is talking about putting in an atom bomb test range in the desert north of town." Doyle frowned as Sharp's drive landed with a bounce in the center right of the fairway.

"So you think the place will grow? Is that what Bugsy was betting on?"

"I don't know, but it's too late for Bugsy. Look, don't worry about him or Las Vegas or Gentry. Your concern is Caples." He used his driver to make his point. "If he's going to make a move, I have to know." For emphasis, he hit the ball a ton, and it landed almost 200 yards down the par 5. Sharp watched the ball roll to a stop thirty yards beyond his own drive and wondered what a guy who would fake being a crappy golfer to win a few bucks would do to someone he thought was threatening his livelihood.

Sharp covered the details he'd uncovered on Caples over the next few holes.

On the fifth hole, he covertly passed the Panther City folder to Doyle, who stashed it in his golf bag. Doyle took some of Sharp's new business cards to pass around, listened intently, and proceeded to play legitimate par and birdie golf.

By the time they reached the eighteenth, Denniker knew as much about Caples as Sharp did, agreed to help him find more business, and won the round by seven strokes. Sharp headed to the clubhouse.

It was always good to play golf with a man who might take your money (which was originally his money) and tell him things that you knew he knew, but he didn't want you to know he knew.

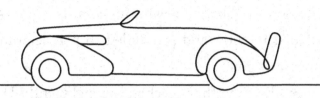

CHAPTER FIFTEEN

Sharp woke with a start at 8:45, then rushed through his morning routine. Sleeping indoors in a real bed was more comfortable, but the sunrise didn't wake him like it did working ranch duty. He paused at his brand-new telephone.

"Jefferson Sharp Investigations." The answering service girls had silky-smooth voices.

"Messages for BElmont twelve twenty-five?" he asked.

"There are no messages, sir."

"Thanks."

That felt like a waste of money. He needed to spread some cards around. Running late, he skipped the coffee shop and drove straight to Consolidated, where he hunted for a better place to surveil the parking lot to make sure George Griffin's Oldsmobile was in its usual place. He executed a near-perfect parallel parking job and was quite pleased with himself. He uncased the Bausch and Lombs and had just found Griffin's car when a tap came on the LaSalle's window. He looked up to the billy club of a patrolling military policeman. This was a change from the Consolidated security guys that usually handled the perimeter rounds. Sharp slid over on the seat and cranked down the window.

"Good morning, Sergeant." Sharp always tried to be pleasant to a man carrying a large stick.

"Can you tell me what you're doing here, sir?"

"I'm just waiting on someone. Keeping an eye on things."

"What kind of things?"

Sharp reached into the pocket of his jacket and retrieved a business card. He made the MP the third person in the world to learn of his new trade.

"Private eye, huh?"

"Yes, sir."

The non-com tapped the stripes on his sleeve with the billy. "I'm no sir, I work for a living."

In four years in the Army, Sharp and maybe one other guy were the only ones who didn't use that lame joke left over from Valley Forge. But he respected the billy club and chuckled dutifully.

"I crawled all over Italy. Never met anybody with three stripes who minded being called 'sir,'" he said.

"So, what are you doing here?" The MP was on the job. Sharp decided the truth wouldn't be a bad thing.

"Tailing a guy whose wife thinks he's cheating on her." He shook out a Lucky Strike and offered the MP the pack.

He declined.

"Sounds exciting."

"It's a living. What's up with you? You guys are usually on the other side of the fence." Sharp snapped the Zippo shut and blew the drag out the driver's side window, away from the MP.

"Test flights. Extra security."

"For the B-36? Kinda tough to keep that a secret, isn't it?"

"Orders. You need to move along, sir." The MP was serious.

Sharp checked the parking lot; all was quiet. "I'm just sitting here ..."

The billy club became a pointer. "With binoculars, a camera, and I'm pretty sure that bulge in your jacket is a pistol."

Okay, he was better than Sharp thought. "Look, really, I—"

"You should go, sir."

Right then, a B-36 roared over like a manmade thunderstorm. The thing was huge, it looked much more substantial than three times the size of the old Liberators. This was the new prototype with six rear-facing piston engines driving propellers and a pair of jet engines hanging under each wing. "Six turning and four burning" was the gag.

The ground shook, and the LaSalle's windows rattled.

The MP looked up. Sharp started the LaSalle and leaned over to the window so he could see the MP.

"It'll just be our little secret!" he yelled over the roar and eased the LaSalle from the curb.

Peggy gave him the evil eye when he walked into the Blackstone.

"What'd I do?" He gave the palms-up gesture that men universally use to acknowledge that they had done something stupid but had no idea what it was.

"You missed her." She spun and went to refill two coffees down the counter as he took a seat.

"Missed who? Roni?"

His cup and saucer clattered to the countertop, and she sloshed half a cup into it.

"She just sat there. Waiting. I bet she was late to work because of you."

"Because of me? How is that? I was working!"

"And did you tell her that?" Peggy looked over her pad, wrote down his order without asking, and turned to stab it onto the wheel.

"Wait a second. Why would she be waiting for me? I never said I was going to be here." Sharp was genuinely nonplussed. "This is not my fault."

"All I know is a very nice lady waited for you, and you stood her up." She smacked her gum and sauntered off.

He frowned and then leaned over and scraped together the remains of someone's morning paper.

"Many readers subscribe to the *Examiner*, you know. We have young men on bicycles who deliver it right to your front porch."

Sharp glanced at the gentleman to his left and smiled as Leo returned his pocket watch to his vest. The mercury was headed to a hundred summertime degrees and here was publisher Fuller wearing a three-piece wool suit.

Sharp lifted the newspaper. "People pay for this? I thought they came free with parakeet cages."

Leo fastened a cigarette into his holder. "So what are you up to, Jeff? Found employment yet?"

Sharp retrieved his card case and presented several to the newspaperman. "I'm going to freelance it for a while. See how the world treats me. If you would pass a couple of those along, I'd appreciate it."

Leo nodded his approval.

"Leo, you don't know anything about Robert Caples, do you?"

The newspaperman took a long moment to light up his smoke. "Personally, no. Professionally? Of course. He's quite notorious over there. We've profiled his comings and goings on more than one occasion."

Sharp suppressed a smile. Leo almost never referred to Dallas by name. He always said "over there." One of the legendary stories was that he'd pack sack lunches for meetings across the Trinity River, so he didn't spend taxable money in Fort Worth's sister city to the east.

"I'd like to ask you a few questions. If you have time?"

"Unfortunately, I do not. I have an editorial board meeting in five minutes, and it's a six-minute walk to the Examiner Building. But I do have seats for the Cats' game tomorrow. If you'd care to join me, we could talk then."

"Your treat? I'm in."

"You should know that Irene and the children will join us for at least a few innings." Leo gave a wry smile.

"It's always grand to see your lovely bride, Leo. You know that." The reply was as sincerely sarcastic as he could make it.

"Yes, I'm sure she'll be equally thrilled to see you." Leo smiled.

"I'll be there."

"I'll have Arleen leave your ticket at the box office."

After the late breakfast, he snuck back to Consolidated and waited to follow George to lunch. More barbecue. Sharp was becoming quite the connoisseur. The sausage was a little dry for his palate, but the smoked brisket was excellent. Bailey's sauce was tangy, with a little more vinegar than he preferred. He was also drinking enough Dr Pepper to take care of any irregularity issues for months. They swore it wasn't made of prune juice, but if he drank the stuff at ten, two, and four like they advertised, he figured he'd never leave the john. He followed George back to the plant and tipped his hat to the MP as he slowly drove past. The billy club waved in salute.

With the remainder of the afternoon to kill, he stopped by the camera store and picked up some essential goods: photo paper, trays, and chemistry mix for the darkroom, and then returned to the house to set things up.

He cleaned up two dusty folding tables he found in the back of the garage and moved them into the spare room to serve as workbenches. His photo enlarger went on one table, and he laid out his chemistry trays on the other. He taped some tinfoil to the windows and replaced the overhead light with a red bulb, then tacked some rubber stripping to the edge of the door.

When he closed everything down, the darkroom earned its name. He could transfer film to a developer can in pitch blackness and then turn on the red light to make prints. He mixed up some developer and fix and set the gallon jugs under the table. All he needed now was for George Griffin to do something worthy of being photographed.

He finished in the darkroom and spent five minutes scrubbing the smell of photo fix off his hands when it occurred to him that he needed to make a more regular habit of calling his clients. He flipped through his notebook and found the Griffins' number. Velma answered on the second ring.

"Griffin Residence . . ."

"Mrs. Griffin, this is Jeff Sharp. The investigator you hired?"

She didn't speak. Sharp imagined her preparing for bad news.

"Yes, Mr. Sharp. What is it? What have you found?" He understood the painful hesitation in her voice.

Sharp decided to be quick and to the point. "Nothing, Mrs. Griffin. I've found nothing. Your husband goes to work, gets a barbecue sandwich for lunch, and comes home to you. Every day. I can spend all the money you have, but my hunch is you're wasting your time," he said.

She wasn't so sure. "I can afford two weeks. Then I'll be satisfied. There's been perfume on his shirt, and it's not mine."

"Maybe he hugged his secretary."

"Maybe. But I don't think so. Keep looking, Mr. Sharp." Her tone was quick and final.

"It's your nickel."

"Yes, it is." She hung up.

Sharp knew when he was licked, but there were tougher ways to make a buck than to eat barbecue every day.

He refilled his business card case. Leo had taken his entire stack, and it reminded him to call the service.

"Jefferson Sharp investigations." It was yet another pleasant voice.

"Messages for BElmont twelve twenty-five."

"One message at two fifteen this afternoon. Jimmy at the Four Deuces asks that you call him. He says it's very important." She gave him the number, and he frowned and dialed. He knew Jimmy, but they weren't exactly buddies.

"Hello?"

"Jimmy? This is Jeff Sharp. I had a message to call."

"You need to come quick. Something's up."

The line went dead. Never a good sign. He jumped in the LaSalle and lit out for Thunder Road.

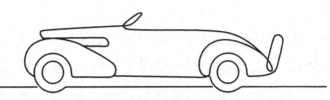

CHAPTER SIXTEEN

S harp walked into Rico's and the namesake proprietor, a short Mexican gentleman in an untucked
white shirt and black pants, immediately led him
through the restaurant to the hidden doorway in the
kitchen. A hundred yards of climbing hallways later, he
passed through the secret door in the side wall of the
Four Deuces.

Sharp was sure they call them nightclubs because they
were never meant to be seen during the day. The bright
lights took the romance and mystery out of the elaborate

decor and the air stank of stale cigarette smoke and old beer.

The housekeeping staff was floor sweeping and silver polishing with an impressive degree of disinterest. He nodded to the help and walked toward the door to Doyle's darkened office, but stopped cold as he saw the lone figure leaning heavily on the empty bar. It was Major Cartwright. Jimmy behind the bar motioned him over with a worried look and cocked his head toward the airman. The major was plastered.

"He came in about two hours ago. Started at Rico's at lunch, then came up here. He's hitting it hard."

Sharp took a seat on the next stool and leaned over the oak bar. The major's wallet was open on the bar with fives and a ten scattered about.

"Buying drinks for the house, Major?"

The pilot didn't say a word.

He slowly turned his head and looked right through Sharp. He was pale and sweating, his eyes were wide, and he stared like Sharp wasn't there.

It gave him the shivers.

The major lifted his glass—a rocks glass half full of Tennessee sour mash. The tall, square bottle next to it was more air than liquor by this point. His hand was trembling, but he drained the glass in a long, slow swallow. This was ninety-proof whiskey, and he poured it down his throat like iced tea. The burn didn't even phase him.

He lowered the glass back to the bar and then turned to Sharp to speak.

He couldn't.

At first, Sharp thought, the alcohol had him. He'd seen plenty of drunks in his day. Sometimes in the mirror. This was different. The man was physically unable to form words.

"Major, are you okay?"

He poured another drink and stared at it. "I . . ."

Nothing. He downed the amber whiskey like soda.

This was a man Roni had indicated was a teetotaler. Sharp looked from him to Jimmy and back, then slid the bottle away from him. "Let's ease up there, soldier."

Sharp's gaze went back to Jimmy. "Can you build us a couple of coffees?"

The bartender nodded and prepared the stainless-steel brewer.

Sharp eyed the major and then turned back to Jimmy again. "Ever see him do this before?"

"Never. He's been coming here for the Tuesday-night game for months. Always a Coke with two cherries."

Jimmy set two steaming cups and saucers on the bar. Sharp pushed one in front of the major. "What say we get something in you that's not booze."

The major looked at the cup, then picked it up and set it aside. Then he began to play with the saucer. Staring at it. Studying it. Looking it all over, up and down.

Sharp had seen this before. Shell shock.

Guys who'd been too close to a grenade or an incoming arty round. Guys who'd found themselves wearing blood and guts when a moment before they'd been talking to a buddy they'd never see again except in nightmares. That one he knew himself. Something could hit you again out of nowhere, days, weeks, even years later. One unexpected jolt and the mind would shut down to protect itself.

Behind them, Doyle walked in. He was in a summer suit and tie, carrying a suitcase. He paused at the gathering at the bar and Sharp intercepted him a few feet away.

Doyle nodded to the bar. "What's up?"

"Something's wrong with the major. He's drunk off his ass," Sharp said.

"Our major? Cartwright?" Doyle couldn't believe it any more than Jimmy could. Doyle stepped closer and watched as the Major played with his cup and saucer.

"I need to get him home before he fries his mind. Or at least his liver. It's not used to this kind of abuse. Can you get ahold of Leo?"

Doyle looked at him with the question, "Leo?"

"He plays golf with the base commander. He can see what's up and if somebody can keep an eye on him."

Doyle nodded his understanding and headed for his office. Sharp went back to the bar and replaced a swig of his own coffee with some of the major's liquor. Nobody ought to drink alone.

"So, what's going on, Jerry?" he asked.

The major looked up from his saucer and found his voice. "It all changes now."

That was interesting, Sharp thought.

"What changes?" He was trying to be as soothing as he knew how. The major's grasp on the here and now was a little tenuous, and Sharp was in uncharted waters.

The major's eyes looked almost hollow. "Everything. Changes."

Sharp stared at Jimmy, waiting for more. But the Major just shrugged and turned away, his elbow tagging a tray of glassware and sending it crashing to the floor.

Major Cartwright leaped backward from the bar like he'd been shot, scrambling, and tripping and crabbing away until he cornered himself against the wall. Sharp carefully moved closer. This guy was wearing ribbons for valor, a Purple Heart, and a Distinguished Flying Cross, but he was as terrified as a puppy in a thunderstorm.

Sharp helped him up, and he was a mess—shaking, eyes darting, wearing a sweating, panicked expression that said his train was leaving the station and not everyone was aboard. He looked at Jimmy, and even the bartender was rattled. Sharp grabbed the billfold from the bar and checked the address on the driver's license. He knew the area.

"Tell Doyle I'm taking him home." Sharp threw a shoulder under the major's arm, and they staggered out to the hall and then down to the LaSalle.

He was putting the flyer in the passenger seat when Jimmy came out.

"Doyle asked if you'd call him once you dropped him off."

Sharp nodded as he slammed the door and pulled onto Thunder Road.

The major didn't say a word on the trip. He stared out the window. Sharp thought he'd passed out, but it didn't feel like he was asleep. He found the small frame house not far from the base and pulled to the curb. He opened the car door, and the flyer stood up without help, but he was shaky, so Sharp ducked under his arm. They got him up the short concrete walk to the three steps to the small, covered porch. The front door was unlocked.

The major's house wasn't anything surprising. Standard-issue bachelor Army Air Force. A few photos of him and some other fliers in front of P-38s hung alongside a portrait of a couple that might be his mom and dad. The furniture was simple and utilitarian, but neat and well kept. Everything you'd expect from a squared-away military man.

They shuffled into the house and to the main bedroom, where Sharp dumped him on the bed. Sharp scooped up the major's hat and put it and the pilot's wallet on the dresser. He paused at the door to make sure the major was down for the count and turned to leave.

"Jeff."

Sharp stopped cold. The sound of his first name felt oddly personal.

"You okay, Major?" He asked.

Sharp waited for an answer that didn't come. Cartwright dozed off, so he went to the phone alcove in the short hallway. He tucked one of his cards under the phone and said to the body on the bed, "Call me when you come to."

The center of the dial had the phone number type-written on a small paper disk. He copied it to his note-book: DRake-7246. Then called Doyle.

"The major's tucked in. No problems."

Doyle said, "Can you come back here? Leo's coming here too, after he talks to the commander. Maybe he can tell us what's going on."

"See you in ten minutes." Sharp hung up the phone and looked in on the major one last time. The body was facing the wall so he couldn't tell if he was asleep or not, but he was still. Sharp turned to leave, and the voice stopped him.

"They're here, Jeff. They're here."

"Who's here, major?" he asked.

There was no response.

Sharp got the willies again and took off.

Doyle and Leo were in the office when he got back to the Four Deuces. Sharp grabbed the empty side chair. Doyle didn't offer a cigar this time, so Sharp lit a Lucky.

Leo had a cigar of his own. He was studying it. "How is he?"

"Rocky. I haven't seen a guy break like that since the war," Sharp said.

"He say anything?" Leo was curious.

"Nothing that made sense. Nightmare ramblings. Probably Germans after him," Sharp answered. He knew those himself, but Leo being curious made him curious. He knew Leo the editor and Leo the publisher, but this felt like the old Leo—the reporter. "What did the commander say?"

"He was going to send some men over to get him to the infirmary."

"I don't think there's anything physically wrong with him," Sharp pointed out.

Leo blew a cloud of smoke. "Well, the Army has shrinks that can look at him. They had lots of guys snap during the war. I think he'll be in pretty good hands."

Leo wasn't a veteran, and something about his attitude bristled the hair on the back of Sharp's neck. "Guys like the major don't just snap. You don't go through a Nazi prison camp and come home with a uniform full of chest salad if you're not a pretty tough nut. Nothing personal, Leo, but you weren't there. Some guys did lose it, but I've seen the major in a tough situation. He's not in that camp."

"I understand." Leo slid closer to condescending than Sharp liked. "But Colonel Grayson assures me that everything is SOP over there."

Sharp smelled something. "Is this related to the weather balloon, Leo?"

"What weather balloon?" Leo shot back a look through his cigar smoke.

"The one on the front page of your paper a couple of days ago. With Major Cartwright standing behind it." He jerked his thumb toward the door.

"Oh, that." Leo dismissed it with a wave. "Some nuts found a weather balloon. Tried to make it sound like men from Mars. Orson Welles-type stuff. The base asked us to run the story and clear it up. Nothing to it."

"How many weather balloons make the front page? They send up a couple a week, don't they?" Sharp pushed.

"Jeff, I don't know. The commander called and asked if I could do him a favor and try and head off these nuts. I didn't see any harm in it. It was a slow news day, and it sold a few extra copies." Leo leaned toward him and gestured with his stogie. "What's it to you?"

"I'm an investigator. It's what I do."

"Somebody paying you to look into all this?"

"No."

"Then quit busting my chops. Go chase some cheating husbands." Leo checked his pocket watch and grabbed his hat on the way out the door. "I've got to go see to tomorrow's paper. We still on for the Cats?"

Sharp nodded, and the publisher went on his way.

He left the door open behind him. Doyle got up and closed it. Outside, the staff was gearing up for the evening's arrivals. The Hamilton on Sharp's wrist showed ten till five. Griffin would be getting off soon.

"Can you keep an eye on the major?" Doyle was direct.

"Sure, I want to make sure he's okay," Sharp said.

"Do that. Consider it a job."

"How does that square with the Bobby Caples work?"

"The major's situation concerns me." As usual, Doyle got right to the point. "He's been on a losing streak over the last few months. And I've given him some credit. That's gotten away from me on a couple of plays."

That was unusual for Doyle.

He was fair but rigid on his rules for establishing credit. The house would always win in the end, but Doyle wasn't in business to earn his own money.

Sharp lit another Lucky. "He's a pretty stand-up guy."

"I'm a sucker for helping out servicemen, and Cartwright has been a good customer, so I wasn't terribly worried. But we went double or nothing on the Derby, and he lost his ass."

Sharp snickered. "He lost on the Derby? An Army flyer bet against a horse named Jet Pilot?"

Doyle wasn't laughing. "He owes over seven grand."

An involuntary whistle chased Sharp's grin away. That kind of dough could take a military man years to pay back. He could see why Doyle was concerned. The club owner looked at his detective through the cigarette smoke.

"I want you to understand the delicate and serious nature of this. I do a lot of business with the personnel at the base, and at Consolidated. I absolutely do not want to have to do something rash to get my money. I trust Cartwright, but I can't be seen as letting him off. People would get the idea they could do that too."

Sharp nodded. "You think he'd run off?"

"No, but I didn't think I'd see him in here drunk as a skunk, either. I need a little predictability when the house extends credit."

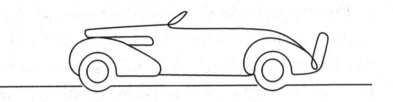

CHAPTER SEVENTEEN

"Mr. . . . .?" The wrinkled man on the other side of the will call window tried hard to place a name to the face.

"Sharp. Jeff Sharp. Might be under Leo Fuller."

"That's right." Arthritic fingers snapped and went to the battered box of tickets on his counter. Behind him, a felt replica of the Cats' 1946 Texas League pennant adorned his cramped cubbyhole of the LaGrave Field box office.

"Good to see you again, Mr. Sharp. Enjoy the game." The old man slid the ticket through the hole in the glass.

Sharp nabbed a program and made his way to where Leo and the *Examiner* kept a plum box behind the Cats' dugout to entertain their higher-paying advertising clientele.

Leo Fuller was waiting alone in the box, decked out for the ball game in a cream seersucker suit and a natty straw boater.

Sharp took one of the five remaining empty seats. "Nobody famous tonight? I was hoping to meet a radio starlet, or at least the Welterweight Champion of the World."

Leo scoffed. "You're spoiled. This box is an advertising expense. Not to hobnob with celebrities."

"Uh-huh. Didn't you have Miss Texas in here last time?"

"That was part of a promotional tour. Strictly business."

"What business was that, dear?" The lovely Irene Fuller ushered twelve-year-old Leo Jr. and his little sister into the box, making sure to leave an empty seat between Sharp and the children to avoid contamination by a lesser grade of human. "Hello, Jeff."

It impressed him that she could make her distaste for her husband's buddies clear in the tone of just two words.

Sharp stood and politely doffed his hat. "Irene, it's grand to see you again," he lied.

"Daddy says you got shot at by cattle rustlers!" Junior interrupted.

Sharp winked and fired a pointed finger back at the boy. "I did, and I shot right back."

Leo Junior couldn't tell if he was kidding or not, so he immediately ran from the box seats to find a peanut vendor.

Irene frowned. "Really, Jeff, I do wish you wouldn't tease the children."

He started to explain that he wasn't teasing, but Irene wasn't interested in conversation with him. "What business, Leonard?" She pronounced it like Leonardo, but omitted the final *o*, failing to give it the intended European flavor. Sharp thought it was ridiculous.

"A promotional package for the paper, dear. Nothing interesting."

Sharp had hoped to get a few minutes with Leo to discuss recent events. That would be a challenge with the kids and Irene.

Eight-year-old Mary had decided to stare at him. Without saying anything. Sharp crossed his eyes and stuck out his tongue. Irene caught the look and turned

Mary in her seat so the obnoxious cowboy wouldn't bother her.

Kids today, Sharp thought, *don't go to the ball game to watch the game. They want to run around.* The new left-hander for the Cats had San Antonio whiffing like a General Electric fan, but Junior begged for an ice cream, so Irene took off with the children.

"So, what do you know about what's going on at the base?" he asked as the Cats' second baseman juggled a grounder and the runner beat it out.

Leo scribbled an E-4 on his scorecard. "You mean, why did Major Cartwright break down? His commander said he thought it was overwork—he's been on several assignments over the last few weeks."

"Overwork? Has he met Major Cartwright? The guy was in a POW camp for half the war. He can probably handle pushing a pen around a desk." Sharp stood as Irene and the kids returned with an armload of hotdogs, popcorn, and Cokes. She ignored Sharp as she passed them out, so he flagged his own hotdog vendor. For fifteen cents, it should have been a steak.

Leo successfully juggled his dinner and the score book. "He told me Cartwright has been traveling quite a bit. Regular trips to DC—they've reopened a bombing range in Nevada for A-bomb tests—plus, he's going back and forth to the Consolidated plant in San Diego."

"So sitting in an airplane is overworked?" But then again, Sharp himself charged people to sit in his car and watch other people.

The Cats changed the subject for Leo with a triple off the right-field wall that sent the crowd to their feet and put the Cats up two runs. Leo went deep into his score book but was interrupted by an impressive display of Spanish profanity by a *mamacita* on the third baseline.

"My Spanish isn't that good. Is she yelling at the right fielder, or is that guy with the pencil-thin mustache next to her about to get clobbered?" Sharp said between bites.

"I'm wagering on the latter." Leo tucked another cigarette into his holder and grinned big.

Irene and the kids took off for a restroom trip, and Sharp earned a "not in front of the children" look when he asked if she could bring back beers the next time she took the hoodlums to get snacks.

He leaned over to Leo. "So, what's up that has the major flying all around the countryside?"

"I hear rumors but nothing concrete," Leo said.

"Such as?"

"The Army Air Force wants to build an atomic plane."

Sharp smirked. "That's not exactly a scoop, Mr. Pulitzer. I read *Popular Mechanics* too."

Leo sneered at the inference. "There's a big difference between an article in a barbershop magazine and one landing at the Fort Worth air base."

"You think they're that close?"

The San Antonio shortstop had drawn a walk and then stole second. He was safe by a foot, but the umpire threw his thumb in the air, and the row that followed as the San Antonio skipper charged out of the third-base dugout was easily worth the price of Sharp's free ticket. They stood and booed heartily, then cheered as the ump sent him to an early shower.

"So if the major is working on an atomic-powered B-36, what drove him around the bend? Something go wrong?" Uncle Jeff waved over a cotton-candy vendor and bought the kids some spun sugar. That would have them bouncing off the walls for the next several hours.

Irene glared at him.

Leo scribbled down a backward K in his book for a called third strike, and the inning ended. "There was a rumor of an 'incident,' but I can't find out anything, they've shut down a lot of information lately. I had a good contact inside the base, but he was transferred to Elmendorf."

"Elmendorf?" Sharp asked, sipping his bathwater-warm beer.

"Alaska."

"Damn. So we're out of luck?"

He looked at Sharp under the brim of his straw boater and over the rim of his round spectacles. "We"—Leo paused for effect—"have other sources, just not as close as the other person was."

"Will we keep us in the know when we find something?"

"We might," Leo said.

The seventh-inning stretch came, signaling Leo Jr. that it was time to run up and down the stairs of the box-seat area. The host of evil eyes from the nearby patrons silently judged Irene's mothering skills as lacking, and it pushed her to the edge. "Leonard. It's approaching the children's bedtime."

Sharp thought quickly. He needed more info from Leo. "If you want to go ahead, Irene, I can drop Leo off after the game." He subtly moved his beer out of her view.

Leo was trying to catch up in his score book and didn't even look up. "Yes, dear. Why don't you go ahead?"

The top scoop of Mary's ice cream chose this moment to fall to the ground. She welled up with tears and began to wail. The row of spectators behind groaned, and Irene gave in. She wagged a finger at Sharp. "But you bring him straight home. No four-hour excursions down Thunder Road for 'just one drink.'"

"Cross my heart," he promised and stood to let her out of the row.

Leo passed her the keys to the Caddy. "Just leave it in the drive. Let me put it in the garage this time."

Irene stiffened. "It was just a scratch. Come along, children."

Sharp was certain he got a discreet thumbs-up from a fellow in the row behind them as she trooped the kids out of the ballpark.

Sharp sat back down and hurried to the prime subject. "What do you know about Bobby Caples?"

Leo shook his head. "I stay out of that mess."

"Organized crime?"

"Dallas."

Sharp chuckled. Big D was also home to Leo's sworn enemy, the *Dallas Times Herald*.

About that time, the hurricane in the third base stands came ashore, and even the players were watching when Mamacita belted her old man and stormed out of the ballpark. Joe Louis would've been proud of that right hook.

Leo tipped his hat to the woman as she marched past, then leaned close to Sharp. "Caples is acting like he's got a new license to expand his influence. One of our reporters is thinking there's a connection to the Chicago Mob."

Sharp nodded. "Meyer Lansky's outfit. Not the first time I've heard that."

Leo raised a finger in warning. "Don't dig too deep. Lansky has a tendency to remove those who look too hard."

"Like Bugsy?"

"Like the *Chicago Tribune* reporter who was fished out of Lake Michigan last month."

"So, there's more to this?"

"Not that we've seen down here." Leo looked up from his score book. "Yet."

Sharp turned things over in his mind, some things he was sure Leo didn't know. Or at least acted like he didn't know. The crowd roared as the Cats turned a nifty double play, and the game was done. Fort Worth 6, San Antone 4.

He dropped Leo at his ostentatious mansion in the hoity-toity Ryan Place section of town and started home.

He had an old feeling, a sense of premonition that had saved his butt more than once in Italy. He snapped an unexpected U-turn, and there in the headlights was a dark gray Plymouth with a driver ducking behind the brim of his fedora.

The next morning, Sharp made sure he was sitting in his prescribed place at the Blackstone when Roni came in. She smiled politely when Peggy brought their coffees, and succinctly ordered her half grapefruit. Sharp tried to request his usual eggs over hard and sausage but Peggy turned and walked away before he could order.

Roni silently stirred sugar into her cup and then lit a cigarette. She didn't exactly blow the smoke in his face, but he caught the drift.

"You want to tell me what the deal is with you two?" He shot a thumb in Peggy's direction.

"I'm sure I don't know what you mean."

"Between her grilling me about standing you up and your cold shoulder here, I'm about to catch pneumonia."

"The polite thing to do after an evening out is to give a girl a call."

"It was work!" his mouth said while his brain remembered how she felt in his arms.

"Yes. You've made that very clear."

"Roni. Seriously, you and the major are . . . I mean Cartwright is your . . . I'm not getting in the middle of that. You should know me better than that."

"Me and the major are what?" She leaned in with a harsh whisper: "You think you know what I have going on?"

"Apparently not. But still, there's Dave and Frenchy. It's just not right for a guy to—"

"And Evelyn?"

"And Evelyn." He'd conveniently let that slip his mind.

Peggy arrived with their breakfasts and a dirty look for Sharp. She refilled Roni's coffee but left his cup empty. He noticed his eggs were runny, his sausage came out as burnt bacon, and Roni's eyes were getting moist.

"Hey. I'm sorry. I thought it might have been a way to combine work and—" He stopped short.

"And pleasure?" She took another drag and the exhale streamed from the side of her mouth.

"I am not going to do this, Roni."

"What makes you think I want to?" She played with her grapefruit spoon. "Jeff, when you guys all shipped out, I was left alone. We all were. Then, those telegrams came and it's . . . it's like a big part of me has been dead inside and I'm just dragging it around." She met his eyes. "And then Saturday night when you told me about you and Jerry in the woods, it all came back again." Her lower lip trembled, and he felt his stomach knot.

"Roni. Honest, the last thing I want to do is cause you any more pain. I really don't."

"No, no, I asked for it. I'm a big girl. I wanted to hear what it was like out there. What happened to my guys? Was my brother scared? Did my husband suffer? None of you who came back seem to want to talk about it."

Sharp swallowed hard. "I'm not proud of a lot of the things we had to do just to survive."

"I get that. But when we were dancing, for a little bit it was just you and me. No past. No pain. Almost peaceful. That surprised me."

"Yeah, me too," he admitted. "I mean I know I am a great dancer, but it rarely has a mind-altering effect."

He had no idea why in intimate moments like these he had to revert to jokes, but there it was. She chuckled, so at least the joke didn't do any harm. But then her eyes left.

"When Jerry and I started going out I thought maybe I could get closer to my guys by talking to him. But he won't say a word. Says he wants good times. Movies. Dinners. That kind of thing."

"It doesn't sound like you're exactly falling for him."

"Well, it's not easy. He's a nice guy and all, and good-looking, but even when he's around, which isn't very often, he's one big secret." She took a long drag on her cigarette and Sharp reached for his fork.

"Well, now I feel awful for roping you into this, Roni. I am sorry."

She searched his face. "You mean that?"

"Of course I do." He looked at her and realized that he really did.

She pulled out her compact to see if she'd done any damage to her makeup. "I think you're just saying that so you can eat."

He reached for the Tabasco. "Of course I am. Groveling makes me hungry."

"You are not getting off this easy, mister."

He made no sudden moves with the Tabasco bottle. "Veronica, I am truly sorry. I have no excuse, and I sincerely apologize."

She pointed the serrated spoon at him. He hoped it wasn't loaded. "Damn right, you do," she said with one more angry look to show she was serious. "But know this.

I'm fully capable of making my own decisions about who I see, who I go out with, and who I dump. Got it?"

He held up both hands. "Yes, ma'am."

Then she turned the weapon to her grapefruit. "So, what happened? Where were you the other day? It's got to be pretty big to get between you and breakfast."

"Your major went off the deep end. When was the last time you talked to him?"

"It's been a week, I think. Is he okay?"

He explained the situation as they ate, and she gave him rapt attention.

"So, is he all right?" She appeared genuinely concerned.

"Leo says they've got good docs at the base and that he'll be taken care of."

"Any idea what it is?" She spooned a section of grapefruit to her mouth, and he found it slightly exciting. His brain pushed that aside.

"I have a hunch. I think they have a couple of secret projects going on over at the base, and our buddy Major Cartwright is right in the middle of it." He explained about the lights he'd seen at the Rafter B. "I think that they've been building something amazing. Something we've never seen before and that it crashed. That's what's got him in a jam."

She thought for a second. "It's not little green men from Mars?"

"It's just enough of a red herring to make people think that. Leo thinks it's an atomic plane. I think it's a type of helicopter."

"Heli-what?"

"A helicopter. It's got the propeller on top, and it can fly straight up. Even hover in one place. I'm pretty certain that's what I saw on the Rafter B."

"Huh." She squeezed her empty grapefruit and filled the spoon with the last of its juice. She stole a look at the wall clock. "I'm going to be late."

"Can I walk you over?"

"Is that an apology?" A trickle of juice moistened her lips. His collar seemed to warm.

"I'm apologizing?"

"You can make it up to me."

"Wait. Make up what?"

"There's a new Bing Crosby movie over at the Seventh Street Theater. You can take me and we won't talk about the major."

"Or your late husband? Or Dave?"

"Or your ex-wife. Just you and me." She grabbed her purse and put coins on the table for Peggy.

"Did you just ask me out?" Sharp frowned. "Or are we just old friends?"

"Maybe." She shot him a wry smile. "Let's just call it work and then there won't be any expectations."

"So it's not a date."

"Of course not."

He gulped a last swallow of coffee and his mind sorted through all the baggage they carried. Then he remembered how she'd felt in his arms on the dance floor.

That afternoon Sharp arrived at the bomber factory early and took a moment from dodging MPs and watching George Griffin's Olds sit in a parking lot to step into his favorite corner phone booth. He was starting to think of it as his office. He'd handled quite a bit of business from it. He'd secured divorce attorney Tom Hall in his battle against Evelyn and the forces of evil. He'd fed it dozens of dimes calling long distance trying to track down Bobby Caples information.

Today's phone chore was to check up on Cartwright for Doyle. He found the main base number in his notebook, plugged in a pair of nickels, and waited to be connected to the major. It seemed like an unusually long time before a stranger's voice answered. "Who are you holding for?"

"Major Cartwright."

"Who's calling?" The stranger was gruff and not happy.

"I'm an old friend of his from Italy."

"The major isn't in today, if I can have a number, I can have him call you back."

"That's okay, I'll try him later."

The man on the other end started to say something, but Sharp closed the connection. Well, Roni had told him Cartwright occasionally ran off on a moment's notice. He called his home number, but the phone just rang.

As he stepped out, an enormous B-36 roared in for a landing, just a hundred feet over his head. He thought about the atomic plane and felt his skin glow from radioactivity. Some of that might have been because it was 94 degrees' worth of summer in the phone booth, but he wasn't discounting the possibility of uranium-235.

He settled into what had become routine. Once George was inside each morning, he'd head off to do research on Bobby Caples. He'd been through the Dallas and Tarrant Court public records, both the Dallas and

Fort Worth libraries, and almost filled his notebook with dead ends and theories that led nowhere and uncovered little.

Then he'd call the answering service to hear he had no messages before heading back to Consolidated and trying not to be noticed during George's routine barbecue lunch. Every afternoon, George would leave between 4:30 and 5:00, drive down the road in front of the plant and make the right turn toward their house over by Monkey Ward.

Sharp blinked twice and got a legitimate thrill when the Oldsmobile turned left, away from Velma and the little white house, and toward Thunder Road.

One simple left turn could make life so much more interesting.

He tailed Griffin down the Jacksboro Highway. Past several of Thunder Road's lesser-known bars and gaming halls, the Rocket Club, and the Skyliner Ballroom. Just beyond the 2222 Club was a block or two of motor hotels and tourist courts. George was a man on a mission. This, Sharp figured, was cheating-husband territory.

The Olds slowed and turned past the fake palm trees and faintly Arabian look of the Caravan Tourist Court. Sharp slowed at the Texaco down the street, pulled a

U-turn at the pumps, and parked at the Williams Ranch House restaurant across the street. He had a clear view of the motel entry as George stepped out of the office with the room key.

Sharp pulled his prized Argus 35 mm camera from its case and double-checked the film counter. A fresh roll of twelve exposures. He had another roll of film at the ready hanging in a leather container on the strap. George walked to bungalow number 3 and Sharp focused, snapped off three frames, then checked his watch. He figured to have about two hours of usable daylight remaining.

Five minutes later, an absolute knockout stepped from a yellow cab. A large-brimmed hat hid her face, but she was nervous and her head darted, taking in the scene. Sharp ducked behind the afternoon's *Examiner*. This dame wasn't in Roni's class, but she was a looker. She glanced around as if she thought she was being followed, and that gave him a good shot with her head up and her hat out of her eyes. He fired most of the roll of film through the camera. He felt like he had a good one of the mystery woman and George in the doorway. Days and days of boredom, watching parked cars and eating most of a herd of barbecued cattle to get to forty-five seconds of panic and fast photos.

Sharp figured he'd have at least an hour to kill. He hit the phone booth on the porch of the steakhouse. He called the answering service and discovered Doyle wanted him to swing by. He dropped another dime and told Doyle he was on a stakeout, and it might be late. Doyle promised to have the kitchen stay open.

He hung up and looked at the receiver. A familiar female voice echoed in his head. "The polite thing to do is give a girl a call." Roni. The movie. Dammit. She answered on the second ring.

"Bing Crosby starts in ten minutes."

"I'm stuck on a stakeout. The guy just took a gal to a motel."

"You're following a cheating husband? Really?"

"Too cliché?"

"Well, at least I know you're not standing me up to go to Doyle's."

Roni might know him a little too well. "Nah, that's later. Wanna come?"

"So you're moving me from spot number one on this evening's list to just behind a cheating husband and the hideaway club?"

The tinge of amusement in her voice made him cringe. He wondered if he was inventing ways around getting involved with Roni. Between her dating the major, being his late friend's sister, and his partner's widow, there was a lot to navigate.

"That's not exactly how I'd phrase it."

"You should work on that." And she hung up.

He shuffled back to the car to fool with his camera, watch bungalow number 3. Yes, he and Roni had a lot to work through, but somewhere deep inside he wondered if he might be missing out on more than just a movie.

The better shots came at 8:15, and he almost missed them. The light was golden, and the summer sun was setting as the lovers parted. He snapped off a shot, clicking off the last frame on the roll. He cursed and cranked the film through, then fumbled the small canister trying to get another roll of film. He loaded the roll, snapped the back in place, and brought the camera up to find George and Miss X in an embrace at the door. He snapped it. Her hand in his. He snapped it. One last hug. Big George helping her into the cab. He snapped it. He thought that Mrs. Griffin might very well snap too.

By 10:15, he was pulling the last prints out of the flat tray of chemical fixative in the darkroom. They were good shots. Here was Miss X wiping lipstick from George's cheek. Another print of her walking directly into the camera, George locking the bungalow door in the background. Sharp admired his art.

He hung the prints to dry and realized he was starved.

Most people don't have dinner at eleven, but that was not unusual for Doyle or, as Sharp was discovering, the take-what-you-can-get private eye. For Doyle Denniker, the definition of *late* was different from that of the rest of the world. It could be three or four in the morning if a high-roller was pushing his luck; the dining room would be open until that last mark went home. Doyle believed if the customer was having a good time, it lasted as long as they wanted.

The next time they'd stick around losing dough, just knowing they'd get hot again.

Doyle was perched at his standard corner table, overseeing his world from the kitchen door to the main gaming floor. Sharp took a seat across from him that didn't leave his back entirely to the room. Doyle ordered dinner for them both. Sharp started to protest, but his host requested prime rib, so Sharp did the smart thing and shut up. Like the Bamboo Room across the Trinity River, the 2222 Club had a top-rate chef.

As the shrimp cocktails came, Doyle asked. "Have you talked to the major?"

"I called the base. He was out of town. I believe he's been traveling a lot recently." The shrimp was swell. Knowing Doyle, it had been swimming in the gulf yesterday.

"So nothing? You don't know any more than when you left here?" Doyle had an ominous frown.

He didn't want to admit that he'd been a little busy following men and aggravating women. "I'll go see him in the morning."

"Do that." Doyle fixed him with the stern look he used to reprimand his gorillas.

Sharp felt slightly uncomfortable, but another shrimp took care of that.

The waiter brought another round of drinks, and Doyle excused himself to make a pass through the casino to be seen and make sure the patrons were having a good time. Sharp lit a smoke and tried to think.

Across the room, Doyle and Gentry Ferguson were sharing a word. The big movie cowboy had a glamorous woman on his arm, a woman Sharp had met once before. Elise-Marie had left the Normandy countryside and come home from the war with him. Gentry had gone in at Omaha Beach, and his demolitions team had taken out German 88s, destroying the big guns so the Allies could establish a beachhead. The movie studio played that up to boost his patriotic box-office draw, but Sharp had heard enough war stories around the poker table to know the big cowboy knew his way around a battlefield.

Sharp had a phone brought over, the waiter stretching the cord to the table in a method that made Sharp feel this was a regular occurrence at Doyle's table. It was a lot of work for nothing.

"Jefferson Sharp Investigations," answered this evening's pleasant voice.

"Messages for BElmont twelve twenty-five."

"You have no messages at the time, sir."

"Thanks." He placed the handset on the cradle, and the phone was whisked away as Doyle returned.

"Anything new on Caples?" Doyle straightened his coat as he sat down.

"Nothing in Dallas. Nothing on this side of the river." Sharp detailed his research trips to the courthouses and that neither Caples, Capellini, nor any of his known aliases or associated businesses seemed to have anything going around the Fort Worth side of North Texas. That didn't satisfy Doyle, so he pulled his notebook and showed some of the information he'd gleaned from the catacombs in Dallas. Addresses, club names, warehouse locations. The gangster tore a page from the notebook. "This is exactly what I need to know."

Then Sharp saw it. The glint in Doyle's eye confirmed there was more to this than a fact-finding mission. As a cop, he'd learned when talking to a witness or a suspect, sometimes there's a look, maybe a gesture or just a feeling, that says there's more beneath the surface.

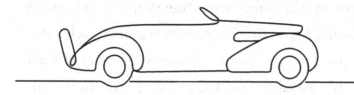

CHAPTER EIGHTEEN

S harp scraped the Gillette Blue Blade down his face and explained the situation to the guy in the mirror. The late night meant he'd overslept again and missed running into Roni at breakfast. So, Peggy would be full of friendly advice on how he was screwing up his personal life. The reflection winked and had a solution for that.

He parked the LaSalle in front of the Paris Coffee Shop and enjoyed a different take on his morning routine. He wouldn't be sweating his day away at Consolidated today, George Griffin had solved that, but detective Sharp did have more than a few errands to run before he could mark his very first case closed.

Between the police department, the Army, and the Stockmen's Association, he'd written more than his share of reports. He walked out of Thomas Office Supply with a portable Royal typewriter, carbon paper, and various sizes of stationery and envelopes.

Back at the world headquarters of Jefferson Sharp Investigations, he set up the reporting, accounting, and record-keeping departments on the kitchen table. He stacked two carbons between three pieces of paper and rolled them into the Royal, then hammered the keys extra hard to make the two copies. He tried not to think about the hornet's nest he was going to be stirring up when Velma Griffin saw the photos, but then again—at ten bucks a week, she was getting exactly what she asked for.

It seemed to Sharp that this was a cut-and-dried case. Velma would cut George bad and then hang him out to dry. She'd make a bundle, and George would have that 115-pound growth removed without surgery. The procedure wouldn't be pleasant, but once the dust settled, Sharp figured everyone would be happier.

He dialed the answering service, which, predictably, had nothing, then tried the base again for the major. The clerk who answered the phone said the major wasn't in today. His home phone just rang. *Major Cartwright,* Sharp thought, *could be in Alaska, Guam, or the bathroom.*

He slid Mrs. Griffin's report and the eight by tens into a manila envelope and then banged out a quick invoice. He grabbed his hat and was out the door before 11:15. A good morning's work.

He parked one door down and across the street from the Griffins' frame house, deciding that a little discretion couldn't hurt in these matters. Sharp knocked at the front door, and Mrs. Griffin called, "Just a minute."

She opened the door and looked at him for a moment through the screen before she recognized what this meant.

"Mr. Sharp?"

"Good morning, Mrs. Griffin. I'm afraid I'm here with not so good news."

She looked at the large brown envelope he was holding. He could almost hear her brain go *click*.

"Oh, no. He couldn't. No . . . he had a lodge meeting last night. He was at the Pythians . . ."

Sharp shook his head. She glanced right and left to check if any neighbors might see, then jerked him into the house.

Inside was neat as a pin.

An oval rug on a polished wooden floor. A knickknack cabinet in one corner between a sofa and a man-sized club chair. Across from that, a floor-standing RCA console radio sat next to a fake fireplace with gas logs sleeping in the Texas summer. A baking apple pie scented the air. *Homey*, Sharp thought.

Velma Griffin was trembling. He couldn't tell if she was mad, hurt, angry, homicidal, or all of the above. He opened the envelope, and she stared at it as if Sharp was bringing out a snake. A snake would have been easier on her, he thought.

"I just didn't want to believe it," she said quietly as she finally brought herself to look at the prints.

"Edna Maguire?" Her switch flipped to furious. "He's screwing Edna Maguire? That limey bitch!"

"You know her?"

"We have the same hairdresser. I see her every Tuesday at the beauty shop."

She started sobbing and wailing, and she clenched her eyes tight as her face went red and veins popped out. Sharp started to say that she was getting screwed at the beauty shop in more ways than one, but for once, he reined in his smart mouth.

"I need a moment, Mr. Sharp, would you excuse me?"

Velma gestured to his right, and he took a seat in a floral-print wingback chair behind him. Velma hurried to the back of the house. Either she honked into a handkerchief or a flock of geese landed on the roof.

He sat there fooling with his hat, admiring her knick-knack cabinet and wondering what possessed people to collect tiny ceramic figurines, when the door opened and George Griffin walked in, filling the small den. He seemed even larger than he looked in photos, across parking lots, or even on the other side of a barbecue stand. Sharp guessed six-four and easily 280. He carried his necktie in one hand; the navy-blue stain on the other matched the inkblot at the corner of his shirt pocket.

"Velma—this damned pen leaked again. This is the second time in—"

George got to the dining room and then turned to face the stranger in his least-favorite chair. Sharp got his first good look at George's broken nose and overbite, and he could see now that the big man and the homely Velma were perfect for each other.

"Who the hell are you?" George demanded.

Velma stomped into the dining room behind him, red eyed and redder faced.

"He's the man who took these!" She scooped the photos from the table and threw them at George, then turned on her heel and marched out.

George watched her and then looked at Sharp with a question. Sharp looked at the door. He suddenly had at least a dozen other places he needed to be. George lifted the facedown photos from the floor and turned one over.

"Oh, damn."

For just a moment, Sharp thought things were going to be okay. George leafed through the shots and winced as he did. Then he started to follow Velma.

"Honey, it's not what it . . ." Then he stopped. And turned around. Sharp stood up and—

But George was quick for a big man. His large mitt shoved him back down in the floral print. "You sonuvabitch. I'm going to—"

He balled an ink-stained fist and pressed Sharp back in the chair.

"Whoa now, George, I'm just the hired help here. I'm—"

He was interrupted by the mechanical sound of a shell being racked into the breach of a shotgun. George froze like an iceman on overtime.

Behind him, Velma had the Browning 12-gauge pointed at George's back. And by luck of geometry, at

Sharp, if George didn't prove quite solid enough to stop the blast. Griffin's eyes were wide and sneaking around his head to see if he was about to become an obituary.

Velma was shaking, even madder than George. Her finger twitched on the trigger. Sharp hadn't been this close to dead since a winter afternoon in Italy and remembered he didn't like it then either.

George slowly turned his head, "Velma . . . honey . . ."

Sharp winced. Velma screamed, "Don't you 'honey' me, you two-timing bastard!"

She shouldered the gun and Sharp kicked George as hard as he could at the ankles, sweeping the giant's legs and the rug right out from under him on the polished floor. Sharp rolled left, George went down right, and the Browning went boom. The air instantly filled with a cloud of floral-print upholstery. George landed hard, and so did Velma, the recoil putting her flat on her ass. Sharp bounced up and grabbed the shotgun and slung it onto the couch. George started rolling around on the ground, screaming like an Apache. Velma wailed as the pain in her shoulder overtook the anguish in her heart.

Sharp had the quick thought that he was getting all of ten bucks a week for this. "Jesus, lady," he yelled. "You trying to kill us all?"

His head was ringing from the blast. Velma was sobbing, and George was bleeding, the red wicking from a couple of pellet wounds at the shoulder of his white shirt. He let out a low moan.

That single moan transformed Velma. Suddenly, he wasn't a lying, cheating bastard. She seemed to realize that she'd very nearly killed the man she loved. She rushed to his side. "Baby! Oh, George, I didn't mean to . . ."

George looked to her eyes. "Honey, it's not what it looks like. It's work, I swear. There's nothing to it. If he hadn't given you those . . ." He winced again. She cooed. Sharp felt sick.

All of a sudden, they were both looking at him, and it was pretty clear who they thought the bad guy was.

"I'll put your bill in the mail." Sharp was out the door and across the street in a flash.

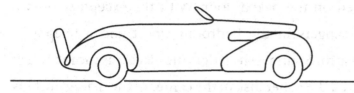

CHAPTER NINETEEN

His late breakfast and having nearly been blown to kingdom come meant Sharp wasn't feeling terribly hungry. He decided to swing by the major's house before lunch and see if the pilot had recovered from his ordeal. He didn't expect to find anyone there, but what he did find changed his world. The major didn't answer the locked front door, and when Sharp peeked in the picture window, the house was empty.

Not just nobody-home empty. It was bare, barren, deserted. Furniture, photos, everything was gone. Sharp

Colin Holmes

double-checked the address, then slipped through the side gate. The back door opened and his bootheels echoed on the naked floor. With the exception of two coat hangers in the bedroom closet and a telephone waiting for Southwestern Bell, the place was vacant. Sharp checked the paper disk in the center of the dial against his notepad: DRake-7246. It was the same phone. He was in the right place. But the business card he'd left under the phone was gone.

The instrument still had a dial tone, and he dialed the number he had for Doyle.

"Denniker residence," Monica, Doyle's housekeeper, answered.

"I need to speak to Doyle," he said.

"I'm sorry, Mr. Denniker isn't available right now. Would you like me to take a message, or would you prefer to call back later?"

"Neither. Wake him up, please." He made it more of an order than a request.

"I'm sorry, sir, Mr. Denniker is not—"

Sharp's patience deserted him. "Look, I was with Doyle last night, and he was going strong at one thirty. Tell him it's Jeff Sharp, and I need to talk to him right fucking now."

The phone went quiet, and after a moment, Doyle came on the line.

"Sharp? What the hell? Why are you getting profane with Monica? She's all upset, this better be—"

"The major is gone."

"What?"

"I'm at his house. The entire place has been cleaned out. Furniture, clothes . . . everything. It's like he was never here."

Brakes squealed outside. Sharp stretched the phone cord to the limit to look through the window. A government-gray Plymouth parked behind his LaSalle, and two MPs climbed from a jeep behind it.

Sharp lowered his voice to a whisper: "Somebody's here, I'm—"

And then the whole world went dark.

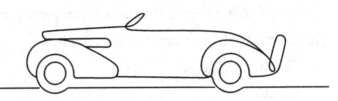

CHAPTER TWENTY

Sharp blinked himself conscious and looked around. Thanks to a recent career change, he was no longer intimately involved with livestock, but he did recognize the inside of a barn when he woke up in one. Even if this was the first time.

He was tied to a chair. His feet bound on either side of the legs with what appeared to be parachute cord. The tight binds behind his back bit into his wrists, and he had a headache that made his teeth hurt.

"He's waking up." A man's gravel voice.

The rickety chair wobbled. The packed dirt of the well-worn barn floor was hard as concrete. Stalls flanked both sides, the rotting wood of the gates collapsing in on itself, and bird shit covered the entire place. The dusty sunbeams coming through the broken windows made him guess it was late afternoon.

A sliding door was falling off its rollers at the end of the alley, and next to it, a walkthrough door hung ajar. In front of the doors sat a decaying table of a workbench and behind it, two men. One about Sharp's age—late thirties—the other older, forty-five or fifty. They were both in dark suits and ordinary ties. Medium build, brown hair. The kind of description that gives police detectives fits because it could mean anything.

"Welcome back, Captain Sharp." The older man sounded like he'd be the good cop. "I hadn't meant for us to meet under these circumstances."

Sharp just looked at him. He wasn't going to say anything if he didn't have to. The fact that he used his last rank in the Army caught him a little off guard.

"I'm Lieutenant Colonel Martin. This is Captain Billings. We're with Army Intelligence," he continued.

Sharp had met his share of Army Intelligence types across the pond; if these guys were Army Intel, then he was Bob Hope. Martin found a place to lean on the edge of the table, and Billings took up a station to Sharp's left.

Martin began: "We'd like to keep this conversation and this event off the record."

So they had something to hide.

"Who did you call?" Martin asked.

Sharp looked at Martin with the eye of somebody who'd been on both sides of an interrogation table. Did this colonel really think he was going to tell him anything?

The punch caught him off guard. Billings hit him on the side of the head right above the temple, and stars spun everywhere. His head cleared enough to appreciate the shot. Above the hairline, so it wouldn't show a bruise.

These guys might not be Army Intel, but they knew what they were doing.

"Who did you call, Captain?" Martin was persistent.

Sharp didn't say anything, and this brought a shot to the ribs. He bit his lip. He hadn't tasted his own blood since Dollar went down.

He gave the Billings character a stare. "You hit me again, and I'm going to stuff this chair so far up your ass you'll shit toothpicks for a month."

"So, you can talk." Martin rose from where he'd been sitting on the edge of the table. He stood and began pacing, almost strolling. "I know I heard you speaking to someone. Who was it?"

Sharp noticed the table had his hat and coat on it. As well as his holster and Colt.

"My answering service," he said.

"Your answering service—why would you do that?"

Sharp thought a second, "I was checking calls. It's what you do when you have an answering service."

"Uh-huh." Martin looked out the window. "How do you know Major Jerome Cartwright, Captain?"

"Cartwright? Don't recognize the name."

The knuckles rapped his head again and he seethed at Billings.

"Okay. I see." Sharp stalled. "Did he have a cup of coffee as my CO in the war?"

Colonel Martin lifted a folder with a sheaf of papers from a briefcase. "Not according to your personnel files."

"Maybe we belong to the same sorority."

That smart remark earned another smack to the noggin.

"Once again. How do you know Major Jerry Cartwright?" He was studying his nails, trying to look bored. Sharp had used the same trick before.

It didn't work for him either.

Sharp decided this wasn't going anywhere.

"Look, we can go around this all day if you want. Why don't you just get to the point and save us all some time?"

"Here's the point, Captain. You were trespassing on a federal installation, and we want to know why."

His head hurt, and this clown was making him mad. "First, I'm a civilian. I haven't been a captain of anything since Uncle Sam cut me loose two years ago. Second, I was in a private residence checking on the last known occupant. When I dropped him off there last, he was under the weather. I hadn't heard from him since, so I was making sure he was okay."

Sharp admitted his tone was a little condescending, but these assholes were acting like they were second graders on a field trip.

"And this occupant was a Major Jerry Cartwright, correct?"

"I didn't say that."

"How do you know Major Cartwright, Captain?"

"Look, if you guys want to arrest me, and I don't know how you'd do that as I'm a civilian in spite of how many times you want to call me Captain, but if you can, then let's go somewhere official and get this done. If you can't do it and your idea of interrogation is to have Sugar Ray here beat me to a pulp, then let's get started."

"We are simply here to get some answers. Did Major Cartwright leave you anything?" Martin had walked to the broken window and was looking outside.

Leave him anything? Sharp thought hard. He didn't even know Cartwright was going anywhere. But they didn't seem to know that. "No, but if he left you a pocketknife, maybe you could cut me loose."

With that, Billings took another poke, but Sharp jerked his head at the last moment.

The punch didn't land solidly but did catch him under his left eye. He slumped against the chair and played possum.

"Not that hard, dammit." Martin sounded angry.

"I think his skull's pretty thick." Billings even sounded stupid.

"Probably, but I don't think he's responding well to fists. Wake him up."

The water Billings threw wasn't cool and refreshing. The metal bucket had been cooking in the sun. Sharp came up, gasping.

Martin opened the folder on the desk. "You were a field promotion to the officer corps, weren't you?"

If those were his records, Sharp figured the colonel knew that.

"Had you been in a nice stateside military installation, they would have explained that your separation from the U.S. Army was conditional, and you could be recalled as a reserve officer if necessary. Captain."

Actually, he knew that. But he also knew it had to be a national emergency, and as far as he could tell, nothing was happening to warrant that.

Martin closed the folder and looked up at Sharp. "So you've not spoken to Major Cartwright at the Fort Worth air base."

"Never." It was mostly the truth. Of all the times he and Cartwright had talked, none had been at the base.

"I'm perfectly capable of having your commission restored and bringing you up on charges," Martin said.

"So you can court-martial me and kick me out of the Army? Sounds terrifying." These guys were trying to threaten him, but why?

The colonel gave an evil smile. "No, so we can lock you away in Fort Leavenworth and forget you exist."

"This isn't Major Cartwright, is it?" Martin held up an eight-by-ten photo that Sharp instantly recognized as having been taken through a window at the Blackstone from over his shoulder. Roni was looking into the camera like a lens into his soul. "She's very attractive. It would be a shame if—"

"Hey, now . . . she's got nothing to do with any of this."

"Perhaps. Still, people have accidents all the time." He paused to light a thin cigar. "What do you know about Major Cartwright? Perhaps we can help you find him."

He touched his lighter to the corner of the photo, and Sharp watched as Roni's pretty face was consumed by flame. The detached professional part of his brain thought that was a nice touch. The part beating in his chest got the message loud and clear.

The colonel dropped the flaming photo into the empty water bucket, and the barn began to stink of smoldering chemical paper.

"Cartwright's working on the atomic plane and he's disappeared," Sharp said.

"The atomic plane?" Martin almost seemed to relax. "The major told you this?"

"No, but it's pretty obvious. He's super-secretive about it, but everybody knows that's what it is." The two Army "Intel" agents shared a knowing look, and Sharp knew he'd said something they liked.

"Yes, they do." Martin smiled.

He nodded to Billings, and the goon made a move toward Sharp, who pitched forward onto his toes and hopped as high and as far back as he could. The ratty chair cracked down and shattered on the hard-as-concrete floor. The move broke loose the spreader on the chair legs, and his ankles came free from the ropes. Billings kept coming. Sharp rolled onto his back and kicked out as hard as he could. The heel of his boot hit just under Billings's kneecap with an audible pop as his patella dislodged. Sharp smiled. That had to hurt. The goon went down hard with a howl. Sharp did a shoulder roll and came up with his hands still tied behind him and Martin pointing a .45 Colt at him. His .45 Colt.

"I will shoot you, Captain."

Billings got up slowly. His leg wasn't working well. He winced as he tried to stand and glared at Sharp, who smiled in return. Billings flashed over in anger and pulled a pistol of his own. A short-barreled .38 revolver. Sharp hated those things. He was always on the wrong end.

"Wait." Martin opened his briefcase. He tucked Sharp's paperwork inside and dropped the magazine from the Colt in for good measure. Then he jacked the round from the chamber, caught it snappily in midair, and dropped it in as well. "Can you walk?"

Sharp took a step, "Yeah."

"Not you."

"Oh, well, I'm OK, just so you know." Sharp winked at Billings.

He didn't wink back. Instead, he simply said, "Enjoy your stay."

Martin dropped the pistol on the desk, and they left.

Sharp watched through the broken window as the gray Plymouth pulled away, then used the busted glass to slice the ropes, damn near slitting his wrist in the process. His watch surprised him by showing 10:15. What he'd thought was late afternoon sun was midmorning sun. He'd been out a whole night. He shrugged into his shoulder holster and put the now empty Colt into its socket, then headed out to see where the hell he was.

Judging by the not late-afternoon sun, the Plymouth had headed south. He followed the overgrown dirt road in that direction. After about a mile, it connected with a strip of asphalt. No visible marking. It ran east-west, and he had no clue. Just miles of empty ranchland in every direction.

Nice place to be in the middle of a 95-degree summer morning with no water. But he was last in Fort Worth and figured they wouldn't drive him east through Dallas, so he guessed he was west of town. He started hiking back toward what he thought might be civilization.

He'd been walking for about forty-five minutes along the scrub ranchland, trying to figure out what the hell that had been about when a Model T pickup clattered alongside him. The old farmer inside sized him up in one glance. "Hop in. Unless you'd rather..."

Sharp shook his head, and the bump on the side of his head made him regret it. "Much obliged," he said, wincing. He settled onto the dust-covered leather seat with a long, worn-out sigh.

A half mile later, they turned south, and he was dropped off at the depot in Weatherford, thirty miles west of Fort Worth. Sharp didn't care. He found a water fountain and drank it dry.

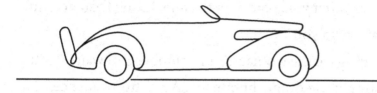

CHAPTER TWENTY-ONE

The modest train depot had a row of three phone booths on the wall. Sharp went immediately to the nearest one and spun the dial all the way around.

"Operator, how may I help you?" It seemed every telephone operator in the world had the same voice.

"Long Distance, please. Collect. I need to reach a number in Fort Worth."

"One moment."

Sharp waited as the line clicked. He looked through the glass of the booth to the schedule board above the teller windows of the train station. The next T&P train of the day was due in forty-five minutes.

Another voice came on the line. "Long Distance, how may I help you?"

He gave the woman Roni's number and waited as the phone clicked and hummed. "Arquette residence." He could hear the radio playing in Roni's living room.

"Southwestern Bell, I have a long-distance collect call, will you accept the charges?"

"Roni, it's Jeff. Are you okay?" he interrupted.

"Am I okay? Sure. I'm not the one calling collect. What's wrong?" She sounded annoyed, then paused a beat. "Yes, Operator, I'll accept."

"Thank you for using the Bell system." The operator clicked off.

"Jeff? Where are you?" Now she sounded concerned. Jeff liked that a lot better.

"I'm in Weatherford. It's tough to explain, can I bum a ride?"

"What in the world are you doing in Weatherford? You want me to come all the way out there?"

"No, not all the way out here, but can you pick me up at the T&P station?" He twisted in the booth to see the timetables on the wall. "In about an hour and a half?"

She didn't respond right away, so he added, "You're the only person I trust right now."

There was a considered pause before Roni agreed, but she was there when he entered the enormous art deco terminal of Fort Worth's main station. The look on her face told him he was a mess.

"What in the cat hair hit you?" Her hand went to his swelling black eye.

He flinched. "I had a little disagreement with a couple of guys."

"Do we need to take you to the hospital?"

"Nah, I wouldn't want to run into them there."

He took her arm and escorted her outside, where her little yellow coupe waited by the curb.

"Why don't you let me drive?" Sharp offered.

"My car? Why would I do that?"

"So, we can go find mine."

She didn't follow any logic that might have been there but dug into her purse anyway. Her hand came out with a mess of a key chain that sported a lucky rabbit's foot, a pom-pom with a pink ribbon, a St. Christopher medallion, and four keys.

"What?" She answered his frown. "It's easier to find this way."

Sharp determined which was the door key to the Pontiac and opened the passenger door for her. Then dug through the mess and found the ignition key. He lit a Lucky and pointed them toward the base. "When's the last time you talked to the major?"

She thought for a beat. "When we saw you at the Four Deuces. He was very interested in you. More than he was me. Wanted to know all about you. How long I've known you. All sorts of details. Why?"

"He's disappeared."

"I told you he does that." She rolled her eyes. "Off in an instant. Sometimes I'll get a phone call and sometimes not. Why can't men use a telephone?"

Sharp ignored the jab. "Does he usually clean out his house and pack up his furniture when he leaves?"

"What do you mean?"

"I dropped by to check on him. He was out of sorts at the club the other day. When I went to his house, it had been cleaned out. Empty as a pocket."

"That's odd." She blew the obvious out her window.

"You think?"

They turned the corner to the major's small house and found a vacant spot where Sharp had last seen his LaSalle.

He pulled to the curb. A pair of grammar school-age kids were playing tag on the major's lawn.

"This is the right house, isn't it?" asked Roni.

"Well, I've only been here once, but it's the right address."

A set of metal street numbers Sharp hadn't noticed before were nailed by the door. There were also potted plants on a small stand on the porch. It looked homey. Lived in.

He rapped on the door frame. The screen was closed, but the front door stood open behind it, the radio was playing.

A petite woman answered. She was pleasant-looking, wearing an apron and drying her hands on a dishtowel. "May I help you?"

"Good afternoon, ma'am. I'm Jeff Sharp, and this is Roni Arquette. We're looking for a friend of ours, Major Jerry Cartwright, who I believe used to live at this address."

The woman paused. "I don't recognize the name. How long ago did he live here?"

Roni leaned in. "Fairly recently."

The housewife concentrated on folding the towel. "Couldn't be too recently—we've been here almost three years."

"Three years?" Roni repeated the address back to the woman.

"Yes, that's this address, but as I say . . . there's no Major Cartwheel here."

Sharp nodded. "Cartwright. We must be mistaken then. Sorry to have bothered you."

Roni started to argue, but he took her elbow and steered her back to the car.

He pulled away from the house, deep in thought. Roni surfaced first.

"What the hell was that Jeff-er-son? What have you done with Jerry?"

Sharp checked the rearview. No Plymouth. "I haven't done anything."

"Well, people don't just disappear into thin air."

"I think he had some help. And I may have met the squad that did it."

"The guy that gave you the shiner?" Roni asked.

"Guys. More than one."

She smiled, thinking back.

"Like that time in school when you took on the Fitzsimmons brothers?"

He remembered that ass-kicking to this day. "All four of them. That wasn't a fair fight."

"Isn't that the way fights go? Fair isn't really a consideration." She blew the smoke from her cigarette out the window.

"Your brother didn't see it that way." He slowed the car to a stoplight. "Ducked out on me just as it started to heat up."

"David was never much for fighting. Especially four on two."

"Yeah, four on one is much better odds."

"It was for him."

His LaSalle sat in the driveway of his rental house, making the hair on the back of his neck stand up. The only set of keys to the car were still in his pocket.

"Jeff." Roni's voice had a note of concern. She nodded toward the front door.

His handsomely crafted repair to the front door facing was splintered, and the new paint scarred. The lock was busted, and the door stood open to the world.

Inside was a shambles. Someone had done a thorough job of ransacking the place. The one decent club chair had been sliced open, and the cushion stuffing thrown about. The kitchen table and chairs overturned, every cabinet open and drawers and contents scattered across the floor.

"Honestly, I thought you'd keep a little nicer house, Jefferson." Her voice had a little quiver to it.

It brought him back to the moment, and he pulled the Colt. It's light weight reminded him that the ammunition was hiding in Colonel Martin's briefcase and he was holding a finely machined steel rock.

He whispered, "They might still be here." Her eyes got wide as he motioned her to get behind him. They listened hard into the silence.

The bedroom was a wreck too. The mattress leaned against the window, and all the dresser drawers were dumped on the floor, along with the contents of the closet. An attic opening in the closet ceiling had been broken through as well.

In his newly converted darkroom, the intruders had busted open ten bucks' worth of film and photo paper and broken the enlarger when they'd flipped over the tables. The chemistry trays were scattered across the wood floor. From the faint smell of dried developer and fixative, he guessed whoever did this had been gone for a while.

Unless they were in the garage.

He told Roni to call the cops while he checked the garage. But whoever had done the tornado impersonation was long gone. They'd been through the detached garage, but there wasn't as much to destroy out there.

Roni met him at the back door. "The phone doesn't work."

"That figures. These guys look to be pros." The cord from the phone to the wall had been ripped out of the wall mount. He went to the area near the hall closet, where his toolbox had been neatly stored yesterday and found a screwdriver hiding in the pile of tools dumped on the floor. He stripped the phone wires with his pocketknife and reconnected it. The dial tone hummed his success.

He found the phone book under a pile of paperwork and flipped to the inside of the cover. He found the number for the police and reported the break-in.

"You should call your landlord too." Roni started in to straighten things up, uprighting his hat tree to discover one of the legs had been snapped off, and it wouldn't stand.

He flipped open his notebook for Mrs. Hunnakee's number and discovered that any pages with information on them, including the landlady's phone number, had been ripped out during his unexpected nap. He riffled through the thin pages of the phonebook, found the number for "N. Hunnakee," and reported the chaos to Norma. The cops arrived first, two guys he didn't know and who didn't know him. They looked around, took a few notes. He couldn't think of anything missing, so it was nothing more than breaking and entering. He gave them the details on Martin and Billings, but he and the cops assumed those weren't real names.

The cops were on their way out when his landlady arrived.

She teetered in and surveyed the damage. "I thought we talked about no wild parties."

Sharp smiled weakly and introduced Roni. "Most of this is her fault—she's taking judo lessons."

She raised an eyebrow at his shiner. "Looks like she's used it on you." She wound her way through the debris to the kitchen. Sharp flipped the table over and found her a chair. She sat heavily, and her oversize purse thumped to the floor.

"Did they leave you any ice?" Mrs. Hunnakee pulled a pint of bourbon from her purse.

Sharp opened his empty fridge and flipped down the freezer door to discover that they had indeed gone through that as well.

Roni held up two empty ice trays that had been thrown in the sink. "All gone. And melted too."

Sharp frowned. "Yeah, I think this happened quite a while ago."

She filled the trays and returned them to the freezer while he maneuvered a drawer that once held silverware back into the cabinet.

Mrs. Hunnakee waved her bottle. "We'll just do neat. I need a drink, and you need to tell me what's going on."

Roni found glasses, and Mrs. Hunnakee filled them with whiskey. Roni took a sip and winced.

Mrs. Hunnakee nodded. "Hundred and one proof. When you get old, you can't taste anymore. Takes a good kick so you even know it's going down." She took a purposeful sip. "So who did this to my house, Mr. Sharp?"

He thought a moment and realized he really didn't know. "They said they were Army Intelligence, but I've known a few of those types, and they don't play these kinds of games. I'm really not sure who it is."

"Ohhh. A mystery." Roni earned a scowl.

"This is not exactly Thursday night's episode of *The Shadow*." Sharp took a second to light a Lucky.

Mrs. Hunnakee waved her glass. "Damn right, it's not. Radio plays don't wreck your house."

"I will get this cleaned up, and everything put back as good or better than it was," Sharp promised.

"What makes you think I want you sticking around here to do that?"

"Well now, ma'am, I—"

"I can't have this." Mrs. Hunnakee looked him square in the eye. "I won't have this. I wanted a nice quiet renter, Mr. Sharp. You told me that wouldn't be a problem. Now you've torn my place all to hell, and you haven't been here a month. Why on God's green Earth would I let you stay?"

"Ma'am, I thought we had an agreement."

"We did, and you broke it. Look at this place." She frowned. "This is my property, not something you can just tear up as you please."

The accusation hung in the air. The old woman took a healthy drink. Sharp and Roni shared a look. Roni came to his rescue.

"Jeff, would you excuse us for a moment?"

He looked at her with a question, and she offered a sweet smile. "Please."

He wandered into the den and set about straightening the room, turning over the chairs and kicking the debris into a pile that he could sweep up later. In the kitchen, Roni and his landlady were talking in hushed tones. He gave them five minutes and walked back in.

Mrs. Hunnakee gazed into the distance, thinking, then shook her head and sighed. "Well, with Mrs. Matthews dying and now this, I'll be damned lucky if I can find any-one else to take the place." She scowled. "So you in the Army?"

"Was. Back in the war, but not since. I have no idea why these guys did this." He shrugged.

She started to stand and wobbled a little. She shot the rest of the drink down and returned the bottle to her giant purse.

"If I give you a second chance . . ." She nodded to Roni and let the fact that she still wasn't sold hang in the air, then pointed the empty glass at directly him. "But if anything like this happens again—you're out on your ass before the dust settles."

"Yes, ma'am."

"And I'm raising your rent to thirty bucks." She shouldered the purse.

"That's not what we agreed to, Mrs. Hunnakee."

She waved her arm at the destruction. "No, it's not. Thirty bucks, Mr. Sharp."

He tried to amend the loss. "How about twenty-eight and a bottle of Wild Turkey with the rent check?"

She paused at the door and cocked her head.

"I can do that. Due on the first."

Sharp grinned, "Yes, ma'am." And she closed the door behind her.

Roni smiled at her good work. "That went well."

Sharp tipped his footstool back upright. "Yeah, but next time, let's just not call the landlord."

They cleaned the place up and returned drawers, shelves, and belongings to their proper homes.

Sharp dug out the remains of his notebook and made a list of things he'd need from the lumberyard and the hardware store to once again repair the house.

He also was going to need to hit the secondhand furniture store and replace the club chair and the hat rack.

They sat down at the kitchen table for a break, and he smacked his head with his palm. "Doyle. Dammit."

He moved his chair to the phone and dialed the number from memory.

"Denniker."

"Doyle, it's Jeff Sharp."

"Where are you?"

"I'm at my house, it's been ransacked."

"What happened at the major's?" Doyle was direct.

Sharp told the tale as best he could remember. Doyle listened silently.

There was a pause before Doyle spoke. "I don't think they're Army Intelligence."

"Me neither. But they had my records, knew all about what I did in the war. If it's Caples's people, I don't know where that would have come from."

"Bobby has access to some pretty impressive resources."

"You mean Meyer Lansky does." Sharp played a card he didn't think Doyle knew he had.

The voice on the other end of the line went quiet for a long moment. Finally, Doyle admitted it. "Yes, that too. Have you seen Bobby? I mean, seen where he works, lives, eats?"

"I haven't tailed him, but it's next on the list." He remembered that somebody else now had his list.

"Find out what's going on. I can't have this visiting my place next." Doyle hung up.

Sharp offered to buy Roni dinner, but she was supposed to have dinner with her parents and invited him to tag along. He passed. He'd always liked her folks and had even gone by to see them and remember Dave a few times, but he didn't feel like that kind of homey family dinner. He walked her to the car.

"Thanks for coming to get me." He looked over his shoulder at the broken door frame. "And everything else." He moved to give her a peck on the cheek, but she stopped him.

"You be careful, mister." She wrapped her arms around his neck and gave him a hug, which hurt because his head had been bashed around. But then she surprised him with a deep kiss and looked into his eyes when they parted. "Can we not make a habit of this?"

Then she was off, and he was alone in the dusk watching her car disappear around the corner. He thought about her burning photograph falling into the bucket. Roni had been through much more than her fair share of tragedy. On top of everything else, was he putting her in harm's way right now? For a few lousy bucks? He felt his lips burning with her kiss and his mind was made up: he'd have to keep his distance. For her sake.

He went in and found his hammer and a few nails and secured the front door. He opted for a two-course dinner of aspirin to calm his headache. And his backache, the slight aggravation that remained in his shoulder, and various other discomforts. He dialed his answering service.

"Jefferson Sharp Investigations." He knew this silky-smooth voice from previous calls.

"Messages for BElmont twelve twenty-five?" he asked.

"There are no messages, sir."

"Thank God."

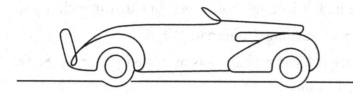

CHAPTER TWENTY-TWO

S harp woke to the sound of someone banging on his door. He grabbed his pants and headed for the front door, only to find that some moron had nailed it shut. "You'll have to come around back."

The two Mutt and Jeff police detectives came to the back door. Sharp opened the screen to badges and mumbled names.

"What's up?" he asked tall, thin Detective Mutt.

"Jefferson Sharp?"

"Yes?"

"Does the name "Evelyn" mean anything to you, Mr. Sharp?" Short, round Detective Jeff asked.

He hadn't had any coffee yet, but that question got some gears turning. "It used to. Why?"

"Evelyn Lavelle Sharp was assaulted yesterday. She's your wife, right?"

"Was. She's filed for divorce. Why?"

"She was abducted, and whoever did it got a little rough." They paused a moment and silently negotiated finger points to see who'd be the bad cop while Sharp ground his mental transmission into overdrive. "She says she escaped and suggested you might know something about it."

Detective Mutt asked, "Mind telling us where you were yesterday afternoon?"

Sharp explained his own predicament over the last twenty-four hours and pointed out there would be a police record. He gave Roni's name as an alibi and told the cops to check with the Bell telephone people. Their records should show his long-distance call from Weatherford.

"Any idea why someone would want to hurt her, Sharp?" asked Detective Jeff.

"Well, she's an aggravating, two-timing, backstabbing bitch, but you have to know her pretty well to find that out." Sharp yawned so wide his jaws popped. "Have you talked to Smitty Smithson?"

"He suggested we speak to you," Detective Mutt said.

"He would." Sharp frowned. "Did he have this address?"

Detective Mutt scribbled on his notepad. "We're detectives, Mr. Sharp. We find these kinds of things out. Mr. Smithson was not a great deal of help."

"Yep. That's Smitty."

The cops took their notes and nosed around, then left. A part of Sharp gave a moment's sympathy for Evelyn, but the flicker died quickly. He showered and dressed for surveillance in Dallas, stopping at the Blackstone for breakfast and some sass from Peggy for missing Roni yet again. He called Roni's office from the phone booth and warned her about the police and what had happened to Evelyn.

She wasn't concerned and gave the impression that Evelyn might have even deserved it. Women, Sharp thought, were indeed the more dangerous sex.

After breakfast, he headed for the police supply store to reload before he set off to find whatever Caples was up to in Dallas. He bought two boxes of .45 ACP ammunition and a pair of new magazines. With the Colt back to its usual self, he felt a little more secure.

Restocking the armory put a dent in his cash situation, and he had some time to kill before the bank opened. It occurred to him that he hadn't really grilled the one guy who might be in a position to know. He looked up at Leo's office high above the street and then followed his nose to the *Examiner's* offices. Sharp had known Leo for a lot of years, but he'd known his secretary, Arleen Clark, almost his whole life. She and her brother Henry had been in the neighborhood bunch with Sharp and Roni's late brother Dave; they'd all been buddies growing up. Henry worked for Texas and Pacific now as a conductor, and no one saw much of him, but Sharp knew he could always find Arleen's ample frame guarding Leo's office door.

He'd long ago discovered a good way to get Leo's goat on the odd occasion when he needed to talk to the senior executive publishing magnate was to tell his old buddy Arleen that Leo had told him to just wait in the office. Leo would return to his office to find Sharp with his size elevens perched on the desk, next to the framed picture of the publisher and FDR on Leo's boat at Eagle Mountain Lake.

"Arleen, how many times have I told you—quit letting this son of a bitch in my private office." Leo smiled when he said it, but the tone was hard.

Sharp took a long puff on the cigar and offered Leo his humidor. "These are nice. Cuban?"

"Yes, Upmann's. Now, get your ass out of my chair." Leo took the humidor, closed the lid without getting a smoke, and dropped the morning's *Examiner* on the desk.

"Yessir, Mr. Publisher, sir." Sharp saluted and scurried to the visitor's side of the desk.

"I'm busy, Sharp, and you look like hell. What do you want?"

"I'm looking for information. Seemed to me, a newspaper might be a good place to start. I need to know about Bobby Caples." He took a seat and leaned in toward Leo.

Leo nodded. "That who beat you up?"

"Nah, I've ticked off a whole different group of people."

"You do have a gift." Leo reconsidered the cigar and took his time lighting up. "Caples, huh? We talked about how Bugsy got himself murdered in California, right?"

"Yeah, and it was on the newsreels."

"The *Examiner* had the scoop on that." Leo smiled around his stogie. "You should read more than the sports page."

"I read the comics too. Snuffy Smith is a riot."

Leo rolled his eyes. "Word has it that Meyer Lansky and the Chicago Outfit have been bankrolling a casino

Siegel was running. They were tired of losing their collective ass."

"And this casino is what got Bugsy killed?" Sharp asked.

"Nevada has legalized gambling. Siegel thought if he could build a first-class resort and casino in Las Vegas, the Hollywood types would come out in droves from LA. Doesn't seem to have worked out that way." Leo knew his stuff. It jibed with the information Sharp had gotten from Gentry.

"At least not for Bugsy. So you think Lansky is looking west?" Sharp took a drag on the Upmann. Nice cigar.

"Nevada is in the middle of nowhere. But Dallas is a different story. Centrally located. It gets you from Chicago to the West Coast or Las Vegas. It's a quick jaunt to New Orleans or even Mexico and the Gulf. It's a natural stepping-stone. It makes sense, and if Lansky is making a move on Dallas, then Caples needs somewhere to go."

"Like Fort Worth." Sharp calculated.

"Where he runs smack into Doyle. Which means he and Doyle—"

The office door flew open, and E. G. Lavelle strode in with an armload of blueprints tucked against his ample gut, still talking to Arleen as he barged in.

"... he'll see me, he'll always see me—"

The look on Lavelle's face when he saw Sharp was priceless.

"Well, well, well. Top of the morning to you, E. G." Sharp blew a smoke ring.

Sharp's soon to be former father-in-law almost dropped his bundles. Then caught himself and the cheap cigar wallowed its way to a corner of the mustache.

"Sharp." A slight nod was all the acknowledgment he gave. "Leo, here are those pla—um, documents, we spoke about. I wanted you to see them before we ..."

Sharp noticed Leo was visibly irked with the man.

"Thank you, E. G. If you'll just leave them with Arleen, I'll look them over, and let's talk after I've finished here." Leo waved a hand in Sharp's general direction.

Sharp stood up. "Oh, no, Leo. I've taken far too much of your valuable time. I need to take off." He saluted his former employer. "Always a pleasure to see you, E. G. Leo, I'll give you a shout later."

He winked at Arleen on the way out.

Sharp walked to the elevator, deep in thought. The Stockmen's Association had just built a new headquarters building, so why in the heck would the executive director be in Leo's office with a bunch of blueprints? Why take blueprints to the newspaper? And while Sharp didn't know much about architecture, it looked like a lot of plans were tied up in those fat rolls of paperwork. That was one large building. Or a bunch of small ones. Like the Panther City contracts he'd seen in Bobby Caples's files.

He stepped into the bright sun of the warming summer morning and added this to his list of things to investigate the next time he descended into the bowels of the courthouse records room.

The bank had just unlocked its doors, and he tipped his hat to the security guard as the door swung open, and he went straight to the clerk manning the safe deposit desk.

He refilled his cash reserves from the dwindling supply in his lockbox. Plus, a bit to buy home-repair supplies and replace the destroyed club chair. Between the Griffins' floral-print wingback, the busted chair in the barn, and Mrs. Hunnakee's club chair, he'd been hell on furniture lately.

The drive to surveil Bobby Caples was almost an hour across Fort Worth, Arlington, and Grand Prairie to RC Distributing, just off Harry Hines Boulevard in Dallas. He'd established that the short pink brick office building at that address was the nerve center of Caples enterprises. Nondescript, it blended into the surroundings of the light industrial area with a set of concrete steps leading to an office in front, while a row of docks out back waited for one of the very few delivery vehicles passing by.

Rather unimpressive for the headquarters of an organized-crime syndicate.

He pulled up across the street and retrieved his binoculars and camera case from the trunk. The same caring souls who had knocked his noggin around and destroyed his house had bashed in the lenses on the Bausch and Lombs. The camera case held a similar story. These guys were really getting on his nerves.

He remembered from his missing notes that Caples had a Packard, and a gray-over-maroon late-model Clipper was parked by the front stairs. With nothing left to do but wait, he cooked a bit as the summer morning heated up until a guy he was reasonably sure was Caples and another associate emerged and headed to the Packard. He wrote down the license number.

He followed them downtown, where they headed into the Adolfus Hotel. Sharp cursed. Parking in downtown Dallas was a pain in the butt, and he momentarily agreed with Leo that there just wasn't much on this side of the river to make one leave Fort Worth. Inside the lavish hotel, he discovered that the ballroom was the setting for a luncheon—a fundraiser for the Salvation Army. Caples was putting forth his charitable side to support the community and help those less fortunate. Sharp wondered if that included those who would beat up women.

He found a seat at the bar and ordered a Budweiser and a sandwich. He figured if Mr. Busch could put up a hotel this grand, he could at least sample the family's product. But when the barkeep came around to offer a second, he opted for his preferred Pearl.

The luncheon broke up, and he dropped a buck on the bar as he spotted Caples coming down the massive stairs. He lost him trying to get to the LaSalle from around the corner. That was aggravating.

He sweated across from the distributorship on Harry Hines, figuring that Caples had to bring the other guy back at some point, if for no other reason than his car was still there. The Packard finally arrived, and the gentlemen returned to what Sharp wagered was an office with at least a fan.

Two o'clock became three, and 95 degrees became 100. Nothing. His sore spots ached, and he grew stiff as he sat. His two-beer lunch wasn't sitting well either. He got out to stretch his legs and moseyed to the corner phone booth to check in with the answering service.

The pleasant-voiced operator had one call. A Jerry Cartwright at 9:25 that morning. No message, but he left a number: Continental-25-7-32-16. Sharp wrote it in his blank notebook and tried to call it back. Nothing happened.

He tried again and then transposed some numbers. Nothing. He called the answering service back and confirmed the number. He'd written it down correctly.

Finally, he dialed zero.

"I'm sorry, sir, that's not a Bell exchange." The operator sounded like she had said this more than once.

"Maybe long distance?" he asked.

"I can check, sir. Can you hold?" She clicked off the line and Sharp lit a smoke and thought for a full minute, trying to remember the addresses and business names he'd so carefully committed to his notebook. Pages that someone was probably trying to decipher right now. He flipped through the phone book and scribbled down addresses. He knew Caples kept an office at the Bamboo Room. He remembered the Carousel Club because it not only had a risqué reputation as the region's most notorious strip club but someone got shot there every couple of months.

He was interrupted by a series of clicks on the phone, and another female voice came on the line.

"Sir?"

"Yes?"

"Sir, this isn't a telephone number."

Across the parking lot, Bobby Caples walked down the set of steps and climbed into the Packard.

"Dammit."

"I beg your pardon, sir?"

"Uh, sorry. Thank you, Operator."

"Thank you for using the Bell system, sir."

Sharp hurried across the parking lot to the LaSalle. The Clipper was turning down the block, and he was going to have to step on it to catch up. He reached the corner, and the car had vanished. He'd lost him twice in one day.

He headed for the Bamboo Room. It looked decidedly less upscale in daylight hours. The fake palm trees out front looked extremely fake in the summer sun, and Sharp wondered why they didn't have real ones. It was hard to remember in the baking summer sun that North Texas also got ice in January.

He circled the nightclub and parked down the street from where it appeared employees parked. He gave it an hour, turning over the mystery of Jerry's message in his head. Who would leave a phone number that didn't go anywhere? Was it a phone number? What else could it be?

He mulled it over for a couple of hours, watching for Bobby Caples to never arrive. He gave up and headed for the Carousel Club. On the way, he remembered Dallas had a Continental Avenue. It was a small detour to find an address matching the number 25-7 he'd written down, but the 2500 block was a vacant lot.

The strip club had nothing either. He was seeing two sides of this private-eye gig. The part where someone was trying to beat you silly and the boring-as-toast part where you watched paint peel for hours on end. Of the two, right now, he could handle a little boredom.

He sat and watched. A few cars stopped, and girls got out but none were in a Packard Clipper.

When the lieutenant's watch read 6:00, he decided Caples might not be that interested in scantily clad young ladies either, and maybe he could catch him at home. The address was off Greenville Avenue in a nice neighborhood of well-tended lawns and modest but attractive homes. He parked down a couple of houses and across the street from a cozy little place with tan bricks and hunter-green trim and shutters. The steep roof had matching green shingles. The yard was landscaped with shrubs around the porch, pink crepe myrtle and a large pecan tree shaded a wide picture window that looked out over the front lawn. It seemed a little domesticated for a mobster, but maybe that wasn't something he and the neighbors talked about over the fence.

Sharp sat down the street, watching the house as the sun sank through the trees. He watched couples out for an evening stroll. A group of kids down the road played red rover, while he sat and sweated and swatted mosquitoes. Dusk came, and the kids broke up to go home. A few porch lights began to come on, and about the time Sharp convinced himself that he'd wasted an entire day, the Packard rolled slowly past and turned into the driveway. At least he had the right place.

Caples was alone. He pulled the car up to the garage and left it running while he got out and opened the doors. He pulled it in and then pushed the swinging doors closed. This Sharp could see from his vantage point, but when Caples went to the house, he couldn't see anything from where he sat. He stepped out of the car and stretched, then crossed the street and lit a cigarette as he ambled down the sidewalk.

Inside the house, the lights came on. Caples pulled open the drapes, and a front window slid up to let in a little air. Sharp strolled to the driveway and heard the telephone ring inside.

The mobster answered, "Yeah, this is he."

And then the house exploded.

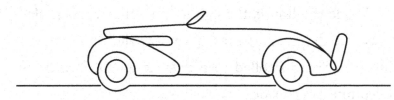

CHAPTER TWENTY-THREE

S harp had some experience coming to in the back of an ambulance. The rattle and shake of the gurney flying around woke him as the driver did his best impression of an Indy 500 competitor. The siren screamed, the world spun, and his head roared, as a guy in a white coat wrapped gauze everywhere.

The guy in the white coat saw the signs and dodged as Sharp blurted vomit all over the shoes of a balding man squatting beside the gurney. A balding guy with a badge hanging out of his jacket pocket.

The balding cop pulled a hanky and put it over his nose while the wannabe Barney Oldfield at the wheel slid the meat wagon around another corner.

Sharp was still too cloudy when the cop mouthed, "Why'd you kill Caples?"

The response was another round of bile. The detective jerked back as far as he could against the wall of the ambulance and cut loose with a string of profanity. Sharp watched him cuss and realized he couldn't hear a thing over the roaring in his ears.

The ambulance jerked to a stop, and the back doors flew open, and somebody yanked the stretcher out into the hot, humid night. It crashed into a green curtained room amid the pandemonium of the emergency department. Sharp tried to sit up, and a grandmotherly nurse shoved him back down on the stretcher, and a couple of other guys rolled him onto a gurney like a piece of meat. A cheap piece of meat.

His head was ringing, and he could only hear a muffled sort of mumbling when they tried to ask questions. He had a weird sense of déjà vu that took him back to Italy. For some reason, that calmed him down.

The docs and nurses were worrying over him. But he knew this feeling and Parkland Hospital was much better equipped than the field hospital in Monte Cassino. Sharp knew he was going to be all right. He'd been here before.

That didn't mean it wasn't bad. A flying something had clipped his forehead, and as with most head wounds, it bled like crazy. The orderlies wiped him down with bloodstained towels, and the nurses looked to be yelling. They kept mouthing him questions, and he yelled back that he couldn't hear them. They seemed to be having a problem understanding that.

Finally, they wrapped him in enough fabric to cause a cotton shortage, and the doc stepped in to stitch up his head. The cut was just to the side of his left eye, and Sharp flinched when the nurse jabbed a needle in his temple to numb it. He'd been blown up, and his stomach had turned inside out, but the one thing that really hurt was that needle.

His eyes watered.

Slowly, his hearing came back, and he could make out some conversation on the right side. The balding cop came back, and it looked like he had changed pants. He had a big guy in a bad tie with him. He introduced themselves as Detectives Jennings and Sloan.

They were going to be his tag team partners for the evening.

"Why'd you kill Caples?" Sharp was lip-reading as much as hearing and understanding.

"I didn't."

"We found you across the street, and the keys in your pocket fit the LaSalle down the block," Jennings said. "You look like a human pincushion."

"Yeah. So?" He was sitting up, but still a little dizzy.

"We found a list of Caples's businesses and notes on his dealings in your pocket. You want to explain that?"

"I'm doing an investigation on Caples for a client." Sharp worked his jaw to clear his ears.

"So you're a private eye?" Sloan had one of his business cards.

"Livestock detective. Cattle rustlers. That kind of thing. Also, a semiprofessional poker player." Sharp blinked hard to focus his eyes.

"What the hell does that mean?" The big guy leaned in close. Sharp decided they were taking themselves way too seriously.

"It means I'm not good enough to make a living at it." Shaking his head emphasized the pain.

"Who's your client?"

Sharp looked at the policemen and explained something he shouldn't have had to.

"I really can't say. An expectation of confidentiality comes with the business."

"The cattle business? Enough to go to jail over?" Sloan toyed with the card.

"If I have to. That's the whole idea behind the 'private' in *private investigator*." He wasn't going to give these guys Doyle, even though he was having some gears mesh in the back of his head that said it might come down to him or Doyle.

Jennings read his mind. "The name Denniker mean anything to you?"

"It does."

"And he put you up to kill Caples." Sloan jumped in.

"Nobody put me up to anything." His head was starting to hurt, and these guys weren't helping.

"You were just walking down the street, and the house happened to blow up." Sloan crossed his arms.

"Believe it or not, fellows, the only person more surprised than Caples was me."

"You had no idea." Jennings took his turn.

"No clue at all." Sharp thought that baffled them. They were confident they had an open-and-shut murder case with the culprit right there in front of them.

Sloan and Jennings conferred a moment. He watched a nurse light up across the way and wished for a smoke.

And a glass of water.

Sloan took his turn. "We can make this very easy on you—you might only get life instead of the chair—if you cooperate."

Sharp smiled, knowing this was part of the game, and truthfully, these guys weren't very good at it.

"I am cooperating. I've answered every question you've asked with the complete truth."

"Who's your client?" Sloan was at least persistent.

"I can't tell you that, but our agreement had nothing to do with killing Caples. All I was asked to do was get as much information as I could on Caples or Cappellini. That's what I was doing." He tried to get the nurse's attention and beg a cigarette.

"Right. Little Miss Innocent." So the big guy was going to get rude.

Sharp got cranky. "Look, Lieutenant Lard Ass, you've been through my car. Did you find any kind of explosives, detonators, wiring—anything that might lead you to think I had a bomb anywhere?"

"I found a cut down .45 in your shoulder holster," Jennings said.

"You blow up a house with a handgun? Check it. It hasn't been fired since I cleaned it last. And there'll be a

record of that weapon at the Fort Worth PD gun range."
Sharp still shot with a few friends on the force. "Look,
guys, I didn't do it. I don't know who did. I know Caples
is into some shady stuff, and there are dozens of people
who might want him dead. I'm not one of 'em."

"You have no idea who did this?" Jennings scribbled
in his notebook.

"I have lots of ideas. How many people benefit if
Bobby Caples is dead? It's a damn long list." Sharp
watched the nurse disappear without a look.

"And I'd bet my pension your client is on it." Sloan
lit a match and touched it to his Pall Mall. If Sharp were
going to kill anyone, right then, it would've been to get
that cigarette.

"Hell, I bet your boss is on it. The mayor of Dallas is
probably on it. Like I said—it's a long list. But I'm not on
it." Sharp twisted his head to pop his neck. It didn't help.

Jennings looked convinced.

Sharp thought Sloan looked like he needed a piece
of pie. Maybe he always looked that way. They told him
they'd be in touch, and Sharp wrote his home address and
phone number on the back of one of his private-eye cards.

"I'm available most any time you need me, fellows."
He could be a helpful citizen when there was a slight

chance that otherwise he'd get a box seat in an electric chair.

By the time Detectives Abbott and Costello had finished with him, his head had cleared a bit, and the roar in his ears was down to a high-pitched whine.

He flagged down the nurse and wrangled permission to put on pants and get dressed. His clothes were tattered and scorched. Dried blood dotted his left side, to show it was nearest the explosion. The doc came back by and looked in on his handiwork. He shined a light in Sharp's eyes and ran through a few questions, then recommended an overnight stay for observation. Sharp declined the offer.

Detective Jennings was stationed at the front desk, sparking an attractive nurse. She went through the paperwork and took down Sharp's billing information. Jennings watched closely. Mostly the nurse.

"Can I get a cab? I think my car's still over off Green-ville somewhere," Sharp asked.

Jennings leaned in. "I can drop you off."

Sharp met his eyes and considered it. Some cops would offer a ride and then rough a suspect up on the way to get information. His gut told him that wasn't this guy's style.

Jennings led them out to an unmarked Nash. He was in Homicide and gotten the call off the wheel—the rotating assignment board that sent detectives out based on who was next up.

It meant that, as a detective, you knew when you'd get a new case but you had no idea what it would be. Sharp mentioned he'd been a Fort Worth PD dick when the war started. So they had a little common experience.

"You notice anything before the explosion?" asked Jennings.

"His phone rang. He answered, and then the show started."

"He answered?"

"Yeah, so it wasn't wired to the telephone. Somebody had to call to see if Caples was home. You guys find any wires?"

"Not yet, but I haven't been back over there. I'll look when I drop you off." And that was it.

The sun was rising behind his house by the time he climbed the steps before remembering someone had nailed the front door shut.

Sharp took a few tablets from his shrinking supply of aspirin and thought that he'd just bought this bottle. Then he crashed into bed and slept like a dead guy.

The rapping at the front door woke him. The lieutenant's Hamilton read 5:20. He thought a beat and found his Colt and headed for the door wearing nothing but his boxers, an A-shirt, and a handgun.

Roni stood impatiently on the front porch. He directed her to the back door and put the gun away and pants on as he made his way through the house.

"Is this the way it's going to be Jeff-er-son? Either you or the house is going to be torn to hell every day?" She touched his bandaged face.

"Yeah, it's not really my preference, but I think this whole mess is about to wrap up. It seems the guy Doyle hired me to watch is a little hard to lay eyes on right now."

"No kidding. He's scattered all over the front pages." She waved the evening edition of the *Examiner* at him. The headline screamed, GANG WAR RAGES ACROSS DALLAS.

"Ahhh, Leo's taking the subtle approach to sticking it to Big D."

"Yeah, seems a little extreme, even for Leo." She opened the refrigerator and frowned. "I thought I might make you some dinner, but you don't have any food."

He peeked over her shoulder, knowing he'd yet to put anything in the fridge. "There's ice in the freezer. Scotch in the cabinet."

She bopped him with the paper. Right on the area with the highest concentration of lacerations. He shut his eyes with a wince. "If you're going to hit me, swat the side that's not still bleeding."

"Oh? Is there a side that's not still bleeding? Seriously, Jeff, what are you doing? Your house is a wreck. People are trying to kill you, you've been out on your own for a while now and still haven't bought any food? How do you live like this?"

"It's not ideal, but I do think there's a light ahead." He went to the cabinet and retrieved two glasses and a bottle.

"You sure it's not a train?" Roni nodded at the offer.

"I don't think so. How about I buy dinner?" He pulled the ice tray from the freezing compartment and cracked the lever.

She found a bowl, and he dumped in the ice. "At Doyle's?"

"Well, he and I need to have a little chat, but I can do that another time. I know you're not wild about the place." He poured two fingers in one glass and three in the other.

Roni took the full one with a wink. "No. That was Evelyn. I like it just fine. I just don't want to get shunted off to a corner to play slots while my date goes off and plays poker all night."

"Speaking of your date— I think I got a message from Jerry." He found his notepad. "Does the number COntinental-25-7-32-16 mean anything to you?"

"Is it a phone number?" She turned to the cabinets to search for a snack. Anything that might cushion the scotch.

He watched her open and close cabinets without success. Then he evened up his drink with hers. "Southwestern Bell says no."

Her eyes met his and for once it was just those big browns.

Then she blinked.

"Your head's bleeding again." She spun on her heel and headed for the bathroom.

He spun the ice in his drink. "Right."

She returned with tape, gauze and his trusty bottle of mercurochrome. "You don't own any cooking utensils and there's no food in the house, but the medicine cabinet is fully stocked. I think I see where your priorities are, Jeff-er-son."

She pulled a chair from the table and repositioned it for better light, then bade him to sit.

"I didn't learn to cook in the Army, but bandages were a way of life," he explained.

She pulled the taped gauze from his seeping stitches and some eyebrow went with it.

"Ow!"

"Oh, stop it, you big baby. Let me look at this."

She leaned in and he caught a whiff of her familiar perfume. The swell of her breast was even with his chin as she examined his wound. Her delicate fingers lightly danced across the stitches.

"They did a pretty good job on this." She moved and he caught a glimpse of undergarment lace peeking from the collar of her blouse. A thin gold chain played across the smooth skin of her collarbone.

"Is that your professional opinion, Nurse?"

She turned to the table for the gauze.

The view of her backside held his attention as much as the décolletage.

"Well, being married to a cop who worked Hell's Half Acre, you get a feel for how doctors handle bumps, bruises, and stitches."

A beer bottle shattered his moment as the memory of he and her late husband busting up a bar fight made itself known. "Yeah. We had a few interesting times."

"Interesting? While I was home with a book, the radio and nothing but time to worry about you two lunkheads."

"Right." He and Frenchy had battled more than a few drunks, johns, and card sharps who'd rather take their chances with a cop's billy club than the city jail.

She taped the fresh patch over his stitches and stepped back to admire her work with a hand on the curve of her hip. "Better. So—dinner at Doyle's?"

He swallowed his whiskey and the moment. "That'll work," he said, silently reminding himself of his promise to step back. He locked the back door as they stepped out into a light summer sprinkle. "I'll drive."

"So just leave my car here? I don't think so." She dug through her purse for her giant mess of a key ring.

"What do you mean?"

"I know how this works. You'll start talking to Doyle or get roped into a card game, and I'll be stuck there all by myself. No, thanks." Roni scurried to her car between the raindrops.

Sharp frowned. "But you said you liked—"

"And I do. And if I meet you there we can have dinner, I can play a little if I want while you and Doyle do whatever you and Doyle do, and I can go home when I want." She ducked into the Pontiac.

The rain started in earnest, so he followed her logic as best he could and decided that simply agreeing was the easiest course of action. Twenty minutes later, they were seated and ordering dinner. The crowd at the 2222 was not large, as it was still early for the night owls, but the kitchen was doing a brisk business. Dessert and coffees came, and then Doyle Denniker waltzed through the room in a crisp linen suit, waving a Churchill cigar and giving the world a thousand-watt smile.

Denniker kissed Roni's hand and smiled at Sharp. "Drop by the office before you leave." He handed Roni a ten-dollar chip. "For good luck."

Roni took the chip to the wheels, and Sharp watched her play a few spins of roulette. She was up a buck and seemed to be enjoying that. He leaned down and kissed her cheek, surprising them both. He recovered quickly.

"Um, yeah. For luck."

She returned a soft smile and he nodded, then headed for Doyle's office. The door gorilla announced him, and Doyle waved him to a chair across from him.

An envelope slid across the desktop. "For your medical expenses."

Sharp shook out a Lucky and lit it. He contemplated the thick envelope for a heartbeat and then put it in his pocket. He could be angry and not stupid at the same time. "Doyle, I'll be honest. I'm not happy about being used for bait."

Doyle waved the concerns away. "You weren't bait. I needed every bit of information you passed along."

"So you could knock off Caples?"

Doyle studied the glowing tip of his cigar. Then he looked up with cold eyes.

"Sharp, you're a smart guy." He paused for drama. "Don't be too smart."

Sharp didn't feel very smart.

But he was cool enough to leave the issue behind and move on. "How about the major? Is that still an open subject?"

"It is. The house is still sitting on a sizable debt. I want him found."

"I've got one clue I haven't been able to track down. The good news is, I don't think he's dead." Sharp blew smoke high overhead.

That seemed to give Doyle pause, as if he hadn't considered that something like that could have happened to the major. "Keep looking. And keep me informed."

He stood as he said it, and Sharp understood that he'd been dismissed.

A strange chill went through him as he closed the office door. He scanned the room and found Roni still laying money on the roulette table. His smile ran away as standing right next to her was Billings, the Army Intel goon who'd played handball with his head in the barn. Billings caught him looking and winked.

Roni grinned big as Sharp took station next to her. "I'm winning! I'm up nearly ten bucks!"

"That's great. We need to get out of here."

Billings looked around Roni, "Oh, you can't just run off."

Roni smiled sweetly. "Jeff, this is Vernon Billings; he's a friend of Jerry's. Vern, this is Jeff Sharp."

Sharp locked his eyes on the oversized rat. "You two know each other?"

"Oh, no. We just met, Vern's teaching me the finer points of roulette."

"Have we met before, Mr. Sharp?" Billings gave a shrewd crooked smile and rubbed one hand across the knuckles of the other. "Your face seems familiar to me."

"Could be, I used to be a livestock detective. Didn't we talk about a jackass with a bad leg in your barn?" He turned his attention to Roni: "We need to be going."

"Jefferson, this is why I brought my car. You can go, but I'm having fun. I'm sticking around." She selectively placed a handful of twenty-five-cent chips on the table and nodded to the croupier.

Billings leaned in close and put his arm around Roni. "Yes, Jefferson, we're having fun. Why don't you scram?" The roulette wheel spun.

She didn't seem to like that, and Sharp nearly lost his cool. "Don't touch her." He had iron in his voice and stared a hole right through Billings.

He laughed. "My, my, my. Aren't we possessive? Why don't you beat it, bub? The lady and I are having a time."

Roni looked at him with a question. He looked into her eyes, so she understood his meaning when he asked the goon, "Haven't you beaten up enough women lately, asshole?"

He saw Roni's brain put two and two together behind the big browns. "Evelyn?" she asked.

Sharp nodded, and Billings looked confused.

On the wheel, the white ball caromed from number to random number.

"You can take your mitts off her, or I can take your mitts off her, but it's happening right now."

Billings dropped his arm and gave his evil grin. "Another time then, smart guy." He stepped back and never took his eyes off Sharp as he walked to the door.

The roulette wheel stopped, the ball came to rest, and none of Roni's numbers paid off.

She looked at Sharp, and for the first time, he saw she was genuinely frightened.

"I need to be going." She couldn't meet his eyes while she gathered her chips. She paused when she collected them as if she wanted to say something, but then turned and went directly to the cashier.

He followed. "Let me take you home."

"Is that supposed to make me feel safer, Jeff? Why in the world would I go to my house? Knowing these . . . these . . . goons could be there waiting? Why in the hell would I do that?"

Her voice got a little shrill. People were looking.

"Look. They are only trying to use you to get to me. They think I know something that I don't and they—"

She threw up a forbidding hand. "Hold it, buster. You mean you knew about this? That this could happen? That they might . . ."

"Look, Roni," he stammered. "I didn't think they—"

"And you didn't tell me?"

Every person in the room could feel the slap when she hit him. The world went still and silent. She spun on her heel and strode to the door.

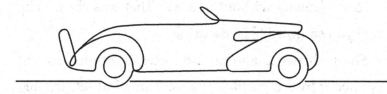

CHAPTER TWENTY-FOUR

The door gorilla stopped him. "The lady seems to prefer her own company."

The guy was huge and rooted to the floor in a way that meant Sharp wasn't going anywhere either. He faced the obstruction straight on. "This is none of your damn business. Now get out of my way."

"Sir, you need to settle down."

Sharp started around the gorilla, and a big hand went to his shoulder to hold him. Sharp stepped back and raised an open hand.

"Don't. Just don't. I need to talk to her. This is important."

"She's leaving without you, sir. That was clear. Why don't you sit down? Have a drink."

Sharp shrugged and in one violent motion, brought his knee into the gorilla's jewels. The wind left the big man in a gasp, and when he doubled over, Sharp jabbed him in the jaw with a right and a left, then shoved him to the floor and jumped past.

He sprinted down the hallway and burst into the dark rain just as Roni and her little yellow coupe shot through a puddle of water, splashing mud across his suit. He shouted after her, but she skidded out onto the wet asphalt of Thunder Road with no regard for traffic, man, nor beast.

Sharp stood in the downpour as a rumble of thunder turned into the sound of an engine revving to life behind him. He turned and saw the headlights come on in the back row of the parking lot. He'd seen this gray Plymouth one time too many. The sedan roared into the drive, the headlights cutting the rain into streaks. He knew this car and pulled his Colt.

The Plymouth turned straight toward him and accelerated. He leveled the front sight on the driver's side of the windshield and fired twice. The windshield shattered, and the car veered as the driver ducked. The gray whale of an auto clipped the curb, and a tire blew out.

The wounded vehicle skidded back toward him. He dove out of the way and caught sight of Billings, laughing behind the wheel as he roared past.

Sharp dashed to the end of the driveway in time to see the blown front tire unspool from the sedan. Two blocks down the highway, Billings was limping it to the far side of the roadway. Sharp holstered the Colt and thought that at least that would let Roni get someplace safe.

He trotted through the rain to the LaSalle and waved as he passed Billings cursing on the side of the road.

Roni's car wasn't at her house. He set up camp and waited. The rain came and went, then came again. Thunder rumbled, and lightning blew open the sky, and it poured for a few minutes, but the neighborhood was quiet. The only traffic came after midnight, 1:17 by the lieutenant's watch, when a Mercury sedan rolled past, slowed, and then splashed into a neighbor's drive. Someone was coming home late to trouble. The clouds marched east, and the stars came out.

At 5:35, the Vandervoort's milkman stopped at a couple of houses. Just after 6:00, a paperboy bicycled by flinging the morning edition of the *Examiner* to still wet porches. And more than a few bushes. The kid needed to work on his aim.

But no sign of Roni. And, more important, none of Billings.

He drove home and again forgot that he'd nailed the front door shut. He took a restless nap and then ran down to the Blackstone. Roni wasn't there either. Peggy hadn't even seen her. He double-timed it over to the courthouse. Maybe she'd gone straight to work. He found his way through the building to Judge Rowan's office. A dark-haired woman about Roni's age was hammering away on an old Underwood typewriter and paid him no attention as he stepped to the desk. A plaque on the desk indicated she was Delores Cantu.

"Excuse me," Sharp said. "I'm looking for Veronica Arquette."

A finger went up, signaling him to wait. Given the small headset under her hair and with his incredible detective skills, Sharp figured out she was doing dictation. After a moment, she paused and pulled the headset down.

"I'm looking for Veronica Arquette," he repeated.

Delores sighed. "I swear, she is little Miss Popular today. But she's not here."

"Somebody else came by looking?"

"Two guys, about an hour ago. Same thing I told them—Roni called in sick."

"Two guys?" He gave her a quick description of Martin and Billings.

She nodded. "Sounds like them. Nice guys."

"Till you get to know them. Can I leave her a note?"

"Sure." Delores keyed her Dictaphone and went back to work.

He pulled his notebook and scribbled out a quick apology and said that this might be a good time to visit her sister. He hoped she still lived in Tulsa. He folded it, and Delores stuck it in an envelope and sealed it.

He made four stops on the way home. The lumberyard, so he could use his front door again, Sears for a coffeepot, and he wound up buying a frying pan, a cheap barbecue grill, and a bag of charcoal as well. Then back downtown, waiting for the bank to open. He unsealed the envelope Doyle had given him and blinked. The first payment he'd received from Doyle had been fives and tens. This was a thick stack of hundred-dollar bills.

He shot a look over his shoulder. He was alone in the safe deposit area. A quick count put the total at $2,500. He swallowed hard. It was the most cash he'd ever held.

It seemed Doyle had pegged this as the going rate for amnesia when it came to Bobby Caples. He shook his head. The devil on one shoulder began to argue: he hadn't done anything wrong.

Somebody else had killed Caples, but if the Dallas PD could trace this amount of cash—he was an accessory. He slid the entire stack back into the envelope and hid it under his car title in the safe deposit box. He opened Doyle's first envelope and pulled out three fives and the last ten.

He took that cash to Roy Pope's grocery and bought the first actual food he'd picked out himself in almost ten years. A steak, potatoes, coffee, bread, bologna, a little jar of mustard, and a six-pack of Pearl beer. It was a modest start.

He re-repaired the front door and pushed the cash out of his mind by concentrating on the major. He seemed to be at the center of his current issues. If the Army Intel guys were trying to find Cartwright through old girlfriends and army buddies, they didn't seem to be having any more luck than he was. He wondered if they knew about the phone number. The Continental business could be a scam to head him off in the wrong direction, but as the only lead he had, he'd follow it wherever he could.

The door worked. It took more shims than he'd expected, but the doorframe had a rough life of late. He knew the feeling.

The house was pretty much back to some semblance of what might have been normal if he'd ever been there for more than a few days of normal. While straightening up, he'd also rediscovered the remains of the divorce filing Evelyn had served him with. He needed to get those to attorney Tom Hall. He called and made an appointment and added that to his to-do list. Lunch, an errand or two, and working on the major's mystery might take his mind off worrying about Roni.

The bologna-sandwich lunch mirrored his mood. Lonely, ordinary, and depressing. He washed it down with a beer and looked at Major Jerry Cartwright's phone number in his notebook.

COntinental-25-7-32-16. Only he now knew it wasn't a phone number. But he also had no idea what it was. It seemed that some good old-fashioned research was in order. He locked his new doorknob and reminded himself he'd need to give a copy of the new key to the lady who owned the house.

He spent the afternoon in the downtown Fort Worth Library. He checked the Continental Congress, Lincoln

Continentals, and the Continental Oil Company. He checked every reference he could find—dates, times, places. He went through the Criss-cross directory, *Encyclopedia Britannica*, copies of *The Old Farmers Almanac*, and phone books. As far as he could tell, it wasn't latitude, longitude, altitude, or somebody's birthday. The whole afternoon was wasted.

No Roni, no major.

He walked out and wandered around downtown deep in thought. In front of the Examiner Building, he saw a familiar automobile—a sparkling maroon Buick Roadmaster with a gray mohair interior. He didn't see the interior, but he'd parked next to it at the golf course and recognized Doyle's car when he saw it. He looked up at Leo's office windows to see if that meant a meeting of the minds was taking place.

The divorce lawyer's office was in the Sinclair Oil Building, just across the corner from the Blackstone and around the corner from the Mexican Inn. The lobby featured shiny black marble with stainless-steel trim and polished terrazzo flooring. It looked expensive, but he considered that getting Evelyn out of his world was worth it. He pressed the elevator call button and nodded to the shoeshine man.

Tom Hall's suite was a small one-man shop on the eighth floor with a single secretary in the outer office. She was a young girl with a victory-roll hairdo and bright red lipstick. She introduced herself as Josephine and then went to the door and told the lawyer he had a client. Hall was a compact man with a broad smile and a firm handshake. He asked direct questions and gave straight answers. Sharp had no interest in fighting over the house or divvying up the silverware, Evelyn could keep what was there and just let him go about his business. Hall counseled him to push a little, but all Sharp wanted was out.

To his surprise, Hall quoted him an affordable price to represent him in an uncontested proceeding, and the entire meeting took less than forty-five minutes. He wished all his dealings were as quick and easy.

He decided to treat himself to the arroz con pollo around the corner at the Mexican Inn. He had just ordered when the boom rattled the windows. In the back of his mind, he knew what to expect before he even got to the door. He ran to the middle of the street and saw the Buick down the block engulfed in flames.

A crowd had gathered, and he saw Leo and Doyle on the far side of the roasting Roadmaster. He started toward them, but Doyle saw him and waved him off. That was unusual. The fire brigade arrived and began moving people back and hosing down the flames. In a matter of moments, Doyle's beautiful new car was a smoldering pile of twisted metal.

Sharp stuck around until Leo and Doyle returned to the Examiner Building, and the crowd thinned out. He wondered how Leo would spin this one. He'd been on a tear lately promoting what a safe, wonderful city Fort Worth was, compared to the gang violence that gripped Dallas. Having a local gambling-joint proprietor's car bombed in front of the newspaper offices would take some creative writing, even for Leo.

As he stepped off the curb against the traffic light to head back to his dinner, a bus nearly plastered him. That would be his luck today. Shot at, beaten up, blown up, and then hit by a bus. Come to think of it, getting hit by a bus might be an improvement. A bus.

A Trailways bus.

A *Continental* Trailways bus.

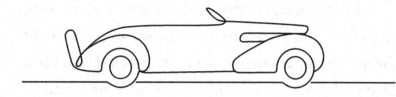

CHAPTER TWENTY-FIVE

S harp watched the bus disappear down the street toward the bright neon of the Trailways terminal, and his own lightbulb came on. Two minutes later, he was standing in front of a wall of lockers and looking at the combination lock holding number 25 closed. Sharp pulled out his notebook. COntinental-25-7-32-16. He spun the dial, and the lock popped open.

Inside the locker was a rectangular olive-drab Army-issue ammunition can. He hefted it and guessed it weighed about thirty pounds. About the same as the ammo cans he'd moved in Italy. He hauled it to the trunk of the LaSalle and drove to the house.

It had taken him a lot of work to repair the front door, so naturally, he parked deep in the driveway and carried the ammo can in through the back. He cracked it open on the kitchen table. On top were two envelopes marked in the neat hand of a career Army pilot. One said "Sharp," the other "Doyle."

He opened his.

The envelope held a postcard with the same neat lettering

Sharp—
Here is the bulk of what I owe DD.
The other item is for you. Keep it safe for me.
See what you can find.
—JEC

He turned it over. The western-themed picture-postcard featured a seductively illustrated pinup cowgirl posed on a split-rail fence and the simple inscription: Visit Fabulous Las Vegas! He smiled and tucked it into his pocket. Beneath the envelopes were four bundles wrapped in kraft paper, folded crisply and tied with cotton string. Inside the first was $2,000 in ten-dollar bills. He checked the other three and then counted all of it. It came to exactly $7,100. Sharp let out an impressed whistle. Today was a day for large amounts of cash.

At the bottom was one more, larger, envelope.

It contained a rectangular piece of what looked like ordinary tinfoil. The surface had strange symbols embossed along the edges of the two short sides, but nothing Sharp recognized. Something about it struck him as familiar, but at the same time, he'd never seen anything like it before. Odd.

The tinfoil had rounded corners and was as thin as onionskin, but when he folded it or wadded it up, it slowly flattened itself back out. A little bigger than the postcard, but it weighed next to nothing. He had no clue what it was, nor could he see any rhyme or reason to the markings.

He'd seen plenty of German military kit, Italian, even Russian, and some Egyptian stuff the guys who'd been to North Africa had brought back with them. This wasn't any of that. Thanks, Major. Sharp solved one mystery, and now the missing man had handed him another.

He looked around the room for a safe place and decided with the recent rash of break-ins, his best bet was to get the cash to Doyle as soon as possible and keep the tinfoil handy.

Sharp shrugged into his shoulder holster and plugged in the Colt. He loaded the cash back into the ammo can, and with a silent thank-you to Woo the tailor, tucked the tinfoil into the secret pocket in his jacket. He was especially vigilant for tails as he turned out of the neighborhood. The coast appeared to be clear.

At the Four Deuces, he parked next to Leo's Cadillac and trucked the ammo can up the hallway and across the game floor.

The door gorilla still sported a tinge of the blackened eye Sharp had left him with. He stopped the detective with an angry glare and a massive hand. "He's busy, asshole."

Sharp shifted the ammo can to his left side. Just in case. "I told you it was none of your business."

"You get to decide what my business is? I don't think so, bub." The gorilla puffed out his chest, fully blocking the doorway.

"You want we should let Doyle decide?" Sharp offered. "You might not have any business."

"I said he's busy."

"Is it Leo? Fuller? I'm pretty sure they'll be okay with me."

The gorilla frowned in confusion. People usually knew better than to question him.

"Fine, then." Sharp tried to look exasperated and handed him the ammo can. "Would you give this to him, then?"

The gorilla took the can with both hands by reflex, Sharp turned and opened the office door, then reached back and took the can.

"Thanks. I'll take it from here."

The gorilla just stared as Sharp gave the door a hip and it closed behind him. He surveyed the room's occupants and had two immediate thoughts. One: Doyle and Leo had been in a conversation they didn't want to continue while he was there. Second: judging from the ash on their respective cigars, they'd been there a while. Doyle didn't look happy.

Leo stood up with a jolt and collected his fedora. "Sharp, what's the news?"

Sharp hefted the ammo can. "Just here to return some things to Doyle. You?"

"I dropped him off after the fire," Leo said.

Sharp nodded to Doyle, "Sorry about the car. Brand new, wasn't it?"

He shrugged.

"The forty-eights will be out in the fall, the new one is supposed to have the Dynaflow transmission."

If Sharp just had a three-thousand-dollar car blown to bits, he'd have a little more to say, but Doyle looked distracted. Leo tipped his hat and closed the door behind him.

"You okay, Doyle?" Sharp asked.

"Yeah, Leo just had some interesting news."

"And you get the early scoop?"

"Strictly as a courtesy. The *Times Herald* jumped all over the Caples explosion and is about to publish a series on what they're calling gang warfare in Dallas and Fort Worth. Leo heard it from a reporter there who used to work for him."

Sharp nodded. "And there's nothing Leo would hate more than the *Times Herald* digging in his dirt."

"That's the size of it." Doyle seemed resigned to the fact.

"Not a great time for your car to blow up," Sharp observed.

"No. It looks like someone was out to get a little revenge."

"Looked that way. Were they?"

Doyle's eyes narrowed. "Didn't we talk about how smart you're getting? Why are you here?"

He hoisted the ammo can to the desk. "I brought you a gift from a mutual friend."

Doyle shot him a questioning look. He removed the envelope and read the enclosed letter twice.

"All of it?" Doyle asked.

"I counted it twice," Sharp said. "Looks like he had some cash squirreled away. Lot of that going around."

"Or he sold his house." Doyle was counting.

"Yeah, right." His hand went to the sore spot where Billings had rapped on the back of his skull. "Doyle, I'm not getting the full skinny. What's going on here?"

"You don't want the full skinny. It's messy. And huge." He peeled off a small stack of tens and handed it to Sharp. "Finder's fee."

"I was going to ask Leo."

He tucked the untainted cash in his jacket.

"Don't bother." Doyle's cigar had gone out, and he took a moment to relight. "Turns out Leo is running a little scheme of his own—real estate."

"I ran into E. G. Lavelle in Leo's office with some blueprints. I wondered about that at the time, but I've been a little too busy to check it out."

Doyle raised an eyebrow. "E. G.'s on this? Well, that fits."

Sharp shook his head. "Just saw him in Leo's office. That's all I know."

"Well, you know Leo. Mr. Civic Booster. Now he's got a way to make it pay off. He's buttonholed every mover and shaker in town in this deal. He's setting up to build entire neighborhoods. Subdivisions, he calls them." Doyle considered his cigar and blew an angry cloud of Montecristo to the side of the room.

"How'd you find this out?"

"Leo told me. Asked if I wanted in. He needs investors. He's mortgaged the *Examiner* to the hilt for this play."

"So he can't have anything about the town looking undesirable for potential home buyers." Lights were finally beginning to come on for Sharp.

"Yeah, it's not just that he doesn't sell more newspapers. He can't have the competition in Dallas reporting gang wars." Doyle sneered. "And what's worse, the hypocritical son of a bitch is going to start a campaign to clean up the city."

"Do what?"

"He's going to go to the police, the DA, and the sheriff. He can blackmail them into going along with it." Doyle was getting riled up.

"So, Leo wants to shut down Thunder Road?"

Doyle slammed a fist on the desk. "And if I do anything to stop Leo, then I lose the DA, the sheriff, and everything else anyway when the Dallas fucking *Times Herald* runs the story. I'll still be screwed."

Sharp let out a low whistle.

"He just told me that's exactly what's coming." Doyle fumed. "I was worried about Caples, Meyer Lansky, and the Chicago Outfit, and the whole time, the biggest threat was right across the poker table in my own place. I'll tell you something, Sharp, the day that son of a—"

The phone on his desk interrupted him.

Sharp stared in disbelief. He'd been in Doyle's office dozens of times, and the standing rule was you didn't interrupt him for anything short of a fire or a police raid.

Doyle grabbed the phone and listened, then shot out of his chair like it was spring-loaded. "Come with me." It was an order. He sprinted out of the office, leaving the cash sitting on the desk.

Sharp followed as Doyle hurried to the stairwell and down the hallway under the hill. He had to walk fast to keep up. They rounded the corner of the building to see Rico, Dutch, and Doyle's door gorilla crowded around the driver's side of a familiar burgundy Cord 812 convertible. The big coffin-nosed car was parked at a weird angle, one wheel up on the parking block like it'd been put there by a drunk. Dutch had the driver's door open, and Sharp could see the blood from twenty yards away.

Gentry Ferguson was slumped over the wheel. Somebody had done a thorough job of beating the pulp out of him. Sharp grabbed the big cowboy under his arms and tried to help him out of the car. He needed a hospital. Now. Blood was coming out of his mouth, nose, and ears, and Sharp had seen enough men die to know the preliminaries were well underway. If he didn't have help soon, the movie star was a goner.

Sharp pulled the Cord back off the parking rock, and Doyle, the gatekeeper, and the gorilla got Ferguson into the passenger seat. They settled him in as best they could, and then Sharp lit out to get him to St. Joseph Hospital. He'd only driven the front-wheel drive, supercharged car once before, and it took him about half a block down Thunder Road to thank the Lord for the high-performance missile. He tried to get some answers on the way, but Gentry faded in and out.

"Who did this?" Sharp asked.

The big man shifted in the passenger seat and coughed. "Two guys. I didn't get . . . a good look. They had a pipe . . . or a ball bat . . ."

He was having a tough time breathing. Sharp sliced through the sparse evening traffic, trying to look at Gentry and dodge cars who weren't in as big a hurry as he was.

"They wanted to know about Caples," Gentry mumbled. "About who killed . . ." He was slipping away.

"Was that you, Gent?"

He never said, but between traffic lights and the slight panic of just missing T-boning the downtown trolley, Sharp swore he saw a small grin. Gentry had a front tooth missing behind the busted lip.

He swerved and scared the hell out of a Vandervoort's milkman crossing South Main. Gentry wheezed. Sharp stole a look at him. He was bad. "Were they a couple of tough guys, Gent? Army Intelligence?"

The actor raised his head in a flash of recognition. "Not like the Intel guys I met during the war . . ."

Sharp wedged the big convertible into the emergency entrance to the hospital and bolted inside, yelling for help. The charge nurse and a couple of orderlies sprinted out with a gurney. Gentry was almost six-four and weighed every bit of 245. It took the three of them to get him out of the car. He grunted when they pulled him free with a shudder that Sharp recognized as busted ribs. He tried to keep the big guy talking as they wheeled him in and parked him in the hallway.

"Gent, talk to me," Sharp pleaded. "What's going on?"

Then a doc was there, elbowing him out of the way, poking and prodding the cowboy—sounded like ribs, skull, and upper arm. The doc was worried about a punctured lung and internal organ damage. Sharp would've been impressed, but he'd made the same basic conclusion just getting him there. His mom always wanted him to be a doctor. The nurse shooed him out so they could work, and Sharp went and parked the car.

When he got back inside, the orderlies and nurse had returned, and they told him Gentry was headed for X-ray, then surgery. They started wheeling him down the hall, and Sharp walked alongside as best he could.

Gentry grabbed his arm. "Sharp . . . you need to get to . . ." His voice was little more than a wheeze.

The charge nurse grabbed Sharp's other arm and pulled him away. "Sir, you can't go back there." The gurney banged through a set of swinging double doors. She held on tight. Like an anchor.

Sharp stopped.

"Sir, your friend is very, very hurt, but don't you worry. Dr. Anders is very, very good and he'll do the very, very best he can to get your friend well. But you have to stay out here. It's for your own safety."

She pointed to the large sign painted on the wall and kept talking. He quit listening. An arrow pointed through the doors, and the lettering read, CAUTION—X-RAY DEPARTMENT.

Sharp looked at the doors. Doyle wanted to tell him something. Gentry wanted to tell him something. He needed someone to tell him what the hell was going on. He ran his hand over his face and paced a small circle in the hallway. Suddenly, he noticed his jacket was getting very, very warm. Not warm—hot. And the heat was coming from his secret pocket. The Major's tinfoil in the lining was heating up. He spotted a men's room down the hall and left Nurse Very-Very in midsentence.

The john was empty of everything but porcelain. He pulled the tinfoil out of the lining, to find it wasn't tinfoil anymore. It had become a rigid piece of metal, as solid as Sears when he tried to bend it. He tapped it on the washbasin with a metallic *tink*. It felt thicker and was still getting warm. The symbols were gone and in their place was a dark shiny rectangle on the surface. It hadn't been there before. The rectangle blinked and then, three . . . creatures . . . appeared on the face of the now metal plate. He had no other word for what he saw. And then one looked at him and cocked its head. He dropped the solid sheet of metal like a hot rock, and it rattled into the sink. Sharp's knees wobbled and he stumbled back, grabbing the stall door behind him for support.

He was breathing heavily, his eyes never leaving the creatures on the tinfoil. He swallowed hard and retrieved it from the washbasin. It was like an old tintype photograph, but the images, the creatures, moved. And they were in color. It struck him that the tinfoil was like a tiny movie screen, the size of his hand.

Sharp watched, transfixed. The beings on the screen had round heads that were too large for their bodies and big almond-shaped eyes that made up most of those heads. Like an insect, but not really. One was taller than the others, and He? She? It? had a thin neck holding up the round head. He was gesturing with three long skinny fingers like the creatures were talking to one another.

Sharp sensed they could see him too, because one of them pointed at the screen and frantically waved a slender hand at the others. That shook him. They all stopped talking and looked straight at him like he was an animal in a zoo. The tall one leaned in and waved a three-fingered hand in the air and began to speak. He didn't have a nose, but the small mouth moved. Sound began to come from the tinfoil. A tinny, lyrical noise punctuated with clicks that made no sense at all. The . . . thing was talking, but it was gibberish, and Sharp couldn't understand a thing.

Sharp examined both sides. The back was blank, the symbols gone, but it seemed darker. On the front, the largest of the creatures now dominated the movie screen. The creature blinked and clicked and made a whirring sound.

Sharp ran a hand through his hair.

The creature mimicked the gesture with a three fin-gered hand.

"What the hell?" Sharp was dumbfounded.

The creature seemed to react to the words. The head cocked slightly and a tinny voice came from the tinfoil. "Whad da hail."

Ever so slowly, the image began to fade.

"Wait, come back!" Sharp shook the softening metal sheet.

The beings on the other side began pointing, waving, whirring, and clicking as the sound faded and photo area went dark, then disappeared. The symbols had returned, but they were different symbols and in different places. At least, Sharp thought they were different.

Sharp took a shaky breath. He turned the piece of thin metal over and examined it again with trembling hands. It was back to being a silver piece of onionskin. He folded it back and forth and examined both blank sides. A piece of tinfoil. Nothing more. Had he been hallucinating?

A noise in the hall made him duck into a stall as two orderlies came in talking baseball.

". . . and Snider goes all the way to the fence and just watches it go over."

"Helluva a way to lose a game."

Sharp stashed the tinfoil back in Woo's secret pocket and exited the stall with a flush. He went to the sink, splashed a little water on his face, and steadied his hands. The beat-up guy in the mirror looked pale and more than a little scared. The orderlies were oblivious.

"Baker got the win, and now they're just two games back."

Sharp took a deep breath, steadied himself, and went to find a chair in the waiting room without even realizing he was walking.

He slumped into a chair off to the side of the sterile-looking lobby. The green tile walls, crappy chairs, linoleum floors, and old copies of *Life* magazine lying around would have fit his mood, but deep in the shock of the moment, he never even noticed them. He sat leaning forward in the chair, thinking. His arms on his knees and head down.

This was why the major was drunk off his ass that afternoon at the Deuces. If he'd stumbled on to these . . . creatures, Sharp could see getting drunk for a month. This piece of tinfoil was like a television. He and Evelyn had seen one at the state fair last fall in Dallas, but that had been an enormous radar-scope gizmo.

This was more like a Technicolor movie screen the size of a postcard. Not just some black-and-white shadows like the television tube. The creatures were a kind of blueish gray, and they were in a big warehouse with blinking red and yellow lights behind them.

He turned the things he knew over in his head, but all it did was lead to more questions. What were these bug people on the screen doing and saying?

Were they puppets? Cartoons like Woody Woodpecker? If it was a movie, how the hell did it get on the tinfoil?

A shadow crossed in front of him, and a nurse stood over him. A different nurse. Something told him he'd been there long enough for a shift change. The lieutenant's watch showed after 11:00. She asked him to come with her. They walked through the swinging door and made a left out of the hallway. The doc was there in a surgical gown and a cap.

Gentry didn't make it.

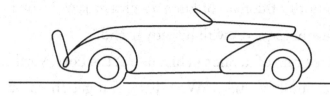

CHAPTER TWENTY-SIX

"Hang on to the car." Doyle was in Mr. Fixit mode. He had plans working, and Sharp was smack in the middle of it and at the same time completely out of it, standing in a hospital phone booth. "Consider it a trade for yours."

"For mine? But I like my car."

The world was spinning at a rapid rate, and Sharp was trying hard to catch up.

"You gonna turn down a custom Cord for a ten-year-old LaSalle?"

"Good point." Behind him, the nurse was waiting outside the door to get his attention. "Doyle, the hospital wants to notify the next of kin and all that jazz. I don't know how that squares with his lady friend."

"I'll take care of it. She's in his suite at the Fort Worth Club. His family is still in West Texas. I'll get ahold of them."

"Can we hang on for just a second, Doyle?" He waved off the nurse. "Just what the hell is going on?"

"You need to lay low."

"Lay low? From what? Who am I staying clear of? I can't hide if I don't know what I'm hiding from. Is this Lansky? The Army Intelligence goons?" He felt the tinfoil crinkle in his pocket. "What the hell is going on, Doyle?"

Doyle's voice went to a whisper. "Look, this is getting bad. I'm heading out of town to see if I can reason with these people. I'm telling you to disappear because these guys are playing hardball. If you don't hear from me for a while, don't sweat it. You're a stand-up guy, Sharp, but you need to drop this and walk away. And whatever you do, stay away from the club."

"Stay away from the club? What the—"

The line was dead. Sharp hung up the phone and looked around the waiting room. Was there a worse place in the world? Entire families huddled together in anticipation of life or death news. Bad coffee, old newspapers, and the oppressing weight of the approaching unknown.

Doyle said this could get bad, and Sharp was pretty sure it already was. Caples blown to bits. Gentry beaten to death. And likely by the same guys who had laid their hands on Sharp too. Yeah, whatever this was, it was bad already.

With nothing else to do, he walked out into the still warm night. He slid into the driver's seat of what seemed to have just become his new car. Leather interior, stainless steel engine-turned dash, and a handful of Martians in his pocket. The world had taken an interesting turn for Mrs. Sharp's little boy.

Gentry had once coached him on the bass-ackward way to start the Cord. Sharp turned the key, stepped on the clutch, and the supercharged motor boomed to life. He reached across to crank up the hidden headlights and heard the crinkle of a newspaper stuffed between the seat back and the bottom. He pulled out an old copy of the *Examiner*. There was a slash of red on the paper. He wasn't squeamish, but there was something about seeing a buddy's blood right there after he died. He started to toss it out the window, but the crimson mark wasn't the bloodstain he'd first thought. A red wax pencil mark circled the photo on the front page. The photo was the one Roni had pointed out—an Army Air Force officer kneeling in his office with the remains of a weather balloon. Sticks and tinfoil and the missing Major Cartwright slipping out the door behind him.

But now Sharp knew that wasn't tinfoil, and he was pretty confident those weren't sticks. And it sure as hell wasn't a weather balloon. Or a helicopter, or even an atomic plane. And he knew the guy who'd put that picture on the front page might have the answers as to where Major Cartwright was headed. Confronting the local newspaper publisher wasn't exactly laying low, but Leo had been playing him fast and loose on the weather balloon, the real-estate scheme, and his plans for Thunder Road. Sharp was tired of games. He wanted some answers. He shifted the transmission lever to first, pulled onto Pennsylvania Avenue, and headed for the silk stocking area of town.

The upscale Eighth-Avenue neighborhood had a decorative entrance to make the residents and their visitors feel they'd found someplace special. At 11:30, when he rolled up to the Mediterranean-style two-story home of the publisher of the *Fort Worth Examiner*, the street was quiet and dark. Two sculptures of leopards flanked the front door. Irene Fuller had exotic tastes. Her husband answered the door in a dressing gown and slippers— maroon velvet with satin lapels and an LF embroidery crest on the pocket, very natty.

"Jeff? Jesus, it's nearly midnight. I've got house guests tonight," Leo said.

"Gentry Ferguson is dead." He waved the paper under Leo's nose. "You and I need to talk." Sharp pushed past him and into the foyer.

Leo peered into the moonlit night. "Is that his car? What the hell did you do?"

He'd been to Leo's more than a few times and turned left from the marble entry directly to the bar in the study, where four decanters and cut crystal rocks glasses needed dusting. He selected the one that was the color of scotch and poured three fingers. It went down in a gulp.

"Can I get you a drink?" Leo asked.

Sharp stared him down. "Yeah, thanks." He poured another, tasting bourbon, not scotch. He didn't care, filling a second glass for Leo and raising his. "To Gentry."

Leo nodded. "To Gentry."

Sharp shot the drink back.

They gave the memory a moment. Leo broke the silence. "What happened?"

"Somebody jumped one of the toughest guys I know and beat him to death." Sharp studied the bottom of the glass. "What's going on, Leo?" He met the publisher's eyes with an angry scowl. "You know something, and I'm not leaving until I do too."

Leo stepped to the study door and pushed it closed. He crossed back to the bar and refilled Sharp's glass, then deliberately returned the decanter to its proper place. He paused a moment to gather his story.

"I know a little, but I don't know if anyone knows the entire story," Leo said.

Sharp shook his head. "Tell me what you do know, I'll piece together what I can."

"I don't even know where to start." Faking innocence was a difficult thing for Leo to pull off.

Sharp sneered and his stomach growled. "Tell you what, let's start with a sandwich. I can't remember the last time I ate."

"Well, the staff has gone for the night and I—"

"What the hell, Leo? You're too good to find your own midnight snack anymore?" Sharp grabbed the bourbon and headed for the kitchen. "Let's start with the weather balloon. Can you get me onto the base to look at it?"

Leo frowned in confusion. "The weather balloon?"

Sharp held up the newspaper. "This weather balloon. This is the front page of your newspaper, isn't it?" He tossed the paper on the counter and found the bread box.

Leo got a faraway look in his eye. As if that photo was a few years old, not a few weeks. "Oh, yeah . . . right. It's not there anymore. They took everything from the crash somewhere else."

"Crash?" Sharp turned. This was news.

"The debris."

"The debris from a weather balloon crash? The Army launches weather balloons all the time. This is the first one I've ever seen crashed. And certainly the first time I've seen one make the front page. What happened?" He pointed the bread knife at Leo.

The publisher glanced at the knife. "This is much bigger than you realize. I don't think you want to be involved."

"I am involved. I'm not leaving until I am satisfied I know what I need to know." Sharp turned to the icebox and rummaged for sandwich makings.

"You could get in a lot of trouble for this," warned Leo.

"I've been beaten up and nearly blown to smithereens. I'm in trouble already, and I don't have any idea what's going on. Gentry knew something, and it got him killed. If you know anything about this, you're in trouble too. You just don't know it yet. Fill me in and maybe we can figure it out before something else blows up."

Leo lowered his voice to a bare whisper. "This can never go beyond this room."

"Can we stop with the melodrama already?" Sharp placed a head of lettuce and a tomato on the counter and waved for Leo to continue.

Leo responded with a pregnant pause. "It wasn't a weather balloon," he whispered.

Sharp rolled his eyes. "Now that the obvious is out of the way, what is it? Or was it? And if it's not at the base, where did it go? You sure this isn't some big government project or a Howard Hughes project like the Spruce Goose? Or maybe it's the atomic plane. They lost one of those?"

Leo studied the floor for a long moment. "All I know is there are three of them. One crashed on a ranch in New Mexico. Near Roswell, not far from the Mescalero Apache reservation."

"Why would they bring it here?" asked Sharp. "The Army has secret bases all over New Mexico."

"These aircraft weren't the Army's."

"Not the Army's? In New Mexico?" Sharp smeared a little mustard on a slice of bread and stacked a thick sandwich. Leave it to Leo—Sharp hadn't had prosciutto since Italy. "We just kicked the crap out of every army of any size in the world. The Brits can't fly anything over here. Last I heard there's not enough of anything left in Russia to build an airplane, much less fly one. Hell, nobody on Earth could just fly across the US without us doing something about it."

"Exactly." Leo got quiet.

Sharp took a bite and chewed on the dots that were connecting.

Nobody on Earth. Lights at the Rafter B. The tinfoil. He'd read a little of Arthur Conan Doyle as a kid. Sherlock Holmes. It had made him want to be a detective.

One thing Holmes said was if you eliminate the impossible, then what remains, however improbable, was the answer.

"You're kidding."

Leo shook his head.

"And these aircraft had pilots, right?" Sharp refilled his glass.

Leo nodded.

Sharp wasn't a praying man, but he said one to himself before stepping across the line. He watched Leo tight. "Skinny blue-gray creatures with big heads, big eyes, and three fingers."

Leo froze. He turned slowly. "You talked to Cartwright?"

"Not yet. Why?" Sharp swallowed the bite and chased it with bourbon. It was an unusual taste combination.

"The sheriff in Roswell called the FBI, and the FBI called the Air Force. They sent Cartwright."

"Air Force? You mean the Army?"

"Not anymore," Leo said. "The Air Force is being split off from the Army. Effective immediately."

"What the hell? Why would they do all that?" Sharp asked.

"Because of this."

"What 'this'? I mean, the Air Force talked about splitting from the Army all through the war. Why now?" The timing didn't make sense.

"Compartmentalization."

It'd been a rough couple of days, and Sharp was beginning to feel the bourbon. "Comm—what?"

"Compartmentalization," Leo said. "The new Air Force does not want the old Army to know what's going on. Or the Navy for that matter."

"So, the right hand won't know what the left hand is doing."

"Pretty much." Leo nodded.

"Well I have bad news, Army Intelligence is all over this like white on rice," Sharp said.

"It's not Army Intelligence."

Sharp chewed some more. "Okay, I think I knew that, but who is it?"

"There's an entirely new group coming out to take over what the old OSS was doing during the war. Truman's calling it Central Intelligence."

"The OSS?" Sharp knew those guys. "Wild Bill Donovan's fraternity for Ivy League spies and saboteurs? I don't think so. These guys hit harder than the Oh-So-Social types I met in Europe. I thought Truman was right to shut them down."

Leo shrugged. "Well, he's rethought it."

"Because of this?" Sharp asked.

"That's what I hear. Executive order, but it's all very hush-hush. It won't even be announced to Congress until they get back after Labor Day. "

Sharp took another bite of his two-dollar sandwich. His mother would not have been happy with him talking with his mouth full.

"So these atomic planes in New Mexico, how big are they?"

"As I understand it, they aren't planes. They're like a big pie pan . . . disks. They had to gut a B-36 to get the wreckage—"

The side door to the kitchen opened, and a tall gent stepped halfway in, also in a dressing gown. He had large ears, a big nose, and a slow drawl. "Leo? Everything all right?" He yawned.

"Oh, Lyndon, did we wake you?" Leo shot Sharp a stern look. "I am so sorry."

Something clicked, and Sharp recognized the politician from the Bamboo Room.

Johnson stepped fully into the room. "No problem at all. I was just . . . say, that sandwich looks tasty." He joined them at the kitchen counter.

"Want one?" He stuck out a free hand. "I'm Jeff Sharp."

"I sure do. Lyndon Johnson, call me Lyndon. Good to know you, Mr. Sharp." His handshake would break a pump handle.

Leo cleared his throat. "Actually, Lyndon, Jeff was just leaving. He came by to tell me that Gentry Ferguson was killed in an automobile crash this evening."

Johnson clouded over. "The movie cowboy? That's tragic. His fans will be crushed."

Sharp gave Leo a dirty look. "Yes, they will. It's terrible."

Johnson took Sharp's hand in his great paw. "Was he a friend?"

"I was at the hospital with him. I came right from there."

Lyndon wasn't letting go. "I'm so sorry for your loss. Lady Bird and I will pray for the family."

Sharp had no clue what religion utilized praying birds, but he acknowledged the sentiment. "Thank you."

Leo grabbed his chance. "I'll see you out, Jeff."

They stepped onto the front porch. An owl hooted in the distance.

"This is your in? Your source? The congressman?" Sharp hissed.

"He'll be a senator come November."

"Oh, come on. You think that rube can beat Governor Stevenson?"

"I don't know if he *can*, but I know he *will*," Leo stated. As if it was a done deal.

"And he trusts you?" Sharp asked. "Why?"

"Lyndon knows I'll never print a word against Texas or Fort Worth."

"Because you need everything to look rosy so you and E. G. can sell your damned subdivisions?" Sharp couldn't tell if it was anger or disappointment that colored his voice.

That took Leo aback. Then he got mad. "Go home, Jeff." The owl flew across the moon, and a dark shadow ran across Leo's face. "While you still can."

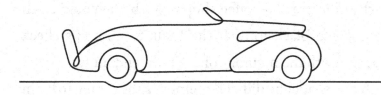

CHAPTER TWENTY-SEVEN

S leep was difficult. Sharp's brain was full of men from Mars doing battle with cowboys and pipe-wielding Earthlings. Finally, he gave up and crawled out of bed. He had no place to be, and after Roni telling him in no uncertain terms what she thought of exposing her to danger, he had no one to be with. It didn't matter that the sun was just beginning to rise.

He shaved, dressed, and tried out his new coffeepot, guessing poorly at the ratio of Maryland Club grounds to water.

The result was as bad as anything he ever had over a campfire or tried to choke down with K-rations. This is why God created coffee shops. Maybe he could catch Roni at the Blackstone. If she'd talk to him. His cheek warmed with the memory of their last encounter.

A newspaper he didn't remember subscribing to lay in the middle of the yard. He unfolded it as he rounded the corner of the house. At the same time he remembered Gentry's Cord was where his LaSalle should be, he noticed that very LaSalle as the lead photo on the front page. His fine old automobile was wrapped around a tree under a two-inch tall headline that screamed WESTERN STAR SAVES CHILD, DIES IN CRASH.

The lead paragraph was poetry. Sharp could imagine Leo hammering it out from his palatial study in his bathrobe:

> *Frequent Fort Worth visitor and friend of the* EXAMINER *Gentry Ferguson was killed in a single-car accident last night when he swerved to avoid a child who had scampered into the path of the borrowed vehicle he was driving. The heroic motion picture star performed one last valiant act, sacrificing his own life to save eight-year old Cubby Carter, who*

was chasing a ball that had rolled into the street. Cubby was uninjured thanks to Ferguson's selfless action.

Sharp rolled his eyes and tossed the paper into the passenger seat. He drove by Roni's empty driveway on his way to do nothing. Outside the Blackstone he learned that the Cord was significantly more difficult to park than his LaSalle.

"All by your lonesome again?" Peggy set a cup of coffee in front of him.

"You haven't seen her, have you?"

"Not this week. What's up with you two? Lovers' spat?"

"We are just friends."

"Right. A shame."

Sharp looked to her as she smacked her gum. She might have meant that.

"Tell me about it."

The gum popped. "So—you gonna eat?"

"Yeah. Number Two, over hard."

Her look told him she already knew that, and then she disappeared to the kitchen window.

He flipped through the rest of his paper. The Cats lost, a city commissioner wanted the city to build a swimming pool, and Monkey Wards was having a big sale. He read the comics and realized he had lied to Leo. Snuffy Smith was not a riot.

He checked his watch and called the courthouse from the phone booth. Delores said Roni had taken some personal time and wasn't expected back the rest of the week. A small part of Sharp thought that was an excellent idea. A more substantial piece of him missed her.

He was at loose ends. He had money in the bank, no responsibilities other than owing rent and nothing to do. He wasn't wild about that, but it beat getting clobbered at every turn, blown up, and spending the day looking over his shoulder. Maybe he should take it easy for a while.

The problem was Major Jerry Cartwright. He was the key to this whole mess, and he'd entrusted Sharp with something valuable. Just how valuable, he wasn't entirely sure. What was he going to do about it? He removed the postcard from his pocket and considered Las Vegas, Nevada. A place he'd never heard of this time last month.

He went to the bank and stashed the postcard and the tinfoil in his safe deposit box. That left him with only one thing he could think of that he needed to do. He had a duplicate of the new house key that Mrs. Hunnakee should have. He drove to the address where his rent check was supposed to go and discovered a familiar yellow Pontiac coupe in the driveway and two very familiar ladies tending plants in the front flower bed.

"What in the world are you doing here?" Sharp unfolded himself from the driver's seat.

"What are you doing in that?" Roni pointed to his new Cord. She was wearing a large sun hat, cotton gardening gloves that were too large, rolled-up jeans with grass stains on the knees, and a smudge of mud on her cheek. She looked fantastic.

"Did you see the paper?" Sharp asked.

Norma Hunnakee waved a trowel at him. "I don't take it. That sonuvabitch Fuller has too much money as it is. I'm not giving him any of mine."

Roni gestured to Mrs. Hunnakee. "Norma is letting me use her spare bedroom. I thought it would take a big leap to find me here."

Solid logic. "They caught up to Gentry last night. He's dead."

Roni's eyes got big, and she clenched her hands to her breast. "Oh, no." She got a little teary as he relayed the details as he knew them.

That caught Sharp off guard. "I thought you didn't like him."

"Well, I didn't want him to be dead," Roni said. "I liked some of his movies." Roni was a caring soul and had a front-row seat at too many funerals lately.

"So, whatever is going on around you is still going?" She sniffed.

"Every time I think this has to be the end, something else happens. But whoever this is, they're running out of people to put the arm on. Caples and Gentry are both dead, the major's disappeared, and Doyle says Leo is launching a campaign to shut down Thunder Road, so he's run off. There's nobody left. At least here."

"There are a few Nobodies left. You. Me. Not that you ever had the courtesy to tell me that I was in the line of fire when I went with you."

"I do owe you an apology. I wasn't trying to hide anything from you."

Roni pointed her trowel at him. "You weren't exactly telling me the whole story either."

Sharp held up a hand. "Guilty. Next time I think there's a chance you could get kidnapped and beaten up, I promise to let you know."

"Do you think it's safe for me to go home?"

"The best I can say is I'm not sure. I don't think it'll be a problem. I think they—whoever 'they' are—have squeezed just about everyone they can squeeze. At least here."

"Here?" Roni tilted her head.

"There's a place in Nevada called Las Vegas," Sharp said. "I might go check it out."

"Nevada? Like out in the desert, Nevada? What are you expecting to find there?"

Sharp shrugged. "There's supposed to be some sort of casino there. I found a clue that leads me to believe that's where Jerry went."

"So, you're going to just take off for the desert?" Roni asked.

Mrs. Hunnakee transplanted a flower from a pot. "You signed a lease. I need five more months' rent out of you."

He grinned. "I didn't say anything about moving."

"If you two run off to Nevada, I'll never see either one of you again." She patted dirt around the flower and struggled to her feet.

"Well, I was planning on going by myself," Sharp said.

Roni put her a hand on her hip. "What if I want to go?"

"I'm not even sure I'm going. I don't have any real—"

"You told me to leave town, to hide out. What better place than Nevada, and what's the town? Lost Vegas?"

"Las. L-A-S. I wanted you to go to your sister's in Tulsa." Sharp reminded her.

"Jeff, she has four kids. Three boys under twelve. That's not where you go if you're trying to get away from trouble."

"Not sure traveling with me is hiding out. I'm following a trail. And to be completely honest, I don't know where it'll take me."

Roni nodded. "I like that."

"The unknown?"

"No, you being honest." Roni tugged one of her gloves off.

"You're welcome to stay here as long as you like, dear." Mrs. Hunnakee headed inside. "You two can stand out here in the sun if you want. I'm going inside for some lemonade."

Roni watched the elderly woman climb the steps and whispered to Sharp, "Her lemonade is almost half vodka. I've never seen anyone put it away like she can."

They went in the house and had spiked lemonade. Mrs. Hunnakee brought out her domino set, and they played until she said she had some steaks if Sharp didn't mind an early dinner. Roni made mashed potatoes and a salad, Sharp gave the grill his best effort and Norma fell asleep in her easy chair with an empty glass still in her hand.

Sharp set the table while Roni changed out of her jeans and freshened up. She woke Norma and Sharp served a first-class steak dinner.

Maybe he'd get the hang of this cooking thing.

When the dishes were done, Sharp stepped out to the front porch for a cigarette. Roni followed.

"So, show me this flashy new car you've inherited."

"It's something to see."

They settled into the Cord, and he showed her how to crank up the passenger side headlight. They put the top down and back up.

She slid a finger across the engine-turned metal of the dash. "This car is so neat. What's that do?" She pointed to a dial on the dash.

"That," said Sharp, "is the radio."

He twisted the key and fired up the beast, then flipped on the radio. Static.

"That's not nearly as impressive as I wanted it to be," she admitted.

Sharp fooled with the tuning knob, and the red line hovered to the left side of the dial. A news announcer's tinny voice came through a hidden speaker: ". . . roof collapsed just moments ago. You can see flames shooting dozens, maybe hundreds of feet into the air above the hill . . . ."

"That's pretty slick." Roni admired the Cord's leather seats. "Somebody thought to put a radio in a car. What'll they think of next? This new gig worked out pretty good for you, didn't it?"

"Yeah, except I don't have any other customers. Doyle was my sugar daddy. I need to cultivate some new clients."

Roni gazed out the windshield, suddenly deep in thought.

"Hey? You there?" Sharp snapped his fingers in her direction, and she shushed him.

"Listen. Did you hear that?"

He turned his non-whining ear toward the radio speaker and dialed up the volume.

The tinny voice sounded excited. ". . . on the telephone from the scene. Porter, what can you tell our listeners?"

An even more excited but less tinny voice came on. "I'm across the Jacksboro Highway from the inferno, Bob. It's tremendous. We just had a major explosion inside the home, and Battalion Chief Burton tells this reporter that they've gone to four alarms. He believes the home was unoccupied at the time, but long-time citizens of Fort

Worth recognize this address as the site of the notorious 2222 Club, a known hideaway linked to organized . . ."

Sharp and Roni shared a look of concern.

He cranked the giant steering wheel, and the radio led them to Thunder Road.

Doyle's stately white house atop the hill was a blackened ruin. The fire department had searchlights playing across the crumbling facade, and hoses reached up the hill from the pumper. Sharp parked around the corner and away from a hydrant with water spewing from the hose coupling. As they scurried across the highway toward Rico's, he wondered how much water pressure was making it to the top of the hill to fight the fire. And they weren't getting one of the Fort Worth Fire Department's trademark white fire engines up the narrow winding drive. He didn't envy the firemen in their turnout gear storming the hill on a hot summer night.

The battalion chief's panel van anchored the center of the parking lot behind the Mexican food joint, and the white-hatted chief directed his teams through a bullhorn. The smoky haze drifted from the club's entrances behind the hill, and Roni put her hand over her mouth to breathe. Sharp nodded toward Rico's, and they hurried to the relative safety of the diner, where a crowd of spectators packed at the windows was gawking at the disaster. Rico spotted him the moment they came in.

He was teary-eyed when he came to them. "Mr. Sharp. It is bad. They cannot put it out. The fire."

"What happened, Rico?" asked Sharp.

"Mr. Doyle came by this evening. He said he was leaving. He shook my hand." Rico looked through the windows as a rumble went through the building.

Sharp wondered if a floor had collapsed next door or if the liquor closet had blown. Or if it even was an accident.

"I think he knew this was coming," Rico continued as another fire engine arrived. "I don't know what to do, Mr. Sharp. He was my friend. He came by every day. But the way he looked when he said good-bye, I don't know if I'll ever see him again."

Sharp turned from the disaster beyond the windows and shared a look with Roni. No one in the crowded diner was eating. The waitstaff was all at their own window. Rico was never going to make a living from his cooking.

Sharp placed a hand on Rico's shoulder. "If I were you, buddy, I'd start looking for another way to make a buck."

Rico watched his world burn beyond the glass. "*Si.*" He sulked back toward the kitchen, disappearing through the double swinging doors. Sharp watched him break down into sobs through the round windows. This was the end of an era.

The end of Thunder Road was driven home by a muffled boom from beneath the hill, as something explosive cooked off. Sharp thought about the impressive wine cellar behind Jimmy's bar.

What a waste.

"Do you think Doyle set it?"

"I'd bet the farm on it. There's a lot of evidence in that place. If Doyle can't have it, this is his way of making sure nobody else can."

"Where do you think he went?" Roni stretched to see over the crowd.

"I have a weird hunch, but that's about it."

She waited for him, then fanned her hand to get him to continue.

"Leo's got a scheme and to make it work, he's got to put Doyle out of business. I think this is Doyle taking the first shot. My bet is Doyle's off to cut a deal with the people Caples was working for. They could use a man with Doyle's resources and abilities."

"You mean the Mob? Wouldn't burning down his club be a little counterproductive?"

"Well if Leo is indeed bringing down the heat, I don't think Doyle or the Mob will bother fighting it out here. If Leo can blackmail the sheriff, the DA, and the police chief about their illicit activities, he can make it more trouble than it's worth to do business here."

A couple moved out of a corner booth and headed to the cash register. Sharp nodded to the empty seats and they took them. Roni looked through the bright window to the flashing lights along Thunder Road.

"Where does that leave you, Mr. Private Eye to the Mob?"

"None of that for me. All I want to do is find the major. You haven't heard from him, have you?"

"Nope. Just one more guy who never calls. You really think he's in Nevada?"

"That's the best clue I've got." He nodded to the blaze as another of the Fort Worth Fire Department's signature white ladder trucks pulled up. "There are a lot of secrets going up in flames out there."

She followed his eyes to the team of firefighters dragging a hose up the hill.

"Maybe you should just let them burn."

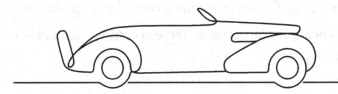

CHAPTER TWENTY-EIGHT

They arranged to meet for breakfast, but to guard against being too predictable, Sharp suggested the Paris Coffee Shop instead of the Blackstone. He arrived first and grabbed a booth in the back where he could see the front door and peruse his paper. The front page screamed MYSTERIOUS FIRE CONSUMES GAMBLING DEN, but he didn't learn anything he hadn't known or guessed last night. A cup of coffee appeared, and he gave the story a better read. The fire department was still on the scene when the paper's deadline hit, and the article ended saying that the latest details would be in the afternoon edition.

The cafe was filling up when he turned to page six, and the small headline buried in a single column near the fold caught his eye.

LOCAL COUPLE FOUND DEAD

Authorities blame a gas leak for the deaths of George and Velma Griffin of Fort Worth, whose bodies were discovered in their west side home . . . .

He choked on his coffee.

Then jumped up and dropped a quarter on the table for the cup. He ran outside just as Roni's Pontiac turned the corner.

He ran to the passenger side and jumped in.

"My house. Now!" Sharp scanned the street, his head on a swivel.

Roni huffed. "I thought we were having breakfast—"

"Drive, Roni!"

She floored it and popped the clutch, jerking him back into the seat as the tires chirped.

"What the hell is going on?" Roni asked.

"We're leaving. We're going to get my gear, then your bags, and we're getting out of here."

"Just a second, Buster." Roni glanced in the rearview mirror. "Don't I have some say in this?"

"Not if you want to live." She shot him a sideways glance to tell him he was being dramatic.

"The cheating husband I was tailing? He worked at Consolidated and played poker at Doyle's. The paper says their house blew up. The same night that the club burns down? I don't think that's a coincidence."

"So what do we do?"

"We get the hell out of town."

"Are you serious?"

"Deadly."

Roni gripped the steering wheel with both hands and double-checked the rearview mirror. "Any idea how long we'll be gone? I need to tell the judge. And my parents."

Sharp had a quick thought. "Tell them two weeks. Say something has come up with an old friend out west, and you have to go tend to them."

She shook her head. "I'm not lying to either of them."

"It's not a lie. Aren't I an old friend?"

"Sometimes, Jeff-er-son, I can't tell." She wheeled the car around the corner and pulled deep into his driveway.

Roni kept an eye out front while he packed his duffel. He put his extra magazines for the Colt on top and grabbed a pair of suits while his brain worked through the things he needed to do.

She dropped him back at the coffee shop to get the Cord, and he stuffed his bag in the tiny trunk. Gentry had a Continental kit added to the maroon missile, so the spare tire on the bumper meant he'd have almost enough room for Roni's makeup case in the trunk.

Sharp followed to her house and stood guard while she packed and made her phone calls. He scribbled out a quick letter and stuck a stamp on it. Roni appeared with three suitcases. Large suitcases. He stole a glance at the burgundy sports car in the driveway. "You need all of that?"

Roni's eyebrows shot up. "For two weeks? I packed light."

He heaved the largest case and then grabbed the second to balance the load. They filled the small backseat to the roof. He struggled to get her smallest case into the trunk and may have bent the hinge trying to get it closed.

She checked her makeup mirror as he pulled to the curb at the bank. "I'll just wait in the car."

"Nope. Stay with me." Sharp gave her a meaningful look.

"I'm fine right here."

"You think so. But the people who killed George and Velma may have a different point of view."

She followed him into the bank, stealing a look around for potential murderers and kidnappers as they crossed the sidewalk.

He cleared all Doyle's cash out of the safe deposit box and tucked his spare Colt in his waistband. One thing he'd learned in the Army was when you needed a gun, having two probably wasn't a bad idea.

He slipped the major's tinfoil and the "Visit Las Vegas" postcard into his detective's pocket and once again gave a silent thanks to Woo the tailor. On his way out, he dropped the letter in the mail slot.

They settled back into the car, and he hesitated. "I want to see one more thing before we leave."

They drove out of town via Thunder Road, which was the wrong way, but Sharp wanted another look at the Four Deuces. He didn't know if it'd be the last time they'd ever see it or not.

At the scene he braked for a ladder truck that was pulling slowly from the devastation and blocking the road.

The bright white-and-gold fire engine took its time.

"Why is it," Sharp wondered aloud, "that every fire truck in the world is red, but in Fort Worth they're all white?"

Roni cocked her head. "You don't know? Really?"

"There's a secret to it?"

"I wrote a report on it in school. Years ago, there was a fire truck race at the State Fair of Texas in Dallas. Somebody told the Fort Worth firemen they couldn't use a truck that was in service, so they took an old run-down pumper and refurbished it. But all they had was white paint, so they used that, trimmed it in gold, and won the race. They've been white ever since." She smiled.

The fireman driving the big white rig tipped his helmet as they finally cleared the intersection and Sharp pulled past the only thing still unscarred: the mailbox reading 2222. It was worse in the late morning sun. The battalion chief's van was still there, and thin white smoke was still drifting from the remaining embers.

The gutter ran deep with water.

Sharp shook his head. "Damn."

"I hope everyone got out." She peered back as he eased slowly past.

"Paper said they did." Sharp pulled into the Texaco station across from the late George Griffin's favorite hideaway motel. The attendant filled the tank, checked the oil, and washed the windshield while the pump chugged three dollars' worth of Sky Chief premium into the Cord.

The station had a map of the Southwest on the wall, but apparently, Rand McNally hadn't yet heard of Las Vegas either, so he bought a handful of individual state maps from the rack by the cash register.

The Nevada map marked the town as a tiny dot.

"You ready for this?" He slid into the seat and found the ignition keyhole.

"Making a break for it?"

"It's called running away. I learned it in the Army. Great way to stay alive."

He fired up the Cord and they waved good-bye to Thunder Road.

Texas stretches for five hundred miles between Fort Worth and El Paso, and there is magnificent scenery for at least four of those miles. They had plenty of time for Sharp to explain the situation and the reasoning for the trip west. It beat playing "count the license plates," because very few other cars were foolish enough to brave the Texas desert in summertime. They left the convertible top up against the blazing sun but rolled both windows down to cool the car. Roni tied a scarf around her hairdo against the breeze but was losing the battle.

Sharp shifted in the seat and tried again to find a comfortable place for his elbow on the Cord's window frame. "So, Doyle figured that the Chicago mob was coming for Caples and Caples answer was to move in on Doyle. Why not beat 'em to the punch? Our mutual friend and former Army demolitions man, Gentry was always up for some action, and knew his way around dynamite, so Doyle and Gent cooked up a deal to take out Caples."

"Why would a movie star even consider that?"

"Yeah, on the surface it seems stupid. But Gentry had his own reasons. Bugsy Siegel had gotten him into a syndicate in an oil play. Gentry told me Caples did the hit on Bugsy for Meyer Lansky—"

"The Chicago mobster? So it really is the Mob." She fought with her headscarf against the breeze from the window.

"Exactly. He tasks Caples with killing Bugsy and as a side benefit, everyone in the syndicate gets a little larger slice of the profits from the drilling."

"So this whole thing is all about money?" She frowned her disappointment.

"Not completely. Gentry had bags of money. But this was also personal. He and Bugsy palled around together. Trips to Fort Worth and Havana. Bugs wanted to be in the movies and Gentry liked that dangerous side of life. He told me he had a piece of the Flamingo."

"They owned a bird?"

"That's the name of the casino—it's Lansky's toehold in Las Vegas, and Bugsy was going to run it."

"So what happened?"

"That I don't know. But it was enough that Lansky sent Caples to take him out."

"And then Gentry takes his revenge and gets an even larger piece of the oil well. No wonder Doyle was paranoid." She retied her scarf as the badlands west of the Texas-New Mexico border unfolded into the horizon.

"Just because he's paranoid doesn't mean he's wrong. But before he died, Gentry said something that makes me think there's more to it."

Sharp checked the speedometer. The Cord had a way of speeding up all on its own.

"And you think we'll find the answer in Nevada?"

"First we'll stop in Roswell. That's where it looks like this whole thing started."

"The weather balloon? You think that photo is a lead?"

Sharp lit a Lucky and blew the smoke out the window. "I have no idea. I'd like to, but the way things have worked lately, just when I think I'm figuring it out, something else happens."

"So, what are we going to do?"

"We?"

"You brought me all the way out here on this romantic desert getaway, Jeff-er-son. I'm in this as much as you are."

"I didn't realize this was your idea of romance." His chuckle faded when he saw her eyes go cold. He was keeping his knack for cracking jokes at the wrong time.

"You're right, sorry. I did drag you out here, you deserve to know everything."

"Yes. I do."

"We're going to see a rancher named J. J. Darnell. It's not exactly in Roswell, but that's the closest town of any size. There's a place called Corona on the map, but I couldn't find anything in the library about it at all."

"Then how do you plan to find it?"

"Hopefully, we can get some information when we get to Roswell."

"We should try the sheriff's office." Roni crossed her arms. "If there's a report that went to the federal authorities, they would've started with the county sheriff's office."

He shot a look into his own eyes in the rearview mirror. She was a smart cookie and not the damsel in distress he'd convinced himself he was rescuing from danger. If anything, he was taking her straight into it.

He watched her staring out the window as the wastelands rolled by, and realized it wasn't that he was concerned for her safety. It was because deep down, he wanted her here with him.

He looked back at the man in the mirror. That guy was a jerk.

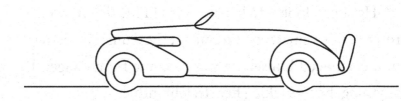

CHAPTER TWENTY-NINE

They'd been on the highway for almost eight hours when Roswell finally came into view. The town was a wide spot in the road that reminded him of his recent trip to the fine community of Weatherford. The map showed an Army air base just south of town.

Sharp figured if Roni's idea about the sheriff didn't turn up any leads, they could always try the USAAF, though he hadn't found those people to be especially helpful of late.

"This will be a little tough for these folks," Sharp said.

"How so?" Roni stubbed out her cigarette and closed the ashtray.

Sharp waved a hand at the scrubland passing by beyond the window. "Well, this is cowboy and Indian country. I doubt they see a car like this on a regular basis."

Roni nodded. "Not many movie stars in rural New Mexico. But they get flying saucers and men from Mars, so it might not be that big of a deal."

He parked in front of the Chaves County sheriff's office and thought she might have a point.

She was wrong.

A half dozen people gathered around the car like it was from Neptune. It was just after dinnertime, and the crowd headed to the movie house was interested.

Sharp tipped his hat to the growing assemblage and double-checked that the tinfoil was in his pocket. He steered Roni inside.

The deputy at the counter had the dark skin, broad face, and high cheekbones of the local Apaches. His name tag read "Arzate." He'd been watching through the plate-glass window since the Cord had stopped. "What kind of car is that?"

"It's a Cord." Sharp wanted to be the one asking questions.

"Foreign car?" Deputy Arzate raised a weathered eyebrow.

"Yes, it's from Indiana."

"Where's the headlights?" Arzate put his hands on his hips. "You have to have headlights to drive at night here."

"They crank down into the fenders," Sharp said. "It's a neat trick. I'll show you later. Is the sheriff around?"

The deputy looked him up and down and took his time admiring Roni. "Who wants to know?"

A business card slid across the counter. "I'm Jeff Sharp. I'm a detective from Fort Worth."

Deputy Arzate took his time studying the plain white card. "The sheriff's not here. Something I can help you with?"

Sharp wasn't betting on it. "I'm looking for the Darnell place out by Corona. I'd like to talk to J. J. Darnell."

The deputy shook his head. "Not his place. Belongs to the Brazel family. J. J. is the foreman."

Roni piped up. "Is that where the sheriff is?" She placed an elbow on the counter and leaned her chin into her hand.

Sharp felt a jealous pang as the deputy gained new interest in this line of questioning. Arzate moved to angle a look down Roni's blouse. "He's in Santa Fe. Him and

Darnell. There's a big meeting there about the weather balloon." From the way he said the last, it sounded like they weren't the first to come poking around.

"Is that what it was?" asked Sharp.

"Dunno." Arzate'e eyes never left Roni. "I don't even know if J. J. knows. He's had so many people out there since they found . . . them."

"Them? As in more than one?" Roni stepped back to the New Mexico state map on the wall and traced the road from Roswell to Corona to Santa Fe.

"Might've been. Nobody's really saying." Deputy Arzate was every bit as much help as Sharp had figured.

However, he did have directions to the ranch, which Sharp scribbled into his notebook as Roni led the conversation. The large map on the wall had a convenient pushpin at the location of the ranch/crash site/mystery. It looked to be seventy miles north of town.

Sharp thanked the deputy for his trouble, but the stout Apache followed them outside for a tour of the sports car. The lawman played with knobs and sat in the seat like he was the King of the West. The small crowd milled around like the circus had come to town. The Cord was a technological wonder with a supercharger, front-wheel drive, a radio, and a Lycoming aircraft engine.

But everyone seemed much more fascinated with the headlights going up and down.

The deputy directed them to the town's hotel, which Sharp would never have found unless he looked across the street.

"Hi-dee, folks!" The desk clerk wore a green eyeshade that didn't hide his comb-over. He had thick glasses, a name tag that read "Lonnie" and a grin that said he was far too thrilled to see paying customers. "Here to see the flying saucer?"

Sharp and Roni shared a look. Sharp bit first. "Flying saucer?"

"It's all everybody can talk about these days! You're in luck, we've got a vacancy!" He leaned toward them conspiratorially, "The Army has had us booked up for weeks."

He spun the registration book around so they could sign in. Sharp picked up the pen and paused. He hadn't thoroughly thought this through. Roni was watching him intently while the clerk rattled on.

"They say it was a weather balloon." Lonnie raised a disbelieving eyebrow. "But we all think that's just some kind of cover story."

"Cover story, huh?" Roni put a hand on her hip and cocked her head to see how Sharp played this.

He winked at her and signed them in.

The clerk read the register upside down and nodded. "Yes, ma'am, Mrs. Sharp. The Army was here for weeks. That's a long time to pick up a weather balloon."

"Is there a place to eat around here?" Sharp tried to look as innocent he could.

"El Palacio, two doors down. Best food for a hundred miles!" He produced the room key from the pigeonholes behind him.

Sharp passed the key to Roni, who was staring at his scrawl on the register. "Honey, I'll go get the luggage."

She took the key in a trance and turned silently to the stairs. Sharp and Lonnie shared a look and both shrugged.

Five minutes later, he was rapping on the room door with four pieces of luggage piled in the hallway. "Roni. Come on. Open the door."

Silence. He shook his head. What had he done now? Then another thought intruded. He pulled his Colt and stepped to the side of the door and rapped harder.

"Roni? Open up. Now." His voice was hard.

It took a long second before the door opened.

He was inside in a single bound. "Are you okay? There's nobody here?" He darted to the window and pulled the curtain back. Nothing. He turned, and her makeup-smeared eyes were riveted on the gun. What the hell?

"I'm fine." Her eyes never left the gun.

Sharp stepped past her, around the corner of the queen-size bed, and into the bathroom. He yanked back the shower curtain on the tub. Empty. He stepped back into the room and holstered the gun. "What's wrong?"

"Nothing."

"Well, something wrong because your makeup is leaking all over." She held a handful of tissue soaked in dark, damp mascara.

"I'm fine."

She sniffed, and he stepped to comfort her. "Hey, Roni, it's okay—"

"Don't." She turned her head away.

It took him aback. "Don't? Don't what?"

She took a deep breath. "At any point, did it ever occur to you that I might not want to be Mrs. Jefferson Sharp? Ever consider that?"

"What?" He drew back. "The hotel register? That's what's got you bawling? Look, Roni—"

She stopped him with a hand and hard look away.

"When we were kids, I thought you were the bees knees. I had the biggest crush on my brother's best friend. I used to practice writing *Mrs. Jefferson Sharp* in my diary. But you never even saw me."

Sharp looked to the window as if his understanding of what was going on might be on the other side of the curtain. "Roni . . . I . . ."

"And then I met Frenchy and everything clicked and it was like a part of me that had been missing was suddenly there. He was truly my better half."

"He was a helluva guy."

"Then one day he walks in with you, his new partner. It was like you were always going to be there."

"I didn't know."

"Of course you didn't. Guys never know. But *I* did. I knew right then I made the right choice. Frenchy made me feel things that making eyes at you never could."

"I see."

"No you don't, because now he's gone. David's gone and I'm here with you and people are trying to kill you. So that little girl's dream of being Mrs. Jefferson Sharp? It's something a whole lot different seeing you write it out in that register. Now it's a nightmare, Buster, and I keep waking up in it."

She dabbed her dark eyes and he searched for words. "Look, I'm sorry about that. It's a crappy deal and—"

"Crappy doesn't cover it, Jeff." She placed her hands on her hips. "I've got my job, the house, and my car, and when I started seeing Jerry, well, I thought I was turning a corner. Now you've gotten me into this and I . . . I . . ." She sobbed, and Sharp went to her, wrapping his arms around her as she cried on his chest. "I'm so damn tired of losing the men I love."

Love? His brain clicked.

"Hey," he whispered. "I'm sorry you're in the middle of this. But I'm going to fix things."

She stepped back, nostrils flaring. "And that's just it! You think that just because you're still alive you have some special power that makes you better than everyone else. Better than David, or Frenchy? How do you fix this? You're taking on the Mob? The goons from the government that beat you up? Vernon Billings? People are getting killed, Jeff! The safest place a person can get is as far away from you as possible. How the hell are you, one pissant out-of-work cowhand, going to fix anything?"

That particular gut punch landed hard. Sharp swallowed and set his pissant cowhand jaw. "I see."

He went to the door and brought in her luggage. "You'll want to lock this door. I'll go see about getting another room."

He carried his duffel back downstairs and went to the desk. The happy clerk was a picture of deep customer-service concern.

"Problem with the room?" Lonnie asked.

Sharp shook his head. "Do you have another? Preferably close to that one?"

"Is there something wrong? The room was in good shape. I checked it myself this afternoon. Everything was working." Lonnie raised a knowing eyebrow. "Is it the bed?"

"The room's fine. Do you have another or not?"

The efficient clerk produced another key from the pigeonholes and handed it across. "Mrs. Sharp not feeling well? I can get Doc Welch over in a jiffy."

"She's fine."

"It's no trouble," Lonnie checked the big Regulator clock on the wall, "Doc's probably home listening to Amos 'n' Andy."

"She. Is. Fine." Sharp scrawled his signature across the next line in the register and slammed the pen down on the counter. He met the clerk's expectant eyes. "That's an exact quote."

Lonnie blinked back his understanding. "Room 203. It's across the hall and down one door."

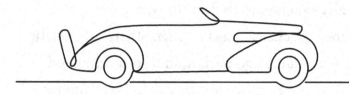

CHAPTER THIRTY

S harp was tired and hungry when the sun rose. He'd sacrificed both dinner and sleep, but both his guns were cleaner than they'd been since boot camp, and he'd gotten to do a lot of thinking. He'd considered the general state of pissant cowhands, women, spacemen, and the Mob, and tried to figure his place amid the whole mess.

At least the Colts were clean.

He dressed in his Dickies and boots for the trip to the ranch, then repacked his duffel. He pulled the piece of tinfoil from his jacket pocket and folded it to fit in his wallet, then headed downstairs. Roni was sitting in the lobby. Her suitcases waited around her.

He took the chair across from her. "There's a bus station here. If you want to go back home. I'd recommend you stay with your parents or maybe talk to Mrs. Hunnakee."

"And get more people involved in this mess?" Roni spoke mainly to the Regulator clock on the wall. "I think you've done enough to her house. I'd hate for Norma to suffer more because of this."

Sharp sighed. "So, what do you want to do?"

"Get breakfast." She stared a hole through him.

Sharp nodded. "I'll load the car and see if there's a place to get some food."

"Yes. Do that."

The huevos rancheros were tasty, but nobody said a word. The morning's paper from El Paso had nothing of real interest. Sharp paid the bill, and they headed north across New Mexico in silence. The fine automobile radio played nothing but static.

An hour later, he found the cutoff to the Brazel ranch, and the rutted dirt road bounced the low-slung car through the dust. Scrub brush and the occasional black boulder, remnants of an ancient volcano that had hurled obsidian rock for hundreds of miles across the prairie, spotted the Badlands' rolling hills.

The road ended through a split-rail fence surrounding a flat-roofed adobe house with a cedar-post porch. Lettering that might have once spelled DARNELL adorned a battered mailbox. Beyond the house sat a small barn and a corral.

Sharp ducked under the low roof of the porch and knocked on the wood-plank door. The house could be a hundred years old. The ancient Mexican woman who opened the door might've been the original occupant.

"*¿Hola?*"

Sharp smiled big and took off his hat. "Mornin', ma'am. My name is Jeff Sharp, and this is Roni Arquette. We're looking for J. J. Darnell."

The elderly woman looked at him with a question. "*¿Que? No savvy. ¿Habla español?*"

Sharp raised his voice. "J. J. Darnell? Is he here?"

Roni rolled her eyes then cut loose with a string of Spanish, the only words of which he understood were Fort Worth and Darnell.

The woman nodded and replied with her own rapid-fire Spanish and then closed the door.

"We're supposed to wait here." Roni lit a cigarette.

"Where did you learn Spanish?" asked Sharp.

"I was treasurer of the Spanish club at Paschal High for two years." Roni blew a stream of smoke at the porch ceiling. "How can you live in Texas and not know Spanish?"

"I can order a beer. And ask directions to the bathroom."

"That must be about all you need." Roni stepped to the other end of the porch.

He gritted his teeth and shoved his fists in his pants pockets.

A thin boy of about twelve or thirteen rounded the corner of the house and stepped onto the porch wiping the sweat off his forehead with a blue bandanna. He had on dirty Levis, worn boots, and a T-shirt that had once been white. He stuffed the bandanna in a hip pocket and covered his red hair with a battered straw hat.

"I'm Rusty. Abuela says you're here about the wreck."

Sharp nodded. "I'm Jeff. This is Roni. And yes, we are."

Rusty eyed Roni's dress and shoes. "Ma'am, you might want to wait here with Abuela. It's a pretty good ride across the ranch. She's got some coffee on."

Roni gave Sharp a cold look. "That sounds good to me. *Gracias.*"

Rusty nodded. "*De nada.*"

He turned and headed back around the corner, Roni stepped through the door, and Sharp found himself alone on the porch. He hustled after the boy, who headed to the corral and the barn.

Sharp stopped near the corral fence, where a saddle and tack hung over the top rail. "We riding out?"

Rusty disappeared into the barn. "Yessir, give me two shakes."

Sharp looked the saddle over. It was a working piece with minimal tooling or decoration. It had been well used but also well kept. It was equipment, not a parade decoration, as so many were becoming.

An engine fired in the barn, and a pre-war REO stake-bed truck bounced into the sunlight with Rusty behind the wheel. Sharp went to the passenger side of the dusty truck and creaked open the door. He moved a coffee can of nails and a pair of fence pliers out of the battered seat and climbed in. Rusty sat with a wooden Coke bottle crate behind him so he could reach the pedals. He eased the clutch out and muscled the truck through the barnyard and out onto the ranch, headed toward the midmorning sun.

"I thought we were going to ride?" Sharp asked as the truck bounced along.

"We are." Rusty dodged the truck around a large black rock. "But not on horses. The livestock won't go near it. Horses or cattle."

"What exactly is 'it'?" Sharp lit a smoke and blew the smoke out his window.

"The crash site." Rusty glanced at him. "The stock gets skittish as all get-out out there."

Sharp nodded to himself. Just like at the Rafter B. "When was it? The crash."

Rusty thought a minute. "Not really sure. Must have been late May, early June. We had a big thunderstorm, and it scattered the herd all over. We were out trying to round 'em up when Pa found it."

"J. J. Darnell your dad?"

Rusty steered down a pair of worn furrows through the bare ranchland. This wasn't the first time for this trip. "Yessir. He saw something shiny, and we rode over until the horses got spooked. Then we walked. It's just over this hill."

They crested the hill, and before them were the remains of a major civil-engineering project. About five acres of ground had been torn up and then graded smooth. Treaded tracks and a makeshift road headed to the west. Rusty eased the truck to a stop.

"Treads?" the infantryman in Sharp asked. "They have tanks out here?"

"Cranes. Great big ones. They put the wreckage on flatbeds and hauled it all off." He pointed to the road. "That leads to the highway. Pa said they hauled it all to the air base outside of town."

They climbed out of the truck and walked down to the excavated area. Sharp squatted to look more closely. "Cranes." He picked up a rock and tossed it. "For a weather balloon."

Rusty shrugged. "Well, that's what they're telling people."

Sharp raised a dubious eyebrow. "Was it?"

"Can't really say," Rusty said. "There was a lot of wreckage. And it was almost sundown when we found it. Pa called the sheriff, and he came out the next morning. That afternoon, when I got done with chores, some Army guys were at the house. They didn't want us to get close to it or touch anything."

Sharp stood and searched the flattened terrain for anything out of place. "Any of it look like tinfoil?"

"Tinfoil?" Rusty's gaze wandered back to the truck. "Yeah, I guess—some of it. There was a bunch of parts. Shiny stuff."

"How big was the biggest piece?" Sharp asked.

Rusty slid his hat back and scratched his head for a moment. "Pretty good size."

Sharp slid into his old cop questioning mode. "As big as the truck?"

"Oh yeah." Rusty nodded. "Easy."

"Were a lot of the pieces that big?" Sharp pointed to the battered farm truck.

Rusty shrugged. "A few."

"Five? Ten?"

"About that." Rusty looked off into space, and Sharp could tell the boy was back there again, on that night.

"Was it muddy?"

"Muddy?" That took the boy out of it.

Sharp looked at the surrounding area. It was desert ranchland, and it hadn't seen rain in a while. "You said it was a thunderstorm."

"Oh yeah." Rusty nodded. "Funny though . . . it didn't rain."

"Are you sure it was a thunderstorm?"

Rusty frowned. "Well, there was wind and thunder, and all kinds of lightning. But it was dark. Night."

Sharp considered his own experience at the Rafter B. "Any of the lightning have color to it?"

"Yeah!" said Rusty. "It did. It was all purple and gold and orange . . . ."

"And the wind, was it more like a whine?" Sharp tried to imitate the sound he'd heard on very similar ranchland.

"That's it!" Rusty's eyes danced, excited. "And it got louder and louder, and then it went all quiet. Real sudden like."

"Yeah," Sharp nodded. "I've heard it too."

Rusty looked at him strangely. "Let me show you something else." He led them back to the truck, and they drove away from the crash site.

It was two rises across to what Sharp thought was the east. The sun was getting higher, and it was harder to tell. Rusty stopped the truck on the side of a hill that was out of view from the main crash area.

"Look at this." Rusty pointed to a depression in the ranchland. An almost perfect rectangle, two feet by four feet and six inches deep in the otherwise undisturbed soil. Like something large and heavy had stamped the earth.

Sharp squatted beside it to get a closer look. The edges were clean, hardly weathered. Whatever it was, it wasn't very old.

"There's a couple of 'em," Rusty said. "I found 'em last week, out here looking for cattle." The excited boy pointed them out, and Sharp walked between them.

Several head of cattle had appeared in the distance. Sharp figured they'd heard the truck, and that might mean food.

Cows had more stomachs than brains.

They were ambling toward them.

"You tell the Army?" Sharp asked. "Or the sheriff?"

Rusty frowned. "First time they were here, they told me they didn't want a kid hanging around. Ran me off when I was trying to find all the stock they scared off. Told me to scram. I figure if they wanted to find 'em, they could hunt on their own."

Sharp grinned. Kids could be great witnesses, and Rusty seemed to have a good feel for when he was being fed a cock-and-bull story.

The cattle had stopped, well clear of the depressions in the ground. They began to bawl at the two humans and the small group split, three or four going left and another half dozen moving right, like the entire region was fenced off with invisible barbed wire.

Rusty glanced in the direction of the ranch house. "Mister, I gotta get back. I've got chores. Pa will want 'em done when he gets back."

"Where is your pa?" Sharp asked. They started walk- ing back to the truck, and then something caught Sharp's eye. Someone had been up here to see these depressions in a vehicle, and he'd seen enough US Army jeep tracks across rugged landscape to know exactly what he was looking at.

Rusty shrugged. "There's a meeting in Santa Fe. Supposed to be back tomorrow night."

Sharp added Santa Fe to his mental itinerary. Another place Roni would be thrilled to visit. "Before we head back, I want to show you something." He pulled the tinfoil out of his wallet and handed it over as it slowly unfolded itself. "Any of it look like this?"

Rusty's eyes got wide. "It sure did! Where'd you get that? You been here?" He narrowed his eyes. "You in the Army?"

"No," Sharp reassured him. "But a guy who is gave this to me. I think he was here. Dark hair, Clark Gable mustache? Walks with a limp?"

Rusty looked at the dirt. "Like I said, they run me off. He coulda been here."

Sharp folded the tinfoil back into his wallet and came out with a dollar bill. "I've got a buck if you'll keep this our secret."

"You don't have to pay me. Nobody wants to talk to me anyway."

"It's my way of saying thanks for taking time away from your chores."

Rusty took the bill and wadded it into the pocket of his Levis.

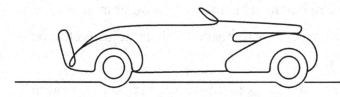

CHAPTER THIRTY-ONE

The trip to Santa Fe started quietly. Roni stared out the passenger window. Sharp was deep in thought. Finally, she broke the ice. "Corona said the number of visitors has dropped."

"Corona?"

"Rusty's grandmother," Roni said. "She's a very nice lady. Said she's been there for seventy-five years."

"Huh."

"She said the Army was there for weeks."

Sharp nodded.

"It looked like it. It was a large-scale operation. Whatever it was, it was bigger than a weather balloon."

"They're having a big meeting about it in Santa Fe."

"That's where we're headed." Sharp adjusted the rearview mirror.

"Were you going to mention that at some point?" Roni lit a cigarette.

Sharp shrugged. "I just did."

She blew smoke out her side of the car.

Sharp slowed the car and pulled to the side of the road. He twisted in the seat to face her.

"We need to get this cleared up. We're stuck out here together, and I can't do a thing about it. But I will be damned if I'm gonna put up with this all the way to Nevada. Spit it out. Why are you so mad at me?"

She looked at him for a moment and bit her lip in that innocent way that took his mind away from being angry and went places he didn't think they'd ever go.

"I'm not mad at you," she said.

"You have an amazing way of showing that."

"I'm upset at the whole mess," Roni waved her hands at the flat land surrounding them for as far as the eye could see. "I don't like not knowing what's going on. I'm not happy that we're on the run. And I'm worried."

"About what?" Sharp asked. There was plenty to choose from.

"I don't know!" said Roni. "That's the whole problem. I feel like there's some boogeyman out there that we can't see, and he's going to get us any minute now. We're out here in the middle of the desert all alone, and you're chasing this story about the Mob and mystery guys who want to kill us and if I think about it too much, it scares me."

Her eyes were getting moist.

"I get it."

"And there's nothing we can do." She sounded miserable. And small.

"There is. We can go to Santa Fe and see what's there," Sharp said. "Then we can go to Las Vegas and see what's there. That's what we can do."

He reached across and took her hand.

"Is that how you get through this?"

"You take one step after the next, prepare as best you can, and keep moving forward."

"That's not exactly a bold plan of action, Mr. Sharp."

"It's what's kept this pissant cowboy alive so far."

She stared at her hand in his, and her voice was quiet. "I'm sorry about that."

"Me too," Sharp admitted. "I didn't want to get you into this."

"I know but . . . that's not what I meant." She leaned in. "I don't think I'm ready to pretend to be Mr. and Mrs. Seeing you write that down caught me off guard."

"I didn't mean to take liberties, honest. I just thought it would—"

She placed her finger on his lips. "You should stop talking now."

He nodded.

She slid her hand from his. "We're a thousand miles from home. In the middle of nowhere. It's just you and me now. There are no bad guys out here, no ghosts of husbands or brothers or ex-wives or missing boyfriends. It might be a good place for a clean sheet to start over, but I'm not there. Not yet."

"I really didn't—"

She shushed him. "And I really am sorry I called you a pissant cowboy. I didn't mean that."

"About that . . ."

"Shush."

He nodded silently and pulled back onto the highway.

The square in Santa Fe looked every bit of the four hundred years old the town was supposed to be, right up until he wheeled the Cord around the burro pulling the cart, and the engine broke the afternoon siesta silence. The Indians selling silver goods and trinkets in the shade of the surrounding covered walkways looked up at the sound and then went back to rearranging their wares on blankets on the ground.

"Corona said they were meeting at the Palace," Roni offered.

"That a hotel?" Sharp heaved the big wheel to get around a tight corner never meant for automobiles.

"The Palace of the Governors," Roni said. "It's kind of like the state capitol building, but it's not."

"Is it near a hotel?" He cranked the wheel around another tight corner and slowed for an Indian woman and her kids crossing the narrow road. Getting through this town was a workout.

Roni stubbed her smoke out. "I bet there's a phone book inside. We could find one in the Yellow Pages."

Sharp parked the Cord on the street, and they headed into the big ancient adobe palace, the original seat of the Spanish government of the territory in the 1620s. It had been replaced as the state capitol by newer buildings with things like electricity and plumbing, but renovations now let it serve as offices and a museum.

There was a row of phone booths along the wall, but Roni pointed to a large counter with a sign reading INFORMATION.

The frumpy woman behind the counter shuffled papers and never acknowledged them. Sharp was sure she was related to the guardians he'd waited on in the Dallas and Tarrant County courthouses.

He cleared his throat with enough volume that it echoed.

She finally raised her eyes in annoyance.

"We're here for the meeting about the crash in Roswell," Sharp announced.

"Names?"

"Jeff Sharp and Veronica Arquette."

She scanned a piece of paper. "And you're with . . .?"

Sharp thought for a second.

He needed a good explanation. But Roni beat him to it, handing over a business card. "Mr. Sharp is an investigator. I'm the chief stenographer with the Sixty-seventh District Court in Fort Worth."

The woman pulled her reading glasses up and examined the card. Then over the frames to scrutinize the two of them before pointing to her left. "Down this hall, third door past the water fountain."

Sharp whispered as they walked. "Chief stenographer? I didn't know you were the head honcho."

She smiled slyly. "It's Judge Rowan's card. Just has the name of the court on it. I kind of gave myself a promotion."

He grinned. "Atta girl."

He cracked the door of the meeting room open slightly for a peek, then pulled it open.

A janitor was erasing a blackboard in the corner, and the U-shaped arrangement of tables was empty of everything but a few half-full water glasses, but no signs that the attendees were coming back.

"They done?" Sharp asked.

The janitor didn't even look over his shoulder. "Broke up half an hour ago."

"Dammit." Sharp slumped. He didn't know what they might have learned, but it would have been better than what they didn't know now.

Roni shook her head. "Now what?"

Sharp shrugged. "Up for some Mexican food?"

"Really? That's the extent of your investigation here?"

"Well, I thought we'd swing by the newspaper and see if they know anything on the way."

The secretary at the *Santa Fe New Mexican* perked up when Sharp mentioned they were from Fort Worth and looking into the crash. She summoned forth a short, slight, balding gentleman with a quick smile who introduced himself as Manuel Garcia, the reporter who'd worked the story.

His first question immediately made him a friend in Sharp. "Have you had lunch?"

He steered them to a hole-in-the-adobe-wall cafe. A few minutes later, they each had a bright red bowl of pozole. Garcia told them the story of the crash, most of which they'd already learned. He'd met and interviewed Darnell but didn't get much. The man was skeptical of anyone from the big city, especially reporters from the big-city newspaper. Sharp nodded. The population of Dallas and Fort Worth probably exceeded all of the souls in New Mexico. Garcia had been to the ranch, but Darnell hadn't taken him to the crash site, so Sharp traded the man his information for goodwill.

"Did you talk to anyone at the Roswell air base?" Garcia was enjoying his soup with one hand and taking rapid notes with the other.

"We haven't had much luck with the Army in our part of the world," said Sharp.

"Same here." Garcia wiped the corner of his mouth. "But the rumor mill says big changes are coming to the Army."

"You mean splitting off the Air Force?" Sharp took a large drink of water to combat the burn of the chili-pepper soup.

Garcia raised an eyebrow. "What makes you say that?"

Sharp shrugged. "I've got information that there's a proposal to do just that. And it's on Truman's desk waiting for Congress to get back in session."

"That's supposed to be classified," said Garcia. "I stumbled on that at the base, and the commandant himself asked me to keep it on the QT."

"You're holding the story just because he asked?"

Garcia waved his soup spoon. "Certainly. If I break that, they may never give me anything again." He paused to give his position a little more gravity. "I believe there is a lot more to this story than just a weather balloon."

Roni looked at Sharp. He nodded but wasn't ready to give away all his cards. "Newspaper in Fort Worth said it was a flying saucer."

"I think it was an experimental aircraft the Army is trying to keep under wraps."

"The atomic plane?" Sharp asked.

"Could be."

"Or a helicopter?"

Garcia frowned. "A what?"

"I saw a helicopter at the air base in Fort Worth," Sharp said. "The propeller's on top. Lifts it straight up and can set it straight down. Doesn't need a runway. Looks like it could go just about anywhere. Even a remote ranch."

"Hmmm." Garcia sat back in his chair. "That could explain a lot. I understand there are some things happening in the Nevada desert. Hard to get more remote than that." He finished his soup and ordered sopaipillas for the table. "So, what's all this to you?"

Sharp looked at Roni. "We have a friend who was at the base. He disappeared right after this happened. We're trying to find him. Nevada is our next stop."

"You with Army Intelligence?" Garcia watched for a reaction.

Sharp held his poker face. "No. I'm a private investigator. We kind of backed into this."

"The Army sent a couple of assholes out here last week." Garcia frowned in disgust. "They didn't make many friends. Threatened the editor. That didn't sit well."

Sharp's hand went to the back of his head.

"We've met. They aren't doing much for Army public relations."

They enjoyed the sopaipillas, and Garcia gave them a little history of New Mexico and the Army, complete with secret laboratories, atom-bomb tests, and other mysteries. He ended the lesson and stood to get back to work. "I think New Mexico is about done as a secret base for the Army. They wore out their welcome with the Manhattan Project. But Nevada is a whole other story. That's the absolute middle of nowhere. If you wanted a place to set up a secret military project and have it stay hidden if everything goes to hell, that's about the perfect spot."

Sharp idled the Cord in the shade of the Tourist Court's adobe portico.

"Wait here. I'll get us checked in."

"Worried after last time?" Roni checked her lipstick in the compact's mirror.

"A little."

He returned with two keys. She raised an eyebrow. "Really?"

"Hey, I'm making sure you understand I have the proper respect for your situation."

He parked in front of rooms 106 and 107.

"Well I didn't mean that we couldn't . . . um . . . use it as cover and—"

He raised a hand. "Mrs. Arquette, you made yourself extremely clear. I'll get the bags."

Sharp shrugged out of his fine Italian leather shoulder holster and tossed the Colt on top of his coat in the side chair.

He pulled his boots off and fell back on the bed.

"Well, this was a bust," Roni said through the wall.

"I think we know more about what's going on than he does." The ceiling had a small edge where the paint was a tad different in the lamplight. He stared at it.

"Is there more in Las Vegas? What if that's a bust too?" Her voice was fainter. Then he heard the shower begin.

"I'm trusting the major. He said visit Las Vegas—"

"Fabulous Las Vegas," Roni interjected.

The sound of the running water changed.

She was in the shower.

Naked.

"Fabulous Las Vegas." He blew smoke at the ceiling as his imagination was running away with him.

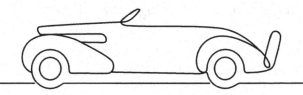

CHAPTER THIRTY-TWO

"The song is a lot more fun than the actual road." Roni fanned herself with the folded map as they turned off Route 66 in the Kingman, Arizona, of the second verse.

"It is not a lot of kicks." Sharp stretched behind the wheel. He rolled his shoulder.

Twenty long hours behind the wheel had stiffened his favorite war injury.

"Nope. I'm tired of kicks. I just want to get there." Roni sighed. "Next time, maybe we should take the train."

"Next time? I'm not planning on a next time. I don't think my butt can take much more time in this seat. But we're gaining on it." He nodded to a giant billboard on the side of the road, imploring them to visit the El Grande Hotel in fabulous Las Vegas, only two hours ahead! Sharp stifled a yawn.

Two and a half hours later, they reached the engineering marvel that was Boulder Dam and Lake Mead. They had seen dozens of billboards for the El Grande offering rooms with refrigerated air; not one, but two swimming pools; casino gambling; the World Famous Chuck Wagon Buffet; live entertainment; and this weekend Jack Benny appearing in the Opera House.

Sharp was pretty sure that out here in the middle of nowhere, the Jack Benny on a desert stage and the Jack Benny on the radio were two completely different guys.

Las Vegas had a single stoplight, so it was that much more impressive than Roswell. Sharp wondered if they had others that might have burned to a crisp in the heat. The late-afternoon sun beat down on the intersection that featured little more than a few two-story buildings, most of which sported new neon signs advertising poker, blackjack, and casino gambling. A now familiar-looking billboard pointed the way toward "the Strip" and the El Grande.

"Any idea where we're staying?" Roni asked.

Sharp cocked his head. "Maybe. The place we're looking for is called the Flamingo. Gentry indicated it was just outside of town on something called the Strip."

"I wonder why they don't all have billboards like the El Grande?" She lit a cigarette and blew the smoke toward downtown as they followed the arrow on the billboard.

The sign in front of the Flamingo answered her question: CLOSED FOR RENOVATIONS. The parking lot was empty and kraft paper covered the interior of the large plate-glass windows. They got out and stretched as the setting sun maintained the hundred-degree heat.

"So, this is what got Bugsy killed." Sharp was both exhausted and impressed. The modern architecture with the giant stonework and expansive glass was much more striking than what the Stockmen's Association back in Fort Worth had tried to do with the same look.

Roni waved her Pall Mall at the building. "How'd they expect it to make money way out here in the middle of nothing?"

"The idea was a resort. A destination. Casino gambling and good times, just a half day's drive from LA." Sharp climbed the steps and cupped his hand to the glass to see if there might be anything visible. There wasn't.

"So, you live in Los Angeles and can drive across town to the beach, or drive across the desert to get . . . here?" Roni shook her head, disbelieving. "Somebody didn't think this through."

Sharp mopped his brow with his handkerchief. "Gent said they spent over five million dollars."

"Wow." Roni flapped the map fan harder and asked the obvious question. "So, now what?"

Sharp looked one last time at the vacant hotel and herded her to the car. "Let's go see about that refrigerated air they're so proud of at the El Grande."

"That might be the best idea you've had this whole trip, Jeff-er-son. I'm sweating like a pig."

Sharp held the door to the Cord open for her. "I thought women didn't sweat. Aren't you supposed to glow or something?"

Roni rolled her eyes. "Fine then. I'm glowing like a pig. Get me to the refrigerated air."

The El Grande was the opposite of Bugsy's Flamingo in every way. The Flamingo was sleek and modern and closed. The El Grande looked like a bunkhouse with a giant windmill on the roof. The wide covered portico fronted a vaguely Spanish Mission style, and the hotel was buzzing with people. Sharp pulled the Cord into the drive and a college-age kid sporting some of the gaudiest western wear he'd ever seen opened his door. The bolo tie, fringed vest, and pants that tucked into pointy-toed boots were topped off by an enormous ten-gallon hat that would have made the boys at the Rafter B laugh their butts off.

"Howdy, folks!" The young man hustled to help Roni out. "Welcome to the El Grande. I'm Kenny. Checking in? Can I get your bags?" Kenny was far too chipper for the triple-digit afternoon.

Sharp looked him up and down. "You a bellboy?"

"Yessir." Kenny doffed his humongous hat. "At your service. Checking in?"

"We don't have reservations," Sharp said. "Who do I see about rooms?"

Roni put her hand on his arm. "Room. Just one."

Sharp gave her a sideways glance and she stuck her arm through his. "Let's see about that refrigerated air they're so proud of, honey."

"Right this way, ma'am." Kenny sidled up to Sharp and nodded to the Cord. "That's a swell car, mister."

Sharp acknowledged the compliment but was undecided about the dude-ranch appeal of the El Grande. They followed Kenny the cowbellboy through the front doors of the hotel, and a blast of frigid air hit them. It was cold, almost frosty.

And magnificent.

Roni swooned as the deliciously chilled air washed over her. "We're staying here."

Sharp patted her hand. "Let's see if we can get a room first."

"Doesn't matter." Roni shook her head. "I'm not leaving."

Sharp's eyes adjusted from the blazing afternoon sun. He ran a tired hand across his five-o'clock shadow and took in the room. If Gentry had gone to cowboy heaven, it would look like this. A huge, wagon-wheel chandelier with lights like old oil lamps hung over the main lobby, barely lighting the expansive room. Tables and chairs made from tree branches that had the bark removed and varnished yellow surrounded the space. Other side chairs made from cattle horns and upholstered in cowhides spiced up the decor. The tile floor had branding-iron impressions all over it. Across the lobby, an authentic-looking Conestoga wagon hid the front desk.

The desk clerk had on the same-style getup as Kenny the cowbellboy. "Checking in today, sir? Do you have a reservation?" A bright gold name tag had HANK stenciled neatly in big black letters. Sharp wondered how long the man's name had been Hank. He looked more like a Rodney.

"I don't," Sharp admitted. "What are your room rates? We'll be here a week."

Hank nodded. "That would be four fifty, sir."

More than reasonable. Even Mrs. Hunnakee wasn't that cheap. Sharp laid five on the counter and paused before signing the register. He looked to Roni, who fanned herself and seemed disinterested.

"Four fifty a night," Hank hastily amended. "Sir."

Roni leaned in against the desk and breathed in the cool air. "It's worth it."

Sharp surrendered and fished three of Doyle's tens out of his wallet.

The clerk rang a dinner triangle, and Kenny popped to attention. Hank slid a sparkling gold room key across the counter. "Room 72. West."

Sharp handed over the keys to the Cord to Kenny and the cowbellboy darted back to the front door.

If Kenny wanted to pretend to be a cowboy, he needed to work harder on his moseying.

Hank pointed out a few of the hotel's amenities, the east and west swimming pools, the full-service bar, the

World Famous Chuck Wagon Buffet, and a twenty-five-cent chip good in the casino for each of them. Their luggage would be delivered to their room promptly.

Sharp picked up the room key and gestured in the general direction of the bar. "I could use a cold drink." He raised an eyebrow at Roni. "How about you?"

Roni nodded. "A drink and refrigerated air? Lead on."

The saloon continued the hokey western theme, as half of the seats at the bar were saddles. That was a little over-the-top for Sharp. "You think Rusty back in Roswell has a saddle he sits on at the dinner table?"

They opted for a side table with ordinary chairs. It was early afternoon, but patrons filled the place with a mix of young and older couples—but no kids. Maybe they were packed around the swimming pools.

Their waitress appeared: a stunning buxom blonde whose too-tight cowgirl outfit was similar to the others, but she wore only the vest and very snug fringed pants. Sharp might've noticed an ample amount of cleavage had Roni not yawned and stretched her arm in front of his face.

"Tired?" he asked innocently.

She took his chin in her hand and turned his head toward her. "Very. I'm bushed and you were the one doing all the driving. You must be gassed."

"A little."

The waitress put a hand on her hip and smacked her gum. "Y'all want anything?"

Sharp paid careful attention to lighting his cigarette rather than the cowgirl. "Scotch and soda and a gin fizz."

"Gotcha." She twirled on a boot and disappeared.

Roni put a cigarette to her lips. He lit it for her.

"Smooth."

"I'm learning."

She blew smoke away and smiled. "I like that." Her eyes swept across the dining room. "So what's the plan, Jeff-er-son?"

"I need a nap," Sharp yawned. "I hadn't planned beyond that."

Roni raised a lovely eyebrow. "I mean now that we're in fabulous Las Vegas. What are we looking for?"

The drinks arrived, and Sharp took the opportunity to check the nonexistent laces in his boots and not ogle the cowgirl. She set the glasses down, and Roni shooed her away.

Sharp took a sip of his more soda than scotch. At least it was wet. And cold. "I'd like to find Jerry Cartwright."

"Yes, I know that. So would I." Roni blew smoke in a huff that for a moment made him wonder how close she and the major had been. "So how are we going to do that?"

Sharp shrugged. "I think it's going to be a lot of looking around and asking questions. Courthouse research to see if he's bought a house here. Checking the phone company to see if he has a new phone . . . see if the PD has any info."

"So, the real danger we are facing on this trip is paper cuts?" Roni asked.

"And dust allergies." He grinned. "Courthouse records rooms are pretty musty."

"You know"—Roni slid a hand up his arm and squeezed—"the private eyes in the movies are a lot more exciting."

"They have editors to cut out all the boring parts."

Two rounds later the small talk died away and the reality of their single room loomed over the table.

"You cooled off?"

She stubbed out her cigarette in their half-full ashtray. "I'm good. Better. The refrigerated air is nice, but after all day in the car, I could use a shower."

His mind went there.

An inquiry at the front desk earned them a bellboy to guide them to the room.

"You folks are in our Cattle Baron's Suite—it features our exclusive king-size bed, a phonograph, console radio, easy access to the west pool . . ."

He carried on, selling the list of amenities all the way to the door.

He unlocked the suite with a flourish and they stepped through.

Roni's eyes went wide. "I didn't know they made beds that big."

"I bet it doubles as a tennis court." Sharp looked to the bellboy.

"We call it king-size. It's exclusive to the El Grande," he said with great pride.

Sharp got the remainder of the nickel tour and tipped the kid a dime. He closed the door and turned to find Roni sitting on the corner of the gigantic bed.

"You sure about this?" he asked, then stifled an exhausted yawn.

"I'm not." She stood up, took two quick steps and stood before him. "But I'm not running from it anymore."

Sharp breathed in the aroma of her perfume and it took him back to the way she'd felt in his arms at the Bamboo Room. Her big browns sparkled, and he pulled her to him. The ghosts, ex-wives, and missing boyfriends faded away and they found each other for a kiss that had been twenty years in the making. Their lips parted and he looked deep into her eyes.

"Roni—"

She put a finger on his lips.

"First, I need that shower."

When she returned, freshly scrubbed and peeking out of the robe the hotel had provided, Sharp was sound asleep.

A cowgirl waitress brought them coffee and asked if they'd like a mimosa.

"Never heard of it. Bring us two." He hunted for a menu and looked to Roni. "Okay?"

"Sure. Might as well."

The waitress directed them to the breakfast buffet. All they could eat for a dime. Sharp was amazed. And starved.

Ten minutes later, he was shoveling down steak and eggs and pancakes.

"I didn't mean to fall asleep."

"It's been a long couple of days. I get it." She smiled. "But your timing could use some work."

The waitress reappeared with tall glasses of orange juice spiked with champagne.

Roni took a sip and instantly motioned for another. "This is delicious. I wonder if I can grow oranges in Fort Worth?"

"I'd rather work on the champagne tree," Sharp said. "I can see why rooms are five bucks if they're giving away booze like this." Every table in the reasonably crowded restaurant was partaking.

He tipped the waitress and asked that they bring the car around. Kenny the cowbellboy opened Roni's door, and Sharp noticed they'd washed the Cord. It looked like a million bucks and he tipped Kenny a dime for his efforts. Kenny's smile faltered a bit as he felt the coin. He probably thought a guy with a car like that would be a bigger tipper.

They headed for the Clark County Courthouse. Sharp had been conditioned to meet yet another civil servant with a dull attitude and the customer-service speed of the average tortoise. Instead, the young woman behind the counter seemed almost glad to have someone ask to see the records room. It wasn't the cavernous dungeon of Dallas County. It was a small room with windows on one wall and a well-cataloged file of the very few records.

Predictably, USAAF Major Jerome Cartwright wasn't in them.

Roni eased a finger through the columns in the ledger. "Are we entirely sure his name is really Jerry Cartwright?"

"I'm not completely sure of any of this," Sharp admitted. "Even the stuff I've seen with my own eyes." He slumped back in the wooden chair and rubbed his eyes. They'd been at this for an hour and a half and were nowhere closer. About the only good thing was having Roni to help. She had spent years in the court system and understood how things worked.

"You weren't kidding about dusty records and paper cuts. You sure you want to do this for a living, Jeff?"

His mind wandered back to the flying lights and he and Dollar racing across the plains in pursuit of the rustlers. "I'll take the paperwork over the fireworks any day."

She slid the cabinet door closed and turned for the door. "Yep, nothing gets your blood pumping like the thrill of a folder being in the wrong drawer."

They thanked the clerk and walked into a blazing morning sun.

"How do people live in this desert?" Roni shaded her eyes.

"That may be the draw of refrigerated air and swimming pools."

"Any chance that's where this research leads?"

Sharp watched something in the distance. The unmistakable silhouette of a B-36 was lumbering across the far sky, headed to the northwest at a steady pace. "It may lead that way." He pointed to a low range of foothills that appeared to be the destination of the big bomber.

"So, we're going to follow an airplane?" Roni sighed. "It's a fast car, hon, but I don't think it's that fast."

"I don't want to follow too close," Sharp said. "I'm pretty sure it's headed to the new atomic bomb test range."

"This place just gets better all the time."

Sharp grinned. "It is fabulous."

Roni didn't grin back.

"You know the hotel has two swimming pools?" She craned her neck and fanned the top of her blouse.

"I saw that." He squinted against the glare and shimmering waves coming off the blacktop. "You're not thinking about skipping out on a fun time chasing Army Air Force aircraft, are you? Lie out by the pool and drink mimosas?"

"That is a great idea, Jeff-er-son. I'll even let you buy me a new swimsuit. Let me know what the flyboys have to say."

"Right after we follow these planes."

"And how do you expect to follow airplanes?"

"Well, first we stop by Sears."

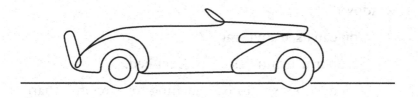

CHAPTER THIRTY-THREE

The Las Vegas outpost of Sears, Roebuck and Co. had a picnic basket. It had a snack bar that packed them sandwiches. They also had replacement binoculars and a Kodak that was on par with his destroyed old Argus and three canteens. Sharp had been thirsty in the middle of nowhere before. Roni found a new pair of cat's-eye sunglasses, a sun hat, and modeled a new swimsuit that made him reconsider the hotel swimming pool.

Instead, they roared off toward a minuscule dot on the map that Rand McNally called Indian Springs.

"This is a whole lot of nothing." Roni's hat fluttered in the breeze as she focused the binoculars out her open window.

"You can't see anything?"

"Scrub brush and desert," she replied.

"You're supposed to be watching for aircraft." Sharp reminded her.

"They're still out there." Roni shifted in her seat. "Way off. Little dots, but that's it."

"Way off is good."

"It is?" asked Roni.

"It is a bombing range." Sharp glanced at her meaningfully. "We don't want to be too close."

"If I'd have known your picnic would put us smack between a bombing range and Death Valley, I definitely would have opted for the pool."

Sharp grinned. "This is a much more entertaining way to get a sunburn."

The entire town of Indian Springs was a lone gas station. They stopped and chatted with the pump jockey about aircraft and the Air Force and the temperature. Sharp gave the guy three bucks for the tank full of Ethyl, and they rumbled back onto Highway 95. Sharp watched the attendant in the rearview mirror as they roared away.

The guy scribbled something in a notepad. And then ran back inside. Strange. To be moving so quickly in this heat. He made a mental note.

They saw no sign of aircraft for the hour's drive to Tonopah before stopping for their picnic and a couple of warm Cokes. The cramped Cord was not the most comfortable place to eat, but it was the only shade they'd seen for miles. The desert was deserted—no other cars, trees, or signs of life for miles around.

Roni shaded her eyes. "I can see why men from Mars would be right at home here."

Outside of the ironically named town of Warm Springs, another car appeared in the rearview mirror, but it stayed back far enough that Sharp couldn't tell the make, model, or even color. But it was back there for more than a dozen miles. He got a bad feeling and put his right foot down. The supercharged aircraft engine under the hood did its thing, and after a moment, Roni looked over. "Just how fast are we going, Mr. Rickenbocker?"

Sharp checked. "Almost a hundred."

"Any reason in particular?" Her voice sounded more than a little concerned.

"There was a car behind us." Sharp checked the mirrors. "He's gone now."

"So we don't have to be going this fast? Defying death out here where even the buzzards couldn't find us?"

He dialed it back.

"Thank—" She was cut off by the shadow that flashed over, and the roar of the engine as a P-51 Mustang fighter buzzed over the car, not a hundred feet off the surface of the road.

"Jesus!" Sharp swerved at the surprise but held on to the car, braking and easing it down. In the distance, the plane banked up and away and arced back toward them. Sharp's mind quickly returned to Italy and remembered a Messerschmitt doing the exact same thing just before it started spitting bullets at his platoon. There, they had some cover.

These were wide-open flatlands. The nearest cover might be back at the El Grande.

The Mustang lined up straight down the highway and headed right at them at 250 miles an hour.

Sharp floored the Cord.

"What are you doing?!" Roni was terrified.

He was too. "Increasing the closing speed. He'll have less time to react." The speedometer hurried toward 70, then 80. The fighter was getting larger in the windshield.

Sharp zigged to the empty left lane, then back to the right, waiting for the guns to erupt. The P-51 screamed over, and he swore he could count the rivets on the underside. Sharp checked the mirrors, but the pilot had taken the plane straight up after the pass.

Roni's eyes were wide as Sharp eased the big car to the side of the road. He grabbed the Bausch and Lombs and jumped out, scanning the skies for the fighter. Nothing. It was as if the plane had vanished.

Roni crawled out, shaken. "What the hell was that? Why would some damned fool do that? We could have been killed!"

In the distance behind them, a car topped a rise. Sharp trained the binoculars on the horizon. The heat radiating from the road made identifying it impossible, but Sharp had the impression it might be a gray Plymouth. He hated gray Plymouths. "Get in the car."

Roni looked at him. "What? Why?"

He pointed at the vehicle in the distance.

She jumped in. "I hate this."

Two painfully quiet hours later, the Cord was covered in road dust and almost out of gas when he pulled under the awning at the El Grande. A cowbellboy who wasn't Kenny took the keys, and Sharp asked him to have it washed and gassed. Roni went straight into the hotel without a word.

He found her in the bar. Her gin was already half gone, and the cigarette in her fingers trembled. Her blank stare reminded him of the last time he'd found someone shell-shocked at the bar.

"Roni—"

"Is this how it was? In the war?"

"What do you mean?"

"Never knowing whether you'd survive the day? Or the next few minutes?"

He gently touched her shoulder. "You just hope you're on good terms with a guardian angel."

She took a long drag on her smoke.

"Stuff like this happened a lot. You got used to it," said Sharp.

"A hell of a thing to get used to." She turned to look him in the eye. "I'm going to the room for a while."

"I'll come with you." He waved to the bartender. "Let me get us a couple to take with us."

"Alone, Jeff. I need some time."

He nodded.

"Thank you. For keeping us alive." She kissed his cheek and walked out.

Sharp watched her leave, then found a stool. The woman behind the bar gave him a friendly smile. Her cowgirl outfit wasn't as revealing as the waitresses—she had a shirt on—but the fringed vest was tight, and the strings of the bolo tie directed his eyes to her cleavage.

"She needs a moment. You need a drink."

"Double scotch. Rocks." He looked at the vacant doorway.

The drink appeared instantly, and he pulled a Lucky. But his Zippo wouldn't fire. That figured. A day in the desert would be hell on lighter fluid. The bartender picked up on his problem and passed him a matchbook with the scotch.

He lit up and noticed the logo on the matches. The Flamingo. He passed it back to the woman. "Thanks. You advertising for the competition?"

She read the cover herself with a smirk. "My last job. Don't tell."

He took a sizable slug of the scotch. It'd been a long day.

"I don't think she was mad at you," the barmaid observed.

Sharp nodded. "No, for once I don't think I flipped her wig."

"Ahh, you don't seem like the aggravating kind." She gave another smile.

"Well, once you get to know me that changes in a hurry." He eyed the matchbook. "I'm curious about the Flamingo . . . . How long's it been closed?"

She took a towel to the glassware she was stacking. "Since the first of the year. They got through Christmas and New Year's. Couldn't keep it going."

Sharp took a deep drag, considering. "What happens to big dead casinos in the middle of the desert?"

"Dunno," she shrugged. "I'm not sure it's ever happened before. But I hear rumors."

Rumors were Sharp's stock in trade lately. He raised an eyebrow.

"I understand some guy from back East is behind the scenes since Mr. Siegel died." She wiped a rocks glass dry and stacked it neatly on the shelf. "Rumor has it he's bringing in new people to run it."

"Mr. Siegel?"

She nodded. "He was always nice to me. It's a shame."

Sharp hesitated, thinking. "Know any of the guys who are coming in?"

"Haven't seen them," she waved a dismissive hand and reached under the counter. "But I'm good here, I won't be back over there." She brought over a bowl of peanuts. "It gives me the creeps now."

He nabbed a few nuts. It'd been a while since the picnic. "Ever meet any of the guys from Chicago there?"

That question was electric. She had her back to him, but in the mirror behind the bar, her eyes darted. "Who are you, mister?"

"Just curious." Sharp washed down the peanuts with the last of his drink. "The story I heard was that Mob money from Chicago had supported it and that not keeping them happy is what got Mr. Siegel taken out. "

"Yeah, I heard that too." She stuck her hand across the bar. "I'm Wanda."

"Jeff." He shook her offered hand. "Where you from, Wanda?"

"Before this? I was in Los Angeles trying to break into the movies." She gave him another smile. She had a charming smile. "Originally, Bowling Green, Kentucky. You?"

"Texas."

"I like Texas." Her smile broadened. She moved to take the order of a couple who sat down in the saddles at the end of the bar. The happy-hour crowd had started to roll in, Wanda got busy, and he decided he should see if Roni had cooled down any. He finished the drink and left a quarter. Something about Wanda ticked a box in his brain, and he didn't think it was the cleavage peeking out from behind the vest.

Sharp entered 72 west to find the room empty, but the bathroom door closed. He knocked.

"Roni? You OK in there?"

There was a sniff from beyond the door. "Yes." Her voice cracked.

"You sure? Sounds like you're on your way to blubbering."

He turned the knob and stepped in. She was soaking in the tub and scrambled, splashing, to cover up.

"What are you doing?!" she asked. "Jeff! Get out of here!"

"Nope." Sharp did his best to keep his eyes where they belonged. "We need to talk this through. What's wrong?"

"What's wrong?" Roni paused. "I've never been scared like that before."

He struck a Flamingo match and lit a cigarette, then handed it to her. She sucked it in and blew the exhale in his general direction.

Sharp shrugged. "Well, I guess this is the exciting part of detective work. Wasn't that what you wanted?"

"No. Not like that." She had one arm wrapped around her knees just above the waterline, her legs pulled tight against her.

Sharp tried to make his voice calming, like talking to a skittish mare. "You can't pick and choose your excitement. This isn't like the carnival at the Fat Stock Show, where you can decide whether you want to go on the Ferris wheel or not."

Roni frowned. "I know that. But I don't like it."

"I'm not exactly doing this because it's fun."

"Then why are you doing it?" Roni asked.

"Jerry Cartwright trusted me with something important. I need to get it back to him. I owe him."

She thought for a moment. And took another drag on the cigarette. "How did you do it?"

"What?"

"Get rid of the fear."

"Today?"

"No, over there."

"Oh," Sharp drew a breath. "I didn't. If you weren't scared, it was because you were stupid."

"So, I'm not being stupid?" Roni's eyebrows rose with the question.

"Not at all," he reassured her.

He lit his own smoke and leaned against the sink. "I think that Mustang was a message. Maybe we're getting close to something." He blew his own cloud away. "But I'll be damned if I know what it is."

"So, now what?"

"Think there's room for two in that tub?"

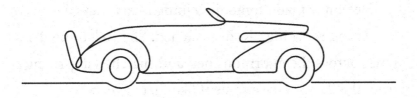

CHAPTER THIRTY-FOUR

As sunlight was streaming through the draperies, Sharp blinked himself conscious and found Roni's head on his shoulder, her hand on his chest.

Las Vegas could indeed be fabulous. The lieutenant's watch said it was 9:30, but the sun was up and that meant they'd slept through dinner and past what he thought of as breakfast time. His stomach growled to emphasize the point. He tried to move his arm and she yawned awake.

"Good morning," he said to the mop of hair in his face.

She paused a moment and raised herself on one arm. He watched for her reaction.

Her smile made something jump in his chest.

"Good morning." Roni stretched. She rolled the distance across the enormous bed and snatched a garment from the floor. "I haven't slept like that in years."

"Me neither." He enjoyed the show as she shrugged into his shirt and padded to the bathroom.

Half an hour later, as she maneuvered her lipstick and he combed his hair, she asked, "Big day planned?"

"Las Vegas air base personnel department." Sharp knotted his tie.

Roni gave him a slow nod. "What if he's back in Fort Worth and not missing at all?"

"The air base and the LVPD are about the only other places to look." He checked his business-card supply. "If he's not here, then yeah, we'll pack it up and head home." He put on his holster and jacket and slipped the tinfoil into his pocket. "Why don't you come with? I'll keep you safe if it gets exciting."

Roni grimaced.

"After yesterday? No, thank you. That swimming pool is all the excitement I need. I'm going to have room-service breakfast and then go read by the pool like I'm on the vacation I told the judge I would take."

He gave her a kiss on the way out the door. "I'll check on you later."

Sharp had gone into the Army as a platoon sergeant. He knew how the wartime Army worked and guessed correctly that even the newly carved off Air Force could bury things under paperwork.

He mopped his head in the triple-digit heat and waited to be introduced to a Lieutenant Evanston in personnel who was glad to be of as little help as possible.

Sharp explained his concerns about the missing major, and the lieutenant nodded politely. He did a cursory search of a file cabinet and found nothing. Sharp pressed Evanston about other records. Which brought in a Captain Miller. He was no help either. The Air Force learned fast. They were every bit as cloudy as the Army had been. Miles of red tape that led nowhere. Why couldn't they be efficient like, say, the Post Office?

You gave those guys two cents for a stamp, and your letter went anywhere and everywhere. One thing he did notice: if these guys were deliberately hiding something, they were as good at it as anybody he'd ever met.

They were either actors on par with Errol Flynn, or they were just desk jockeys shuffling papers. After three hours, he was certain it was the latter.

It was pretty clear no Major Cartwright was assigned to the base. The Captain didn't recall having ever even seen a Major Cartwright, and he said he met all the officers who came through. He was a fountain of knowledge. Sharp looked into his blank face and saw nothing but another dead end. He said his thank-yous and headed back out into the broiling summer sun.

There was a thunderous roar and he looked up as the now familiar silhouette of a giant B-36 Peacemaker rumbled toward the runway. Sharp walked along the cyclone fence, wishing he'd brought his binoculars as the behemoth aircraft touched down and began taxiing toward a group of war surplus bombers. Sticking out like a sore thumb was a triple-tailed Lockheed Constellation, a sparkling jewel in the middle of a field of army-drab paint jobs. The brilliant white-and-red paint scheme of TWA on the graceful airliner was hard to miss.

What, Sharp wondered, would a civilian airliner be doing on an Air Force runway? Roni had mentioned that the major palled around with Howard Hughes, and the millionaire aircraft designer owned Transcontinental and Western Airlines. Another clue? Another mystery? He shook his head and returned to the car.

Back at the fabulous El Grande, Roni had turned a little pink poolside, despite the umbrella and her oversize hat. He ordered a beer and squatted onto a chaise lounge beside her, his summer suit contrasting with her new swimsuit.

She looked at him over her magazine. "So Las Vegas is a bust?"

Sharp nodded. "It is a riddle in the middle of a question surrounded by a mystery."

"Well, the postcards only say come visit fabulous Las Vegas." Roni fanned herself. "They never promise you'll find anything."

"I've got one more idea, but it's a longer longshot than driving out here was."

"We could go on out to California?" She had a note of hope in her voice.

Sharp shook his head. "More like dropping by the LVPD in the morning."

Roni rolled her eyes. "You do know how to show a girl a good time."

"You know, I think I can. Did you bring a dress?"

She was wearing it when they walked past the buffet arm in arm to the less cowboy-styled and more ornate dining salon. That was followed by dancing. The El Grande orchestra was tremendous, and the Jack Benny on the Opera House stage really was that Jack Benny. They laughed until their sides hurt, and Roni got a picture with the radio star after the show. The evening took the stress away, and they slept like contented lovers.

The next morning, Sharp slipped out of bed and tried to make as little noise as possible. He dressed in the bathroom, tucking the Colt into its holster and the tinfoil into Woo's secret pocket. When he opened the door, Roni was awake, watching him from one elbow.

"Is this it? Last day of Fabulous?"

"Last day in Las Vegas. Let's keep working on the fabulous."

"I can do that." She smiled.

He kissed her. "I'll be back as soon as I'm done at the PD."

Sharp told the desk sergeant he wanted to talk to somebody about a missing person.

After a short wait, Detective Lenny Rubenstein met him in a side office looking over the business card he'd given the sarge.

"Private eye, huh?" Rubenstein was slight and olive-skinned. He placed the business card in his breast pocket. "You're a long way from home."

Sharp shrugged. "Not for long. I just want to see if you've got anything on this guy, and then I'm headed home." He gave him the basics, plus or minus a few specific facts.

The cop lit a cigarette and looked at him through the exhale. "I'll tell you, we don't get much cooperation with the Army people. They stay to themselves and have very little do with us."

Standard Army protocol. "Nothing happens when they get in a jam in town?"

"Oh sure," the detective tapped the ashes off his smoke. "We'll have a couple of enlisteds get into it over a broad, or a few too many cocktails on payday and get into a fight. They go in the holding tank until the MPs come get them. We pass along the specifics, and that's it. Judge advocate general takes our paperwork, and that's all we hear of it."

"So if it's something serious like a murder or a kidnapping?" Sharp asked.

Rubenstein nodded. "Same thing. If it's Army jurisdiction, we pass it along."

"Tidy."

The detective narrowed his eyes. "If your major has disappeared, it's because somebody on the Army side of the fence wanted him to. You should talk to them."

"I did." Sharp sighed in exasperation. "Stonewalled. I've tried going over it, around it, and under it."

"Yeah. They're really good at that. They can bury you in paperwork."

They went through the records for the weeks since Cartwright had last been seen in Fort Worth. Nothing. Sharp had pockets full of nothing. Sometimes the evidence and the clues would never yield the answer.

He shook hands with Rubenstein, and the cop showed him out.

Out to a big, wide world full of questions and no answers. People were trying to kill him, and nobody bothered to tell him why. Sharp looked at himself in the rearview mirror. He'd given this his full measure. Maybe gone above and beyond. As he drove through Las Vegas to the El Grande, he knew he was missing something, but it wasn't going to be found at this rate. He needed to start looking down the road.

He had no more clues, no job, no home, and a pretty terrific girl wondering what was next.

The problem was, he had no idea.

Kenny the cowbellboy was back on the job, and he acted oddly. Quiet. Watching him out of the corner of his eye. It was the kind of thing that got Sharp's senses up.

The door to the room was ajar. His first thought was the maid, but stepping in reminded him of the destruction that had visited Mrs. Hunnakee's rental house. The room had been tossed. He yanked the Colt and cursed himself on how cavalier he'd gotten as he stepped around open drawers and their contents on the floor. Their suitcases and clothing thrown about. He followed his gun into the bathroom and found it empty.

He stepped back into the hall and made sure the door latched. Then he sprinted to the pool.

Roni's sunglasses and hat were there, but she wasn't. He bolted to the lifeguard stand, but the kid with white zinc smeared on his nose hadn't seen a thing.

Maybe a man, but he didn't recall. There were a lot of people who walked by the pool.

Sharp made a beeline for the front desk and demanded to see the manager. He was directed to the Saloon, where a tall, distinguished gentleman in a conservative western-cut suit was talking with Wanda behind the bar.

"How may I help you, sir?"

"My . . ." Sharp's brain stumbled over how to classify his relationship with Roni. "My girl has disappeared, and somebody went through our room—72 west."

The manager frowned and snapped his fingers at a passing cowbellboy. "Get Mr. Benton, won't you?" Then turned back to Sharp: "I'm Robert Ogilvy, manager of the El Grande. Mr. Benton is our hotel detective. We'll get this sorted out, Mr. . . . ?"

The question hung in the air as the answer paced back and forth. "Sharp. Jeff Sharp."

"I can assure you, Mr. Sharp, this type of thing is very rare at the El Grande. Whatever the issue is, we will get it resolved quickly and discreetly. You can count on that."

Sharp nodded his understanding. A destination resort that charged five bucks a night couldn't have guests disappearing and rooms getting ransacked. Bad for the reputation.

"Please get Mr. Sharp something." He motioned to Wanda and rechecked his watch. "I'll go see if I can't hurry Mr. Benton along."

Wanda looked like she wanted to say something but instead built a scotch and pushed it and a matchbook across the bar to him. He nodded thanks and lit a Lucky as Ogilvy scurried off, and Wanda disappeared to the far corner of the bar.

Another patron sat down for an early-afternoon refreshment. Having been a cop once upon a time, Sharp knew a thug when he saw one. The thug had a broken nose and cauliflower ears that told Sharp he'd met his share of cops. The cold eyes met Sharp's gaze, and their owner moved to park on the stool next to him.

He swiped the matchbook, lit up and blew the smoke over the bar.

"So youse from Texas." His accent was thick with the south side of Chicago.

Sharp nodded warily. His eyes scurried around. Wanda had disappeared. Everyone had vanished. The thug turned his broken nose to Sharp. "Foit Worth, Texas, by chance?"

"Well, we say it as all one word—For'worth." Sharp took a sip. "What's it to you?"

The thug glanced around the quiet, empty bar. "I got some friends who wanna meet wid you."

The hair on the back of Sharp's neck was doing the samba. He casually checked the Hamilton. "I may be free for dinner. Who is it?"

He shifted on the stool and opened his jacket to show the snubbie revolver tucked in his waistband. "It's guys who don't want to wait until dinner."

Sharp scrubbed out his cigarette, swallowed the drink, put a quarter on the bar for Wanda, and stood up. "Let's go chat."

The thug stood and hitched his pants. Sharp swept the glass off the bar and the thug's eyes followed it all the way to the crash. When he looked up, Sharp belted him on the chin. He fell backward onto a saddle, and Sharp went for his Colt but the world went dark before he got there.

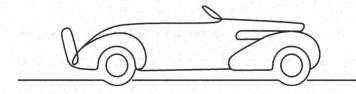

CHAPTER THIRTY-FIVE

S ome people go their entire lives without getting knocked out. Sharp was taking it up as a hobby. He woke up fuzzy, then came to with a start. The late-summer heat in Nevada could have one believe the Sunday school preacher was right, and he was waking up in hell. The room was all wood paneling with a large picture window. This version of hell was much nicer than the last time he'd been KO'd and woke up in a barn. The underworld had a decent padded and upholstered chair, and he wasn't tied to it.

Behind a big modern desk, silhouetted against the neon signs blinking in the Las Vegas twilight, sat the devil himself in the form of Doyle Denniker.

Doyle was shuffling papers and didn't notice Sharp was awake until he tried to sit up with a groan. The mobster finally looked up from his paperwork. "Well, well. Welcome to the world of the living, Jeff."

Then Sharp noticed they weren't alone. His old friends Lieutenant Colonel Martin and sidekick Captain Billings were in chairs by the door.

His hand went to the lump on his noggin. It was on top of the last one.

"This is living in Las Vegas, Doyle?" His eyes finally focused, and someone was missing. "Where's Roni?"

Doyle gave him a lopsided grin. "Las Vegas is what you make of it, Sharp." Then he grew serious. "She's fine. You have my word."

Sharp's head cleared a bit. "If anything happens to her, Doyle. This will get ugly very quickly. Especially for your Central Intelligence buddies, here."

Doyle broke into a broad smile and nodded to them, "I told you he was good. So you know about the CIA, do you?" He seemed quite pleased with himself.

Sharp frowned. "I know as much as anybody."

Billings interrupted. "Then you don't know very much."

He really knew how to get Sharp's goat. "Don't count on it, tough guy." He reached for the Colt. His holster was empty.

Billings cut a crooked grin. "Not so cocky now, huh, tough guy?"

Sharp stared at the guy long enough to get his message across. *First chance I get, buddy.* "Doyle, what are you doing with these guys?"

Martin took over the conversation, "What's a small-time P.I. from Cowtown doing in Las Vegas?"

Sharp shrugged. "I'm on vacation. I collect gangster trading cards and wanted to come see where all the action was."

"You're a riot." Billings smiled without a trace of humor. "Here to open for Jack Benny, funny guy?"

"I know a few good ones." Sharp rubbed the tenderest spot on the bump on his old bump. He needed some ice. Maybe with scotch all around it. "Hear the one about the disappearing Air Force major? The one who never existed?"

Doyle didn't react, but the CIA guys shared a concerned look. *These assholes would last about twenty seconds at a poker table,* Sharp thought.

"And you thought he was here?" Martin asked.

"I'd give it good odds." Sharp shook his throbbing head. "Seems to be a lot of B-36 work here with the new bombing range." It seemed logical that the major would go from one B-36 installation to another.

They seemed to relax with that, and Sharp made a mental note. Something was going on, and it wasn't bombers.

Doyle cleared his throat. "Any luck?"

"Not yet," Sharp admitted. "But I'll find something. It's hard to make someone disappear without a trace."

Billings and Martin shared a look and stood to leave. The larger goon pointed with his hat. "It's not as difficult as you might think."

Sharp took a little pride that Billings still favored one leg as they left.

That brought a smile but it didn't help his sore noggin.

Doyle offered his humidor and Sharp took a Cuban.

"You in bed with these guys, Doyle? You, the Chicago Mob, and the CIA are going to build a city in the desert dedicated to gambling? Or have I just been hit on the head too many times?" He puffed the Montecristo to life and waved out the match. "Which I might add—you didn't have to do. You could have just called."

"That was Billings's idea. He went to get you and said you threw the first punch. I'd have preferred you walk in here on your own accord." The mobster took his own cigar, clipped the end and took his time lighting up. "So, yes, Mr. Lansky's friends from Chicago, the CIA, and you forgot the military—they're chipping in. They're all just a means to an end." He waved his stogie to the room and the darkening evening behind him.

He then changed the subject. It was a gift he had. "How long you staying?"

Sharp stood. "I thought I was due for a nice vacation with a beautiful future and potential Mrs. Sharp. But fate seems to have other plans."

"I understand what you mean." Doyle reached in a drawer and pitched across a copy of the *Fort Worth Examiner*. Two inches tall, all caps, the headline blared: VICE SQUADS SWEEP DOWN THUNDER ROAD. "Happened the night I left."

The photo of the smoldering Four Deuces was taken from the parking lot at Rico's.

Doyle got a little misty. "I was in Chicago. And while I was gone, my home and its expansive game room mysteriously caught fire and burned to the ground. Total loss."

Sharp looked at the glowing tip of his cigar. "You should have come up with a better alibi than Chicago."

Doyle paused. "Oh?"

"Too close to Lansky. It's a red flag."

Doyle eyed him.

Sharp waved his cigar at the big picture window. "I think I've got the deal with you, Gentry, Caples, and Lansky figured out. But this? Las Vegas? I don't think you knew about this until after the major went off the deep end. You showed up at the Deuces with a suitcase and it had an American Airlines baggage tag from Chicago. You were already working a deal with Lansky. None of that made sense until right this minute."

Doyle leaned back and took a deliberate puff. "Go on."

"I know you've always got one eye on the future, Doyle. When you heard about Leo's crusade to shut down Thunder Road, you figured you're done with Texas, and with Bugsy dead, Lansky needs an experienced operator to handle Las Vegas. Everybody wins. Except Caples."

Sharp sat down and took a long draw on the Cuban. His eyes never left Doyle's.

Doyle slowly smiled. "You know that fire destroyed everything. All manner of potential evidence, up in smoke. All the notes and files you gave me. The fire chief—you know, Burt? Helluva good guy, and an unbelievably good blackjack player. He said my wine cellar made it one of the hottest fires they'd ever worked."

Sharp shook his head. "And you happened to be out of town?"

"I was attending a memorial service," Doyle closed a folder on his desk. "In Chicago. For the late Mr. Caples."

"Such a tragic end. Now what?"

"This." Doyle spread his arms as if to encompass the entire desert. "You're right. Las Vegas is the future. Thunder Road was, once; now it's here."

Sharp pointed to the ground where they sat. "The Flamingo?"

Doyle leaned back in his chair and fixed his gaze on Sharp. "I have a contract with ownership to get everything repaired and squared away. We're about a month out."

"So, you're moving here?"

"Already have," Doyle said. "I've got a suite at the El Grande temporarily. I'm building a house. Las Vegas is home now. No game room this time. No highly flammable wine cellar that a single misplaced ember can set fire to." He took a puff, admired the cigar, placed the arsonist's best friend in the ashtray, and pulled Sharp's own .45 Colt from a drawer. Doyle set it on his desk.

"You've got an interesting theory, Sharp. What are you going to do with it?"

"Do with it? Nothing. Like you said, there's no evidence. Gent killed Caples and I have no idea who killed Gentry—"

"I had nothing to do with that. I liked Gentry; he was very useful."

"Which leaves the Central Intelligence guys, and I can't win with them."

"Take it from me, that is very much a stacked deck."

"So now what?" Sharp's poker face deserted him. His eyes flicked to the Colt. "I don't suppose I can have my gun back?"

There was a long pause while Doyle lit his cigarette and Sharp stewed. The mobster picked up the phone and dialed.

"Come get him," he said and hung up.

"I take it that's a no on the gun?"

Doyle broke into a wide grin around his cigar. "I can do better than that." He opened a desk drawer and handed across yet another envelope, along with the Colt. "It's the title to the Cord."

Sharp had to admit Doyle was a devious, manipulative son of a bitch. But he had style.

Doyle blew a perfect smoke ring across the room. "There's a wedding present in the trunk."

"If these goons have gotten to her, I'm pretty sure that'll be the end of that."

"Never argue with a man who can tell the future."

"You don't happen to know where they're keeping her, do you?"

Doyle waved the large cigar. "I've been assured she'll be perfectly fine. You'll meet up with her soon. You two have a lot to talk about."

Sharp automatically checked the Colt's magazine and considered the city beyond the window. "So you'll make a go here in the desert with this bunch and that's it?"

Doyle chuckled. "That's never 'it' with these guys. There's always something else. Another carrot farther down the line to draw you in."

"That get old?"

"Depends on how much you like carrots. Come on, I'll show you out."

They walked through the darkened casino, Doyle pointed out details and changes to be made. Repairs were well underway. It had potential.

Doyle was going to make a fortune if he could get people to come out.

"It looks great, but how are you going to fill it up?" Sharp asked. "Where do the people come from?"

Doyle shot him a knowing look. "The Army is going to get very big here."

"You mean the Air Force."

"Yes." Doyle stopped, and a question came over his face, "Where did you hear that?"

Sharp knew something Doyle didn't think he did. "I'm an investigator, Doyle. Finding things out is what I do."

Doyle paused for a half beat. "Yes, well, the Air Force will be bringing in thousands of personnel. They'll need entertainment here in the middle of the desert."

Sharp stepped around an old can of paint. "And you're just the man to improve morale."

"Recreation, libation, and fornication." Doyle smiled. "That's what I do. Plus, people in California must vacation somewhere. It's not like they can go to Hawaii or something. If we do this right, they'll come here."

They'd reached the front door, Doyle turned the key, and Sharp stuck out his hand. "So long, Doyle. It's been fun."

The mobster shook the offered hand, nodding. "It will be."

The door opened into the growing darkness and Sharp looked around for a phone booth so he could call a cab. He swallowed hard when he saw a government gray Plymouth idling at the curb. These guys would never stop. He strolled to the driver's side and peeked inside.

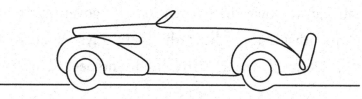

CHAPTER THIRTY-SIX

"You are a hard man to find, Major." Sharp suppressed his surprise.

Cartwright gestured to the front seat. "Well, I've been out of town. Hop in."

Sharp settled inside the gray Plymouth. "You know, that man back there has had me looking all over for you."

"That's been taken care of." Cartwright wheeled them out of the empty parking lot.

"By you or the Central Intelligence goons?"

Cartwright guffawed and slapped the steering wheel as they turned out onto the highway. "I knew you were the right man for the job, Sharp. Very few people have figured out the CIA."

It was then he noticed the major had a general's star on his collar. "Promotion?"

"Of sorts. That was a temporary demotion for security purposes. We discovered very early on that people will tell a major a great many things they'd never tell a brigadier." He slowed the Plymouth and turned onto an unmarked road, away from the safety of the city.

"Uh . . . shouldn't we be going towards town? I'm at the El Grande."

"Well, that depends on the answer to my question. Do you still have the item I sent you?" Cartwright was much more interested in the road.

"The tinfoil?" Sharp instinctively put his hand to his jacket.

Cartwright nodded a smile. "Tinfoil. It does look a little like tinfoil, doesn't it?"

Sharp felt the crinkle through the lining and hesitated. He'd been trusted with it by the major, but if being a major was a lie, could he trust him now? He went with the gut feeling only two men who've been through the crucible of war together can know. "It's in my pocket. My question is: Why is it in my pocket?"

Cartwright lit a Raleigh, cranked his window down a half inch, and blew his smoke out. "I needed an ace in the hole. Things in Fort Worth were moving quickly. Too quickly. I needed to make sure I had some leverage. In case things got . . . difficult."

"The CIA guys? Yeah, they can be difficult." Sharp's hand went to the tender spot on his scalp. "What's going on Major, er, General? I've got some of this pieced together, but not all of it." Sharp lit a Lucky and cracked open his vent window.

"All in due time," Cartwright said as the headlights illuminated a cyclone fence.

A white sign with large red lettering announced that they were entering a live fire-bombing range, and visitors were prohibited unless cleared by the facility commander.

The lone guard checked Cartwright's ID and saluted. He handed Sharp a clipboard.

Sharp gave the document a cursory glance.

"That won't be necessary," Cartwright stated.

The corporal took the clipboard and stepped back crisply. "Yes, sir."

"No record of this visit. Understand?" Cartwright said.

"Sir, yes, sir."

The tone in Cartwright's voice almost made Sharp salute.

The general put the car in gear and pulled out.

Sharp looked back to see the corporal still standing at attention. "General, if you don't mind, I have a few questions."

"Oh no, you'll have a million questions, and I likely can't answer most of them, but I'll tell you what we know." Cartwright slipped his ID wallet into his breast pocket. "Which is far too little."

Five minutes later, they came to another fence. This one had signs saying it was electrified and that trespassers would be shot.

Concertina wire was coiled along the top, and it stretched into the night in each direction. Klieg lights burned in the darkness atop a twenty-five-foot tower with a mounted machine gun. Sharp noted guards with Army Ranger flashes on their shoulders, including the three he could see in the tower.

He could still smell the paint. It all looked brand spanking new. Cartwright stopped the car and motioned for Sharp to get out.

"This is starting to look serious, Jerry."

A captain appeared from the tower. He snapped to a nervous salute. "General Cartwright, sir. We weren't expecting you, sir."

"Process this civilian but make no record of this visit. Secure his sidearm."

Sharp submitted to the body search and reluctantly surrendered his Colt. Neither Cartwright nor he mentioned the tinfoil.

Back inside the Plymouth, Cartwright pointed a thumb behind them as they passed through another fence and gate about a hundred yards inside the outer fence. "You're partly responsible for that. Your damn digging has ruffled some very important feathers."

"It did?" Sharp was genuinely curious.

Cartwright nodded. "I was supposed to just disappear, but you wouldn't let it go. I should've just paid Doyle and been done with it, but I got rushed out of town. I was putting out fires, and by the time things settled down, you were in county tax offices and Army personnel offices trying to uncover all the tracks we'd buried to make me disappear."

"I have a talent for messing up other people's plans," Sharp admitted.

"So I've seen." The major-turned-general gave him a frown as the desert rolled by in the darkness.

"Why not just send it straight to Doyle?" Sharp asked.

Cartwright took a drag from his smoke. "Do you trust Doyle? His relationship with Lansky made that too risky. I have to deal with them, but I do it as infrequently as possible."

"How exactly is the Mob tied into this?"

"Part of the CIA program. We needed a viable cover. Lansky had an operation in place through the Flamingo," Cartwright explained.

Sharp looked out the window, wondering what was beyond the darkness and how much darker this got. "So, what happened to Bugsy?"

Cartwright shifted in the seat. "Mr. Siegel had a difference of opinion about how the operation should be run. Accounting irregularities were found."

"The Mob doesn't account for skimming? I'd figure that would be a cost of doing business with the ethically challenged members of society." Sharp lit another cigarette. This was a long drive, but there seemed to be a glow on the far horizon.

Cartwright checked his watch. "It's one thing to take a little of Meyer Lansky's seed money. He understands a certain amount of grease is necessary to keep wheels moving. It's quite another to pocket most of the operating budget of a brand-new governmental agency."

"So the CIA and the mob kill Bugsy Siegel in Beverly Hills and get it covered on every newsreel and front page in the country? Quite the covert operations group you've got."

General Cartwright chuckled. "Well, I'm trying to limit assassinations. It's one of the reasons you were let go after they found out you didn't know anything."

"I didn't know anything," Sharp admitted. "They beat the tar out of me before I figured out your code games."

"Well, you know enough now." Cartwright squinted through the windshield.

"Like why you got knee-walking, commode-hugging drunk at the Four Deuces?" Sharp blew a stream of smoke at the vent window.

Cartwright shook his head. "Not one of my finer moments."

Sharp looked at him in the glow of the dash lights. He seemed genuinely troubled by the incident. "Aw, your secret's safe with me."

The general remained focused on the highway into the darkness. "Yes, I guess I have to count on that." His head turned and he examined Sharp as if he were choosing a steak at the butcher shop.

"You know, I spent the war in a cockpit and a POW camp. I missed the hell on earth some guys saw. That afternoon was the first time I'd ever seen anything truly shocking."

Sharp thought for a bit. He was right. The flyers shot up trains and planes from a thousand feet away. They didn't see nearly the horrific faces of war the way the infantry grunts did. Sharp's nightmares spoke to the things he'd never shake.

The general looked in the rearview mirror. "It'd be best if no one ever heard about that afternoon."

"Hey, Leo called your base commander, not me."

"Yes. The late Colonel Grayson."

"Late?"

"Automobile accident."

Sharp swallowed hard and changed the subject. "So Lansky needed somebody to run his Las Vegas operation after they took out Bugsy?"

Cartwright looked relieved to talk about mundane things like organized crime. "I suggested Doyle."

"You did?"

"I owed him. And after the turf war started in Fort Worth, I thought I could offer him an out. Then Caples got killed and screwed up just about everything."

There was exasperation in Cartwright's voice.

"Especially for Gentry," Sharp remembered.

"Damn shame. And totally unnecessary. But Doyle and Gentry both wanted Caples gone. Gentry got hooked on the action in Europe and needed his fix. It was not an elegant solution."

"And it got Gentry killed by Lansky?"

"It looked like that, but no. The CIA piled up quite the impressive body count trying to find your tinfoil."

Sharp watched the growing darkness roll by. "Who all knows what's going on here? Doyle? Leo?" Sharp asked.

"No one is supposed to know the entire story. Leo certainly doesn't, even though he thinks he does. And Doyle has only seen the Las Vegas end of things. There are one or two people in DC who know most of it, but the whole key is compartmentalization," Cartwright explained.

"Well, I know all that, so do I know what's going on?" Sharp stubbed out the butt of his Lucky in the Plymouth's half-full ashtray.

"You've put quite a bit of it together. And now you're in for a penny and a pound." Cartwright chucked, but Sharp didn't see anything funny about it. "Only a half dozen people truly know the whole story. Maybe."

"Plus that congressman?" Sharp asked.

Cartwright nearly wrecked the car. "What gives you that idea?"

"I think that's Leo's in."

Cartwright got visibly angry. "Johnson. That son of a bitch. I wondered how Leo figured this out."

Sharp nodded. "Leo knows people."

"People who ought to be able to keep their yaps shut. It is Johnson, isn't it? Leo was in tight with FDR, and now he can't get to Truman, so he's cultivating his own inside man. Dammit, I should have seen that." Cartwright thumped a palm on the steering wheel.

"Leo tells me Johnson'll be a senator come November." Sharp led his witness.

"That's the plan."

Sharp got a cold chill. "The plan?"

"You should forget you heard that phrase," Cartwright said.

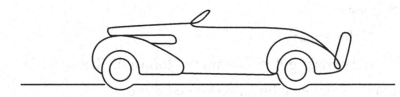

CHAPTER THIRTY-SEVEN

T he glow at the end of the highway had become buildings in the lights—a lot of buildings. The blue-and-white strobe of a manned control tower and bombers turning off onto runways. A gigantic B-36 taxied through the lights. A couple of C-47 cargo aircraft sat off of the apron. Canvas-covered deuce-and-a-half trucks and jeeps zipped everywhere. It was damned busy for the middle of the night.

They paused at an intersection as two flatbeds loaded with lumber and construction materials cut across, followed by a bus full of GIs. A small sign pointed ahead and read AREA 49. Another sign pointed left toward Area 50. Cartwright turned right. There wasn't a sign.

"You've got a lot going on here, General. Working all night?" Sharp looked back at the busy intersection.

"Three shifts. Twenty-four hours a day. Seven days a week."

The hills around a natural box canyon were a beehive of activity. Giant dump trucks emerged from an enormous excavation site. They were loaded with dirt. Huge light standards surrounded the entire place. There must have been fifty acres under construction. Not including the dozen or so Quonset huts and the tent city that stretched into the night.

Sharp was impressed. "That's a whopper of a hole in the ground."

"It'll be a quarter of a mile deep when it's finished." Cartwright slowed for another MP checkpoint and flashed his credentials.

"Damn. What are you burying?"

"Everything we can."

"Back to not giving straight answers, General?" Sharp's head was on a swivel, taking in everything he could see in the darkness.

"I am. You just don't know all the questions yet."

Cartwright steered them to a complex of four aircraft hangars. They parked in front of the farthest one. It was twice as large as it looked from a distance, with doors that would easily take a B-36. Sentries posted all around the compound stood guard. Fully armed like they were expecting the Germans to come over the hill any minute now. Cartwright stepped from the car and waved a hand at a couple of rows of identical small houses. "This is temporary housing for the aeronautics people. We're bringing in the best aviation minds we can find."

He pointed to another vast concrete slab that was being poured. It looked bigger than a football field. "Over there will be electronics and computers. Bell Labs is moving some of their brightest people here, as are Sperry and Westinghouse. Eisenhower calls it the Military Industrial Complex, but he doesn't know what's going on here and what the ramifications are."

Sharp stopped in his tracks and waved to the construction surrounding them. "Ike doesn't know about this?"

The general paused at the door. "The only people who know are those who need to. If they know and shouldn't, we make arrangements."

Arrangements. Sharp looked around. "Where exactly do I fall in those arrangements?"

But Cartwright was already up the steps, opening the door of the hangar's office.

"Welcome to the Rabbit Hole," he said.

They stepped into a garden-variety Army office. A lieutenant typed away at a government-issue desk; a four-drawer file cabinet sat in the corner with a coat and hat tree and a steel trash can. One other door waited on the left side of the room. Sharp had been in these offices a hundred times in everything from tents, to Quonsets, to palaces all over Europe. The lieutenant handed Cartwright some pink message slips, and he read them while the aide fingerprinted Sharp. He used rubbing alcohol and a rag to clean off the ink.

The general handed one slip back to the lieutenant. "Call Kelly Johnson in Burbank and see if he can move that up to Friday. I'll need—"

The phone on the desk jangled, interrupting him. It looked like a regular phone, but it had a row of buttons across the bottom. Sharp had never seen that. One lit up when it rang. Neat trick. The lieutenant lifted the handset and punched the button.

"Liberty 4-3-0-1."

He punched a red button on the phone and handed the handset to Cartwright.

"It's for you, sir." Cartwright took the handset and nodded. The lieutenant punched the red button again.

Cartwright listened to a one-sided conversation and winced.

"Dammit, they're not supposed to be here until tomorrow. Pass them through but take your time. Make sure he knows this is our show, not his."

He cradled the handset; all the lights and buttons on the phone went dark. He motioned Sharp to follow.

They stepped through the office, and through what he thought was a closet door but led to a hallway that turned to another hallway. About the time Sharp felt like a mouse in a maze, they stepped into the hangar. He'd been in more than a few hangars. He'd been through the bomber plant in Fort Worth on a public tour for vets after the war. He'd been to a goat roping, a rattlesnake roundup, and upside down in a Curtiss biplane. Nothing prepared him for this.

Hundreds of workers bustled about. Civilians in white shirts and ties, military in khakis with no insignia. Sharp stepped to the railing. They were on a platform that looked out over the space. As much as he had seen above ground outside, that much was buried below the surface inside.

They hadn't climbed any stairs but were three floors above the bottom level. Sharp gawked as they walked down three flights of stairs to an open bullpen of drafting tables—rows and rows of men hunched over them scratching out drawings and slapping out calculations on slide rules.

The general led the way to a knot of six men in a discussion at the end of the central aisle. A large man had his back to them and was making a firm point. He sensed their approach, and George Griffin turned around. He recognized Sharp instantly.

"You sonuvabitch!"

Big George balled a fist and drew back, and Sharp got ready to duck with a strange sense of déjà vu as three guys behind George grabbed him.

Cartwright stepped between everyone. "Whoa! Whoa. Whoa . . . Griffin, stand down. What the hell is this?"

George wilted. Then he stammered, "He ruined my marriage."

Cartwright was lost. He looked at Sharp.

"You and . . . Velma?"

Sharp was insulted. "Are you kidding me? I was hired by Mrs. Griffin to tail George. I got some rather interesting pictures that . . ."

"You took those?" The general ran a hand through his hair. "Oh, you are a pain in the ass."

"What did I do?" Sharp held up his palms.

Cartwright waved at the large engineer. "Griffin here is one of the best aerodynamicists in the business. That "other woman" you photographed is an agent for the British government. She was a covert liaison to the program, and we couldn't have her seen at Consolidated. You screwed up a significant program."

"Where is she now?" Sharp gritted his teeth.

"Agent MacGuire?" He looked at his watch. "Alice Springs. Australia."

"Wow."

"It was not an enjoyable mess to clean up." He shook his head. "Griffin, I have a VIP on the way in. Can you see to him, while I show Mr. Sharp around?"

"Yes, sir."

He really did look like a guy who had lost the love of his life. Griffin turned back to the engineers and Sharp and Cartwright started down the aisle to where the building was divided by a wall of translucent sheeting.

He shot the general a questioning look.

"It's called 'plastic.' It's a little like glass and a little like metal, a little like paper, and you can synthesize it out of petroleum. We're just starting to figure it out."

They stopped at the door, and Sharp looked back at George. He'd recovered and was back into his heated discussion. "I'm almost afraid to ask . . . what happened to Velma?"

The General paused. "Velma did not want to play ball. Thanks to a very recent change in Nevada State Law"—his look told Sharp that had been hard to arrange—"one can get a divorce or get married here in a matter of hours. Her name is now Henrietta, I believe, and she is this very week opening a bookstore in Fort Walton Beach, Florida."

Sharp thought he was supposed to feel ashamed. He didn't. "That was quick."

"We can do amazing things. Here's one now."

With that, they stepped through the plastic and into the vast open area of the hangar.

That's where they kept the flying saucer.

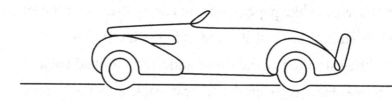

CHAPTER THIRTY-EIGHT

The saucer was huge. It wasn't exactly a saucer—more oval and the edges were rounded like the front of a thick airplane wing, it looked to be three stories tall in the center, he guessed it was 150 feet across.

Sharp stood there. "Holy. Shit."

"Yeah, we say that a lot." Cartwright chuckled.

They walked up to the edge. The craft sat on legs that looked like they retracted into the outer shell. At the bottom of each of the three legs was a rectangular foot. The pads were about two feet by four feet. Sharp was confident the bottoms were covered in New Mexico ranchland dirt. The surface of the craft looked like a rubberized compound. It was a dull, dark gray finish that was scorched and pockmarked like it'd been sandblasted and burned and beaten up. It had either been in New Mexico a long time or traveling across the galaxy wasn't like going to Piggly Wiggly for groceries. Sharp ran his hand across it.

"Feel's weird, doesn't it? It completely absorbs radar waves. Amazing stuff." The general was right, but "amazing" didn't begin to cover it.

"You were right about me having a million questions." Sharp peered under the leading edge of the craft.

"There's more." Cartwright turned to lead him across the hangar.

Sharp stopped. The tinfoil in his pocket had begun to warm up like it had at the hospital. He kept his mouth shut. The craft comprised a couple of layers that got smaller as they got closer to the top, which was a translucent dome. Shapes moved inside the dome, but Sharp couldn't make them out to be anything. Hoses and wires and cables ran all over the craft and from underneath. The general walked him around to a rollaway staircase that led up to a platform set against the side of the ship. Sharp was flummoxed.

Then he noticed that everyone in the hangar had stopped to look at him and the general. Mostly Sharp. The sixty or seventy men stopped work and looked at him like he was the one from Mars.

"You guys get many visitors here, Jerry?" Sharp pushed his hat back and scratched his head.

Cartwright paused to sign a clipboard for a khaki-clad gent. "More than I want; there's almost always someone here to see it. I expect Truman and the Majestic Twelve sometime this week."

Sharp had no idea what that meant.

A team of scientists in white lab coats were in a very animated conversation on a platform to the far side of the craft. They pointed at the general and his guest.

Cartwright nodded to them. "Come on. I'll show you why you're a curiosity."

On the far side of the saucer was what had to be the remains of another. Rusty Darnell had been right: there wasn't much left. The parts were laid out on the floor, and it looked like the fifteen guys walking around in white doctor's coats were trying to reassemble it.

They climbed a set of stairs to a platform erected next to the craft. The White Coat Team was excited. "It's doing it again!"

The general introduced Sharp to a tall, balding gent with glasses, an unlit pipe clenched in his teeth, and a German accent you could hang a coat on.

"Dr. Dandermeyer, this is Jefferson Sharp. Jeff, Dr. Henry Dandermeyer, he's one of our lead astrophysicists."

"It's so very good to meet you in person, Dr. Sharp." It was a hearty handshake and the scientist grasped his hand with both of his, as if he was greeting a long lost friend.

In person? He had a suspicion the doctor's first name had once been Heinrich. "I'm not a doctor, Doctor. I'm just a regular guy."

Heinrich shook his head, "No, you really aren't. You just may not realize it yet."

Dandermeyer gestured to where several of these white coat types were looking at a large piece of black metal hanging on a support wall. They kept looking at Sharp and pointing at clipboards. One or two were arguing. Sharp was lost like a kid in a corn maze.

The general led him over to the group. "Dr. Dandermeyer's team is mostly theoretical physicists working on reverse-engineering the technology of the ship."

"I'm a livestock detective from Fort Worth. I'm here to show you how."

It seemed to be funnier to Sharp than the White Coats.

Cartwright pointed to the black wall. "Usually this is covered with what the techs call snow. It's gray and grainy like a photograph of sand, but it moves."

Dandermeyer leaned in. "Earlier this month, one evening with no warning, it went black. And then a human being appeared on the screen like it was a movie. We all saw it. It was fascinating. And then he disappeared. Until now."

Sharp looked at him with a question.

"It was you. Mr. Sharp. You were on the screen watching us, looking at the Greys. They were fascinated by you. It was a seminal event in our progress."

"The Greys?" Sharp had no clue.

Dandermeyer looked puzzled and then horrified. "He's not been briefed? I had no idea."

"It's all right, Henry. He's in. He just hasn't been briefed to Delta Level yet. Come take a look at this." Cartwright took his arm. "Do you still have the tinfoil?"

Sharp reached into the hidden pocket of his jacket. And when he pulled the now warming and stiff tinfoil panel out, the screen on the wall went wild with a moving kaleidoscope of colors. It spun and danced until he held the tinfoil in front of himself and looked into it. There on the wall in front of Sharp, was Jefferson Sharp.

"It's a television," he said. "I saw one at the state fair."

Dr. Dandermeyer chuckled. "You did not see this at the State Fair of Texas."

"Well, not exactly, but it's the same principle. You point the tinfoil like a camera, and it shows it over there. Simple," Sharp explained.

"I assure you, Mr. Sharp, it is anything but simple."

Sharp moved the tinfoil around, and the doctor and the general came over to look into it and see themselves on the screen. They were like school kids playing with a new toy. The place had gotten very quiet. The lab coats were all looking at them, and as Sharp looked into the screen, he could see the three of them mugging for the camera. And behind them, the taller, larger gray head and insect eyes he'd seen on the screen at the hospital. The doctor and the general stepped away.

Sharp turned slowly around and found himself face-to-face with a creature from outer space.

"Jerry, make that two million questions."

The creature's almond eyes focused on Sharp and its oversized head tilted ever so slightly. A long, thin finger touched his chest.

"Whad da hail," it said.

Sharp remembered the men's room at the hospital.

"Yes. What the hell?" He nodded.

The creature took the tinfoil from him. It looked at the fabric and then turned it over and pressed a small symbol on the back. Almost instantly, the screen went gray and the tinfoil went limp. The Grey gave a slight bow of his head. Sharp did the same and the alien reached out a slender hand. Sharp took it and shook his hand. The Grey bowed again and then walked off the platform and back into the ship. The Grey's skin was cool and moist and left a waxy, slimy film on his hand.

The general stepped beside him. "You okay?"

"I think so. This why you got drunk off your ass at the Deuces?" Sharp asked.

"Yep."

"Got any left?" He looked at his hand and wiped it on his pants.

Dr. Dandermeyer nearly died. "Don't! That's the most contact we've had with them! We'll want a sample!" Except it came out sounding like, "Ve vill vant a sample!"

"Doc's right. That was as close to actual communication as we've had with the Greys." Cartwright gestured to his hand.

"That was communication?" Sharp looked at his palm.

Across the way, an officer in khakis was double-timing it across the hangar toward them.

Cartwright thought a second. "You ever have a dog?"

"Sure, when I was a kid." Sharp thought that came from left field.

"Ever want to be able to talk to it? Ask it how it was? What did it want for dinner? If it needed to go out?" Cartwright waved the aide up to the platform.

"Of course. Who wouldn't want a talking dog?" Sharp said.

"Man and dogs have been living together for thousands, maybe tens of thousands of years," Cartwright explained.

"Yeah . . . ?" Sharp had no idea where this was going.

"We still can't speak Dog."

"I hadn't thought about it," Sharp said.

Cartwright nodded toward where the Gray had disappeared into the saucer. "Well, in this case, we're the dog."

The aide arrived. "Sir? He's here."

"Here at the front gate or here at the hangar?" Cartwright frowned.

"Here at the hangar, sir."

"Damn, that was fast. He was supposed to be in St. Louis." Cartwright was visibly annoyed.

"He flew himself, sir."

"Figures." Cartwright hurried down the steps, and Sharp followed, mostly because he had no clue what the hell he was supposed to do now. Cartwright looked over his shoulder as they headed toward the plastic wall. "I told you we were getting the best aeronautics people we could find?"

"Yeah."

"Some are more difficult to deal with than others."

They went through the plastic wall back into the engineering spaces, and George Griffin backed toward them, trying to wrangle a handful of men in dark suits and one man in a leather flying jacket and a fedora. Sharp recognized the face and a pencil-thin mustache from the newsreels. It was not George's best moment. "Mr. Hughes, we really didn't expect you until tomorrow. The general has prepared an indoctrination so that you can familiarize—"

"Does it fly?" said Howard Hughes. "I'm probably more familiar with it than he is."

George was trying. "Well, this isn't really like—"

"Hello, Howard." Cartwright saved his butt.

"Jerry, what the hell is going on? You tell me it's a national security issue and to come see it. Then when I get here, they don't even want to let me land." Hughes was direct.

"We didn't expect you until tomorrow. I really need to brief you beforehand. This is highly out of the ordinary." Cartwright stepped between Hughes and the door.

Hughes looked at him, then walked right by and through the plastic wall. Sharp followed, to see what was happening, and nobody stopped him.

Hughes was already studying the saucer and yelling to no one in particular. "What the hell is this, Jerry? Is this Northrop? Did Jack do this? After that 'Flying Wing' bullshit, I can see him doing a saucer."

Sharp watched the aircraft genius in Hughes come out. He'd seen a newsreel showing Hughes breaking the transcontinental speed record in a plane of his own design. And then, when the Army didn't want to buy it as a fighter, Hughes said the Japanese copied much of the design to build their Zero. The man knew airplanes.

Hughes was under the craft, running his fingertips over the surface of the hull. "Jack's work has improved. I can't even feel the rivets. That's tight." He nodded in admiration. "How the hell did he seam these? There's not even a butt joint? And where's the propulsion?"

Hughes never noticed the Grey who had come down to investigate on his own. "There's no intake, and if it's a jet there has to—Jerry! Is this thing atomic? I read a paper last month on—"

He backed into the alien. Hughes spun to see who had gotten in his way. The Grey was a foot taller than the millionaire pilot, and the shock to Hughes's system was apparent even to Sharp fifteen yards away. The Grey stood up straight, then gave the same head bow he'd given Sharp and offered his hand. Hughes's eyes went wide, and he took the hand by reflex. The Grey gave a simple handshake, then turned and walked back to the ramp leading up into the craft. Hughes looked at his hand, he began to tremble, and his eyes widened even more, Sharp watched him shrink back into his jacket. He pulled out a handkerchief and began to scrub the film from his hand.

Sharp looked at his own hand. It reminded him a little of handling a fish. But Hughes was scrubbing furiously. His head jerked from side to side, looking from the group to the spot he'd last seen the Grey and back again.

Cartwright spoke for everyone watching the man come apart. "Oh. Shit."

He ran to Hughes, who was shaking like a leaf. "Howard. It's all right. Everything is under control. It's A-okay."

"Wha . . . is that . . . was that a . . .?"

"Yes, it was. Let's get you a chair." Cartwright put his arm around the millionaire and began to steer him to a desk nearby.

"A chair . . ." Hughes blew out a shaky breath.

"Now, Howard . . . I need you to take some deep breaths." Cartwright settled him into a desk chair. Hughes slumped forward, stealing looks over his shoulders and all around.

The general looked from Hughes to Sharp and back again. "This is why we do the indoctrination. If you're not ready for it, this can be . . . difficult." Said the voice of experience.

Sharp got it. He'd had a little preparation, halfway expecting something like this since the evening Gentry died. Maybe it was because he'd seen some really gruesome things in his life. Maybe since he'd seen the Greys on the tinfoil in a hospital bathroom, he was a little harder to shock than the average Joe. Or Howard.

"Where's Odie?" Hughes's voice was hollow.

Cartwright's face was a question. "Odie?"

"Odekirk. Get me Odie!"

One of the Dark Suits stepped forward. "Yessir, Mr. Hughes?"

Hughes rose from the chair to a hunch and then grabbed the man's arm. Cartwright tried to intervene—"Howard, let me help you."

Hughes couldn't even see the general. "Odie, get me out of here."

"Yessir, Mr. Hughes."

They walked toward the stairs, Hughes trembling and stealing looks back over his shoulder, Sharp and the general behind them. Two of the Greys had come down to watch. That seemed to draw Hughes back, but then he retreated. "We'll need a base of operations here, Odie. What's that town?"

"Las Vegas, Mr. Hughes?"

"Las Vegas. We'll need to set some people up here to review this. I'll want to be involved. This will be big." Hughes looked at his hands, still wiping with the hand-kerchief. "Plan on a long-term project; keep my name out of it. For now."

They had made it through engineering and to the stairs. Sharp was trailing the group and tapped one of the Dark Suits on the shoulder. "Is he going to be all right?"

"I don't know, I've never seen him like this."

Sharp and the general followed them out and watched the four cars of Hughes's motorcade tear across the desert, the dust hanging in the headlights of each trailing vehicle.

They both lit cigarettes as they watched the lights disappear. Cartwright blew smoke toward the stars.

"So," he asked. "Got any questions?"

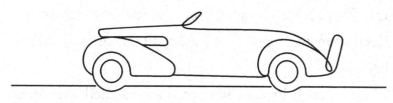

CHAPTER THIRTY-NINE

J erry turned the gray Plymouth onto the road they'd come in on.

"Well, what do you think?"

"Think? What's to think? We just whipped the whole damn planet in a war, and now we find out there are other planets out there?" Sharp shook his head.

"It's a lot to take in."

"High-school algebra was a lot to take in. This changes everything," Sharp said.

"I think I remember telling you that."

"What happens next, Jerry?"

"Truthfully? We're making this up as we go. You've put more of it together than I thought you would. And then you didn't quit. I convinced Martin that if we didn't tell you the whole shebang, you'd have half the world looking for this place. I think there'd have been a simple solution if you hadn't made the tinfoil work." Cartwright accelerated away from the complex.

"A simple solution?"

"The CIA wanted you dead. Then you showed up on the screen and established communication with the Greys. The scientists lobbied hard to keep you alive, sure you could be that communication link." Cartwright said.

"Have I ever told you how much I like scientists?"

"No kidding. When I first came on board this project, it was just the crash site. We had no contact with the Greys. Then one morning at the site, two ships landed. I was the senior officer on site that day, so I took a jeep and went to meet them. It shook me to my core."

Cartwright focused on the darkness.

"I remember that."

"We got back to the base in Fort Worth, and I went straight to the bar," Cartwright said.

"How'd they get here?"

"We worked out getting all the wreckage here for safekeeping. Hidden from everyone, so we thought. Then just like in New Mexico, one day they flew right in like they owned the place. That scared people."

"Like the CIA?" Sharp asked.

"And a lot of others above my pay grade. There's a belief that the human race isn't ready for this news. That knowing the government can't protect us from the Greys and that the perception of limiting what Uncle Sam can do would be a bad thing. That some people in Washington are more afraid of that than beings from outer space."

Cartwright checked the rearview mirror.

Sharp noticed the car was slowing down. He also noticed that sometime between the moment they walked out with Howard Hughes and right this minute, Brigadier General Jerome Cartwright had equipped himself with a sidearm. And Sharp's weapon was somewhere up ahead in a safe in a guard shack surrounded by ten Army Rangers.

No matter what was about to happen, it was not going to be a fair fight.

"We need to talk, Sharp." Cartwright steered the car to the edge of the road.

"Talk? Isn't that what we've been doing?" Cartwright stared straight ahead and Sharp looked around. This really was the middle of nowhere. "Do I have a choice?"

"I'm afraid not. What we're doing here affects mankind. We can learn a lot from the Greys, but it will take years, maybe decades. It'll take hundreds, maybe thousands of men to do it."

Sharp took a stab at it. "So it's the Manhattan Project all over? A hidden town in Nevada, but this one isn't hidden?"

"We learned a lot from the Manhattan Project. This time it's hidden in plain sight. There's a viable cover—the atomic testing range. That should keep people away. And the city we're building across the desert will give those who can't leave a place to enjoy." He cocked his head in the direction of Vegas.

"Those who can't leave?" Sharp parroted. "Howard Hughes just walked away."

"Airplanes crash all the time."

"You'd kill the richest guy in the world?"

There was a long moment and Sharp shifted in his seat. The desert seemed colder at night.

"We need you on this Project, Jeff. You're the first link, the first real communications breakthrough we've had with the Greys. We need to study how you and they seem to be able to communicate."

"I don't know that I'd call it communicating . . . ."

"Dr. Dandermeyer and his team disagree. They think you may be a key to this."

"So you'd fly me back out here? How often?"

"You wouldn't be leaving."

Sharp glanced at the automatic on the General's hip. "I don't suppose I get a bookstore on the beach if I don't play ball?"

"No." Cartwright acknowledged the ultimatum.

"This is it? The solution the CIA and the government have come up with? People who don't get on board get killed?"

"Or disappear." The General nodded to the vast desert around them.

"Is that what happened to you?" Sharp asked.

"At first they weren't sure about me. Getting drunk and coming unglued didn't help."

Sharp nodded.

"That's when I sent you the tinfoil. When they came to discuss it"—Cartwright's glance told Sharp there was a threat involved—"I mentioned that I had passed the tinfoil along, and if they killed me, then others would come forward."

"That took some guts."

"Bluffing is easy when they know you're serious, and what you have is more powerful than they are," Cartwright said.

The man understood the concept of blackmail better than most people who'd done it. The general was more fearless than he gave himself credit for.

Sharp lit what he hoped wasn't his last cigarette.

"So, of the choices you've laid out, I'd rather not get killed. What now?"

"You need to join us on this program. Work with our communications people. Help us reach the Greys."

"Join you? You got a poker room in that big hole? I'm a civilian. What am I supposed to do? I really don't want to go back to being a cop, and I'm definitely not going back in the Army."

"We've got a viable cover for you. Casinos need security. Somebody who knows how to look for things. I'm told the Flamingo is looking for a guy, and it pays almost twenty-five grand a year," Cartwright said.

That was more than Sharp had made in the last five years put together. "What about Roni? She doesn't know anything about this. I've got nothing back in Fort Worth, but she's got family, friends, and a job. You can't keep her here. If I agree to this, she gets to go home like none of this ever happened. No bookstores or banishment to the Australian outback."

"She's being talked through this same scenario right now." Cartwright met his eyes. "Roni's a patriotic American and this is a matter of national security. She's a sworn officer of the court. We trust that she can keep a secret. But know that this is her decision. Not yours. Not mine."

"And if she doesn't want to play ball? Because if you're talking the other option, I'm about to become very uncooperative." Sharp's pissant cowhand jaw tightened.

"We'll keep her here. There are incentives." Cartwright smiled.

"You need to know right now?"

"Yes, I do. There will be some documents to sign up ahead. Secrecy oaths you'll need to take very seriously. Under penalty of death." Cartwright's eyes were as cold as stones.

Sharp thought a second. "Nobody would believe me anyway."

Cartwright grinned. "That's the general idea."

"And I'd work for Doyle?"

"Unless you'd rather be somewhere else." Cartwright's face showed they hadn't considered that.

Sharp let him off the hook. "I think I'd start with the devil I know. Is the whole town in on this?"

"Not everyone. Let's just say that the atomic bomb makes a very good cover story."

"Wanda?" Sharp looked out the window to emphasize that he knew something.

"The bartender? She's one of our best operatives. She spotted you the second you walked into the El Grande," Cartwright said.

"She needs to be better at not letting on. I knew I was getting into something from the way she acted," Sharp said.

"I'll let her know. Are you in or not?" Cartwright wasn't going for his gun, so that was a relief.

Sharp looked out to the darkness. He lit a Lucky and blew the first drag through the window and watched it fade into the desert night.

"Yeah. I'm in." Sharp nodded. "But I don't want to deal with those assholes from the CIA."

"Me neither. I'm pressing Truman to limit their assignments to outside of the US."

"You're pressing Truman?" Sharp was impressed.

"Well me, and Mr. Hoover."

"Oh, the FBI, that's much better." Sharp chuckled.

The general put the car in gear. "At least the FBI is somewhat predictable. The CIA wants to write their own rules."

They drove to the tower, and Sharp signed his life away. Then he got his gun back.

It was a quiet ride back to town. Earlier, he'd thought he had a million questions. Now he didn't think he could handle the answers.

They parked at the entrance of the El Grande, Sharp started to get out, and Cartwright stopped him. "Don't forget about the trunk of the car."

Sharp watched the general disappear into the evening and remembered what Doyle had said about something in the back of the Cord. The cowbellboy brought the car around and Sharp wrestled the spare and the continental kit out of the way. Sure enough, beneath the false panel was a beat-up leather briefcase. He bet his Colt it had $7,100 in it.

He tipped Kenny fifty cents, and asked if he'd put the spare back in place. He seemed to be okay with that. Maybe this was going to work out well, he thought. Right up until he got to the room.

Sharp was all ready to go in and take a load off when the sound of voices came from the other side of the door.

Two of them. Men. And they sounded enough like the guy he'd tagged in the bar.

"... he knows too much."

"Do we kill him or just make sure he gets the message?"

"The boss says we take him out."

Sharp eased the case to the ground, slipped the Colt from its hiding place, and slowly worked the key into the lock. He had the drop on these two—and was betting they'd be associates of Billings and Martin. He was learning to hate the CIA.

In one move, he shoved open the door and followed the .45 into the room.

The perfectly straight, empty hotel room.

The bed was made, the drawers were back in place. It was neat as could be.

With a trumpet fanfare, the radio announced *The Shadow* would return after this message from twenty-mule-team Borax soap flakes.

The air went out of him like a balloon. And then the bathroom door opened.

He spun around and leveled the gun right between the lovely eyes of Veronica Arquette.

She gasped and nearly dropped the towel she was wrapped in. Sharp frowned, and then it got awkward.

"Dammit, Jeff! They said we were done with the guns." She spun into the bathroom while he tucked the Colt away and found his stammering voice.

"Sorry. I had no idea. I mean, I'd never . . . I mean— what the hell are you doing here? Where'd you go? Who said we were done?"

She stepped back out, tying a robe around her. Obviously, she wasn't expecting visitors any more than he was expecting to be one.

"I got a message to meet you at the bar." She pulled a cigarette from her purse, and he found the matchbook and lit it. Even scrubbed clean of makeup and with her hair piled up under a turban, she looked like a dream. "But I knew something was up."

She gave him that look. The one women use to tell you that you weren't getting away with whatever it was you thought you were getting away with.

"My message?"

"Yeah, you didn't write it, and I knew something wasn't on the level."

He frowned.

"Then Doyle called for me. He was with Vernon Billings and an Army colonel at the bar. They told me all about what you've been up to. I just wanted to help."

"I don't know what he told you, but Doyle doesn't quite know the entire story."

Her lip quivered.

"Jeff Sharp, if we came all the way out here, spent all this damn time in the car, everything we've done and you're going to be an ass, I'll . . . I'll . . ."

"Wait. What did they tell you?"

"They said you've uncovered something and it's a matter of national security. That they need you to help Jerry on a secret project."

Sharp ran a hand down his face. It wasn't exactly a lie.

"And they said you might need my help." She took a seat on a corner of the enormous bed. A bare knee slipped from beneath the robe.

Sharp shook out a Lucky and lit up. "Roni, this . . . thing is huge. And it could be dangerous. I doubt they mentioned that."

"In case you didn't notice, Jeff-er-son, it's been dangerous for a while now."

"Yeah, but this is your chance to walk away. You don't have to do this."

"I know that." She balanced her smoldering cigarette on the ashtray and came to him, meeting his eyes. "I'm not agreeing to this because anyone says I have to."

She put her arms around his neck and gently planted her lips on his. The kiss promised a passion he didn't dare imagine she felt. And just as he began to loosen the robe's belt, they were interrupted by a knock at the door. They both looked to Sharp's jacket and the Colt hidden within. He nodded to the bathroom, and she ducked inside. He slid a hand inside his jacket and leaned against the room door.

"Who is it?"

"Hotel staff, sir."

Sharp put his hand on the Colt and positioned his boot as a door stop. He cracked the door open.

It was another cowbellboy, but not Kenny.

"Excuse me, sir, is this your case?"

He'd left the briefcase in the hallway. Sharp thanked him and brought it in.

Roni cocked her head from the bathroom door. "What is it?"

"Unless I miss my guess, it's a couple of thousand bucks."

"I guess running around with you does have an upside, Jeff-er-son."

"And you're okay with that?"

"Are you?"

He set the case on the nightstand and scooped her into his arms. He spun around and deposited her on the enormous bed. "I am much more than okay with that."

This time, the phone interrupted their moment. Sharp ignored it for the first dozen rings, but the bell didn't relent.

"What?" he barked into the receiver.

"Mr. Sharp?"

He had a flashback to Bobby Caples answering the phone and paused. Roni bounced up and approached the briefcase.

"Who is this?"

"This is the maître d'. I'm to remind you of your dinner reservation."

He looked at Roni; she was staring into the case. Her mouth was gaping.

He covered the mouthpiece. "Did you make a dinner reservation?"

She shook her head.

"Nobody here made a reservation . . ."

The other end of the phone was dead. He got a wary feeling and hung up. When he turned back to Roni, she had pulled a small square Tiffany blue box from the briefcase. A crisp white bow adorned the box.

She looked at Sharp, then the box. Then him again.

"Jeff . . . is this?"

A cold shiver ran down his spine that made the one he'd had when the Grey shook his hand feel like the warm fuzzies. Cartwright had given him an ultimatum about moving across the country and starting a new life, but there could be something in that little box that would really change his world. He looked at Roni and made another life-altering decision.

In a snap.

"It is."

"Are you . . .?" Her gaze darted between his and the box.

It seemed like the thing to do, so he dropped to a knee. "I am. Will you?"

She looked deep into his eyes. But she didn't speak.

His heart beat hard. It occurred to him that he wasn't just asking her to join him in a cute little bungalow back home in Fort Worth. She deserved the truth and all of it he knew.

"Before you answer, there are a few things that you need to know."

She put a finger on his lips. "I know we are not talking about a white picket fence, Jeff-er-son. That much became clear to me in the last couple of days. And that is all I need to know."

She opened the box, and the ring was everything one would expect when you have a mobster picking out your jewelry. It was a little overdone. She gasped again.

"Oh, Jeff."

"If you don't like it, we can get something you—"

"It's perfect." One thing he'd learned: Roni could be a little flashy.

"Honey, what I'm involved in . . . there's a lot to it. More than just—"

"Vern mentioned 'a secret government project.' I understand."

"We can't go back to Fort Worth. Ever. We'd have to stay here." Sharp started an explanation he'd never get to finish.

"I can live with that." She admired the ring. "It is a tad gaudy," she said, "but I can live with that too."

He opened the briefcase but didn't find $7,100 in there. It was more like twenty grand. The note inside, written in Doyle's familiar handwriting, said that Gentry wouldn't be needing it.

Roni watched as he pulled wrapped bundles of cash out of the case and placed them on the bed. "This gets more interesting every moment. Any other surprises?"

"I hope not. I've about reached my limit." He set the last bundle on the bed and scratched his head.

"It's been a lot to take in."

"You have no idea."

The phone rang again.

"I told you we didn't make a reser—"

Doyle Denniker cut him off. "No, I did. But take your time. I'm putting most of this on your room tab." The phone went dead in his ear.

"That was Doyle. He's waiting for us." He hung up the receiver.

"Is this how it's going to be? Doyle always pulling our strings?"

"I have no idea, but we should at least go and tell him thanks for the wedding present." He nodded to the cash.

He took the briefcase to the front desk and checked it into the hotel safe while Roni got herself ready. Then they walked to the Chuck Wagon Buffet, where the maître d' wore a Stetson and a bolo tie. It seemed the perfect place for an elegant dinner with the fiancée and new boss he hadn't had at breakfast.

But the buffet buckaroo led them past the warming tables and chafing dishes. Doyle had a private dining room, and one of his gorillas opened the door and ushered them inside. The room actually was quite elegant. Not a hint of western wear in sight. Doyle and his companion Monica were chatting with the general and an attractive woman who was introduced as Mrs. Cartwright. Sharp raised an eyebrow at Jerry, and he just shrugged. He wondered what the man's real story was. And hers.

A waiter brought champagne.

Doyle raised his glass. "A moment, for Gentry Ferguson."

They paused, then toasted. Sharp couldn't help but reflect on the serious nature of this business. He'd once thought that money was serious business. Now, he knew some things could be much more valuable than money. Some were in a currency he couldn't yet fathom, and he didn't know if he ever would. The world had gotten smaller, the stakes larger, and the game had more than changed. They'd be making up rules as they went. And he'd have some interesting help to do it.

Monica and Mrs. Cartwright admired the ring.

"But where do we get married?" Roni asked.

The general winked. "Sharp already took care of that."

"I did?"

He nodded. "Remember me telling you about Velma Griffin? How we had to get a state law put on the books for quickie divorces? The same law allows for expedited marriages here as well."

"So you can come to Las Vegas and get married? Just like that?"

"Yep. You two can be the first to try it out."

"And probably the only ones. Who's going to elope to the middle of nowhere and get married?" Sharp shook his head and took another glass from the waiter. It was one of the dumber ideas he'd heard in a while.

Doyle gave him a smile. "I'm betting there will be lots of folks."

Sharp laughed. "Sure, there will."

The mobster took a sip of champagne. "Never argue with a man who can tell the future."

THE END

ACKNOWLEDGMENTS

I t's customary to thank everyone who has helped a fledgling author get their first work into print and I believe that's a very necessary thing to do.

Especially in this case. My wonderful bride, Elisa, has supported this effort on every level a person can—she's put up with hours of bad dialogue readings as I performed numerous strange voices. She's read and re-read numerous revisions and throughout it all she's believed that this effort would one day see ink on a press. Thank you, dear.

The excellent author Ed Isbell read a draft and gave some of the most insightful notes and clarifying suggestions one could ever hope for. Ed writes hilarious stuff, but his true genius is seeing the spine of a story.

The entire Dallas Fort Worth Writers Workshop listened, commented, critiqued, and pushed me to tighten, lift and edit the original story. They say it takes a village—this is mine. Thanks, guys, it's been a journey.

Jack Thompson first turned me on to the legends and ghosts of Thunder Road. Paula Renfrow read an early version and her appreciation of that effort helped me think this story might have merit. I cannot begin to name all the people who have shared stories of the dangerous days of the Jacksboro Highway, but Sam and Mary Deviney have been a constant source of inspiration. Also, thanks to Mitch, Mike, Beth and Doug for the support and encouragement. My sincere thanks to everyone at CamCat Publishing who have made *Thunder Road* possible—especially my editor, the ever-patient Helga Schier.

Finally my parents. Dad and Dr. Seuss taught me to read, but we lived three blocks from the library and Mom walked us down there every week. It gave my brother and me a love of reading and appreciation for a good story. I think Mom would have liked this one.

FOR FURTHER DISCUSSION

1. The book begins as a western, then becomes a detective story with a science fiction twist. As such, it doesn't fit traditional genres but mashes up several to create the world of *Thunder Road*. Does that work for you or would a simpler take on any of those categories be more readable?

2. Sharp has a single-minded doggedness to return the tinfoil to the major. This is partly because he feels the major once saved his life, but do you think that it's also

a part of his character and that accepting a task means he must complete it at any cost? Do you know anyone who has that stubborn streak to finish what they promise or is that character trait part of a bygone era?

3. During WWII the American government built a secret base in New Mexico to house the Manhattan Project and build the atomic bomb. Do you think it's possible that Area 51 in the Nevada desert could house a similar super-secret project?

4. The character of Doyle Denniker is presented as a charming host who cares for his clientele. At the same time he's a mobster who cheats at golf and hires contract killers. How does Doyle's moral ambiguity impact your impression of the character?

5. There are a great many books, films and television programs detailing the battlefields of World War Two. But Roni spent those war years at home, alone and suffered the loss of her older brother and her husband. Who do you think had the more difficult time dealing with the aftermath of the war? Jeff Sharp the infantryman, or Roni Arquette the widow?

6. The story fictionalizes a lot of history and leans on some real-life elements and personalities. How do you feel when a historic person like a young Lyndon Johnson or Howard Hughes shows up in a story? Does it add to the authenticity of the book, or does it take you out of the fictional world?

7. Sharp and Roni wrestle with their mutual attraction and the history they share. Do you think her losses would make her more vulnerable to wanting a relationship with her first crush? Does the dangerous world he now lives in make him more attractive, or should she have just walked away and lived the safer life with her court reporting job, simple home, and no one trying to kill her?

8. A key point of the book is the end of *Thunder Road* with its nightlife and violence. Most of the places and products from the 1940s mentioned in the book no longer exist. Everyone smokes cigarettes, making a phone call requires a phone booth and in some cases needing an Operator to help place the call. Has the world changed to a better, easier place, or was the simpler life of 1947 more difficult?

9. Do you believe in the idea that aliens have visited the planet Earth? Has anything given you a reason to believe that could have happened?

10. What part of the story seemed the least plausible to you? Was it that the CIA, the Mafia and the Air Force conspired to build Las Vegas, or that aliens crashed near Roswell? Why?

11. Newspaper publisher Leo Fuller is a prominent character. When was the last time you bought a newspaper?

ABOUT THE AUTHOR

Before the pandemic, Colin Holmes toiled in a beige cubical as a mid-level marketing and advertising manager for an international electronics firm. A recovering advertising creative director, he spent far too long at ad agencies and freelancing as a hired gun in the war for capitalism.

As an adman, Holmes has written newspaper classifieds, TV commercials, radio spots, trade journal articles and tweets. His ads have sold cowboy boots and cheeseburgers, 72-ounce steaks, and hazardous waste site clean-up services. He's encountered fascinating characters at every turn.

Now he writes novels, short stories and screenplays in an effort to stay out of the way and not drive his far too patient wife completely crazy. He is an honors graduate of the UCLA Writers Program, a former board member of the DFW Writers Workshop and serves on the steering committee of the DFW Writers Conference. He's a fan of baseball, barbecue, fine automobiles, and unpretentious scotch.

If you enjoyed
Thunder Road by Colin Holmes,
you'll enjoy
Jove Brand Is Near Death by J. A. Crawford.

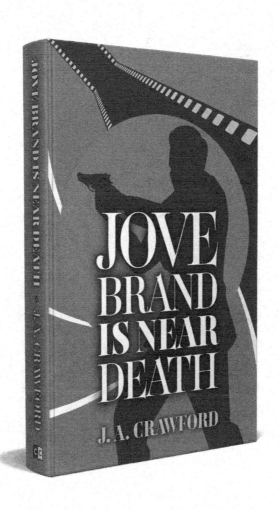

CHAPTER ONE

I was waiting in the wings, staring out at a live studio audience with seven million viewers behind them, and like everything that had ever happened to me worth mentioning, it was because of *Near Death*.

I looked good for my age, trim in my salmon blazer over a blue button-down and brushed-watercolor tie. Vintage Ken Allen, on the bare fringe of pop culture I occupied. For all intents and purposes, I was born in this outfit and had no doubt I would be buried in it. At least the jacket hid the wet patches under my arms.

"We might not even need you."

The executive producer was hoping for the best, but you didn't keep *Beautiful Downtown Burbank* running every Friday night for thirty years without preparing for the worst. Which was why they dug me up. If there was one thing I was good at, it was taking the hit. If the scene needed saving, I would make the perfect sacrifice.

"Keep an eye on the monitors. Come back when the house band wraps up."

It wasn't the most tactful way of telling me to get lost, but the guy had a lot on his mind.

"Just happy to be here," I told him. I'd been living a lie for eighteen years, why not keep it going?

I turned away from the stage that didn't want me and wandered around behind the scenes, following the pre-show progress on the countless monitors mounted in the halls and cramped dressing rooms, both dreading and praying they would need me. On the far side of an open dressing-room door, a drop-dead gorgeous woman was doing her own makeup. I didn't mean to stare, but it was hard not to, with her making those getting-ready faces that, for whatever reason, I had always found hotter than anything a woman did after getting ready. She was glamorous in an evening gown that had Brand Beauty written all over it.

She caught me reflecting. "Yeah?"

"Sorry. Just killing time until someone tells me to go home."

"What are you here for? Like, who are you?"

I wasn't offended. All those fuses were blown long ago. I wasn't surprised either. *Beautiful Downtown Burbank* was known for its young cast.

"I'm nobody," I said. "But once upon a time, I was Jove Brand."

"No you weren't." She looked up to think, ticking off the timeline on her fingers. "First it was the mean guy— so hot— then the prissy guy, before Sir Collin."

"I was between the prissy guy and Sir Collin."

She didn't reply, but her face said it all. Claiming you were Jove Brand was too big of a lie. You'd be better off pretending you were an astronaut or had invented touch screens. I took my phone off airplane mode and typed *Ken Allen Near Death*. It knew what I wanted when I got to the N in *Near Death*.

The first image result was me, eighteen years ago, pointing a pistol at the camera. I was trying for tough but came off looking confused about how this lemon tasted.

Pretend Brand Beauty—though I suppose they were all pretend—snatched my phone and swiped through the sequence of images that all too accurately told my life story. She stopped on the one of me holding up a container of Kick-A-Noodles.

"Nice."

"A week's worth of sodium in one little can." It was one of the ten or so responses I had ready for one-time exchanges. Meet a hundred thousand people sometime and you'll develop a list too.

Brand Beauty handed my phone back with an appraising tilt of the head, trying to decide if she liked what she saw. She stroked the front of my salmon blazer. "This isn't from props."

"I brought my own."

"You got the look, kid," she said, giving my cheek a squeeze.

My blessing and my curse. "You can't get by on looks alone."

I stepped aside to let her pass. She turned back, just out of arm's reach. That was when I caught the act. Until then her performance had been flawless.

"I'm just screwing with you, Ken. Everyone is so hyped you made it. *Near Death* is such a piece of shit. I love it."

I didn't step on her exit. That girl was going places. I hoped they would be good ones. On the monitors, the cold open was crashing hard. The tension in the air said it all—Jove Brand was in the building, and the audience was restless for his entrance.

I reminded myself to breathe on the path back to stage right. Jove Brand almost ran me over, but I stepped aside in time. He walked onstage ready for action, the king of his jungle.

Bone dry under glaring, thousand-degree spotlights and 14 million eyeballs, Collin Prestor—sorry, Sir Collin Prestor—made a tuxedo look like casual wear. There was acting and there was acting and then there was being able to control when you sweat. Whether it came with British blood or was the product of a Shakespearean theater pedigree I would never know. Lawndale, California, wasn't exactly London, England.

The audience went wild. The world's most famous fictional superspy stood before them. Women wanted him. Men wanted to be him. And Jove Brand was about to announce his chosen successor to the waiting world.

That successor now stepped from the shadows to stand beside me in the wings, waiting for his grand entrance. Niles Endsworth would be the next Jove Brand. He bore the same label as his predecessor, but of modern vintage, with a body sculpted by a strict regimen designed to produce a physique like a special effect. I couldn't fault Niles. He was just giving today's audience what they demanded in a hero.

Despite everything Niles had on his mind, I rated a second glance. He had been expecting the Ken Allen of eighteen years past, an image imprisoned in cinematic infamy. The kid was a good actor. He was almost able to mask his disappointment.

When his cue came, Niles snapped to the present and rushed to join his predecessor on stage. The merest sheen of perspiration betrayed the junior man's anxiety. His calculated display won the audience over. They'd be freaking out too, if they had been chosen to be the next Jove Brand. But the next Jove Brand would also have the nerve to mask it.

The two Brands, old and new, discussed the perks of playing an icon of fiction. You wore tailored clothes while driving luxury vehicles to exclusive locales. You could kill anyone who annoyed you. You always got the girl, who either conveniently died or disappeared between escapades. They played their roles to the hilt, master and apprentice. The production assistants could have ditched their cue cards and snagged a sandwich for all the good they were doing.

The problem was no one laughed. The part of Jove Brand had never been cast based on comedic chops. Fault for the only farcical portrayal of the character landed squarely on me and no one was looking to repeat that mistake. Sir Collin and Niles were gifted the perfunctory chuckles any incredibly attractive person with half a sense of humor scores, but the audience rapidly cooled as the initial rush of watching two Jove Brands together faded.

Beautiful Downtown Burbank's executive producer white-knuckled his headset, waving me toward the stage like it was a live grenade in need of a warm body. This is what you're here for, isn't it?

Yes, yes it was.

A life lesson: Go at whatever you're dreading full tilt. Sprint right into it. The worst thing that could happen was the entire world got to witness the train wreck for time eternal. That your epic failure would become an object lesson studied—literally—in college courses.

That you became a walking punch line.

It really wasn't so bad.

I exploded onto the stage with a butterfly twist, transitioning into a flurry of fancy kicks, battling through a horde of unseen foes toward Sir Collin and Niles. I kept the phantom attacks wide and slow to ensure the audience could follow along. This was all on me. I'd choreographed the sequence myself, drawing from an arsenal of techniques made instinctual through decades of dogged repetition.

If you had enough tenacity, you could fool people into believing it was talent.

I hit my mark an arm's length from the two Brands. Right on the bull's-eye. My surprise appearance had shocked the audience into complete silence. A small section of the crowd hooted, then the hoots built to applause and my heart started up again. Some of them were ringers but the rest sounded like my demographic—hipsters in the know.

I stretched the moment, resting my hands on my thighs as if I had come a long way. Pretending to catch my breath let me avoid eye contact not only with the audience but also with the two men who were arguably my contemporaries.

Sir Collin and Niles turned to face the interloper who had fought his way into their conversation. The consummate pro, Sir Collin held his expression through the cheers, freezing the scene for as long as it had legs. Meanwhile, my stomach explored heretofore unknown depths. When the crowd quieted, the time had come for me to deliver my first line.

"Sorry, my good men," I panted. "Bike broke down. Asian imports, you know?"

It was a good thing I was supposed to sound breathless. My American-cum-British accent was atrocious. I could have done better, but who wanted that?

It didn't get a huge laugh, but the audience members in on the joke lost their minds. No one wrote for the audience anymore, anyway. They wrote for the internet, for the bloggers, the tweeters, and the streamers. They let the fans explain the references in postmortem. There was nothing like free labor, and no one worked as hard as someone made to feel smart.

"How did you get in here?" Sir Collin asked. Stressing the did, not the you, kept the question at the appropriate level of condescending. Considering the audience's reaction to my appearance, it was the right choice.

"Who is he?" Niles asked.

Sir Collin moved to block the younger man's view. "No one worth remembering. Now, as I was saying, a gentleman shoots only once, and never first."

I stepped out from behind Sir Collin to add, "But he chops as many throats as required."

Don't ask me why, but that's when I ad-libbed. Not a line, not on live television—I'm not a monster. I offered an unplanned hand to Niles, who furtively extended his own in return. As we were about to touch, I turned my shake into a knife-hand aimed at his Adam's apple. Niles hopped back, genuinely shocked. I threw him a wink and a nod, my eyes a little crazy.

The big screens facing the audience had been playing a *Near Death* highlight montage from the moment I crashed the sketch. Now that everyone was in on the joke that was Ken Allen, the entire studio erupted in laughter at my action and Niles's reaction. It was a dizzying level of hot onstage. I reminded myself to not lock my knees.

Sir Collin moved between us again, precise in rhythm and position. The stage was his native turf, the sacred ground he retreated to when he wasn't playing a super-spy. He was fighting for Niles's attention now.

"He always looks his foe in the eyes." The strain in Sir Collin's voice projected concern his successor was learning all the wrong lessons.

"Then gouges them!" I interrupted, darting my fingers at Niles like a striking snake. I mimed a second, goofier gouge as Sir Collin put an arm around my shoulders. He turned our backs to Niles for a confidential moment as we switched cameras, me and Sir Collin and the millions watching at home.

"Ken, old boy, I'm trying to impart some wisdom on the lad," Sir Collin said. "You understand, don't you?"

Trust me, I did. Sir Collin had starred in six Jove Brand movies over fifteen years, each more successful than the last. If anyone could speak with authority on how to play Brand, it was him. He was so authentic, so genuine, it made me want to leave. But that wasn't the scene.

I hoped my attempt at a wide-eyed, thoughtful nod conveyed understanding. "Oooh. Sorry about that, Sir Collin." I forgot to use my crappy British accent, but breaking character fortuitously worked for the scene. The audience roared at every beat. Opening monologues were tough pitches to hit, and the writers had knocked this one out of the park.

"There's a good man." Sir Collin gave me a pat I liked a little too much before turning to again address Niles. "Now, when a lady demurs—"

"Chop gently, but firmly," I interrupted again, "right where—"

Sir Collin silenced me with a no-look elbow—a short, tight shot, measured to be effective but not punitive. His gentlemen's strike sent me airborne. I managed a full rotation from a dead stance and hit the stage flat with a resounding thud. Not trusting myself to appear unconscious, I buried my face in the crook of my arm.

The crowd cheered while Sir Collin adjusted his cuffs. "And there you have it."

He assured the audience they had a great show lined up, though when he announced the musical guest, it was apparent Sir Collin had no idea who they were. When they cut to commercials, I hopped up as the stagehands broke down the set for the next sketch.

The executive producer flagged me down with one arm while pumping his fist with the other. He wasn't in the best shape and the effort turned his face red. "You killed it. Don't go anywhere. Prestor is a dud. We might work in a callback."

I froze, trying to process this as the producer stomped off to put out the next fire. He said two things I hadn't heard in a long time: that I'd done a good job and that I should hang around. I snapped back to reality and headed toward the green room. Niles Endsworth was there, sipping a sparkling water. Hydrating, but not overhydrating. You never knew when you were going to have to take your shirt off. I shot Niles a friendly, wide-eyed nod as if to say Crazy, huh? but I don't think he saw me. He looked like he was beginning to grasp what it meant to be Jove Brand, his eyes flicking back and forth like he was watching different versions of his future unfold on the monitors. I could relate.

"Hey! Ken! Ken Allen!"

I knew who it was without having to look. Layne Lackey, owner and operator of JoveBrandFan.com, the number-one place for everything Jove Brand on the web. Layne Lackey, equal parts savior and devil.

"Ken, it's Layne Lackey. From JoveBrandFan.com, the number-one—"

"Layne! How're ya!?" I spread my arms for a hug and Layne took a step back. There was nothing like overenthusiasm when it came to setting someone on their heels. "You afraid of doorways?"

"Pass excludes the green room," Layne replied, dangling his lanyard. "Can I get a shot of you and Niles Endsworth for the site?"

A glance back told me Niles would rather drink from the tap than perform fan service right then and there.

"Producers need Niles for promo crap." I stepped to block Layne's line of fire. Niles slipped past us as if he were late for something. Become an actor and never get work. Become a star and never stop acting.

"You were great, Ken." Layne always used your name, like he had to constantly confirm to himself he was really talking to you.

"We'll let trending decide." I guided Layne away from the backstage chaos of live television. "That and my convention take. I have an appearance in Fresno coming up."

"Already plugged it on the site," Layne said. "The platinum pistol is going to be there too. Well, one of the five originals."

"Double billing." I was able to keep most of the salt out of my tone. "Sounds like they're starting up again."

"I'll catch the replay," Layne said, adjusting the settings on too much camera. "I'm going to run Niles down and ask if he's ever thought about doing conventions."

I didn't wish him luck.

The Brand Beauty was on the monitors in a sketch where she brazenly threw herself at Sir Collin, who was more interested in the strapping bartender. He killed it but got few laughs. Sir Collin was simply too understated for the American audience.

I winced at the screen.

Watching other people bomb struck my most tender places. It was an empathy thing. I sought solace in Sir Collin's dressing room, telling myself it was out of everyone's way, but that was just me telling myself. The truth was, I wanted to sit in his chair.

I wasn't bitter. Sir Collin deserved everything he'd earned. His Brand movies really were better than the early ones, though the lens of nostalgia kept the fans from acknowledging it. His performances helped restore the series to the juggernaut it had been in the sixties and seventies.

I wanted to be Sir Collin the way I had once wanted to play guitar in Nirvana. The ability was simply beyond me. It was a pipe dream—only it wasn't. I had been Jove Brand, once.

But *Near Death* was indeed a piece of shit.

"Harsh lights, wouldn't you say?"

Sir Collin's voice was purely chummy, but it launched me out of his chair.

"Sorry, Sir Collin." When in doubt, it was best to come clean. "Guess you caught me."

Sir Collin waved my apology off as he came over to stand with me at the dressing table. "Of all the moments we spend in the light, these are the ones I dread the most. Having to face myself, every flaw exposed."

He was right. His age showed in the bulb-bordered mirror. Jove Brand was not a young man, but he could never be an old one. Four walls and two generations away, the musical guest kicked in as if on cue. If anyone deserved accompaniment, it was Sir Collin.

"You saved me out there. Thanks, old boy."

"I don't have range, but I know my role," I replied.

"I didn't want to do this, you know," Sir Collin said. "Every time such an offer is tendered, I tell myself it's more money for the troupe, to put on the shows we want. Being Jove Brand has given my fellows a life on the stage."

I'd read as much but took it for PR until that moment. "Same here. But I did want to be a great Jove Brand. Problem was, I did my best."

Sir Collin laughed as he rested his hands on my shoulders. "Without your film, I would not be here, and the fifty men and women I support would have been forced to abandon their dreams. Tonight, you again displayed a true player's spirit, putting the show before the man."

It was the nicest thing anyone had said to me in eighteen years. I lost my voice. I couldn't even look at Sir Collin.

"Now if you'll excuse me, I'm off to sneak a drag or two before my next sketch," Sir Collin said. I managed a nod as he gave me a last squeeze and left me in reflection.

Going purely on appearance, I was the spitting image of Jove Brand as described in the books. The passionless killer. The distant lover. Tall and pale, with light blond hair and ice-blue eyes. A face and body reminiscent of renaissance sculpture. But sculpture didn't come to life, which also accurately described my acting.

I looked more the part now. Eighteen years ago I was eighteen years too young, but casting had been tight. *Near Death's* entire pre-production took place on a flight from Kiev to Hong Kong. Had the internet of today existed then, my tender age would have caused the same uproar it did with Niles Endsworth now. A combination of professional discipline and CGI smoothing had sustained Sir Collin for a spell, but his time had come. Soon he would meet his fate—most likely during a pre-credit sequence—and the alias of Jove Brand, Royal Gamesman, would be passed to Niles.

The executive producer burst into the dressing room, breaking my self-indulgent reverie.

"I didn't do it, I swear," I said.

"Where the hell is Sir Collin?"

The executive producer bent over to rest his hands on his knees. The dash to the dressing room had left him about a burpee away from a heart attack.

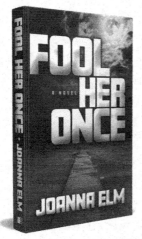
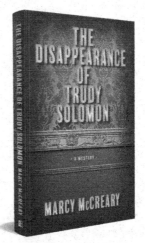

CamCat
Books

VISIT US ONLINE FOR
MORE BOOKS TO LIVE IN:
CAMCATBOOKS.COM

FOLLOW US

CamCatBooks   @CamCatBooks   @CamCat_Books